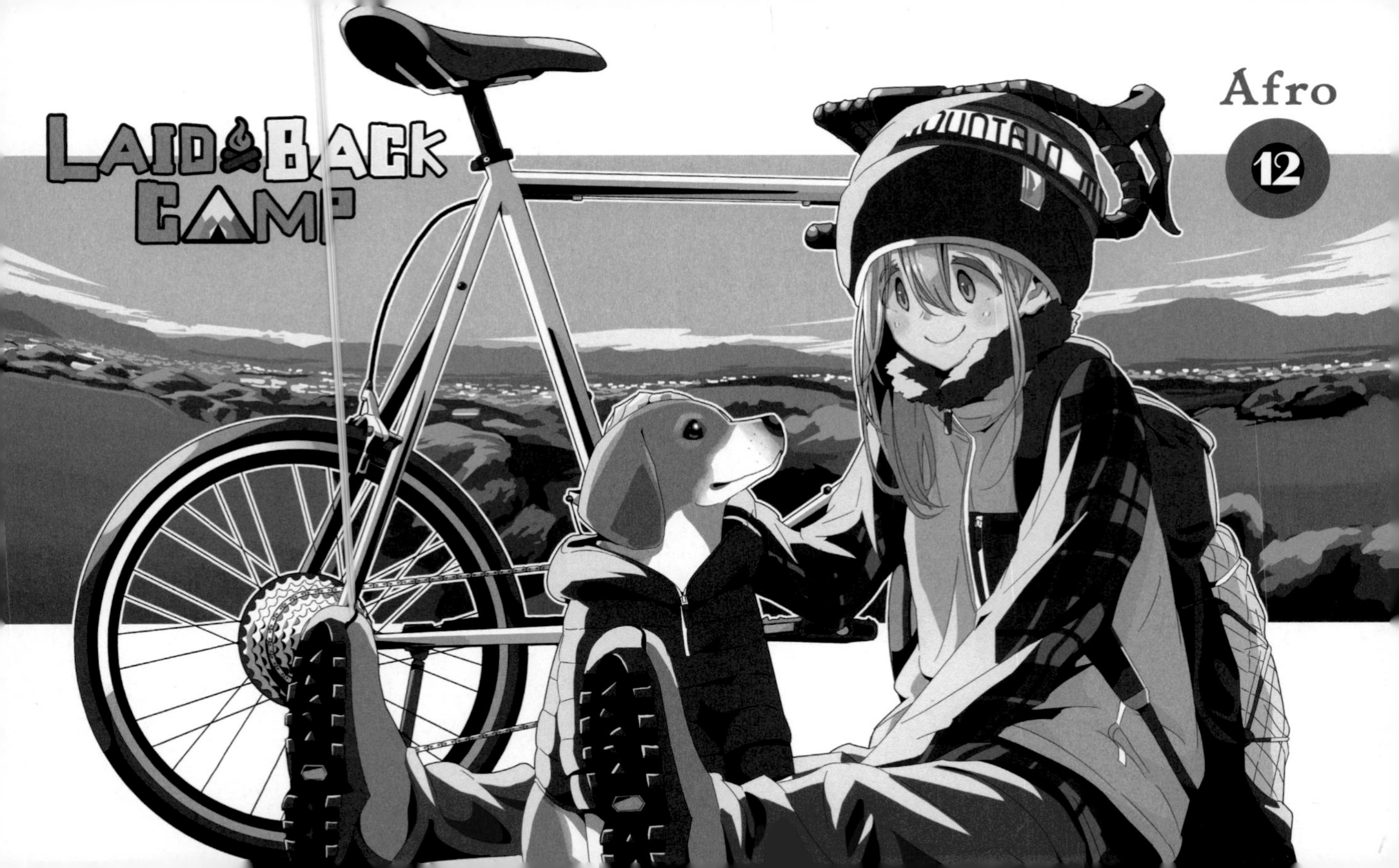
LAID BACK CAMP
Afro
12
MOUNTAIN

12

LAID-BACK CAMP

contents

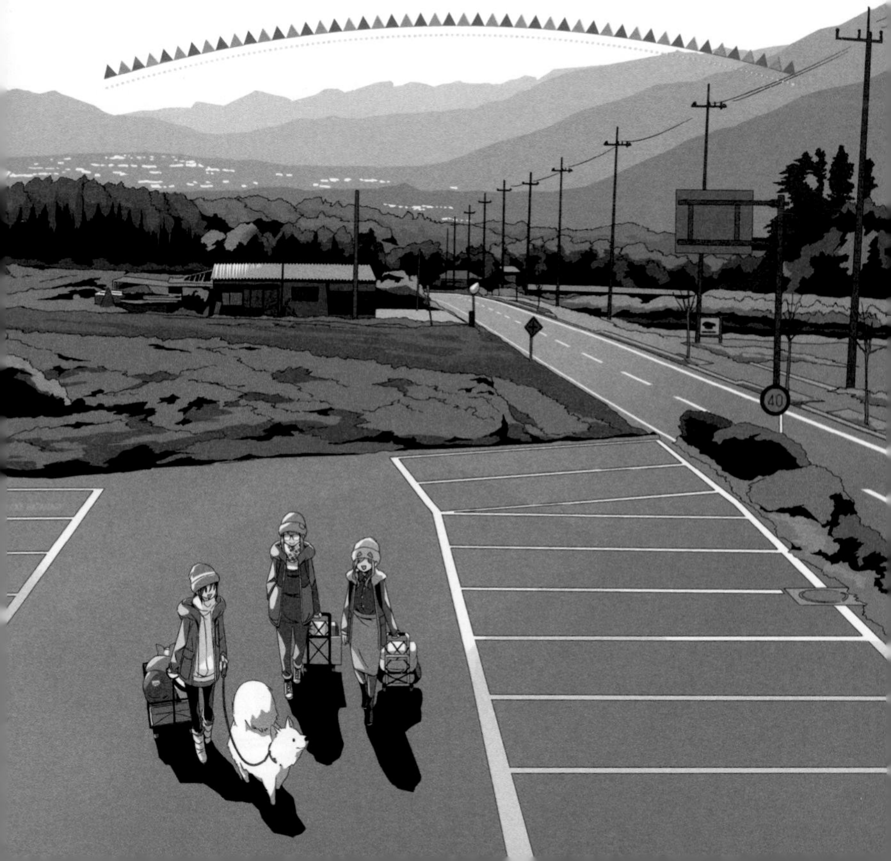

40

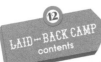

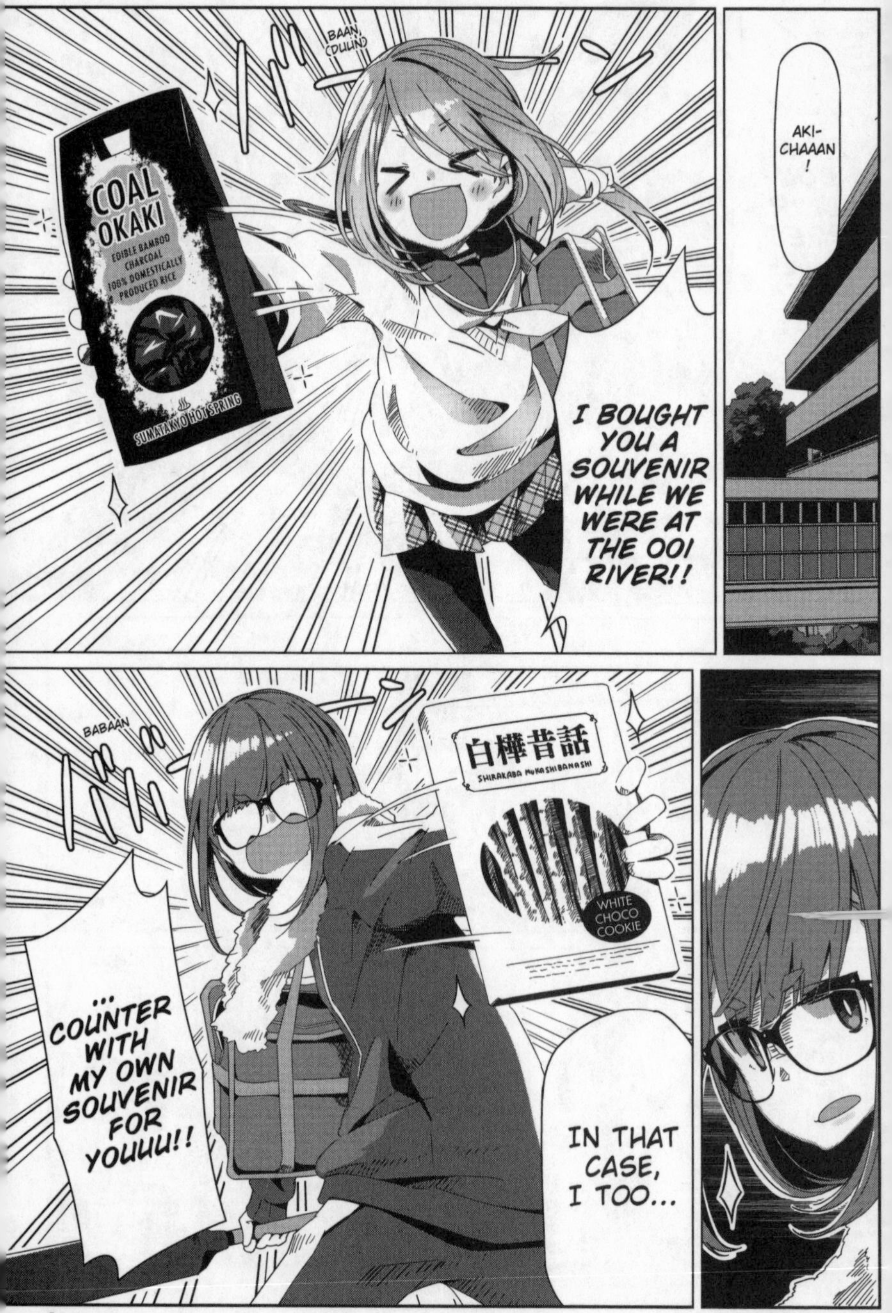
AKI-CHAAAN!
BAAN (DUUN)
COAL OKAKI
EDIBLE BAMBOO CHARCOAL
100% DOMESTICALLY PRODUCED RICE
SUMATAKYO HOT SPRING
I BOUGHT YOU A SOUVENIR WHILE WE WERE AT THE OOI RIVER!!
IN THAT CASE, I TOO...
BABAAN
白樺昔話
SHIRAKABA MUKASHIBANASHI
WHITE CHOCO COOKIE
...COUNTER WITH MY OWN SOUVENIR FOR YOUUU!!

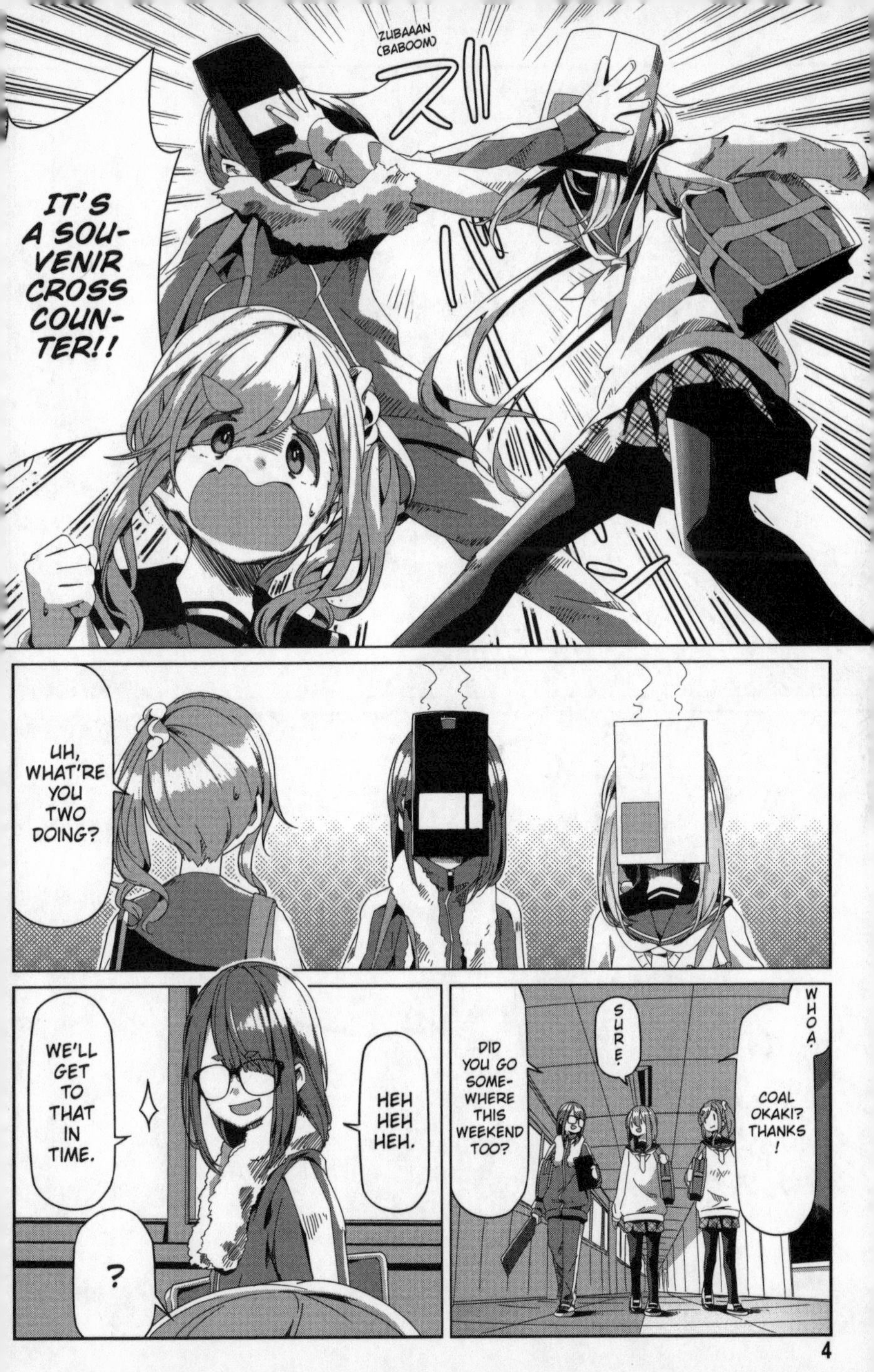
ZUBAAAN (BABOOM)
IT'S A SOU-VENIR CROSS COUN-TER!!
UH, WHAT'RE YOU TWO DOING?
WHOA.
COAL OKAKI? THANKS!
SURE.
DID YOU GO SOME-WHERE THIS WEEKEND TOO?
HEH HEH HEH.
WE'LL GET TO THAT IN TIME.
?

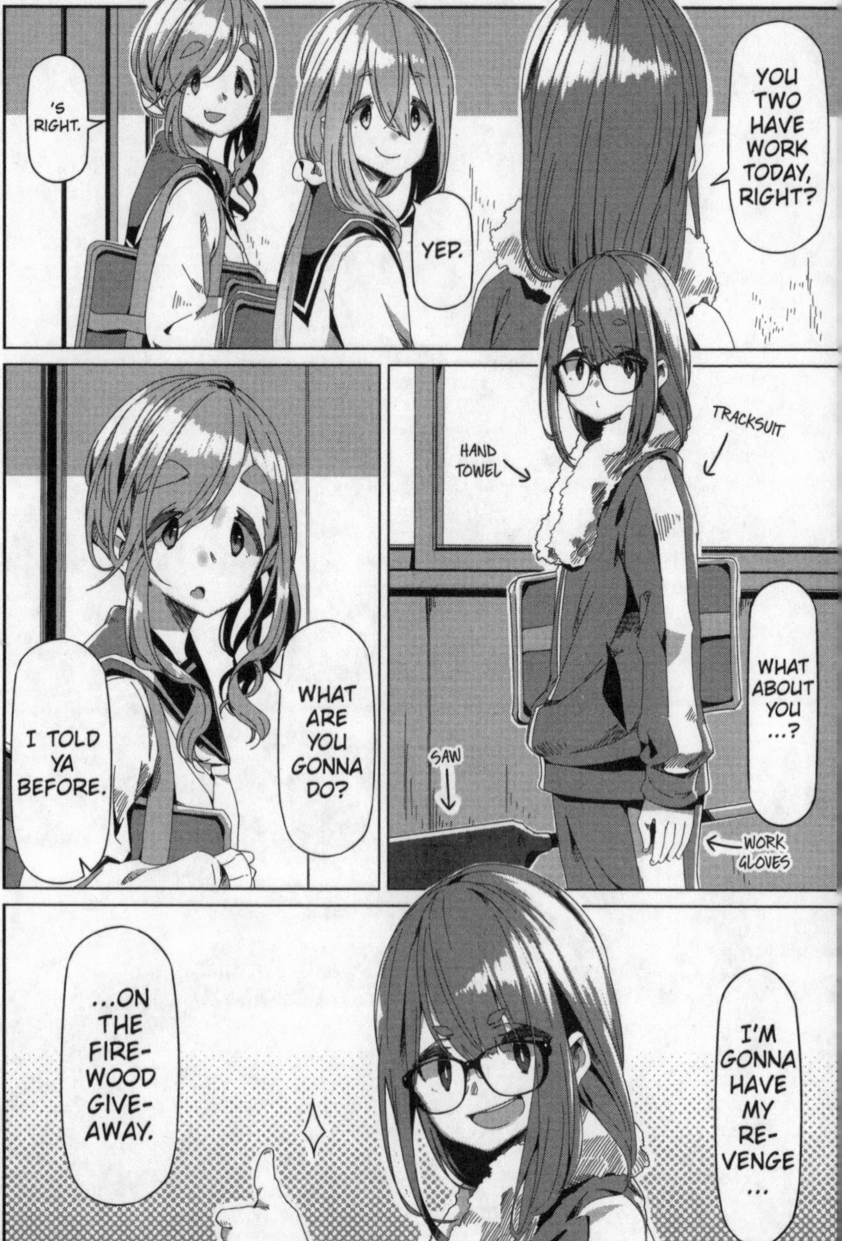
YOU TWO HAVE WORK TODAY, RIGHT?
YEP.
'S RIGHT.
TRACKSUIT
HAND TOWEL
WHAT ABOUT YOU ...?
SAW
WORK GLOVES
WHAT ARE YOU GONNA DO?
I TOLD YA BEFORE.
I'M GONNA HAVE MY RE-VENGE ...
...ON THE FIRE-WOOD GIVE-AWAY.

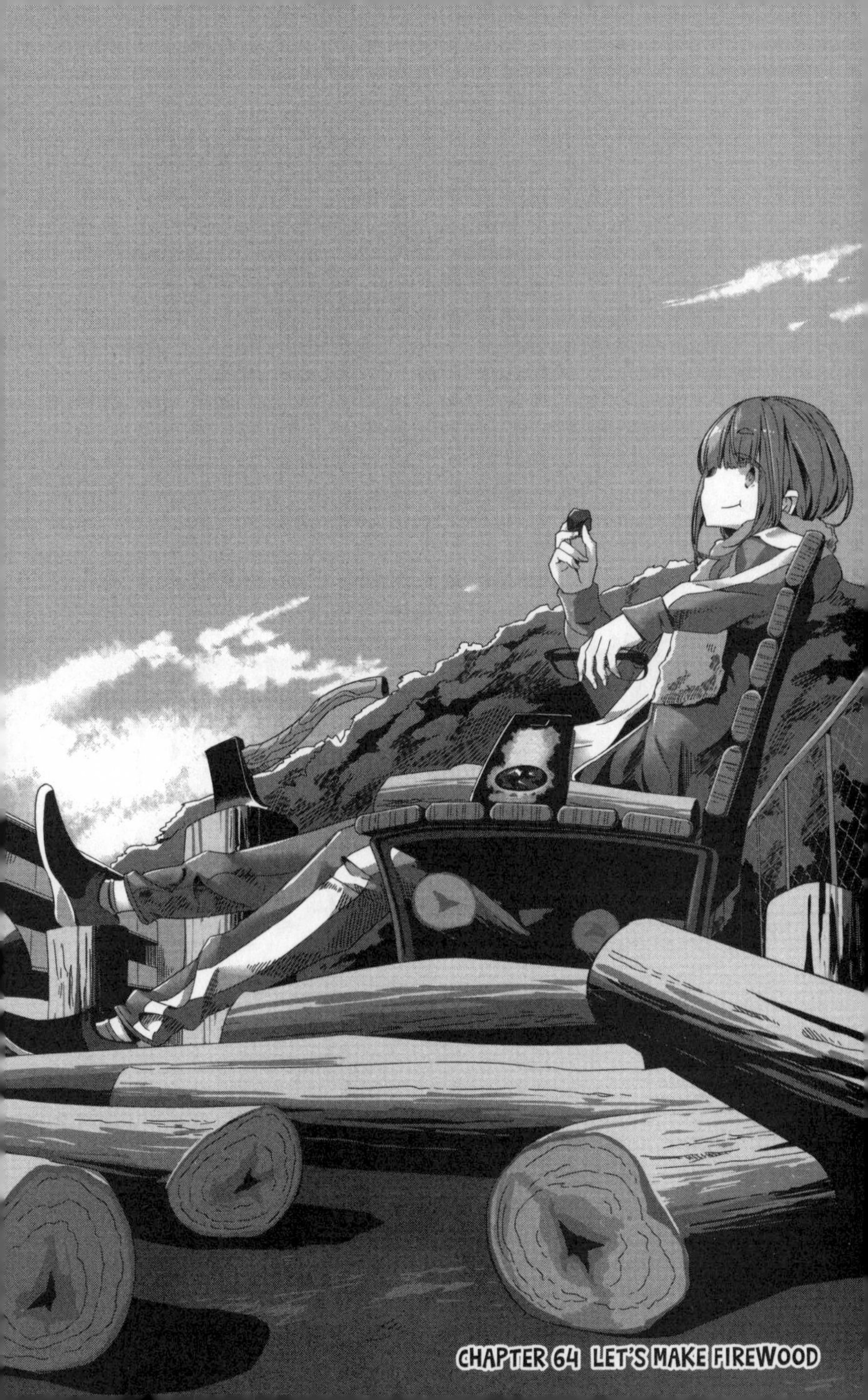
CHAPTER 64 LET'S MAKE FIREWOOD

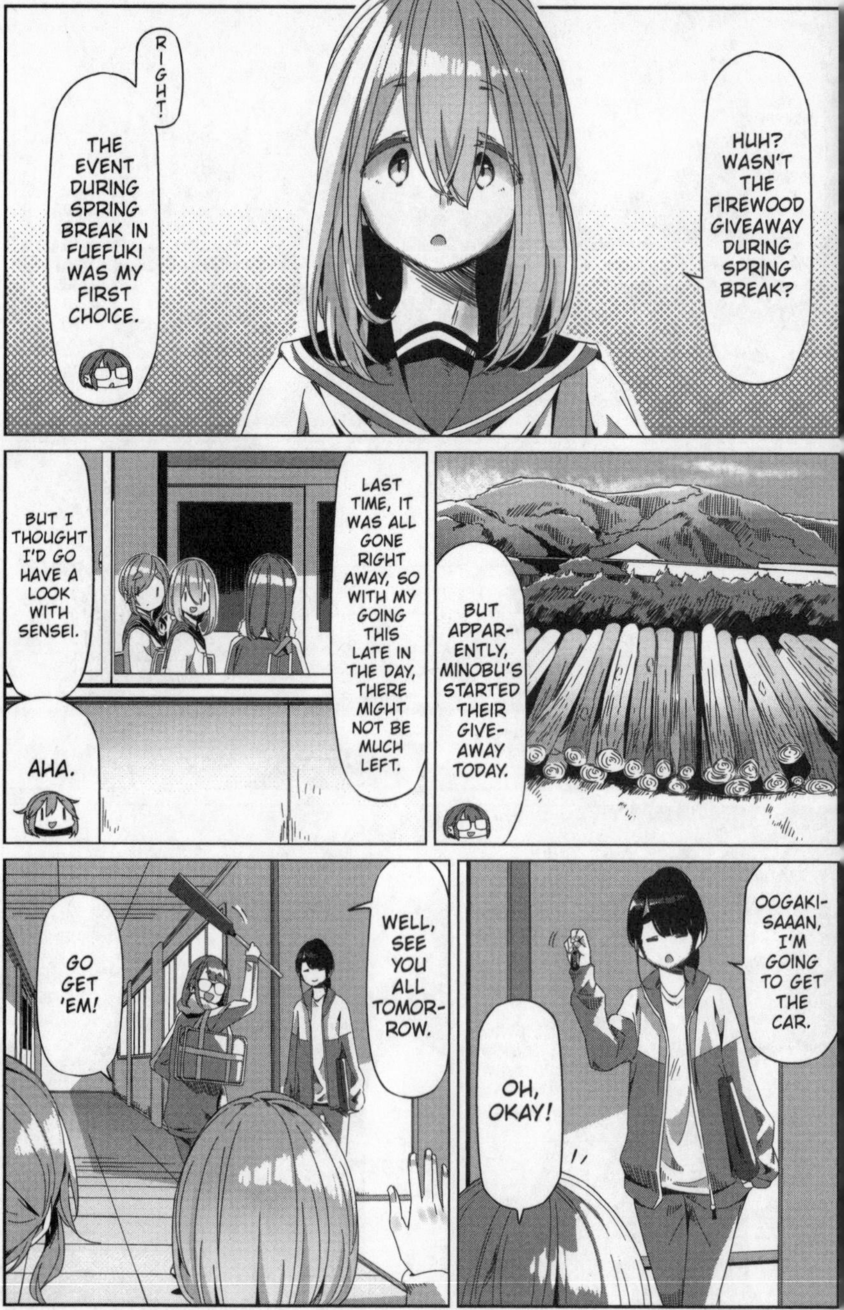
HUH? WASN'T THE FIREWOOD GIVEAWAY DURING SPRING BREAK?
RIGHT!
THE EVENT DURING SPRING BREAK IN FUEFUKI WAS MY FIRST CHOICE.
BUT APPARENTLY, MINOBU'S STARTED THEIR GIVEAWAY TODAY.
LAST TIME, IT WAS ALL GONE RIGHT AWAY, SO WITH MY GOING THIS LATE IN THE DAY, THERE MIGHT NOT BE MUCH LEFT.
BUT I THOUGHT I'D GO HAVE A LOOK WITH SENSEI.
AHA.
OOGAKI-SAAAN, I'M GOING TO GET THE CAR.
OH, OKAY!
WELL, SEE YOU ALL TOMORROW.
GO GET 'EM!

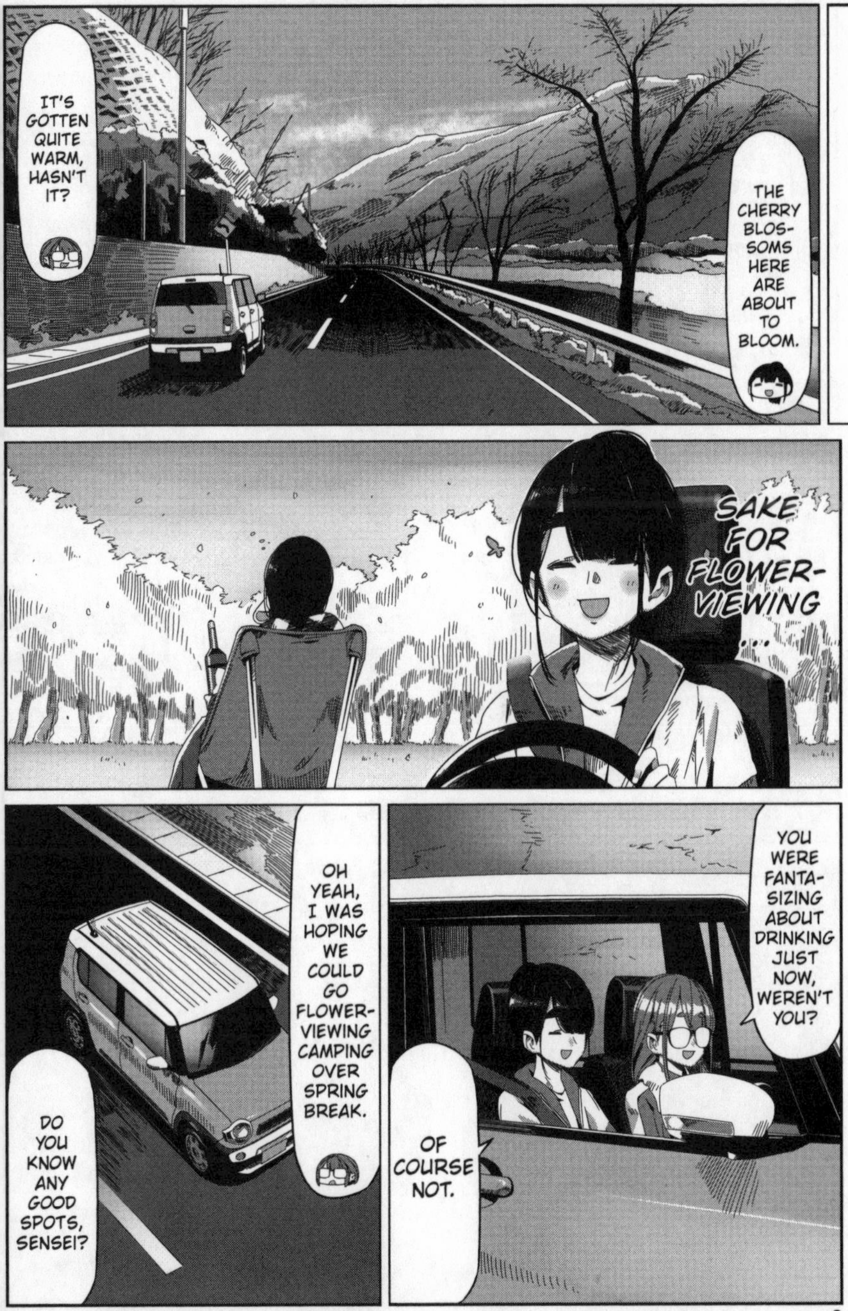
IT'S GOTTEN QUITE WARM, HASN'T IT?
THE CHERRY BLOSSOMS HERE ARE ABOUT TO BLOOM.
SAKE FOR FLOWER-VIEWING...
YOU WERE FANTASIZING ABOUT DRINKING JUST NOW, WEREN'T YOU?
OF COURSE NOT.
OH YEAH, I WAS HOPING WE COULD GO FLOWER-VIEWING CAMPING OVER SPRING BREAK.
DO YOU KNOW ANY GOOD SPOTS, SENSEI?

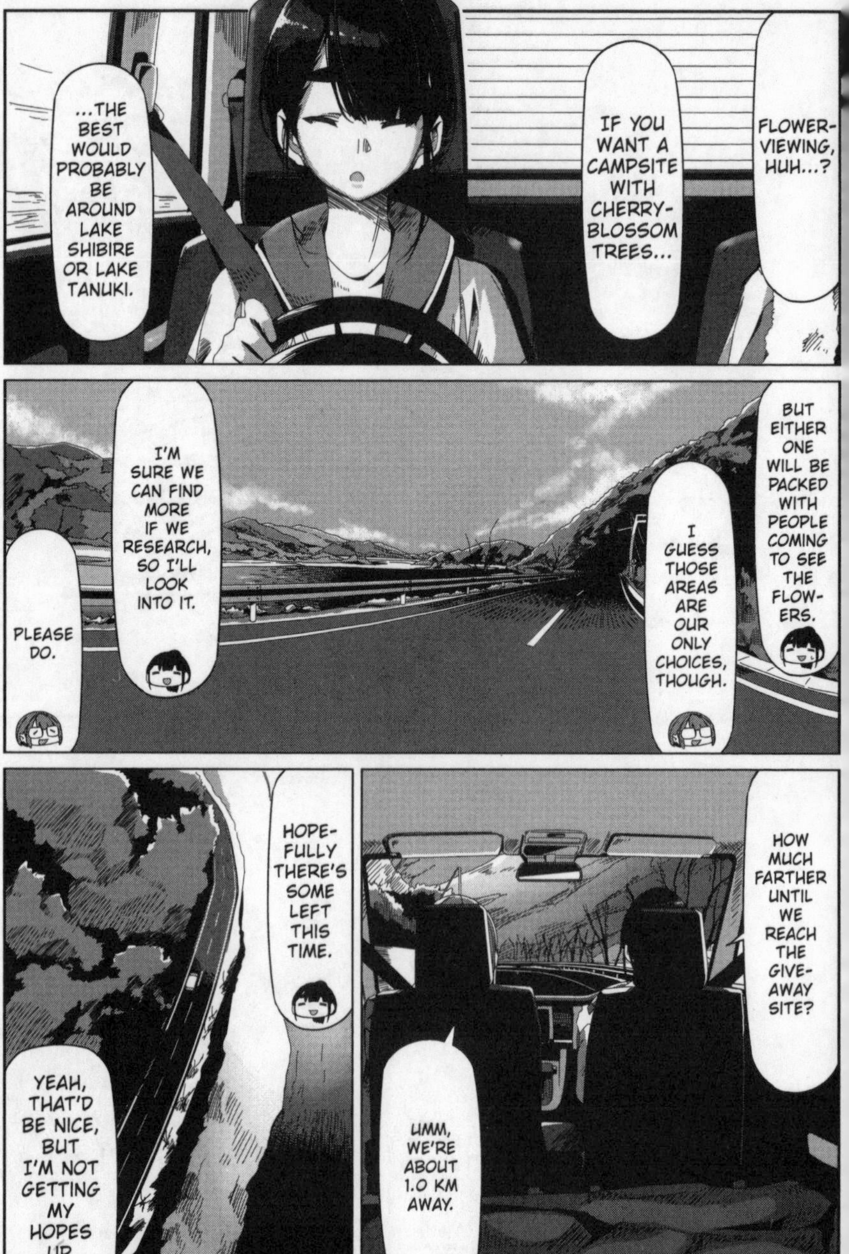
FLOWER-VIEWING, HUH...?
IF YOU WANT A CAMPSITE WITH CHERRY-BLOSSOM TREES...
...THE BEST WOULD PROBABLY BE AROUND LAKE SHIBIRE OR LAKE TANUKI.
BUT EITHER ONE WILL BE PACKED WITH PEOPLE COMING TO SEE THE FLOWERS.
I GUESS THOSE AREAS ARE OUR ONLY CHOICES, THOUGH.
I'M SURE WE CAN FIND MORE IF WE RESEARCH, SO I'LL LOOK INTO IT.
PLEASE DO.
HOW MUCH FARTHER UNTIL WE REACH THE GIVE-AWAY SITE?
UMM, WE'RE ABOUT 1.0 KM AWAY.
HOPE-FULLY THERE'S SOME LEFT THIS TIME.
YEAH, THAT'D BE NICE, BUT I'M NOT GETTING MY HOPES UP.
HA HA HA...

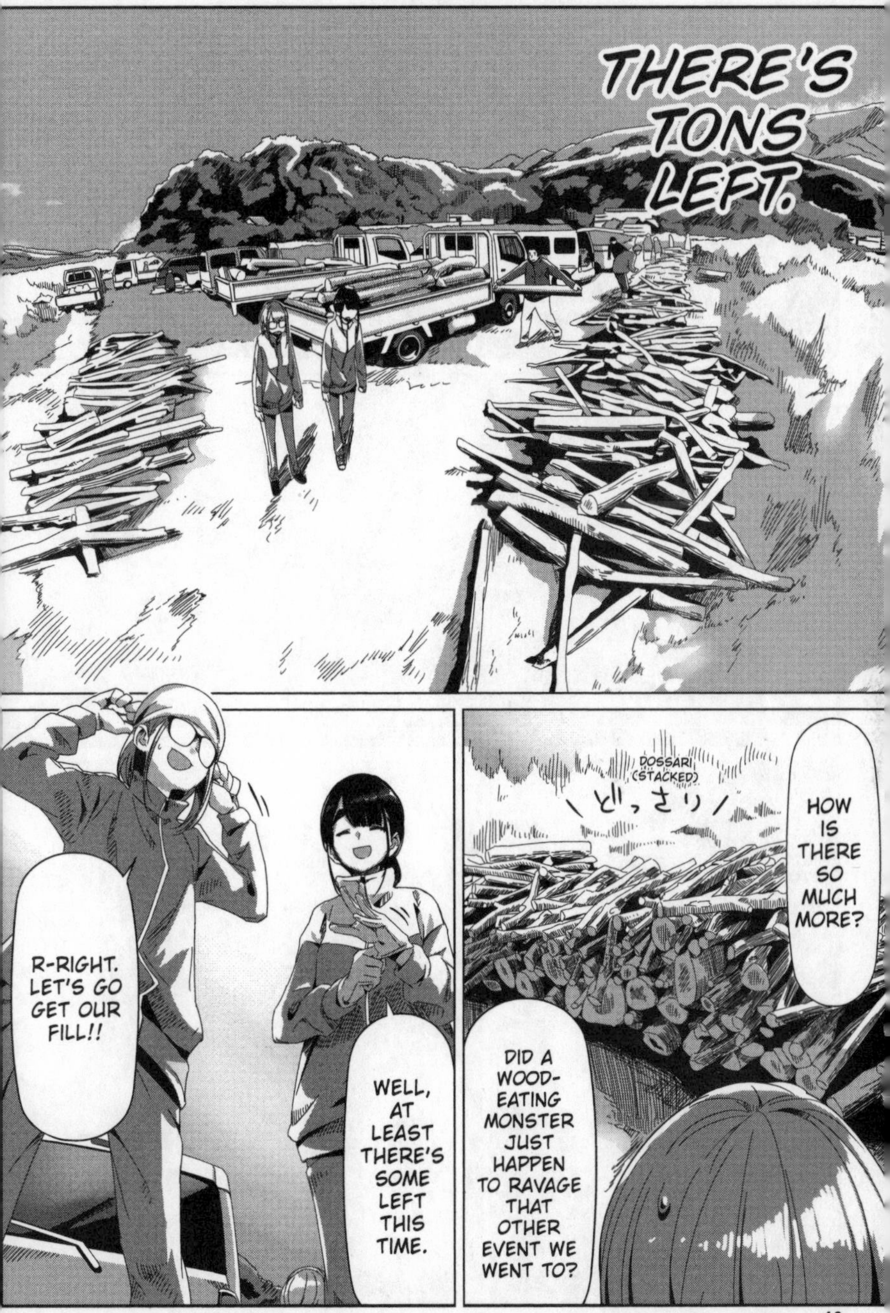
THERE'S TONS LEFT.
HOW IS THERE SO MUCH MORE?
DOSSARI (STACKED)
どっさり
DID A WOOD-EATING MONSTER JUST HAPPEN TO RAVAGE THAT OTHER EVENT WE WENT TO?
WELL, AT LEAST THERE'S SOME LEFT THIS TIME.
R-RIGHT. LET'S GO GET OUR FILL!!

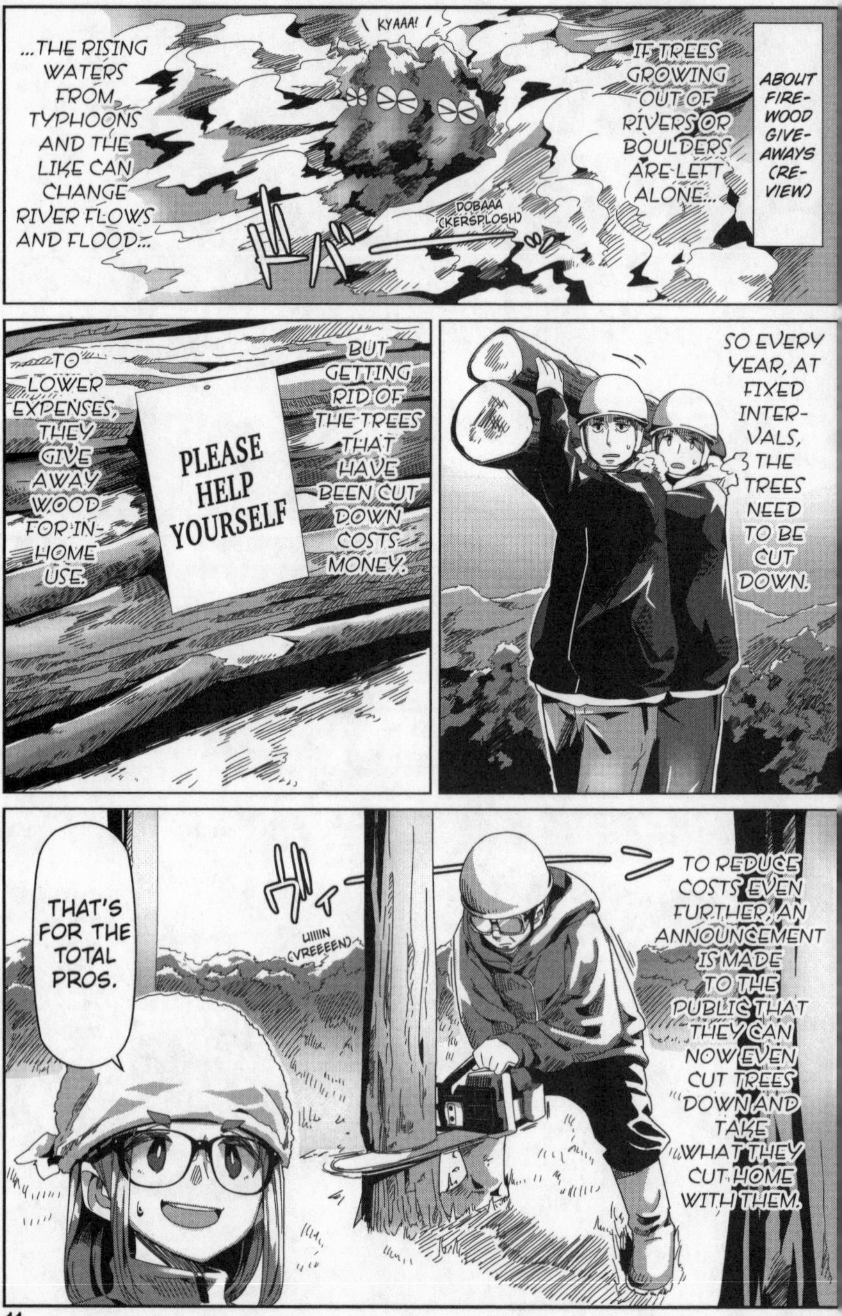
ABOUT FIREWOOD GIVEAWAYS (REVIEW)
IF TREES GROWING OUT OF RIVERS OR BOULDERS ARE LEFT ALONE...
KYAAA!
DOBAAA (KERSPLOSH)
...THE RISING WATERS FROM TYPHOONS AND THE LIKE CAN CHANGE RIVER FLOWS AND FLOOD...
SO EVERY YEAR, AT FIXED INTERVALS, THE TREES NEED TO BE CUT DOWN.
BUT GETTING RID OF THE TREES THAT HAVE BEEN CUT DOWN COSTS MONEY.
PLEASE HELP YOURSELF
TO LOWER EXPENSES, THEY GIVE AWAY WOOD FOR IN-HOME USE.
TO REDUCE COSTS EVEN FURTHER, AN ANNOUNCEMENT IS MADE TO THE PUBLIC THAT THEY CAN NOW EVEN CUT TREES DOWN AND TAKE WHAT THEY CUT HOME WITH THEM.
UIIIIN (VREEEEN)
THAT'S FOR THE TOTAL PROS.

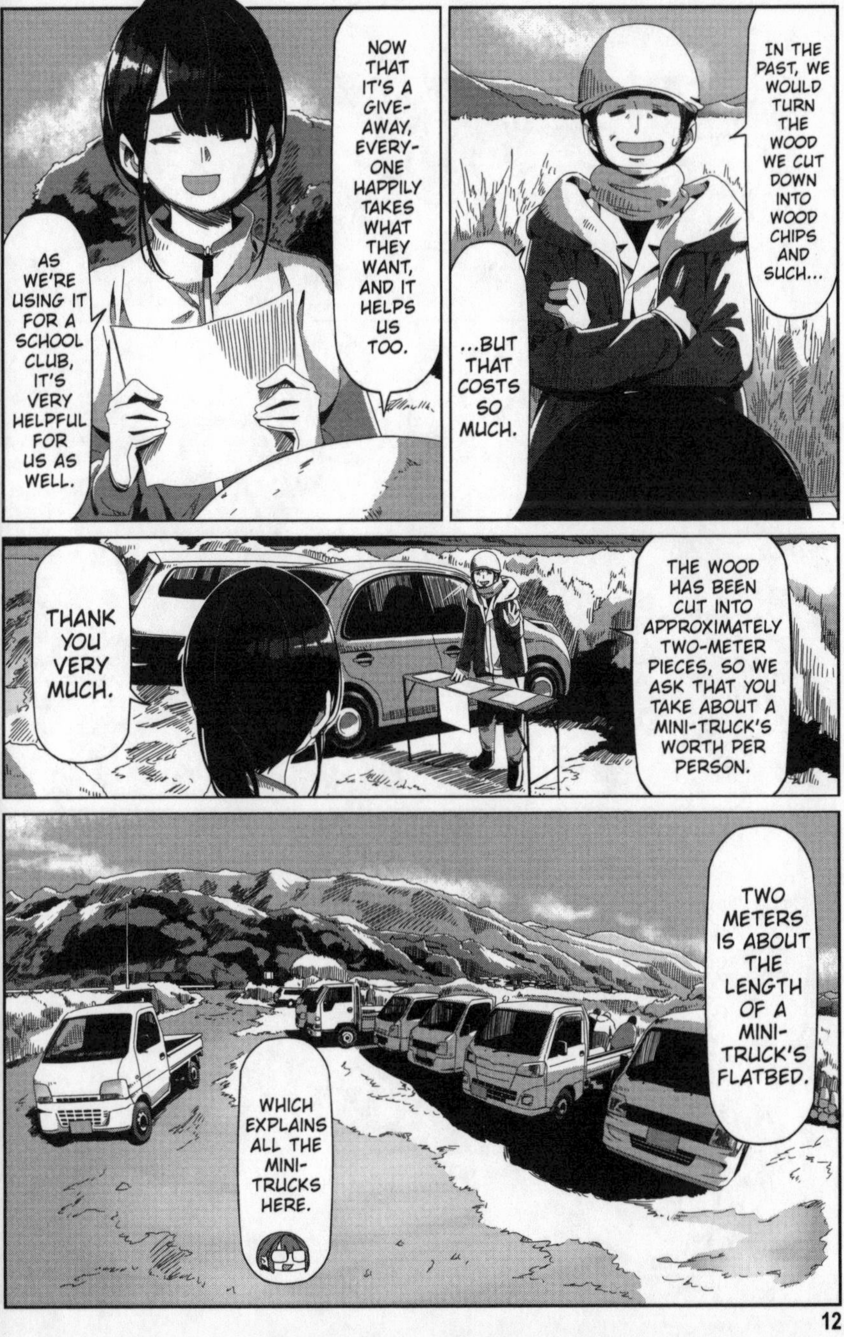

IN THE PAST, WE WOULD TURN THE WOOD WE CUT DOWN INTO WOOD CHIPS AND SUCH...
...BUT THAT COSTS SO MUCH.
NOW THAT IT'S A GIVE-AWAY, EVERY-ONE HAPPILY TAKES WHAT THEY WANT, AND IT HELPS US TOO.
AS WE'RE USING IT FOR A SCHOOL CLUB, IT'S VERY HELPFUL FOR US AS WELL.
THE WOOD HAS BEEN CUT INTO APPROXIMATELY TWO-METER PIECES, SO WE ASK THAT YOU TAKE ABOUT A MINI-TRUCK'S WORTH PER PERSON.
THANK YOU VERY MUCH.
TWO METERS IS ABOUT THE LENGTH OF A MINI-TRUCK'S FLATBED.
WHICH EXPLAINS ALL THE MINI-TRUCKS HERE.

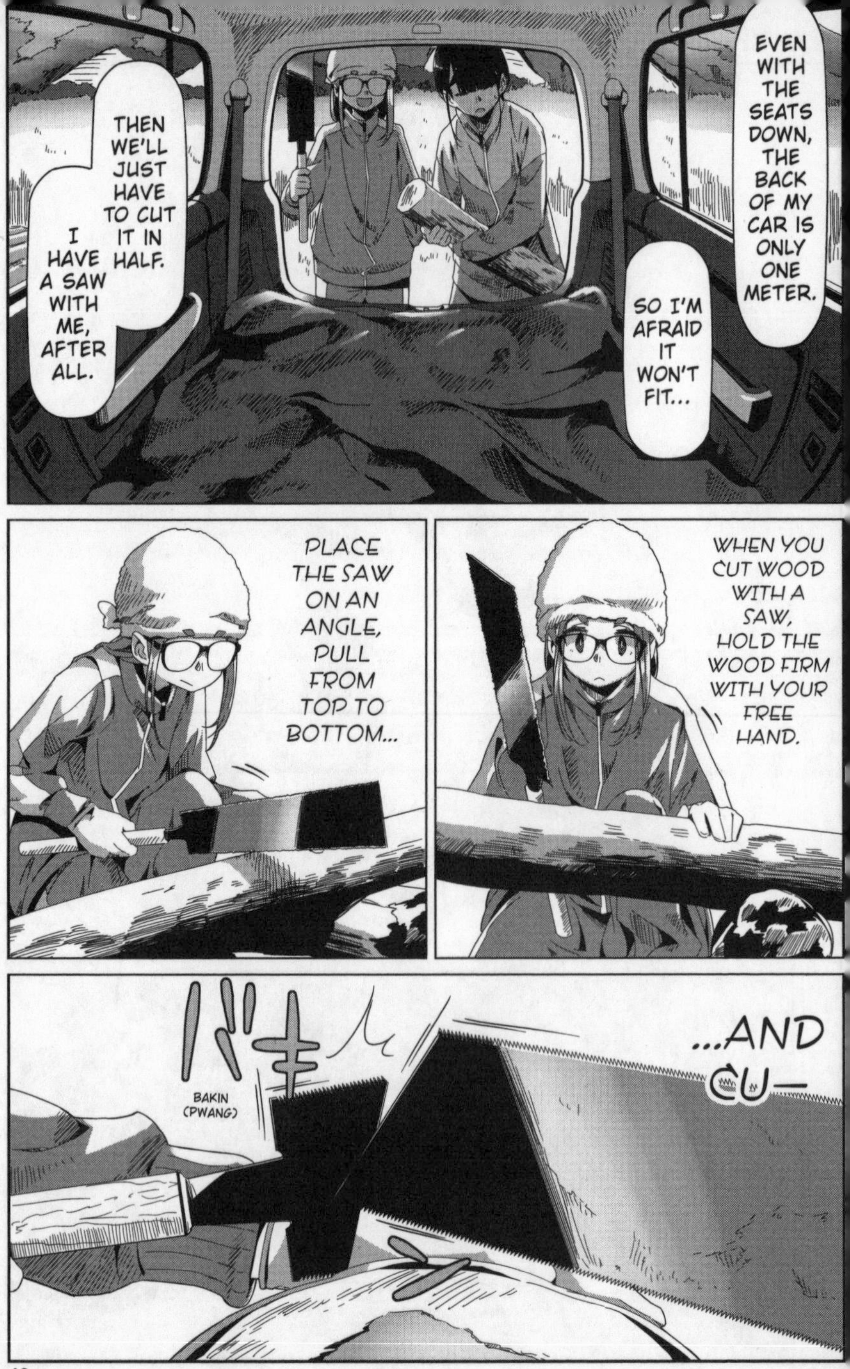
EVEN WITH THE SEATS DOWN, THE BACK OF MY CAR IS ONLY ONE METER.
SO I'M AFRAID IT WON'T FIT...
THEN WE'LL JUST HAVE TO CUT IT IN HALF.
I HAVE A SAW WITH ME, AFTER ALL.
WHEN YOU CUT WOOD WITH A SAW, HOLD THE WOOD FIRM WITH YOUR FREE HAND.
PLACE THE SAW ON AN ANGLE, PULL FROM TOP TO BOTTOM...
...AND CU—
BAKIN (PWANG)

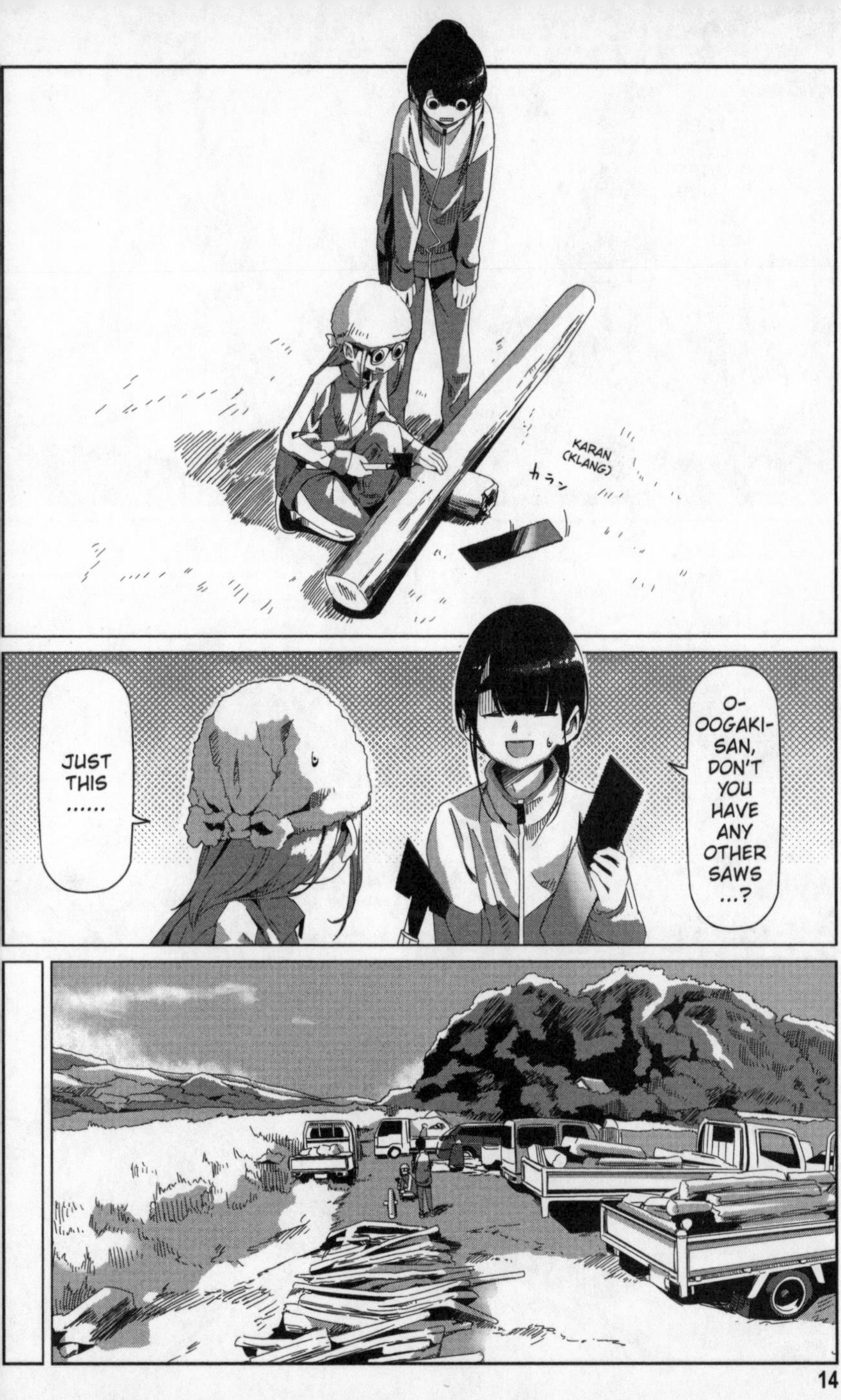
KARAN (KLANG)
カラン
O-OOGAKI-SAN, DON'T YOU HAVE ANY OTHER SAWS ...?
JUST THIS ......

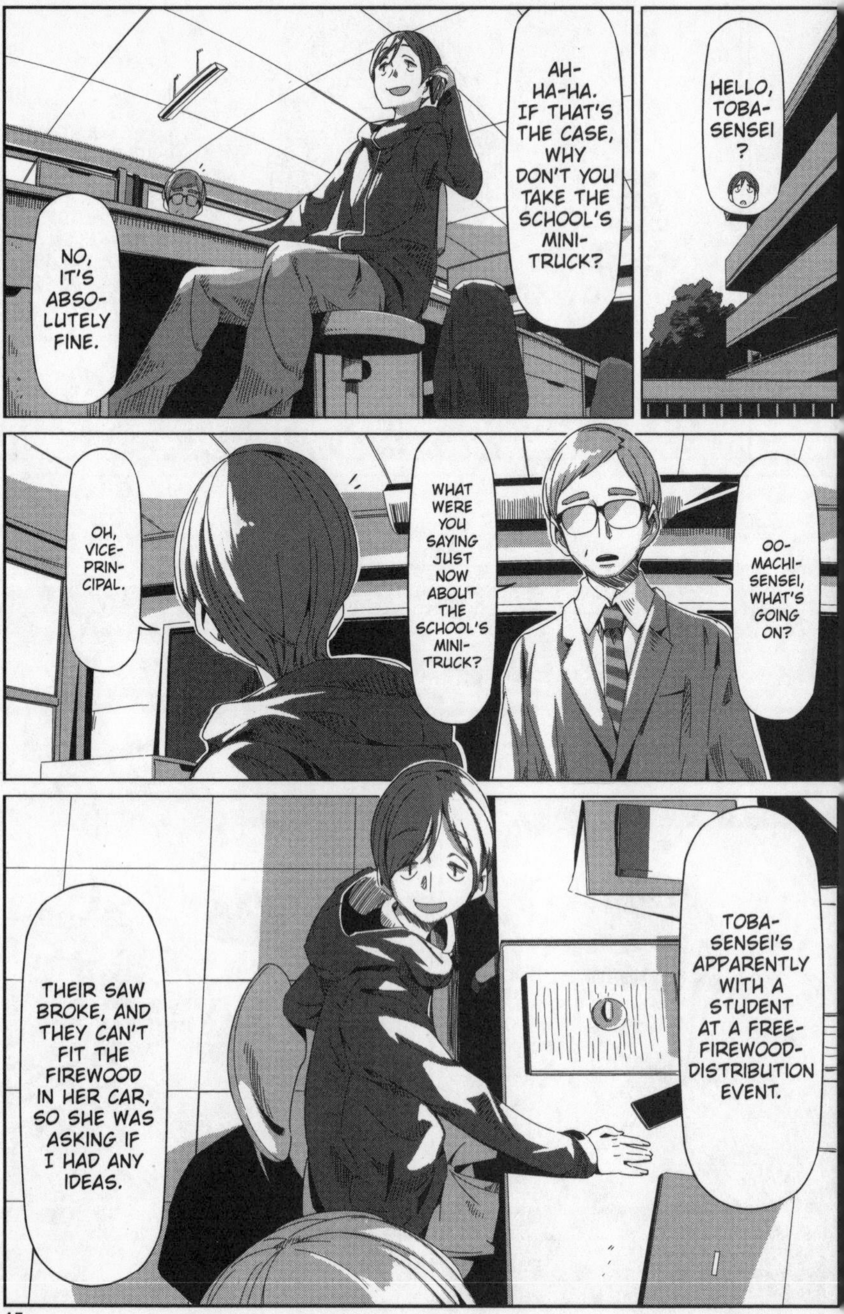
HELLO, TOBA-SENSEI?
AH-HA-HA. IF THAT'S THE CASE, WHY DON'T YOU TAKE THE SCHOOL'S MINI-TRUCK?
NO, IT'S ABSOLUTELY FINE.
OO-MACHI-SENSEI, WHAT'S GOING ON?
WHAT WERE YOU SAYING JUST NOW ABOUT THE SCHOOL'S MINI-TRUCK?
OH, VICE-PRINCIPAL.
TOBA-SENSEI'S APPARENTLY WITH A STUDENT AT A FREE-FIREWOOD-DISTRIBUTION EVENT.
THEIR SAW BROKE, AND THEY CAN'T FIT THE FIREWOOD IN HER CAR, SO SHE WAS ASKING IF I HAD ANY IDEAS.

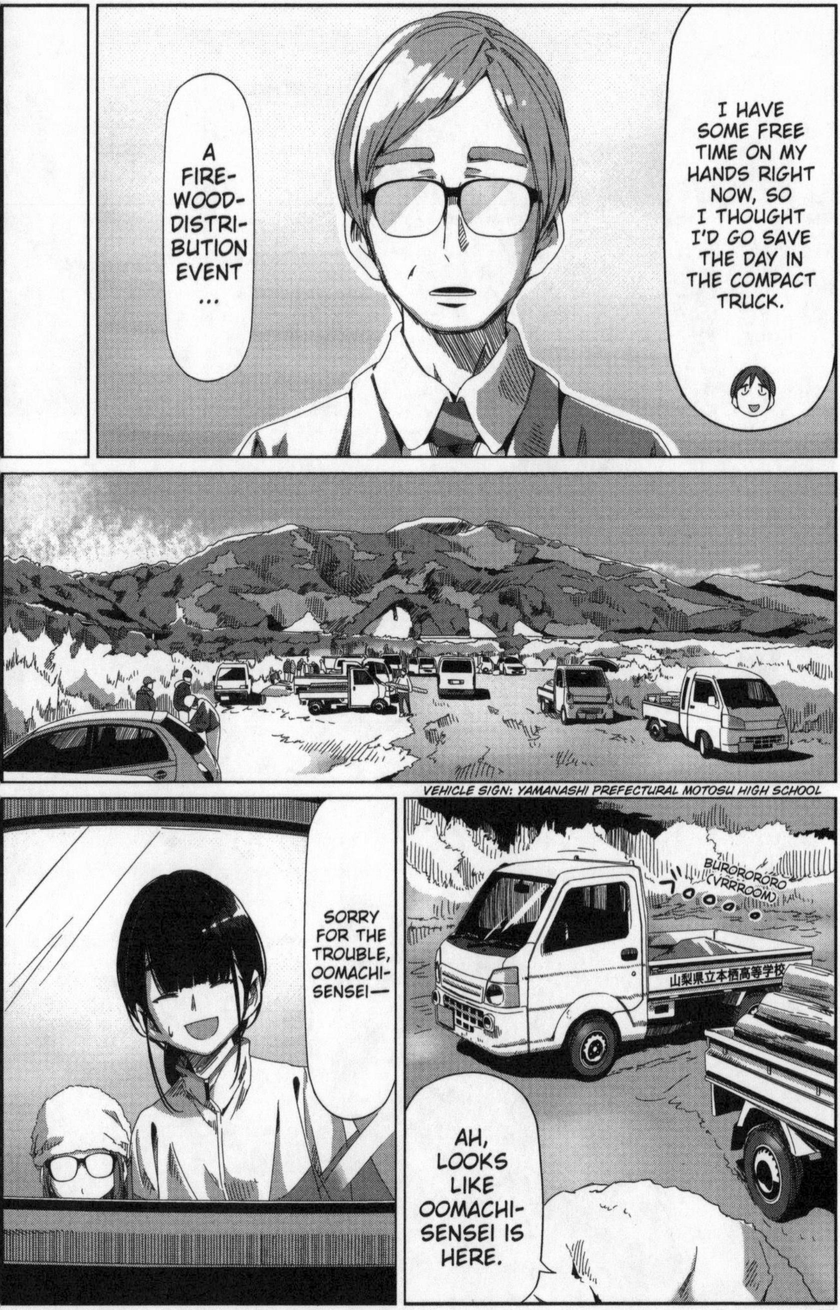
I HAVE SOME FREE TIME ON MY HANDS RIGHT NOW, SO I THOUGHT I'D GO SAVE THE DAY IN THE COMPACT TRUCK.
A FIRE-WOOD-DISTRI-BUTION EVENT ...
BUROROROROR (VRRROOM)
山梨県立本栖高等学校
VEHICLE SIGN: YAMANASHI PREFECTURAL MOTOSU HIGH SCHOOL
AH, LOOKS LIKE OOMACHI-SENSEI IS HERE.
SORRY FOR THE TROUBLE, OOMACHI-SENSEI—

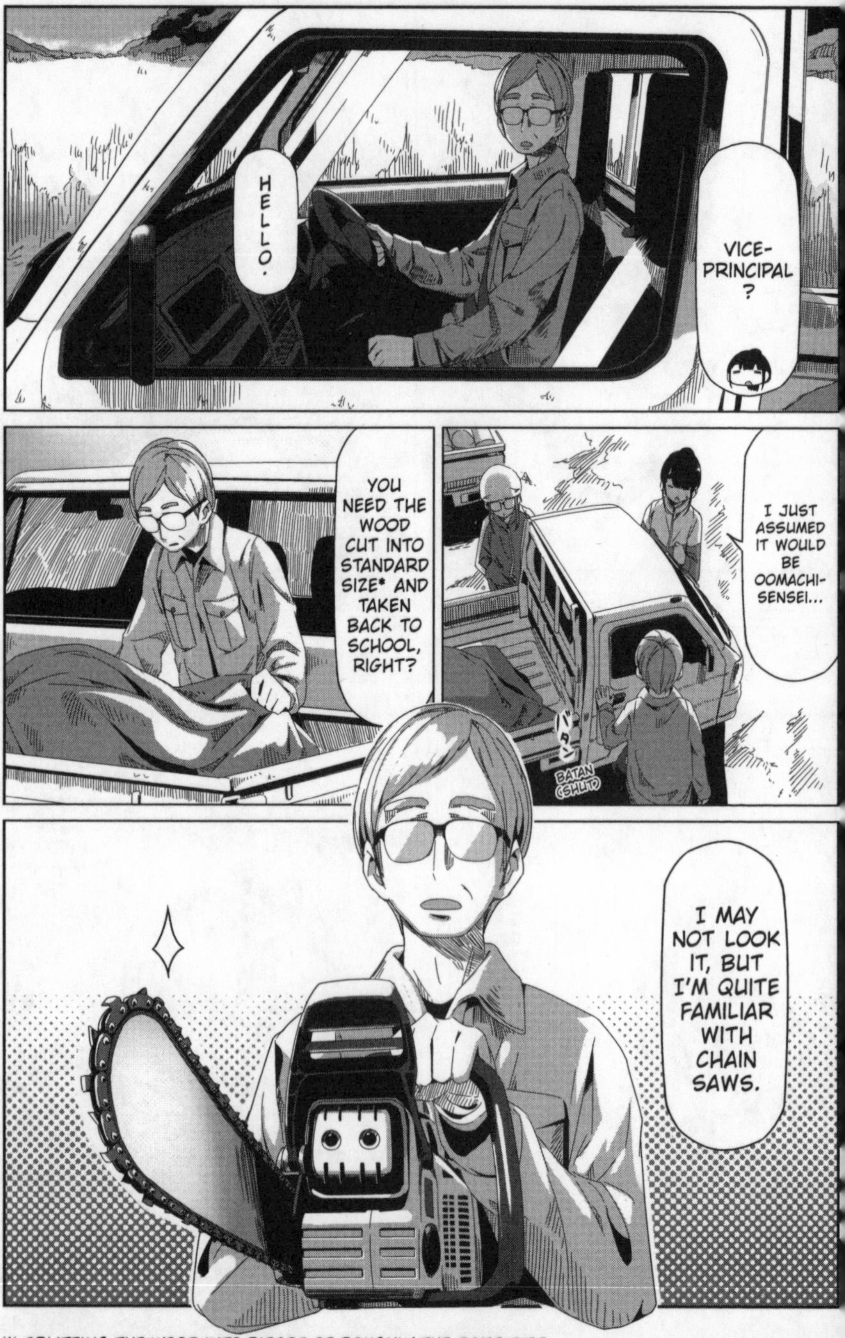
VICE-PRINCIPAL?
HELLO.
I JUST ASSUMED IT WOULD BE OOMACHI-SENSEI...
BATAN (SHUT)
YOU NEED THE WOOD CUT INTO STANDARD SIZE* AND TAKEN BACK TO SCHOOL, RIGHT?
I MAY NOT LOOK IT, BUT I'M QUITE FAMILIAR WITH CHAIN SAWS.

※ *SPLITTING THE WOOD INTO PIECES OF ROUGHLY THE SAME SIZE*

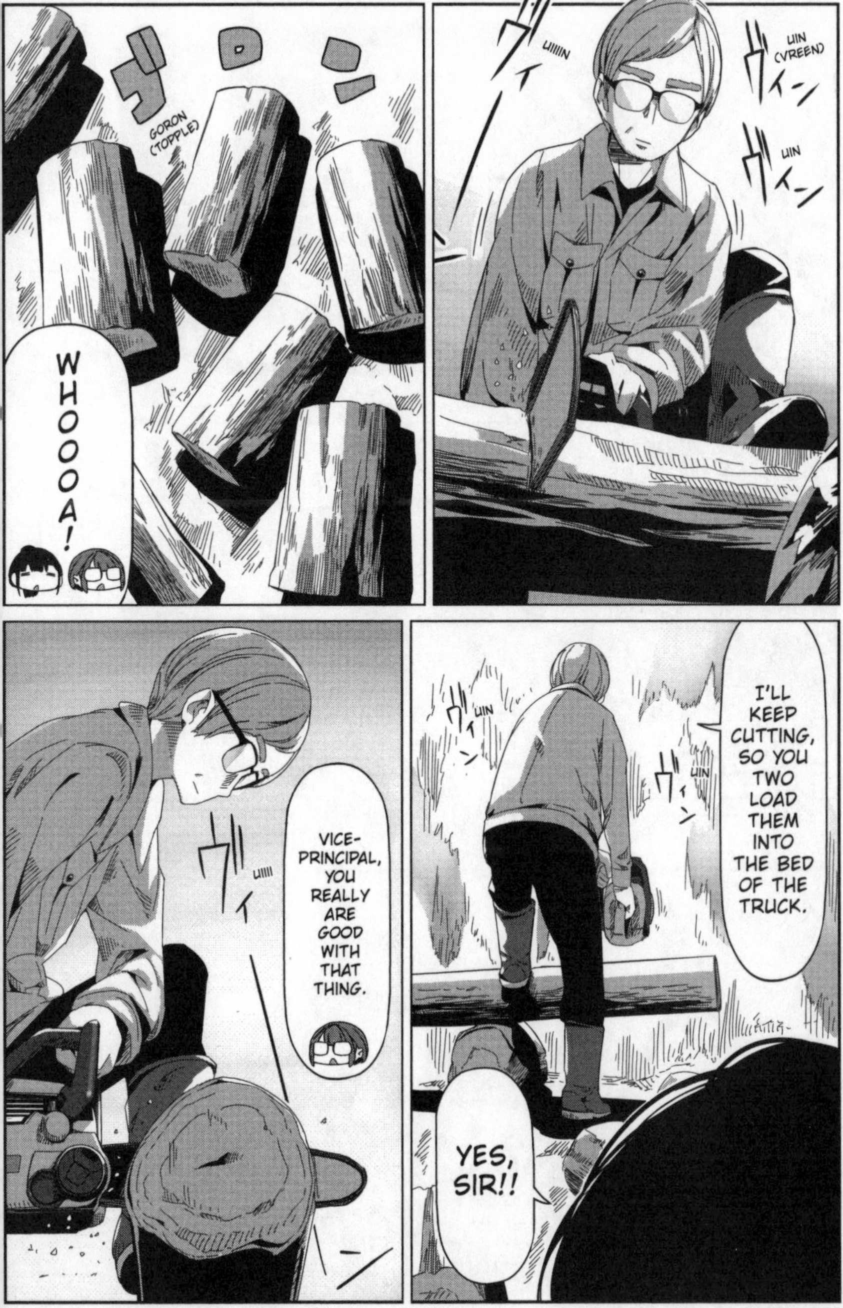
UIIIIN
UIN (VREEN)
UIN
GORON (TOPPLE)
WHOOOOA!
I'LL KEEP CUTTING, SO YOU TWO LOAD THEM INTO THE BED OF THE TRUCK.
UIN
UIN
YES, SIR!!
VICE-PRINCIPAL, YOU REALLY ARE GOOD WITH THAT THING.
UIIII

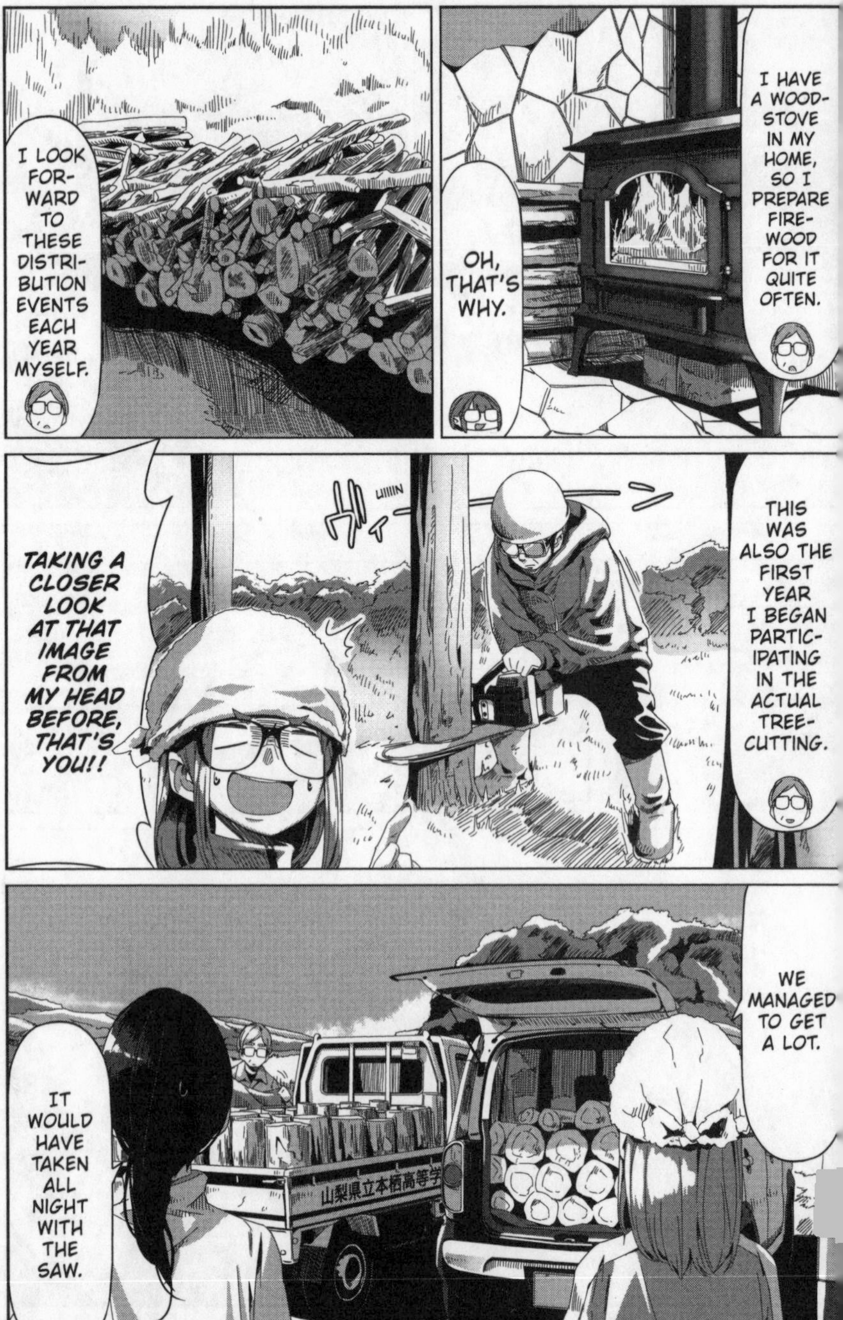
I HAVE A WOODSTOVE IN MY HOME, SO I PREPARE FIREWOOD FOR IT QUITE OFTEN.
OH, THAT'S WHY.
I LOOK FORWARD TO THESE DISTRIBUTION EVENTS EACH YEAR MYSELF.
THIS WAS ALSO THE FIRST YEAR I BEGAN PARTICIPATING IN THE ACTUAL TREE-CUTTING.
ヴィーン
UIIIIN
TAKING A CLOSER LOOK AT THAT IMAGE FROM MY HEAD BEFORE, THAT'S YOU!!
WE MANAGED TO GET A LOT.
山梨県立本栖高等学
IT WOULD HAVE TAKEN ALL NIGHT WITH THE SAW.

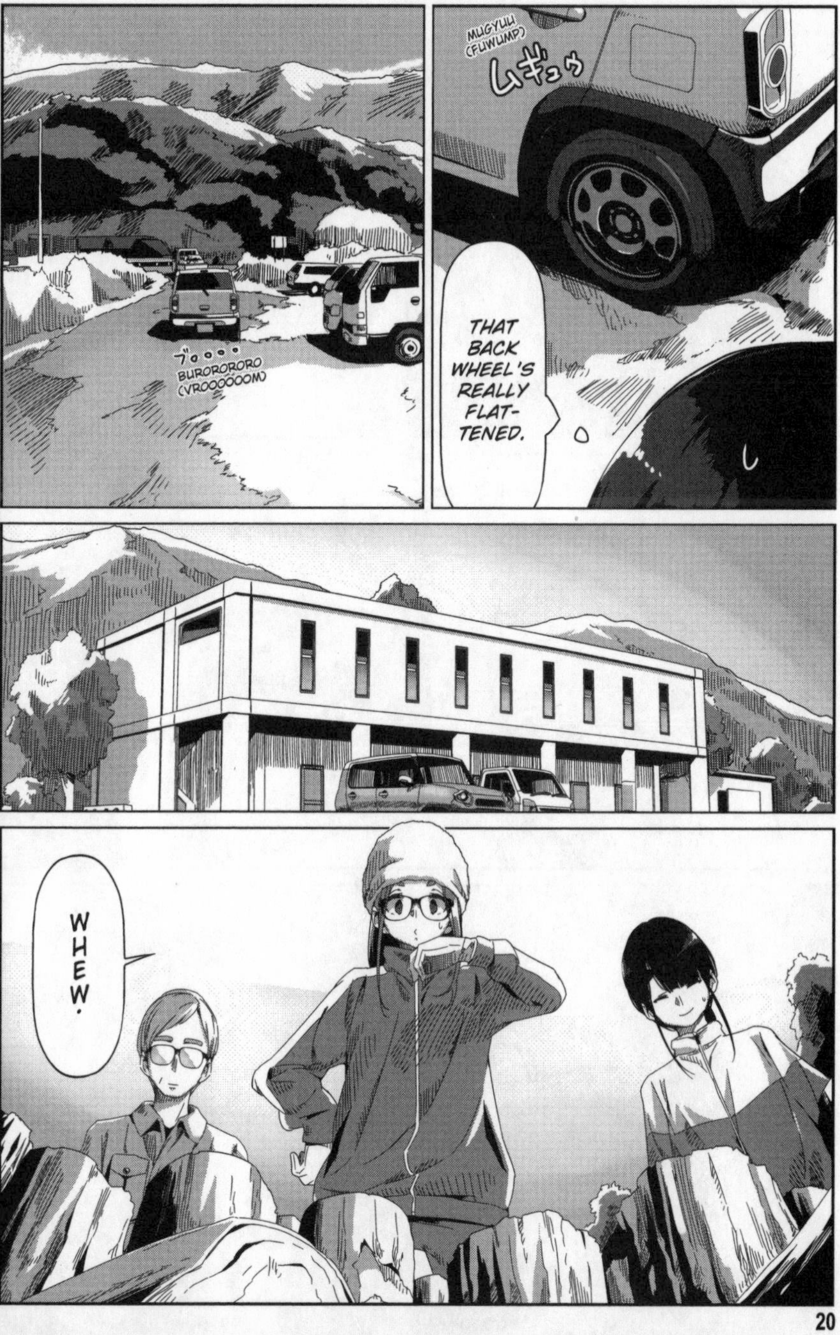
MUGYUU (FUWUMP)
ムギュゥ
THAT BACK WHEEL'S REALLY FLAT-TENED.
BURORORORO (VROOOOOOM)
WHEW.

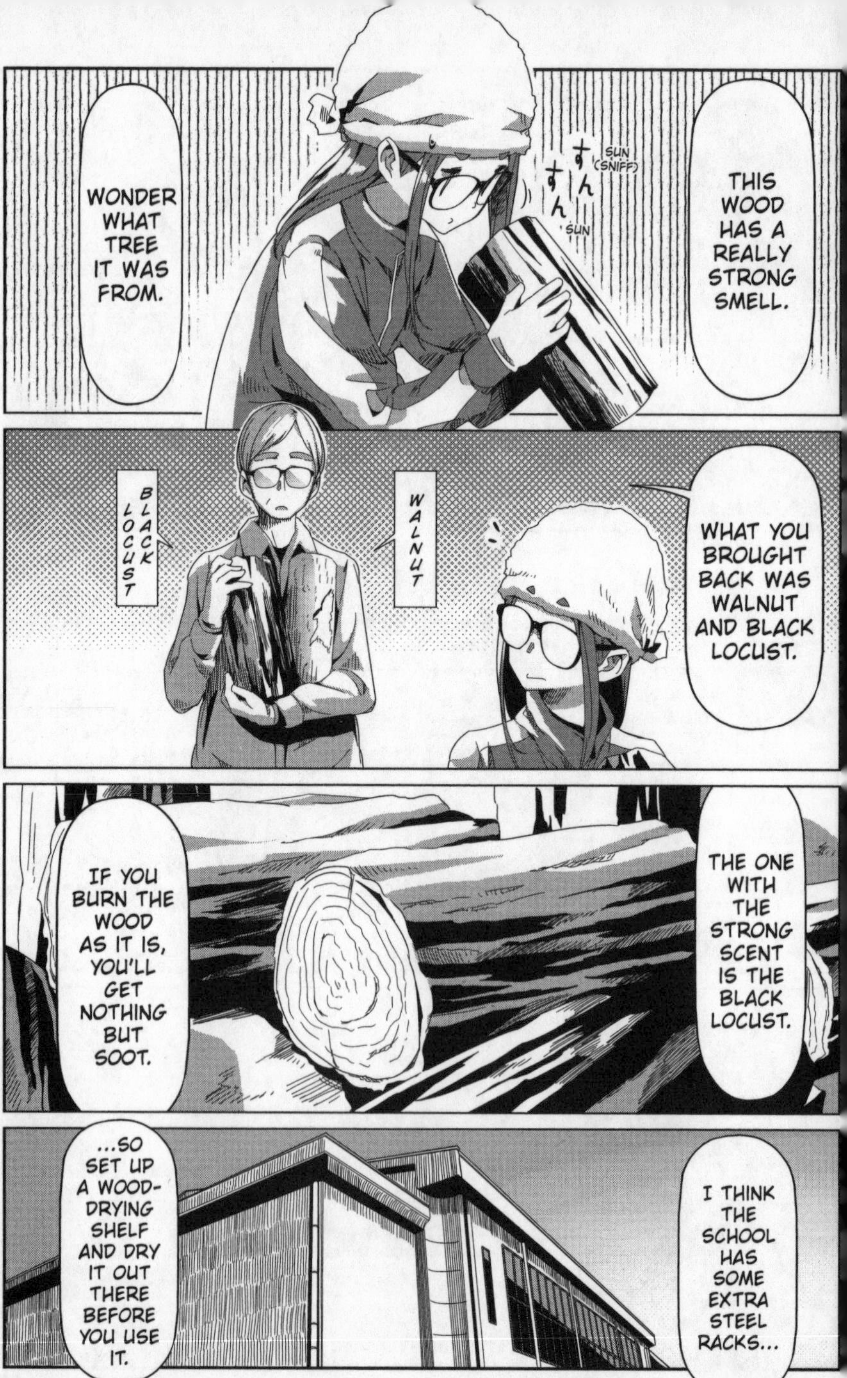
THIS WOOD HAS A REALLY STRONG SMELL.
すん すん
SUN (SNIFF)
SUN
WONDER WHAT TREE IT WAS FROM.
WHAT YOU BROUGHT BACK WAS WALNUT AND BLACK LOCUST.
WALNUT
BLACK LOCUST
THE ONE WITH THE STRONG SCENT IS THE BLACK LOCUST.
IF YOU BURN THE WOOD AS IT IS, YOU'LL GET NOTHING BUT SOOT.
I THINK THE SCHOOL HAS SOME EXTRA STEEL RACKS...
...SO SET UP A WOOD-DRYING SHELF AND DRY IT OUT THERE BEFORE YOU USE IT.

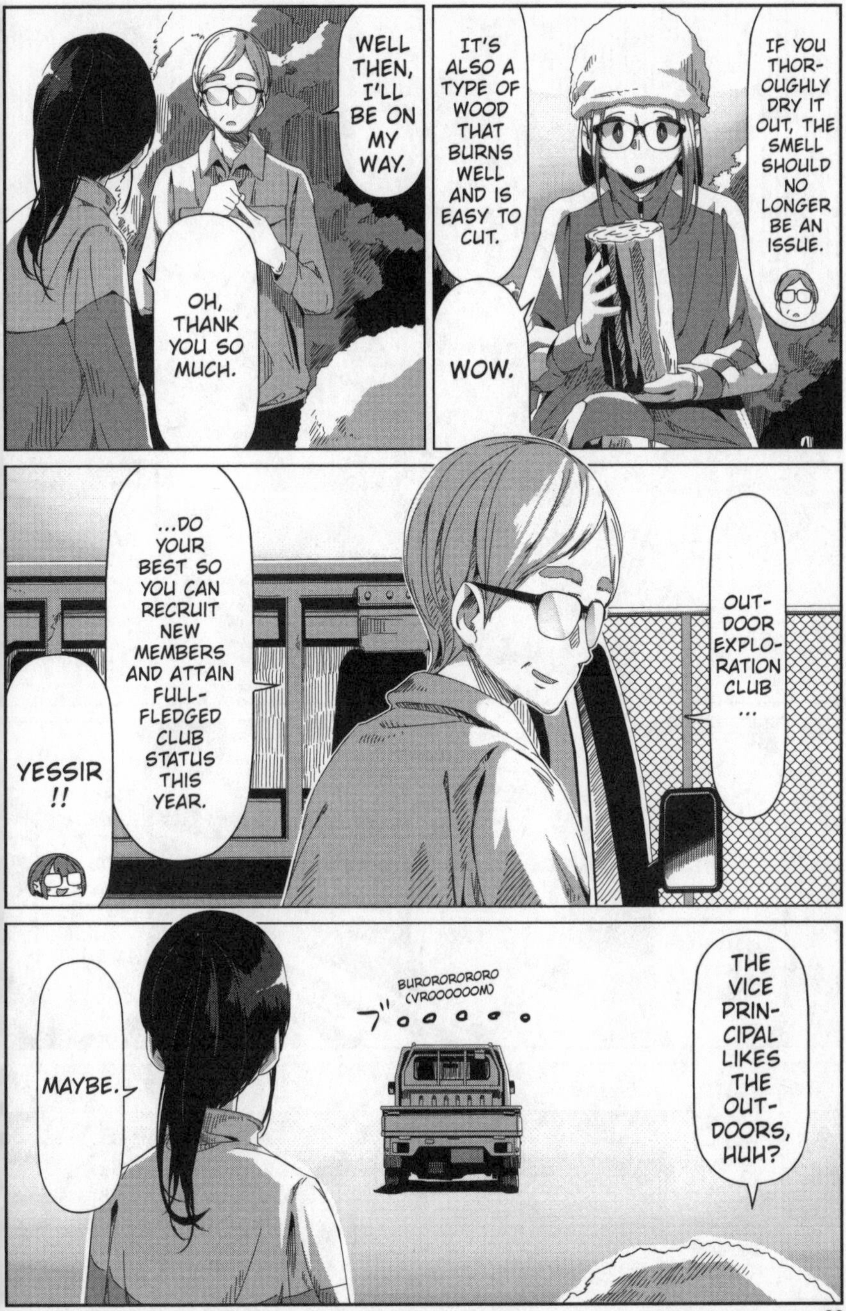
IF YOU THOROUGHLY DRY IT OUT, THE SMELL SHOULD NO LONGER BE AN ISSUE.
IT'S ALSO A TYPE OF WOOD THAT BURNS WELL AND IS EASY TO CUT.
WOW.
WELL THEN, I'LL BE ON MY WAY.
OH, THANK YOU SO MUCH.
OUTDOOR EXPLORATION CLUB...
...DO YOUR BEST SO YOU CAN RECRUIT NEW MEMBERS AND ATTAIN FULL-FLEDGED CLUB STATUS THIS YEAR.
YESSIR!!
THE VICE PRINCIPAL LIKES THE OUTDOORS, HUH?
BURORORORORO (VROOOOOOM)
MAYBE.

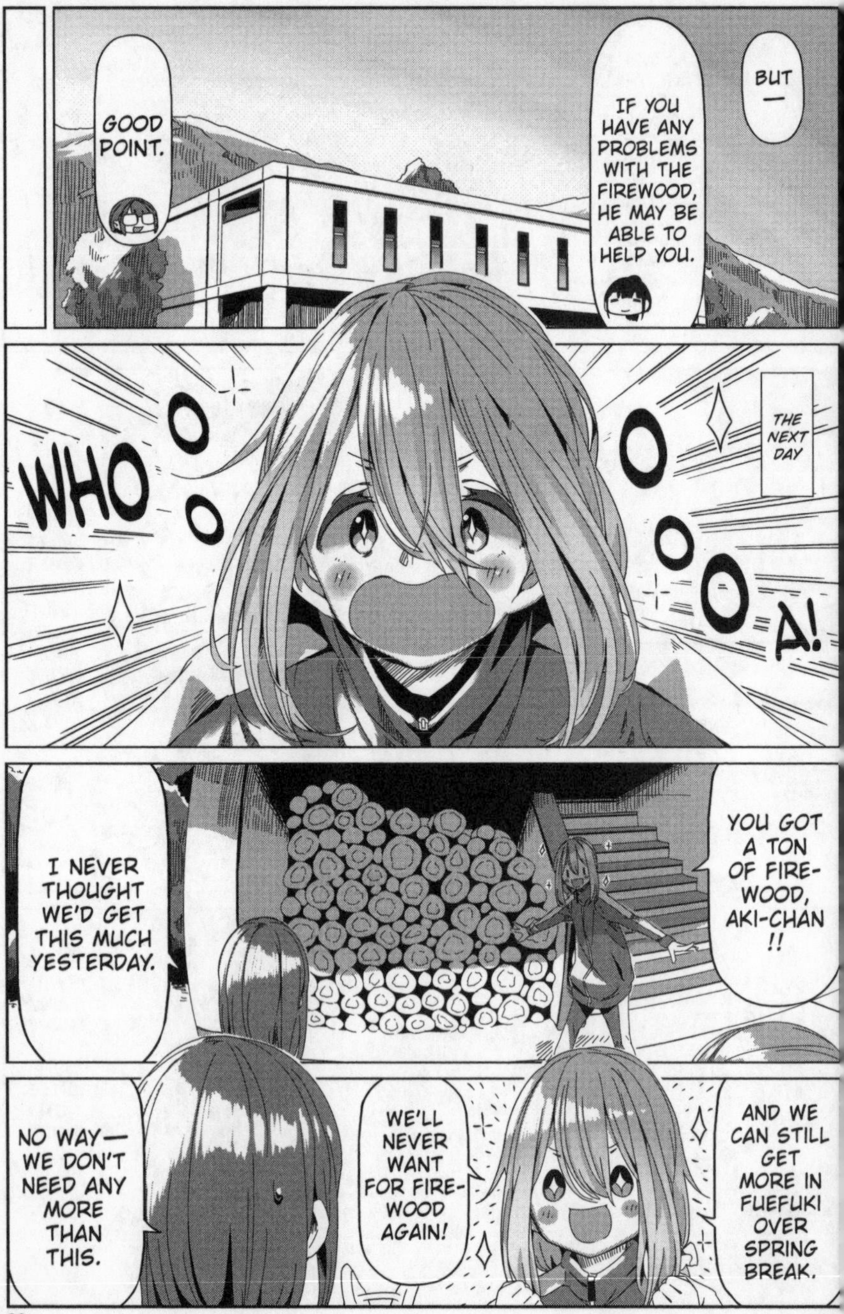
BUT—
IF YOU HAVE ANY PROBLEMS WITH THE FIREWOOD, HE MAY BE ABLE TO HELP YOU.
GOOD POINT.
THE NEXT DAY
WHOOOOOOOA!
YOU GOT A TON OF FIRE-WOOD, AKI-CHAN!!
I NEVER THOUGHT WE'D GET THIS MUCH YESTERDAY.
AND WE CAN STILL GET MORE IN FUEFUKI OVER SPRING BREAK.
WE'LL NEVER WANT FOR FIRE-WOOD AGAIN!
NO WAY— WE DON'T NEED ANY MORE THAN THIS.

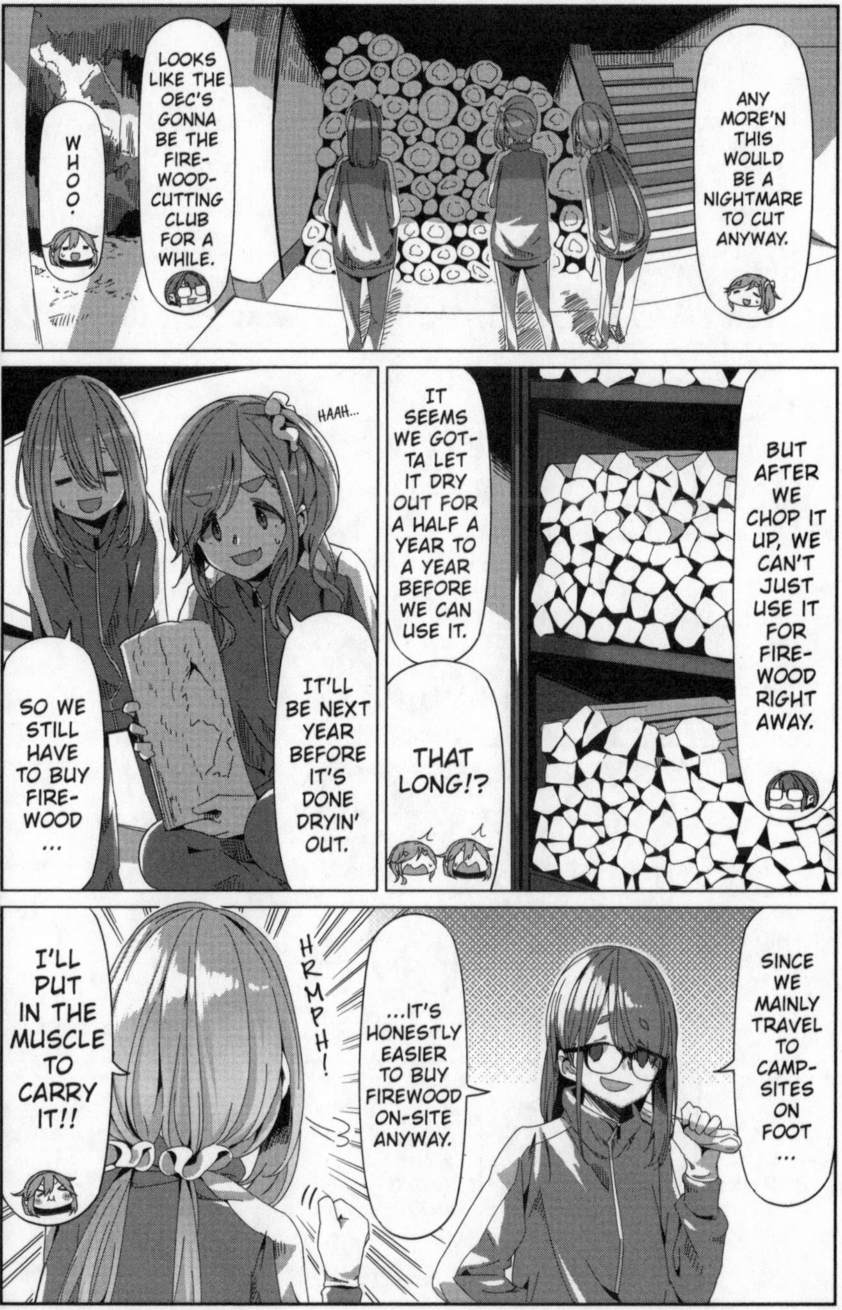
ANY MORE'N THIS WOULD BE A NIGHTMARE TO CUT ANYWAY.
LOOKS LIKE THE OEC'S GONNA BE THE FIRE-WOOD-CUTTING CLUB FOR A WHILE.
WHOO.
BUT AFTER WE CHOP IT UP, WE CAN'T JUST USE IT FOR FIRE-WOOD RIGHT AWAY.
IT SEEMS WE GOT-TA LET IT DRY OUT FOR A HALF A YEAR TO A YEAR BEFORE WE CAN USE IT.
THAT LONG!?
HAAAH...
IT'LL BE NEXT YEAR BEFORE IT'S DONE DRYIN' OUT.
SO WE STILL HAVE TO BUY FIRE-WOOD ...
SINCE WE MAINLY TRAVEL TO CAMP-SITES ON FOOT ...
...IT'S HONESTLY EASIER TO BUY FIREWOOD ON-SITE ANYWAY.
HRMPH!
I'LL PUT IN THE MUSCLE TO CARRY IT!!

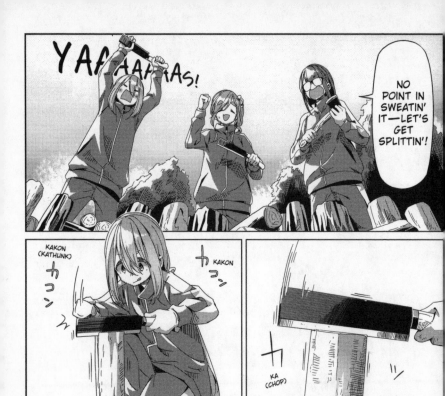

YAAAAHAS!

NO POINT IN SWEATIN' IT—LET'S GET SPLITTIN'!

KAKON (KATHUNK)

KAKON

KA (CHOP)

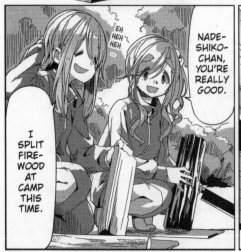

EH HEH HEH.

NADE-SHIKO-CHAN, YOU'RE REALLY GOOD.

I SPLIT FIREWOOD AT CAMP THIS TIME.

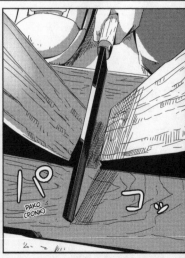

PAKO (PONK)

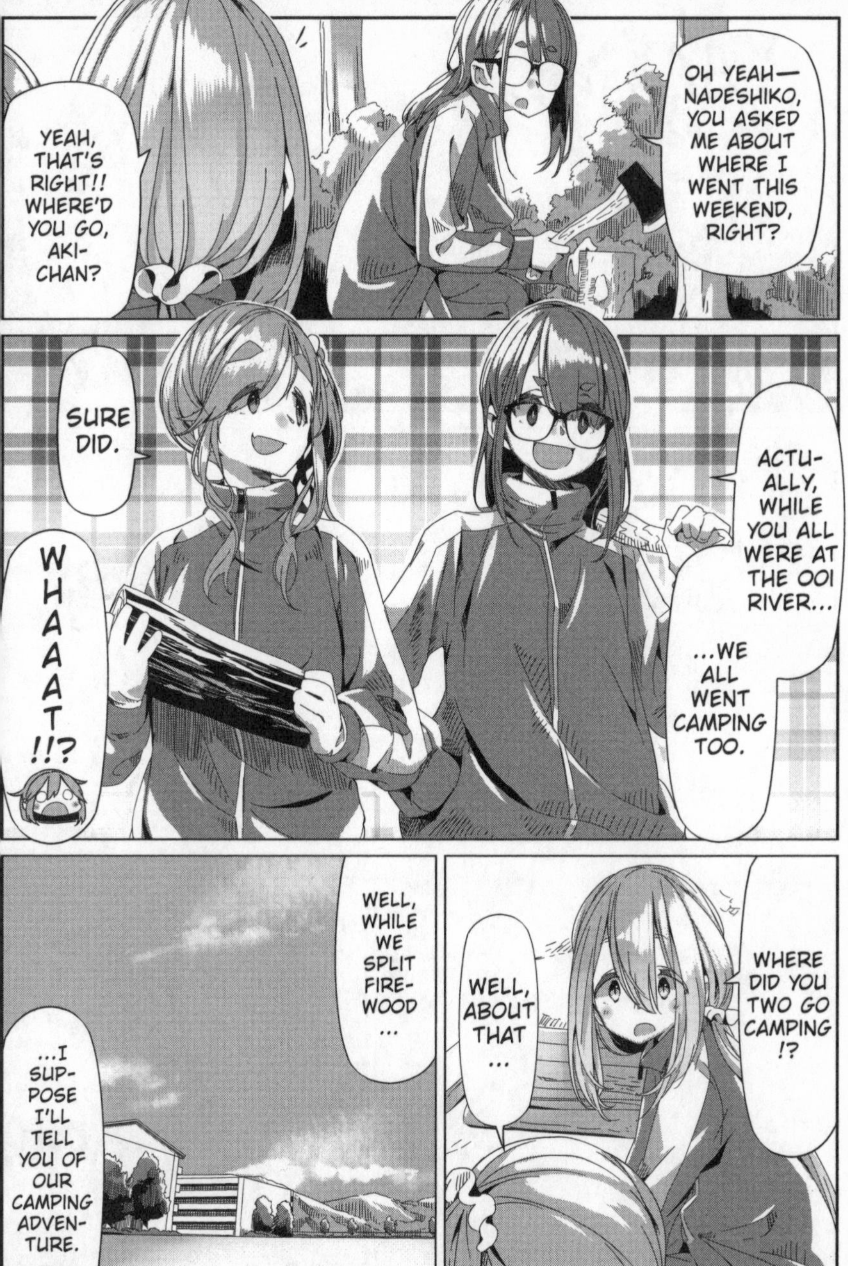
OH YEAH— NADESHIKO, YOU ASKED ME ABOUT WHERE I WENT THIS WEEKEND, RIGHT?
YEAH, THAT'S RIGHT!! WHERE'D YOU GO, AKI-CHAN?
ACTU-ALLY, WHILE YOU ALL WERE AT THE OOI RIVER...
...WE ALL WENT CAMPING TOO.
SURE DID.
WHAAAAT!!?
WHERE DID YOU TWO GO CAMPING!?
WELL, ABOUT THAT...
WELL, WHILE WE SPLIT FIRE-WOOD...
...I SUP-POSE I'LL TELL YOU OF OUR CAMPING ADVEN-TURE.

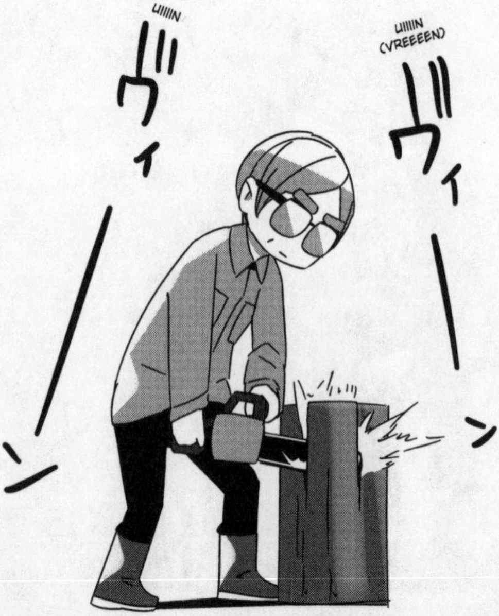
UIIIIN
(VREEEEND)
ヴィーン
UIIIIN
ヴィーン

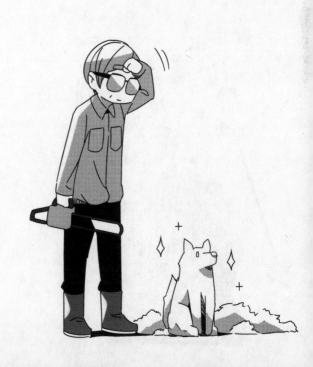

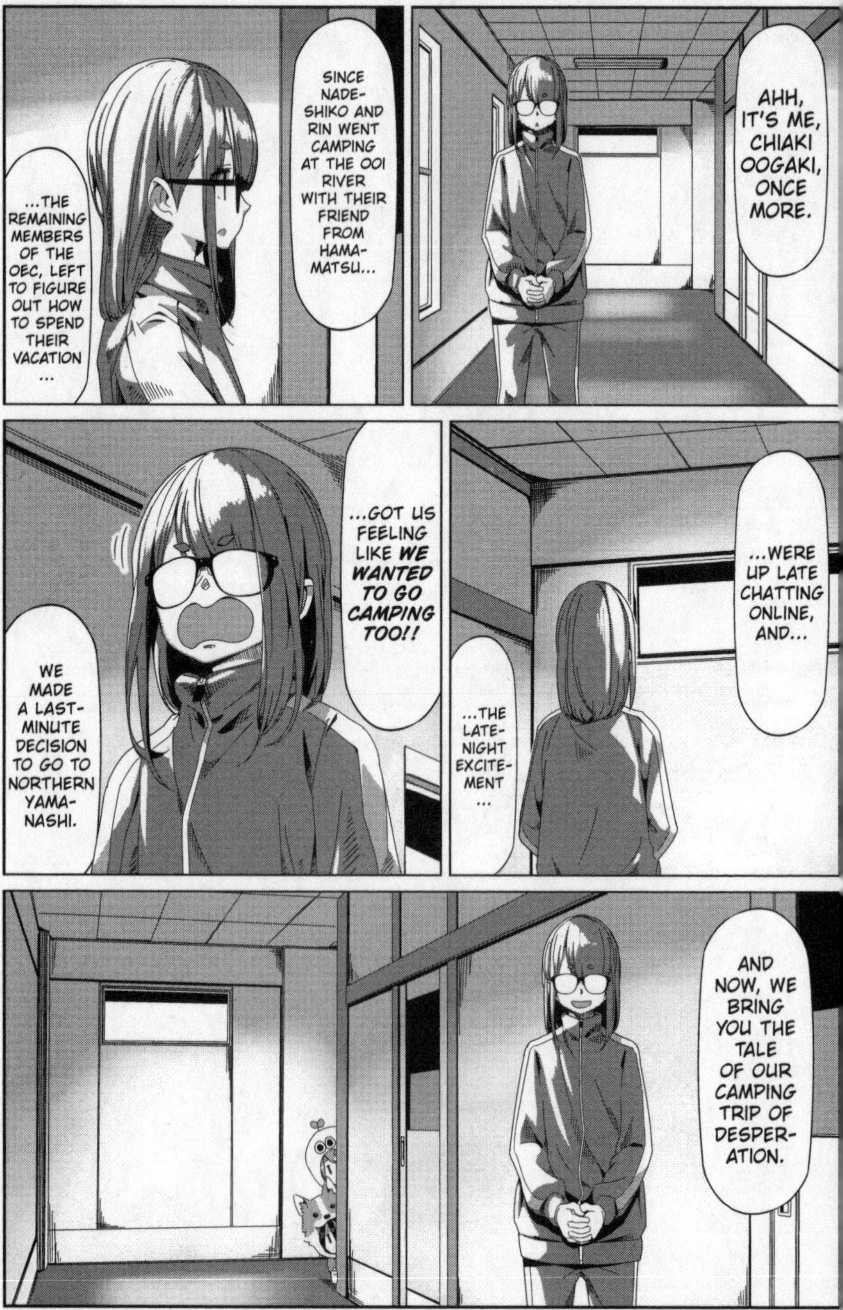
AHH, IT'S ME, CHIAKI OOGAKI, ONCE MORE.
SINCE NADESHIKO AND RIN WENT CAMPING AT THE OOI RIVER WITH THEIR FRIEND FROM HAMAMATSU...
...THE REMAINING MEMBERS OF THE OEC, LEFT TO FIGURE OUT HOW TO SPEND THEIR VACATION...
...WERE UP LATE CHATTING ONLINE, AND...
...THE LATE-NIGHT EXCITEMENT...
...GOT US FEELING LIKE *WE WANTED TO GO CAMPING TOO!!*
WE MADE A LAST-MINUTE DECISION TO GO TO NORTHERN YAMANASHI.
AND NOW, WE BRING YOU THE TALE OF OUR CAMPING TRIP OF DESPERATION.

CHAPTER 65 FLASHBACK CAMP OF TRUTH AND TROLLIN'

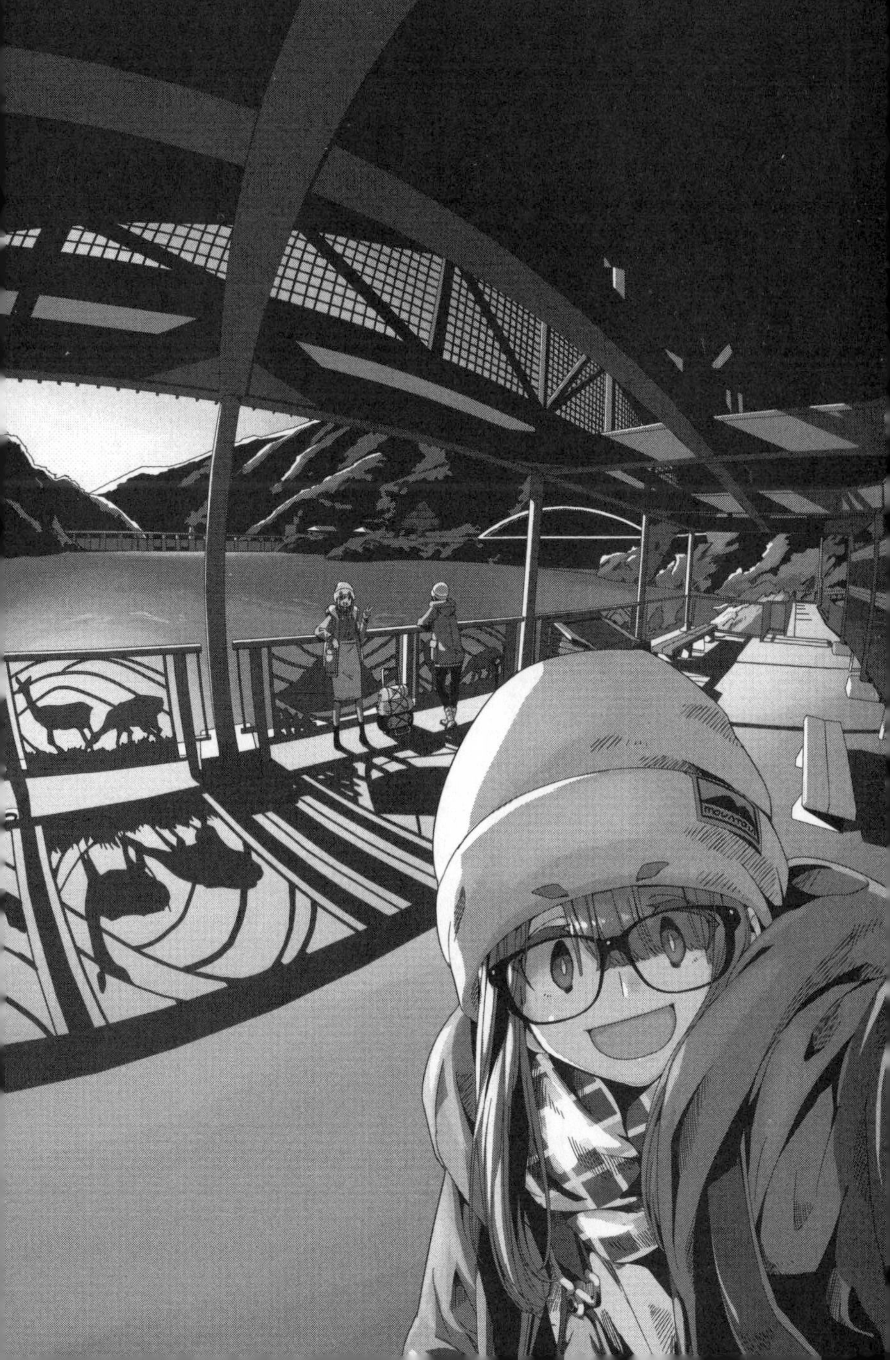

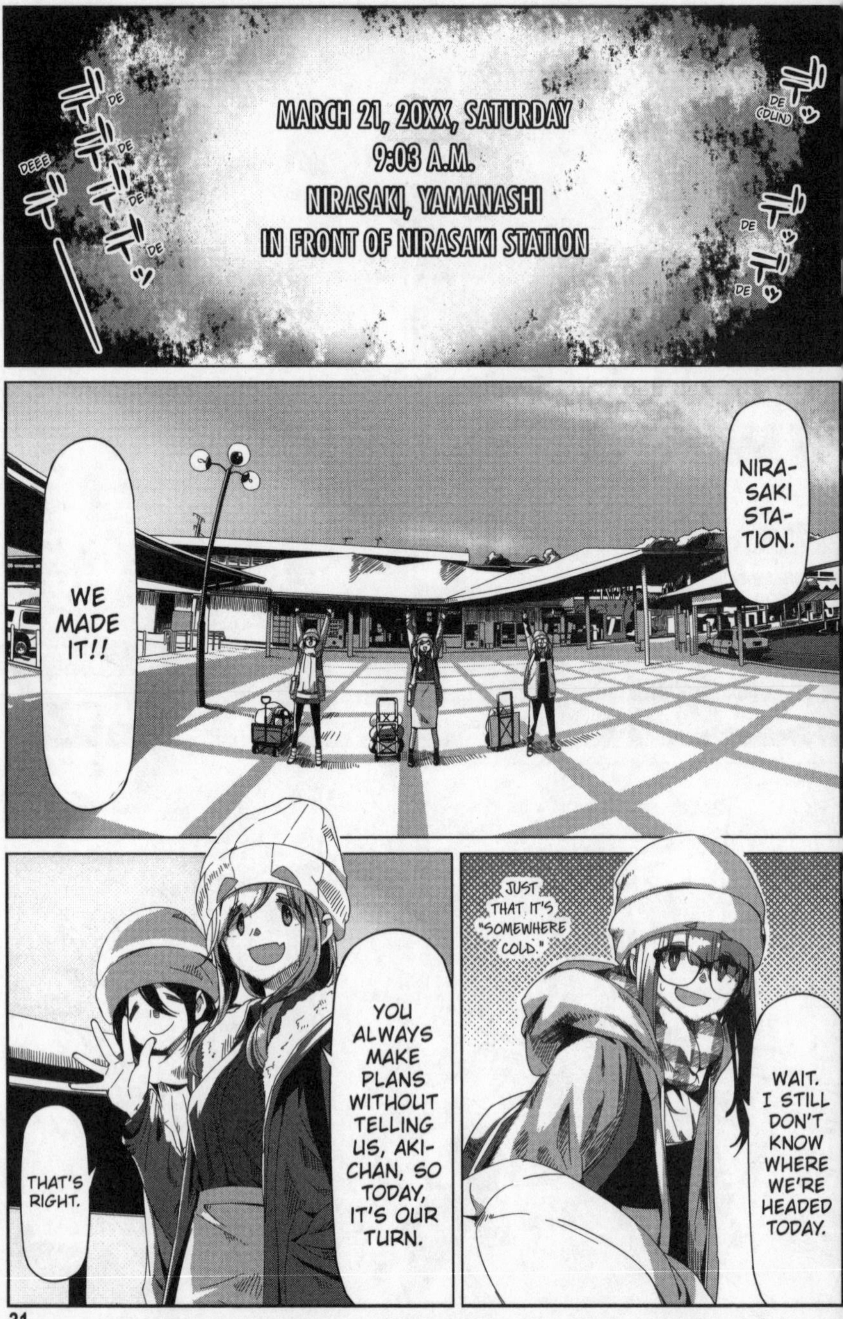
DE (DLIN)
DE
DE
DE
DE
DE
DEEE
MARCH 21, 20XX, SATURDAY
9:03 A.M.
NIRASAKI, YAMANASHI
IN FRONT OF NIRASAKI STATION
NIRA-SAKI STA-TION.
WE MADE IT!!
WAIT. I STILL DON'T KNOW WHERE WE'RE HEADED TODAY.
JUST THAT IT'S "SOMEWHERE COLD."
YOU ALWAYS MAKE PLANS WITHOUT TELLING US, AKI-CHAN, SO TODAY, IT'S OUR TURN.
THAT'S RIGHT.

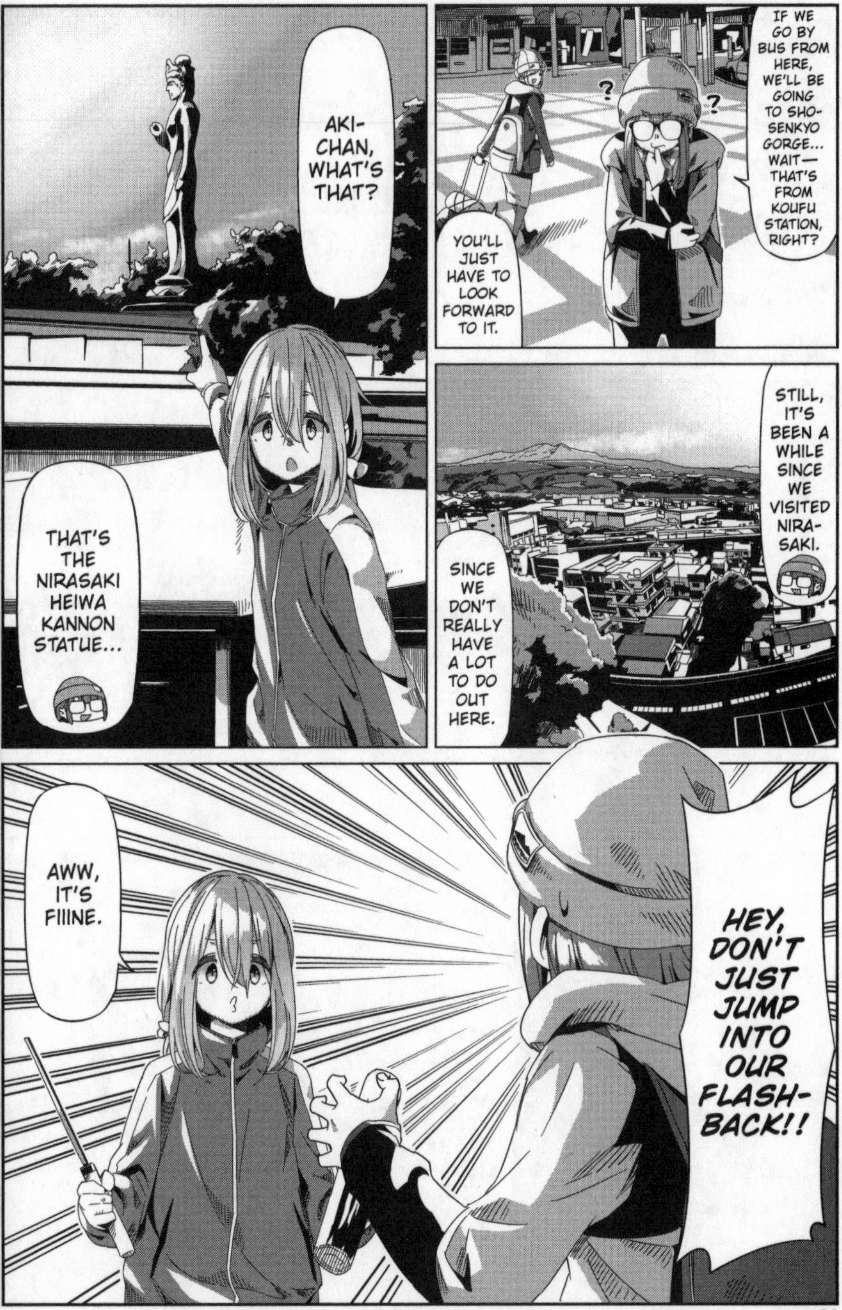
IF WE GO BY BUS FROM HERE, WE'LL BE GOING TO SHO-SENKYO GORGE... WAIT—THAT'S FROM KOUFU STATION, RIGHT?
YOU'LL JUST HAVE TO LOOK FORWARD TO IT.
STILL, IT'S BEEN A WHILE SINCE WE VISITED NIRA-SAKI.
SINCE WE DON'T REALLY HAVE A LOT TO DO OUT HERE.
AKI-CHAN, WHAT'S THAT?
THAT'S THE NIRASAKI HEIWA KANNON STATUE...
HEY, DON'T JUST JUMP INTO OUR FLASH-BACK!!
AWW, IT'S FIIINE.

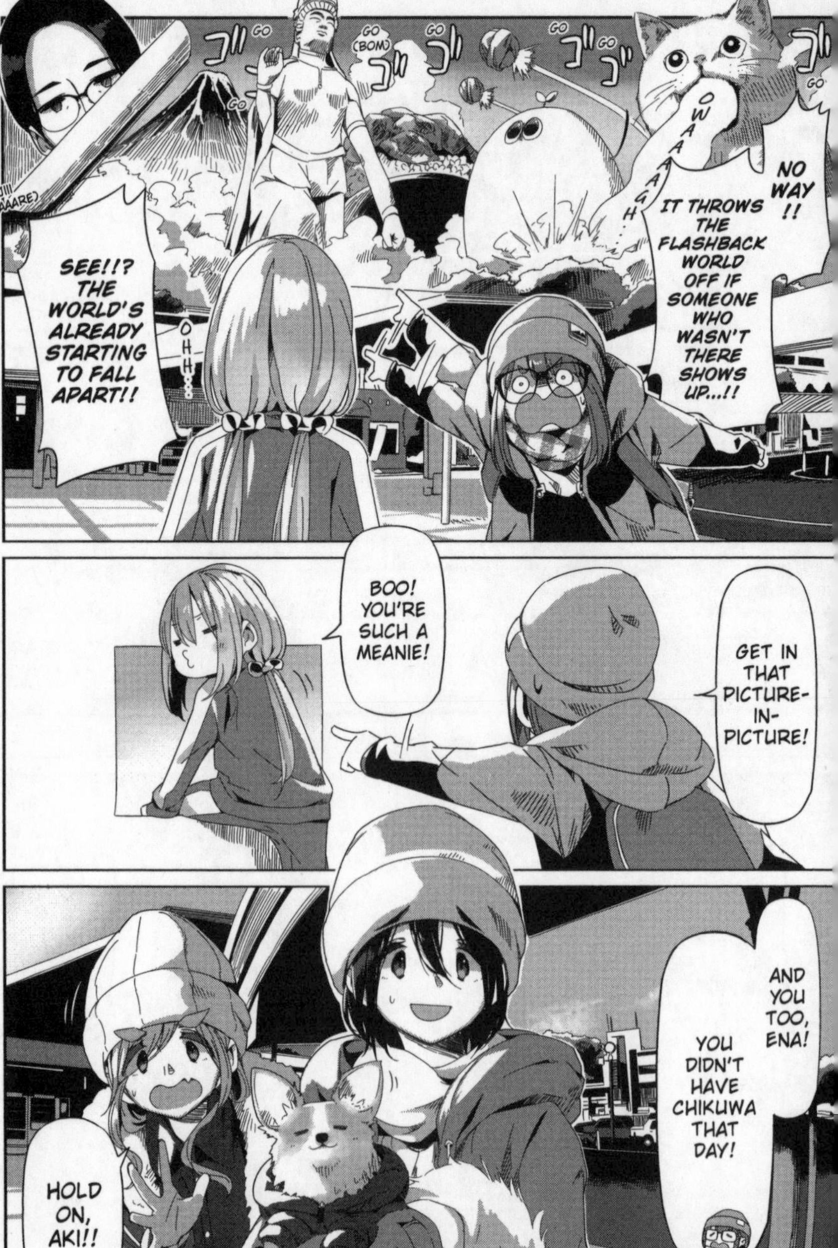
GO
NO WAY!!
IT THROWS THE FLASHBACK WORLD OFF IF SOMEONE WHO WASN'T THERE SHOWS UP...!!
OWAAAAGH...
GO GO
GO
GO (BOM)
GO
JIII (STAAARE)
OHH...
SEE!!? THE WORLD'S ALREADY STARTING TO FALL APART!!
GET IN THAT PICTURE-IN-PICTURE!
BOO! YOU'RE SUCH A MEANIE!
AND YOU TOO, ENA!
YOU DIDN'T HAVE CHIKUWA THAT DAY!
HOLD ON, AKI!!

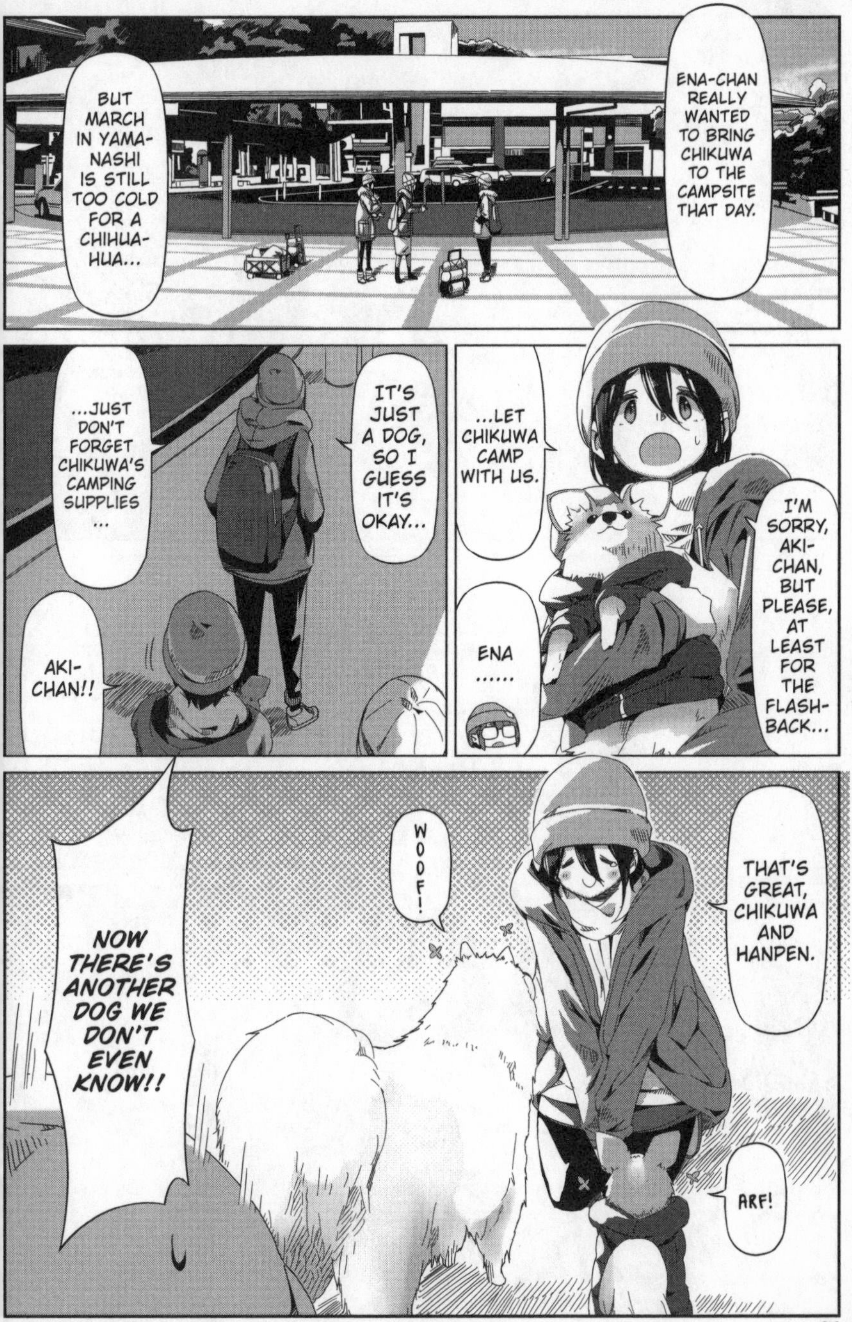
ENA-CHAN REALLY WANTED TO BRING CHIKUWA TO THE CAMPSITE THAT DAY.
BUT MARCH IN YAMA-NASHI IS STILL TOO COLD FOR A CHIHUA-HUA...
I'M SORRY, AKI-CHAN, BUT PLEASE, AT LEAST FOR THE FLASH-BACK...
...LET CHIKUWA CAMP WITH US.
ENA ......
IT'S JUST A DOG, SO I GUESS IT'S OKAY...
...JUST DON'T FORGET CHIKUWA'S CAMPING SUPPLIES ...
AKI-CHAN!!
THAT'S GREAT, CHIKUWA AND HANPEN.
WOOF!
ARF!
NOW THERE'S ANOTHER DOG WE DON'T EVEN KNOW!!

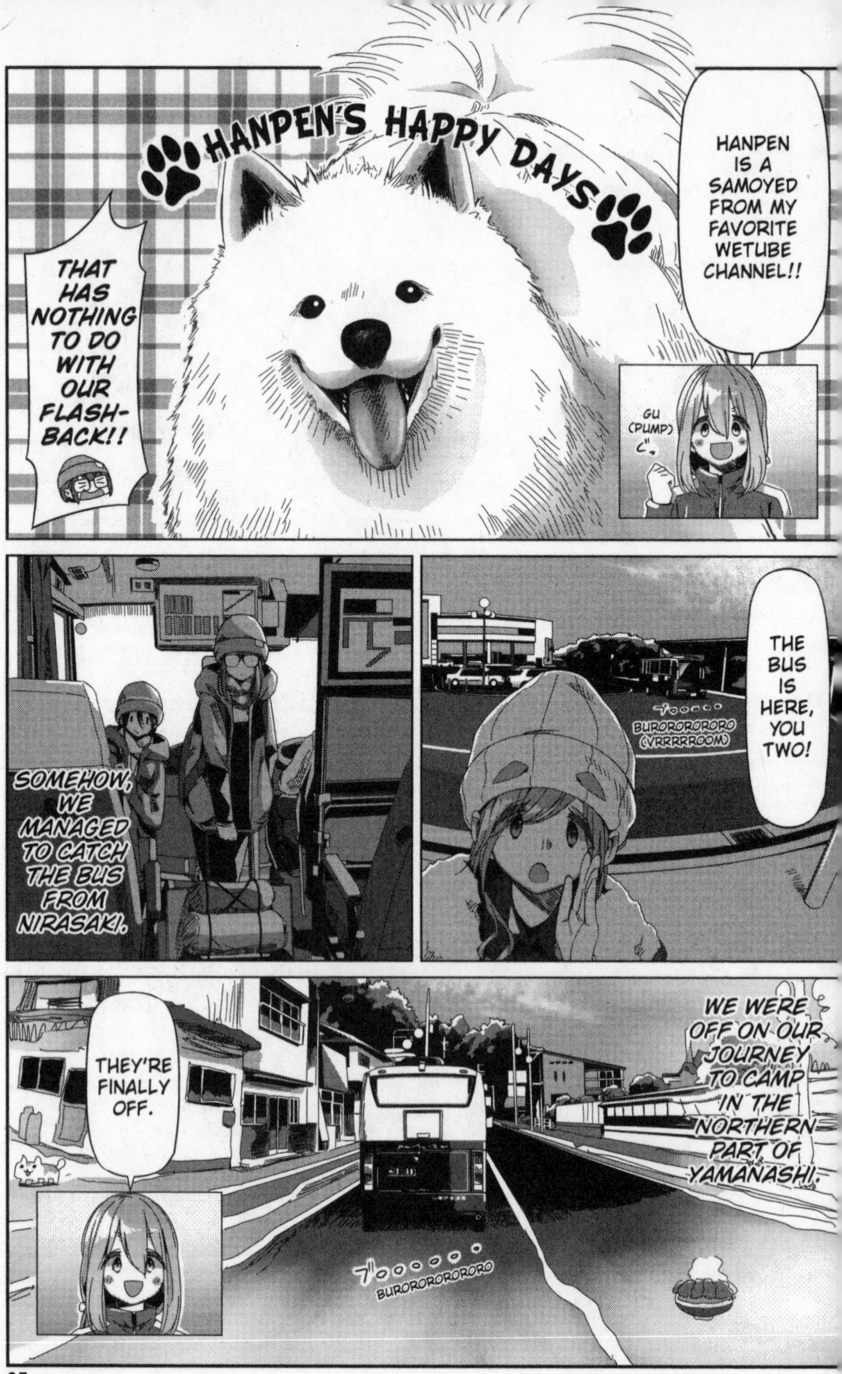
HANPEN IS A SAMOYED FROM MY FAVORITE WETUBE CHANNEL!!
GU (PUMP)
HANPEN'S HAPPY DAYS
THAT HAS NOTHING TO DO WITH OUR FLASH-BACK!!
THE BUS IS HERE, YOU TWO!
BURORORORORO (VRRRRROOM)
SOMEHOW, WE MANAGED TO CATCH THE BUS FROM NIRASAKI.
WE WERE OFF ON OUR JOURNEY TO CAMP IN THE NORTHERN PART OF YAMANASHI.
THEY'RE FINALLY OFF.
BURORORORORORO

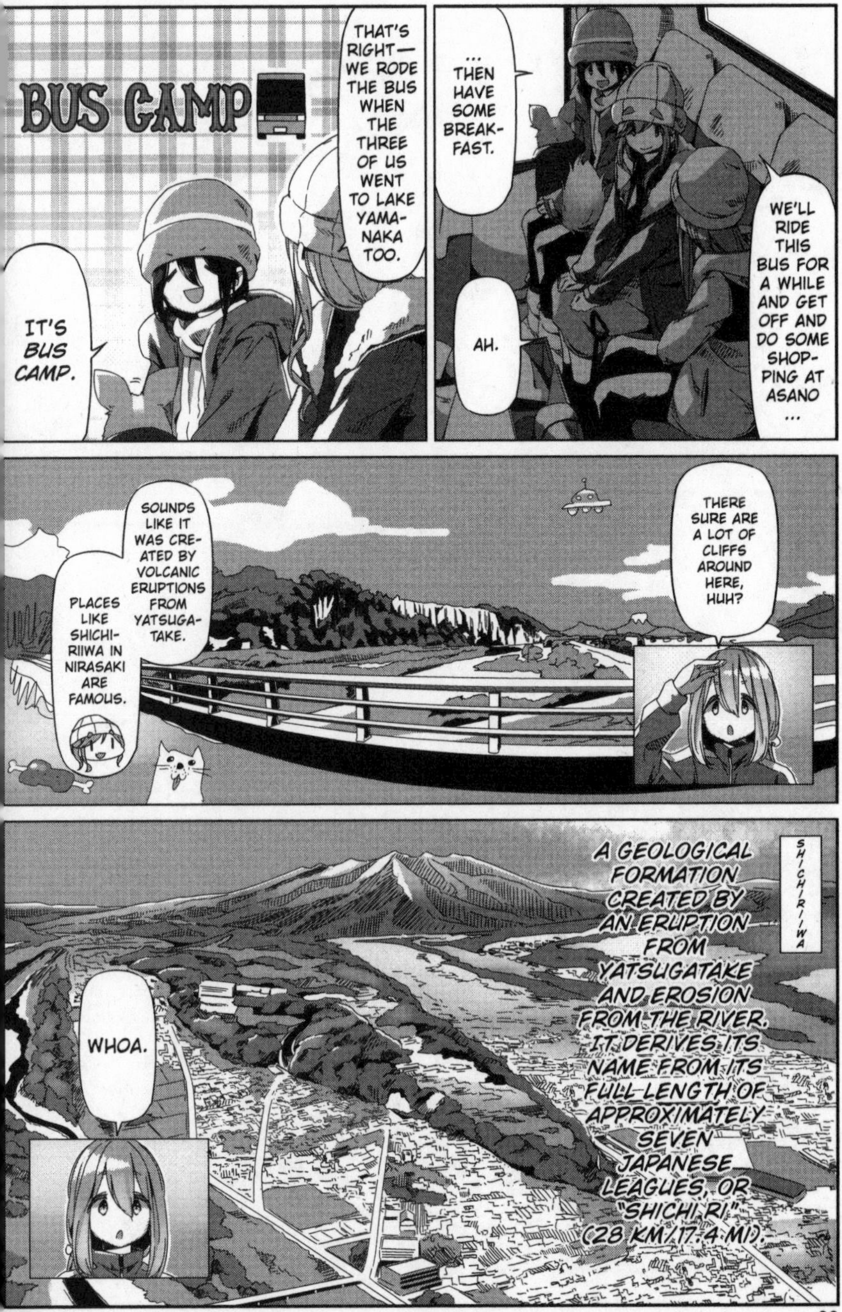
WE'LL RIDE THIS BUS FOR A WHILE AND GET OFF AND DO SOME SHOPPING AT ASANO ...
... THEN HAVE SOME BREAKFAST.
AH.
THAT'S RIGHT—WE RODE THE BUS WHEN THE THREE OF US WENT TO LAKE YAMANAKA TOO.
BUS CAMP
IT'S BUS CAMP.
THERE SURE ARE A LOT OF CLIFFS AROUND HERE, HUH?
SOUNDS LIKE IT WAS CREATED BY VOLCANIC ERUPTIONS FROM YATSUGATAKE.
PLACES LIKE SHICHIRIIWA IN NIRASAKI ARE FAMOUS.
SHICHIRIIWA
A GEOLOGICAL FORMATION CREATED BY AN ERUPTION FROM YATSUGATAKE AND EROSION FROM THE RIVER. IT DERIVES ITS NAME FROM ITS FULL LENGTH OF APPROXIMATELY SEVEN JAPANESE LEAGUES, OR "SHICHI RI" (28 KM/17.4 MI).
WHOA.

IN REAL LIFE, PETS MUST BE IN CARRIERS ON THE BUS.

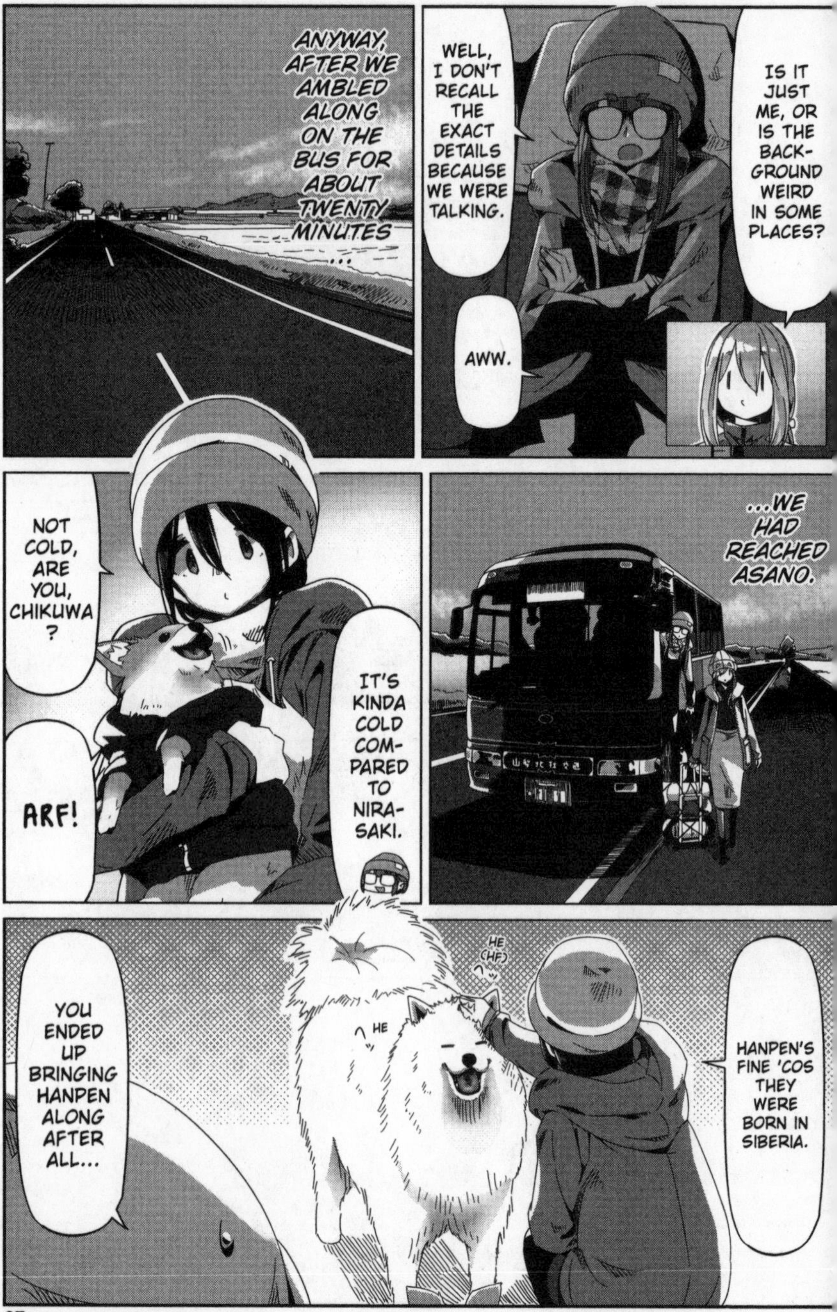
IS IT JUST ME, OR IS THE BACK-GROUND WEIRD IN SOME PLACES?
WELL, I DON'T RECALL THE EXACT DETAILS BECAUSE WE WERE TALKING.
AWW.
ANYWAY, AFTER WE AMBLED ALONG ON THE BUS FOR ABOUT TWENTY MINUTES...
...WE HAD REACHED ASANO.
NOT COLD, ARE YOU, CHIKUWA?
ARF!
IT'S KINDA COLD COMPARED TO NIRA-SAKI.
YOU ENDED UP BRINGING HANPEN ALONG AFTER ALL...
HANPEN'S FINE 'COS THEY WERE BORN IN SIBERIA.
HE (HF)
HE

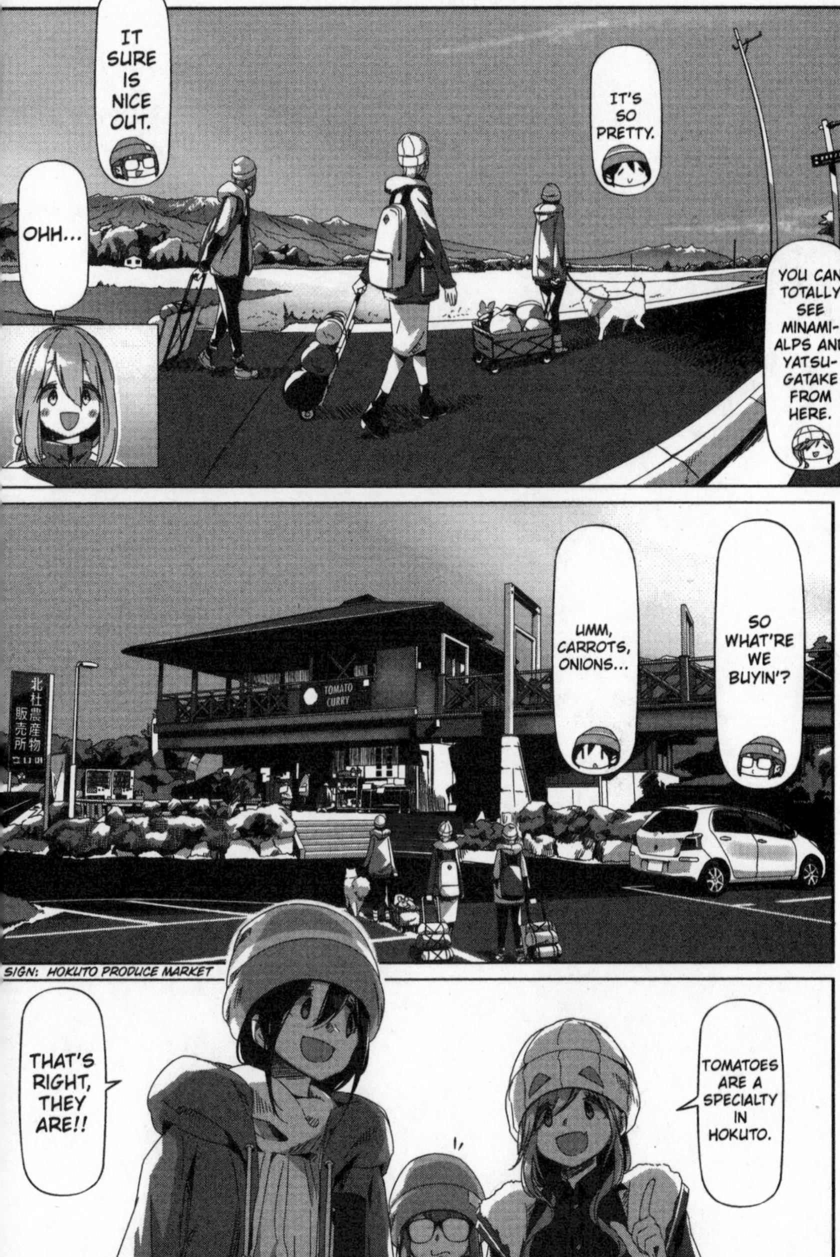
YOU CAN TOTALLY SEE MINAMI-ALPS AND YATSU-GATAKE FROM HERE.
IT'S SO PRETTY.
IT SURE IS NICE OUT.
OHH...
SO WHAT'RE WE BUYIN'?
UMM, CARROTS, ONIONS...
TOMATO CURRY
北杜農産物販売所
SIGN: HOKUTO PRODUCE MARKET
TOMATOES ARE A SPECIALTY IN HOKUTO.
THAT'S RIGHT, THEY ARE!!

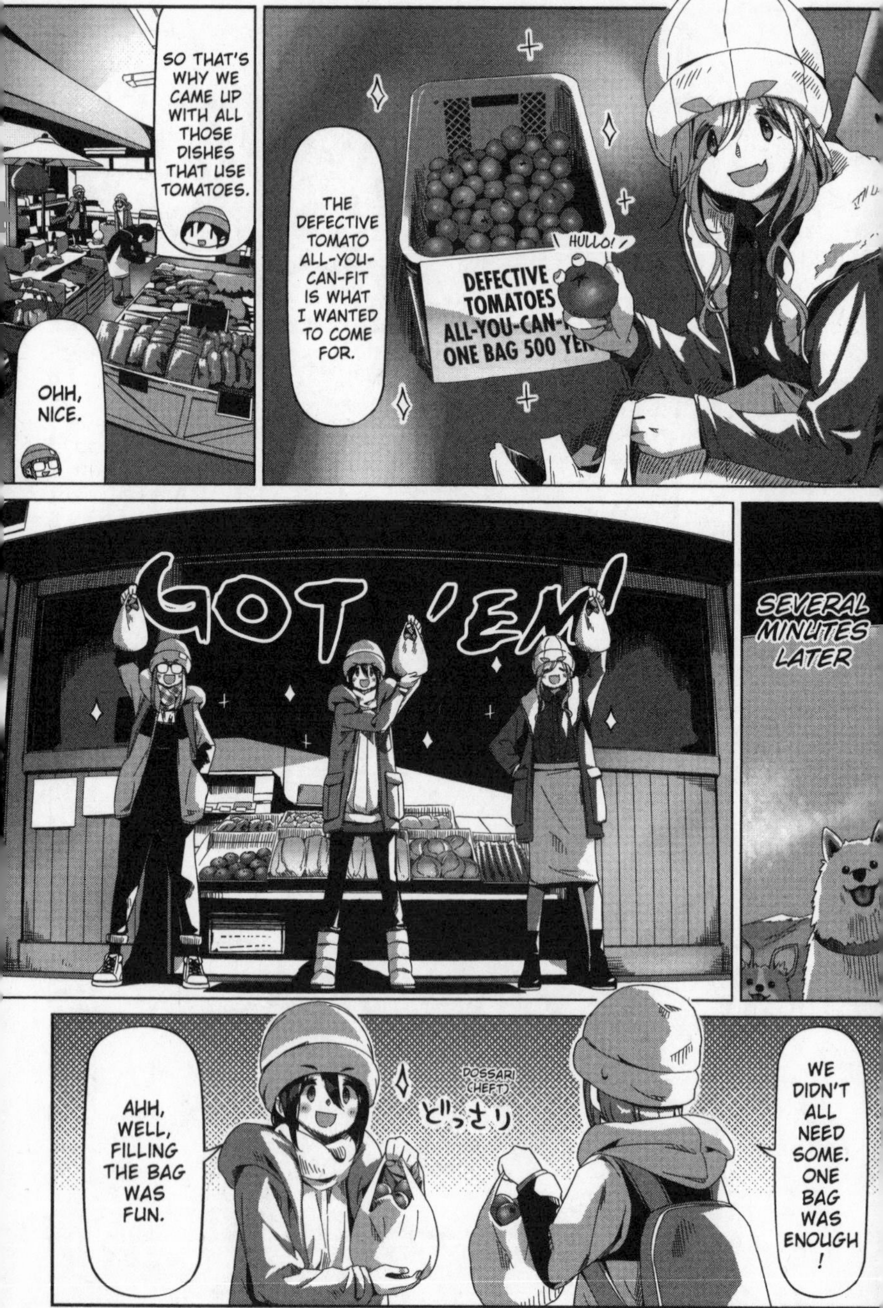
THE DEFECTIVE TOMATO ALL-YOU-CAN-FIT IS WHAT I WANTED TO COME FOR.
DEFECTIVE TOMATOES ALL-YOU-CAN-
ONE BAG 500 YE
HULLO!
SO THAT'S WHY WE CAME UP WITH ALL THOSE DISHES THAT USE TOMATOES.
OHH, NICE.
SEVERAL MINUTES LATER
GOT 'EM!
WE DIDN'T ALL NEED SOME. ONE BAG WAS ENOUGH!
DOSSARI (HEFT)
どっさり
AHH, WELL, FILLING THE BAG WAS FUN.

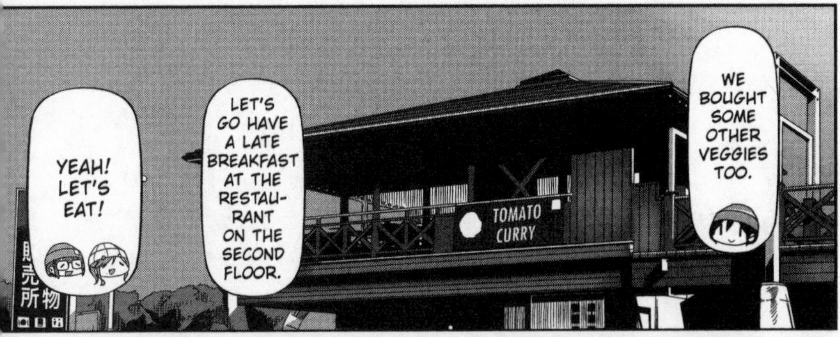
WE BOUGHT SOME OTHER VEGGIES TOO.
TOMATO CURRY
LET'S GO HAVE A LATE BREAKFAST AT THE RESTAU-RANT ON THE SECOND FLOOR.
YEAH! LET'S EAT!

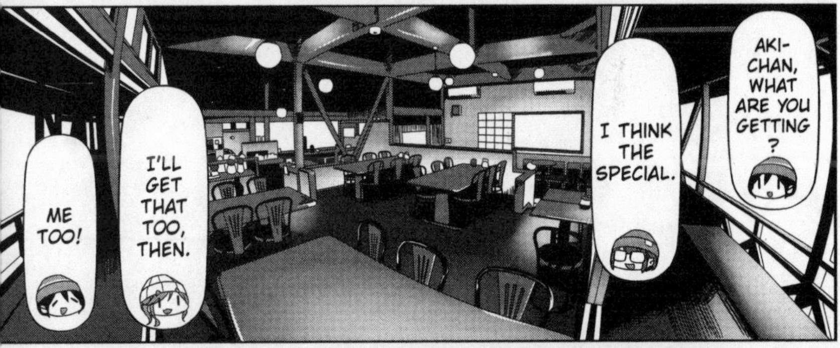
AKI-CHAN, WHAT ARE YOU GETTING?
I THINK THE SPECIAL.
I'LL GET THAT TOO, THEN.
ME TOO!

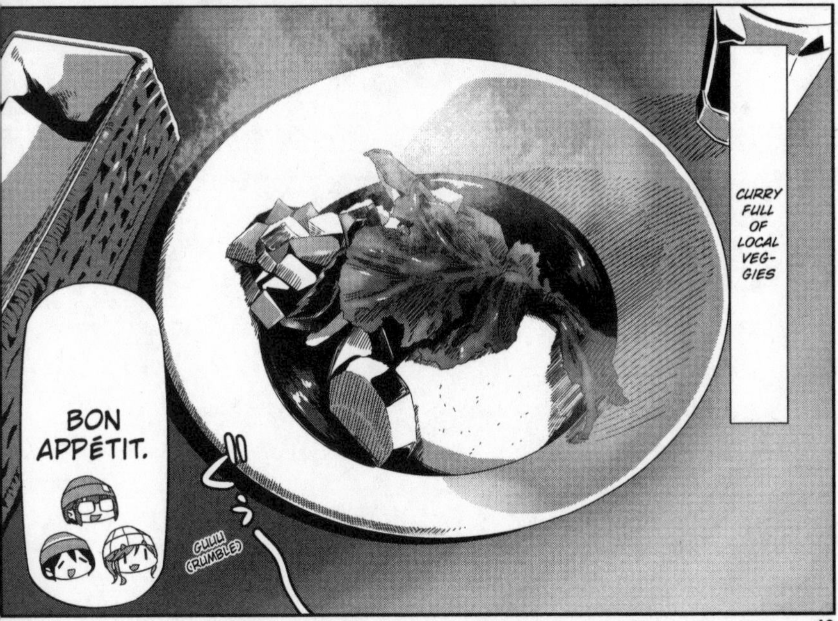
CURRY FULL OF LOCAL VEG-GIES
GULU (RUMBLE)
BON APPÉTIT.

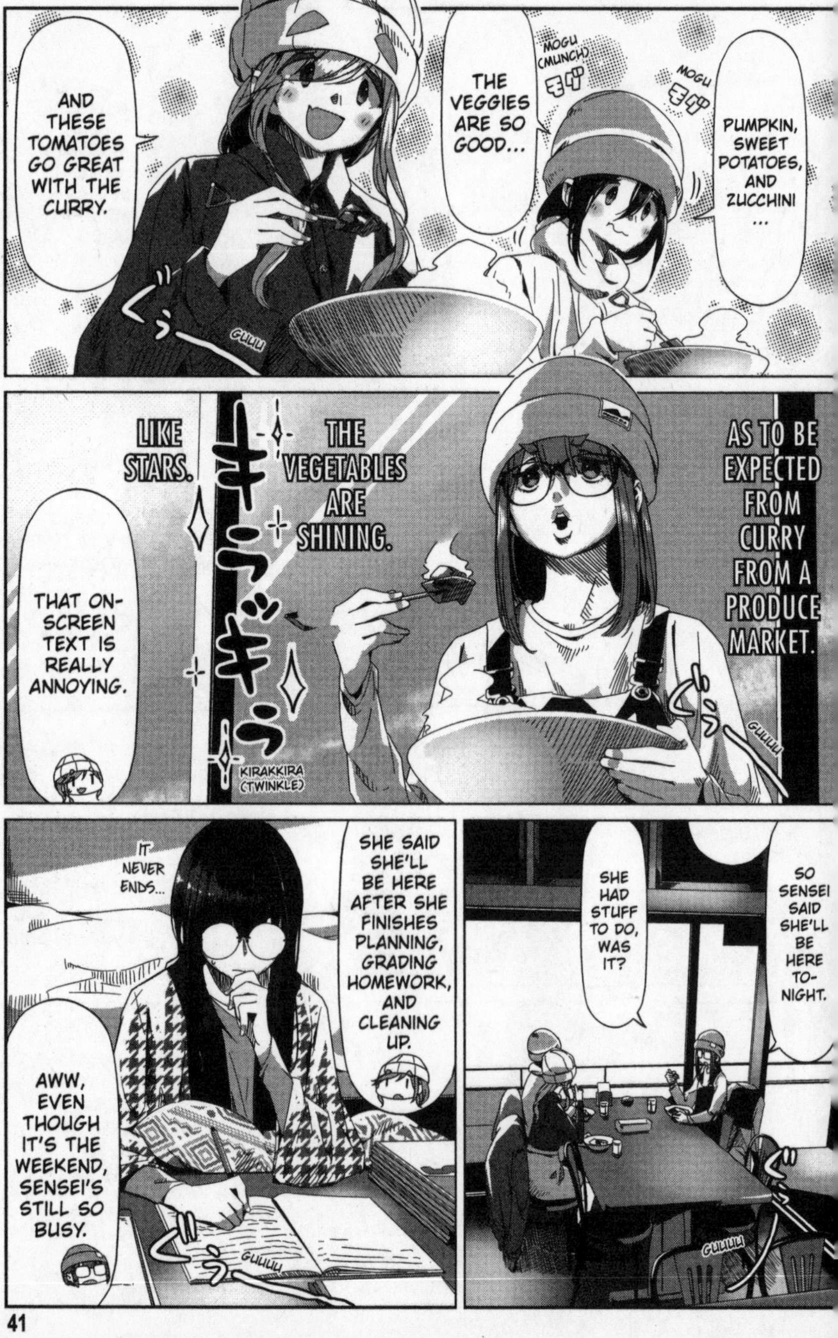
MOGU
PUMPKIN, SWEET POTATOES, AND ZUCCHINI ...
MOGU (MUNCH)
THE VEGGIES ARE SO GOOD...
AND THESE TOMATOES GO GREAT WITH THE CURRY.
GUUU
AS TO BE EXPECTED FROM CURRY FROM A PRODUCE MARKET.
GUUUU
THE VEGETABLES ARE SHINING.
LIKE STARS.
KIRAKKIRA (TWINKLE)
THAT ON-SCREEN TEXT IS REALLY ANNOYING.
SO SENSEI SAID SHE'LL BE HERE TO-NIGHT.
SHE HAD STUFF TO DO, WAS IT?
GUUUU
SHE SAID SHE'LL BE HERE AFTER SHE FINISHES PLANNING, GRADING HOMEWORK, AND CLEANING UP.
IT NEVER ENDS...
AWW, EVEN THOUGH IT'S THE WEEKEND, SENSEI'S STILL SO BUSY.
GUUUU

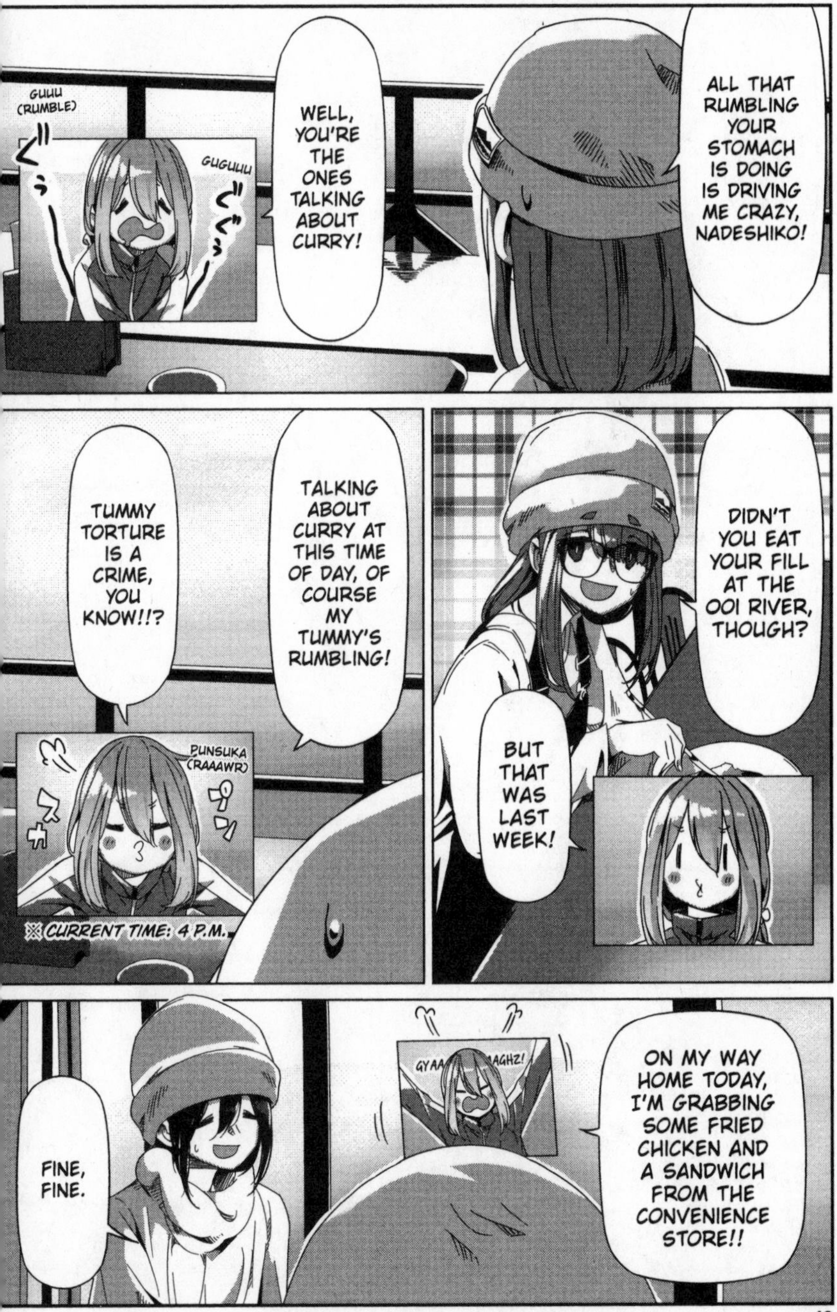
ALL THAT RUMBLING YOUR STOMACH IS DOING IS DRIVING ME CRAZY, NADESHIKO!
WELL, YOU'RE THE ONES TALKING ABOUT CURRY!
GUGUUU
GUUU (RUMBLE)
DIDN'T YOU EAT YOUR FILL AT THE OOI RIVER, THOUGH?
BUT THAT WAS LAST WEEK!
TALKING ABOUT CURRY AT THIS TIME OF DAY, OF COURSE MY TUMMY'S RUMBLING!
TUMMY TORTURE IS A CRIME, YOU KNOW!!?
PUNSUKA (RAAAWR)
※CURRENT TIME: 4 P.M.
ON MY WAY HOME TODAY, I'M GRABBING SOME FRIED CHICKEN AND A SANDWICH FROM THE CONVENIENCE STORE!!
FINE, FINE.

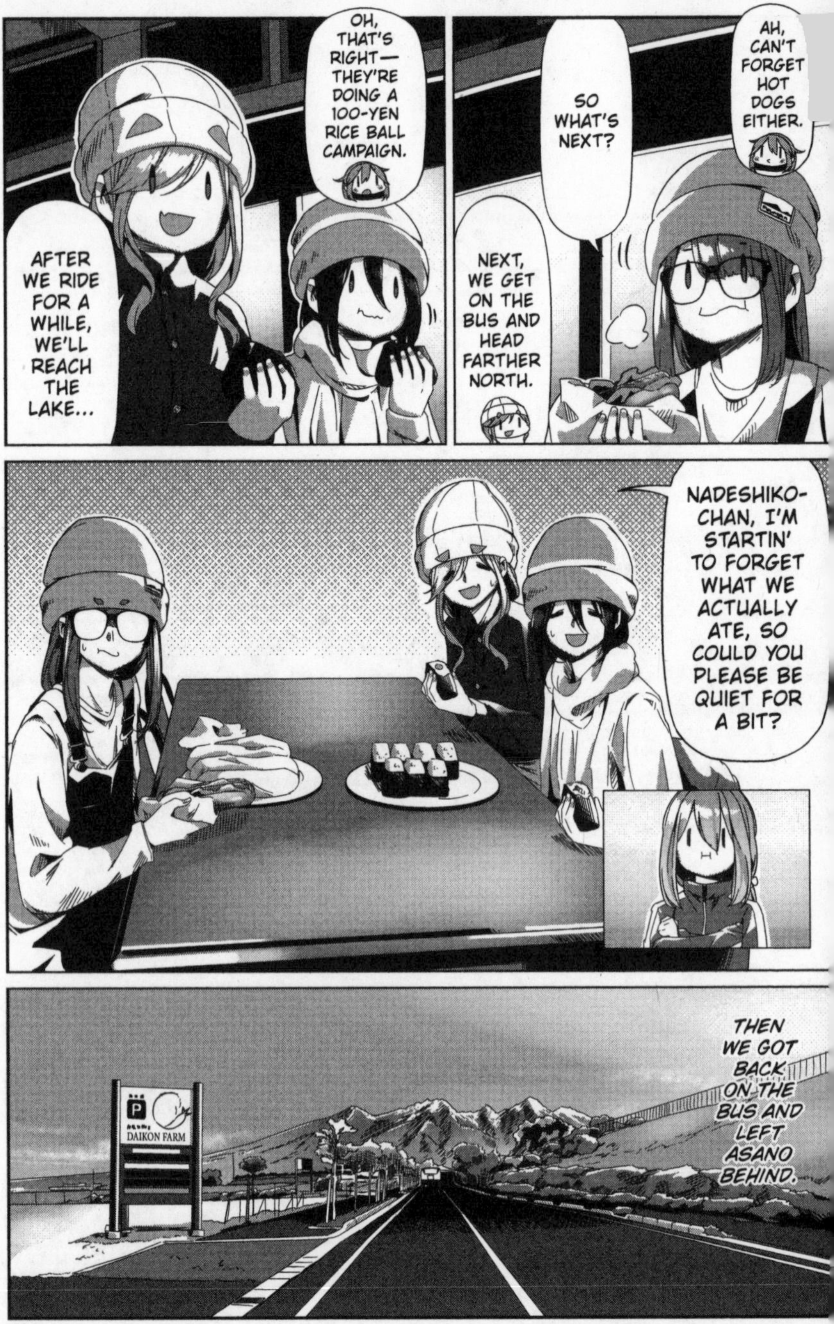
AH, CAN'T FORGET HOT DOGS EITHER.
SO WHAT'S NEXT?
NEXT, WE GET ON THE BUS AND HEAD FARTHER NORTH.
OH, THAT'S RIGHT—THEY'RE DOING A 100-YEN RICE BALL CAMPAIGN.
AFTER WE RIDE FOR A WHILE, WE'LL REACH THE LAKE...
NADESHIKO-CHAN, I'M STARTIN' TO FORGET WHAT WE ACTUALLY ATE, SO COULD YOU PLEASE BE QUIET FOR A BIT?
THEN WE GOT BACK ON THE BUS AND LEFT ASANO BEHIND.
DAIKON FARM

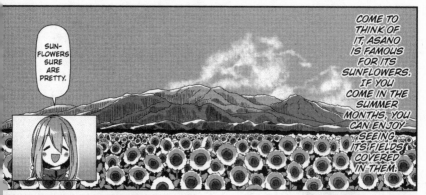

COME TO THINK OF IT, ASANO IS FAMOUS FOR ITS SUNFLOWERS. IF YOU COME IN THE SUMMER MONTHS, YOU CAN ENJOY SEEING ITS FIELDS COVERED IN THEM.

SUN-FLOWERS SURE ARE PRETTY.

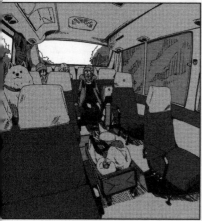

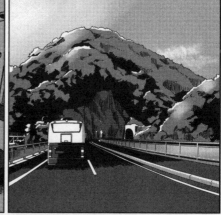

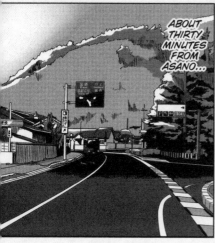

ABOUT THIRTY MINUTES FROM ASANO...

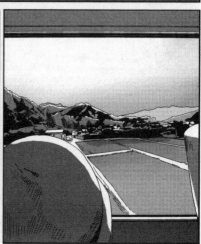

44

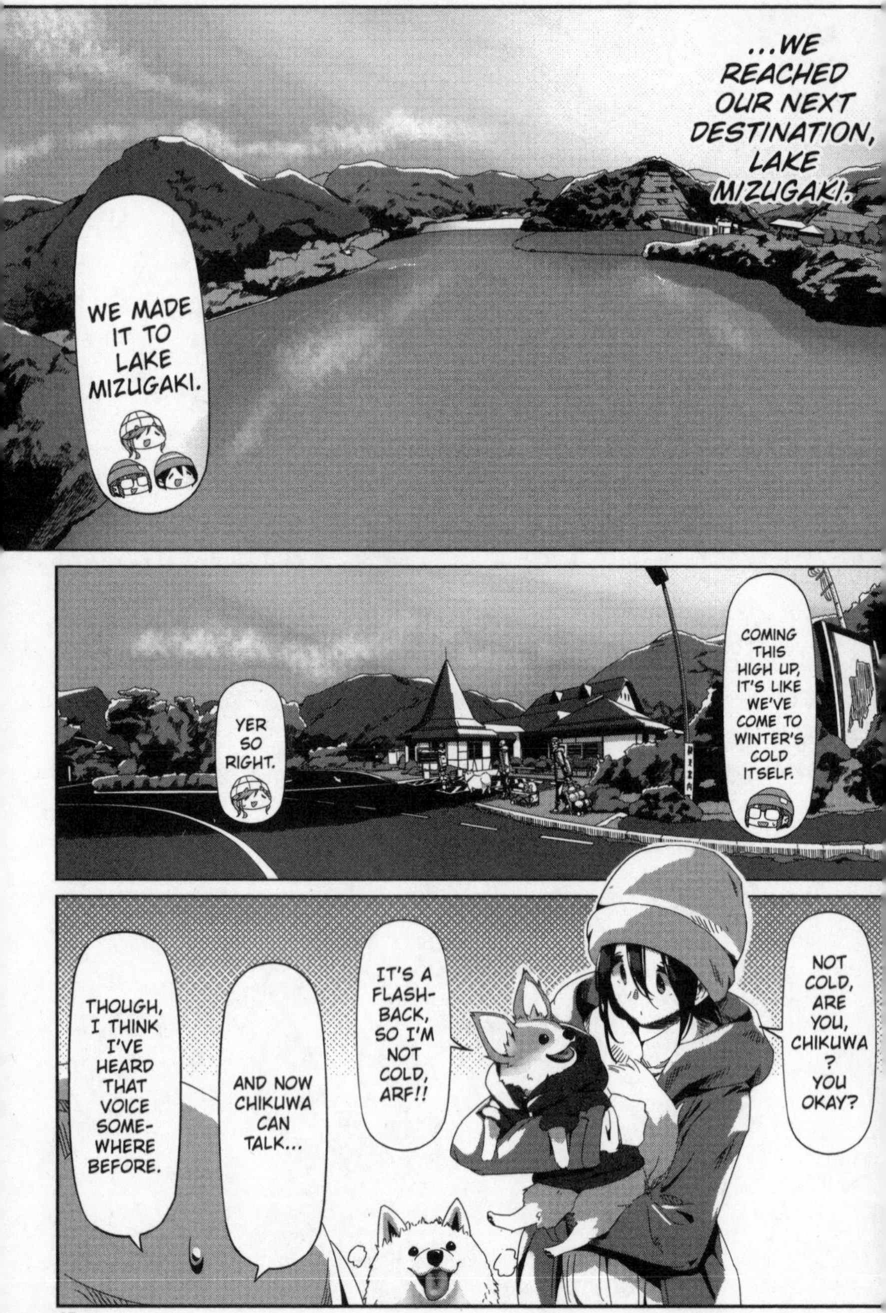
...WE REACHED OUR NEXT DESTINATION, LAKE MIZUGAKI.
WE MADE IT TO LAKE MIZUGAKI.
COMING THIS HIGH UP, IT'S LIKE WE'VE COME TO WINTER'S COLD ITSELF.
YER SO RIGHT.
NOT COLD, ARE YOU, CHIKUWA? YOU OKAY?
IT'S A FLASH-BACK, SO I'M NOT COLD, ARF!!
AND NOW CHIKUWA CAN TALK...
THOUGH, I THINK I'VE HEARD THAT VOICE SOME-WHERE BEFORE.

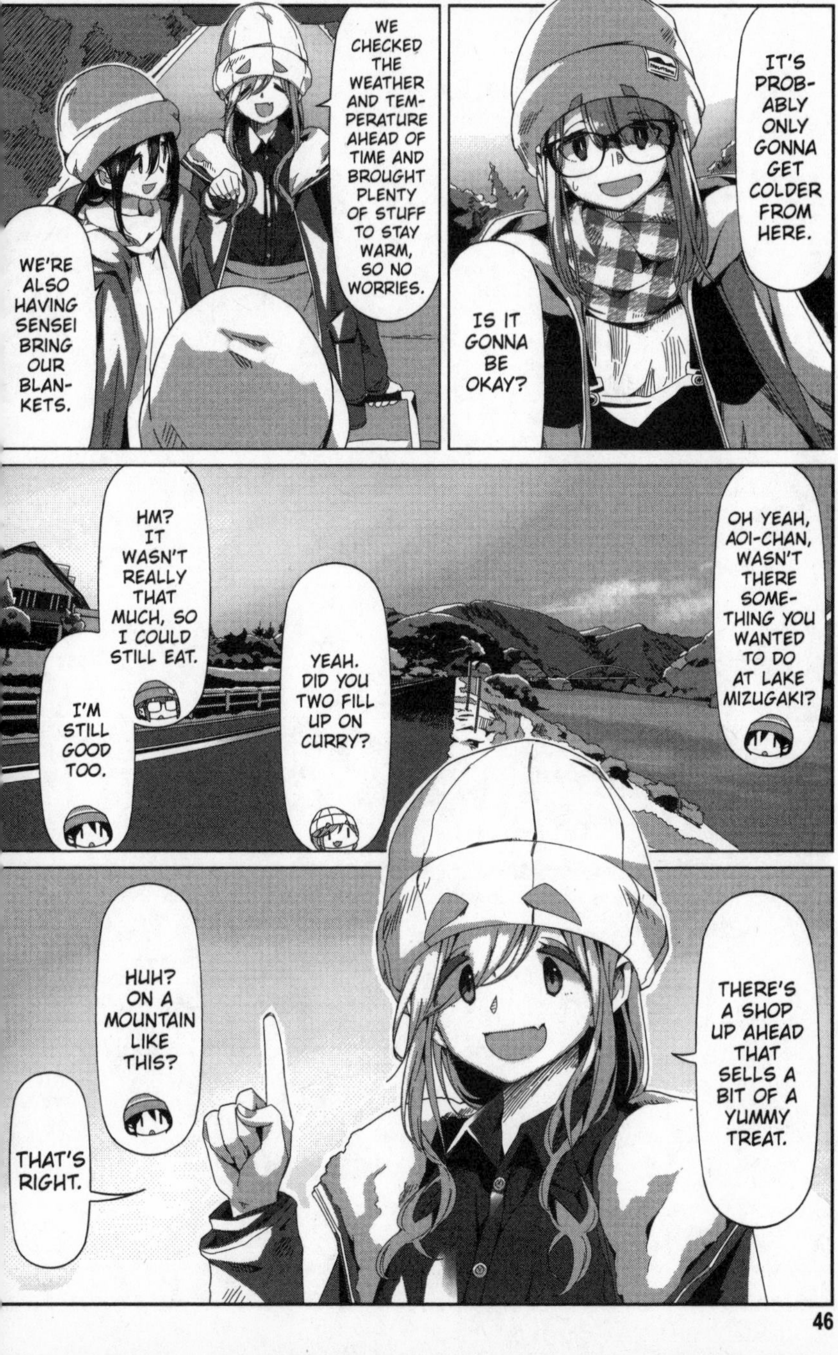
IT'S PROBABLY ONLY GONNA GET COLDER FROM HERE.
IS IT GONNA BE OKAY?
WE CHECKED THE WEATHER AND TEMPERATURE AHEAD OF TIME AND BROUGHT PLENTY OF STUFF TO STAY WARM, SO NO WORRIES.
WE'RE ALSO HAVING SENSEI BRING OUR BLANKETS.
OH YEAH, AOI-CHAN, WASN'T THERE SOMETHING YOU WANTED TO DO AT LAKE MIZUGAKI?
YEAH. DID YOU TWO FILL UP ON CURRY?
HM? IT WASN'T REALLY THAT MUCH, SO I COULD STILL EAT.
I'M STILL GOOD TOO.
THERE'S A SHOP UP AHEAD THAT SELLS A BIT OF A YUMMY TREAT.
HUH? ON A MOUNTAIN LIKE THIS?
THAT'S RIGHT.

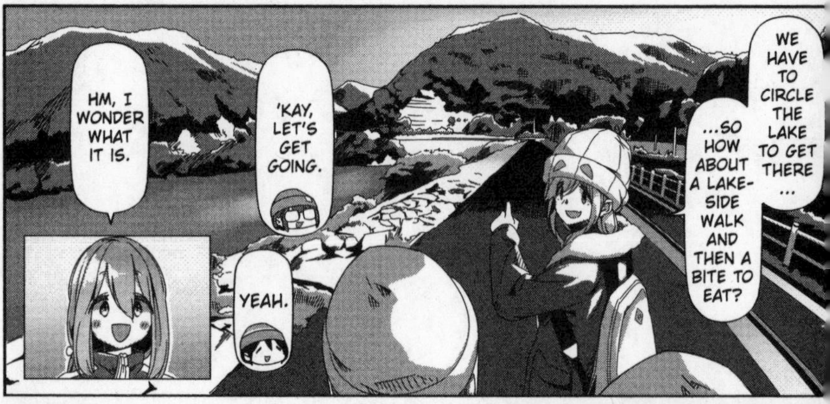
WE HAVE TO CIRCLE THE LAKE TO GET THERE ...
...SO HOW ABOUT A LAKE-SIDE WALK AND THEN A BITE TO EAT?
'KAY, LET'S GET GOING.
YEAH.
HM, I WONDER WHAT IT IS.
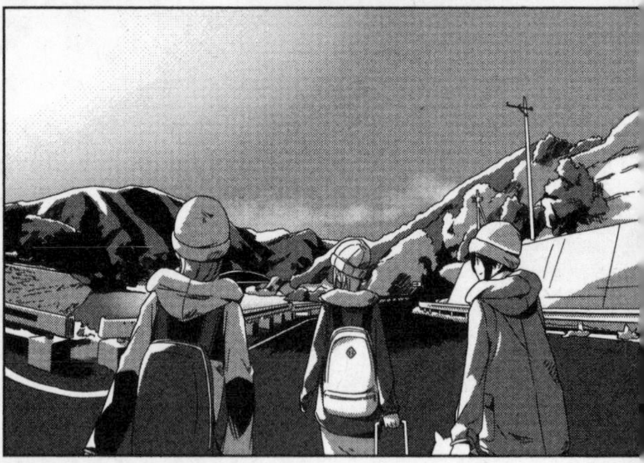
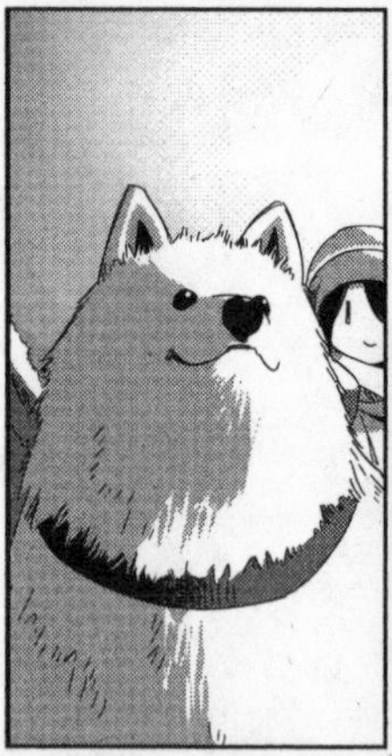
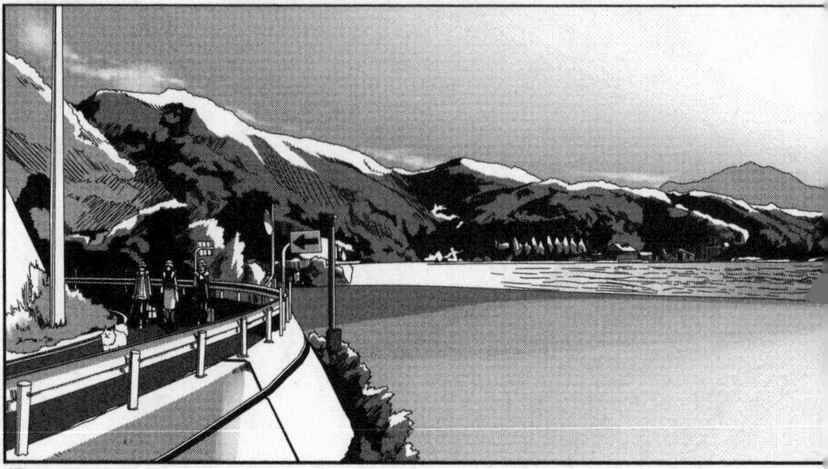

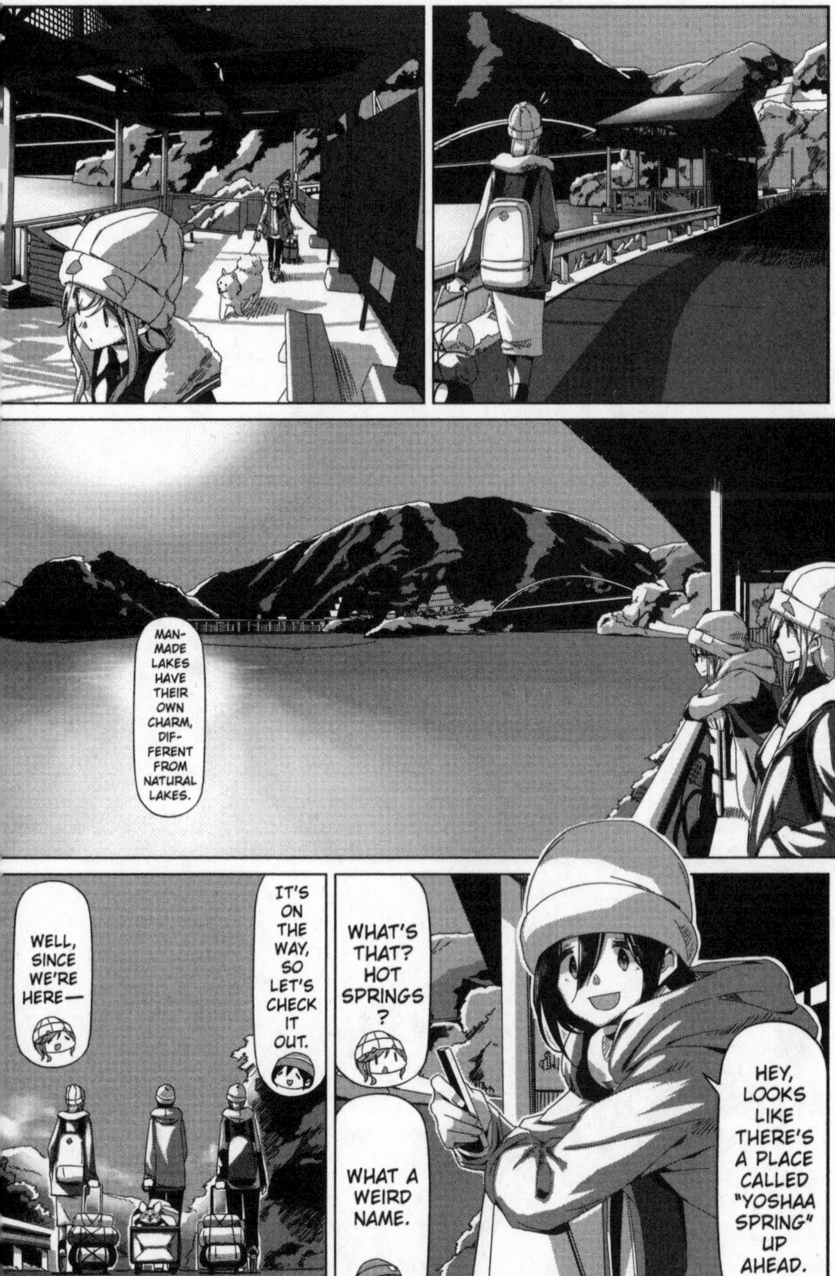
MAN-MADE LAKES HAVE THEIR OWN CHARM, DIF-FERENT FROM NATURAL LAKES.
HEY, LOOKS LIKE THERE'S A PLACE CALLED "YOSHAA SPRING" UP AHEAD.
WHAT'S THAT? HOT SPRINGS?
WHAT A WEIRD NAME.
IT'S ON THE WAY, SO LET'S CHECK IT OUT.
WELL, SINCE WE'RE HERE—

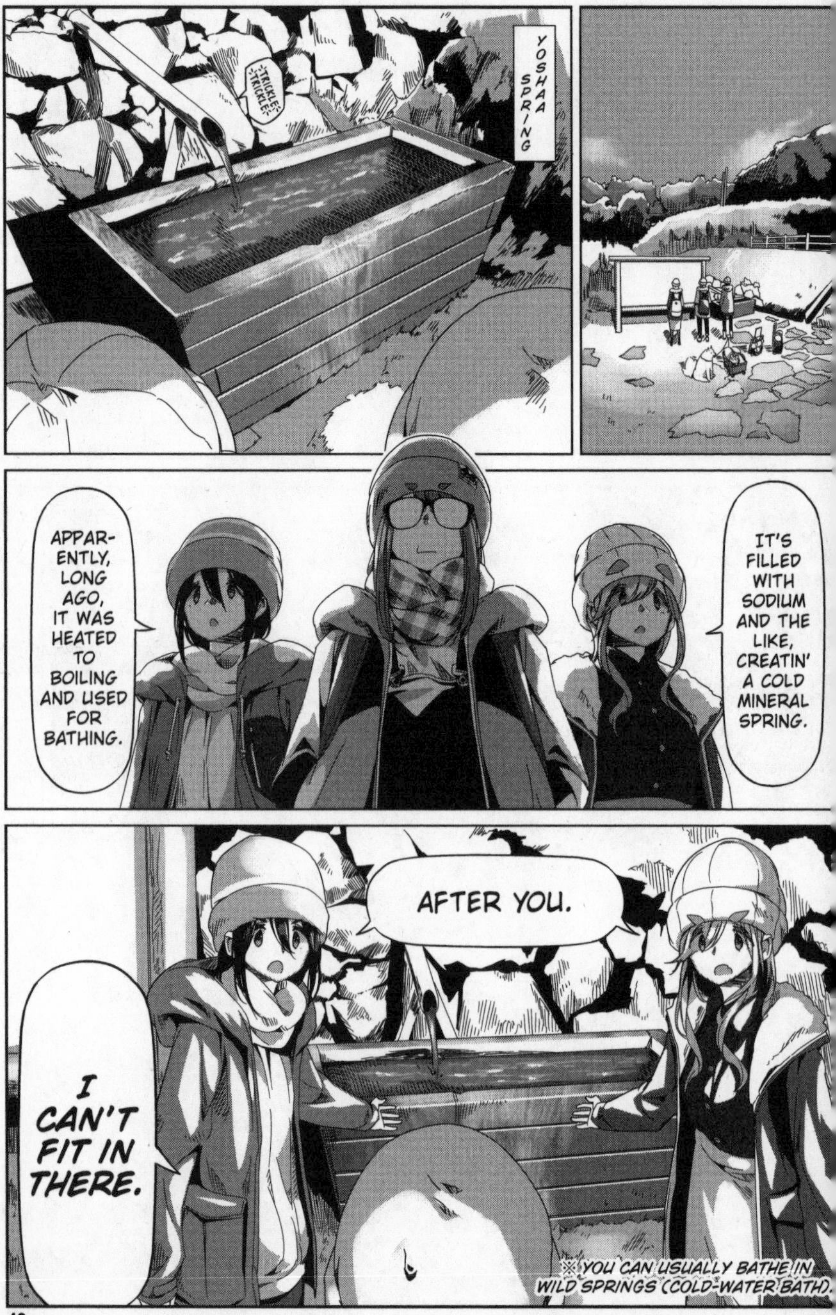
YOSHAA SPRING
TRICKLE TRICKLE
IT'S FILLED WITH SODIUM AND THE LIKE, CREATIN' A COLD MINERAL SPRING.
APPARENTLY, LONG AGO, IT WAS HEATED TO BOILING AND USED FOR BATHING.
AFTER YOU.
I CAN'T FIT IN THERE.
※ YOU CAN USUALLY BATHE IN WILD SPRINGS (COLD-WATER BATH).

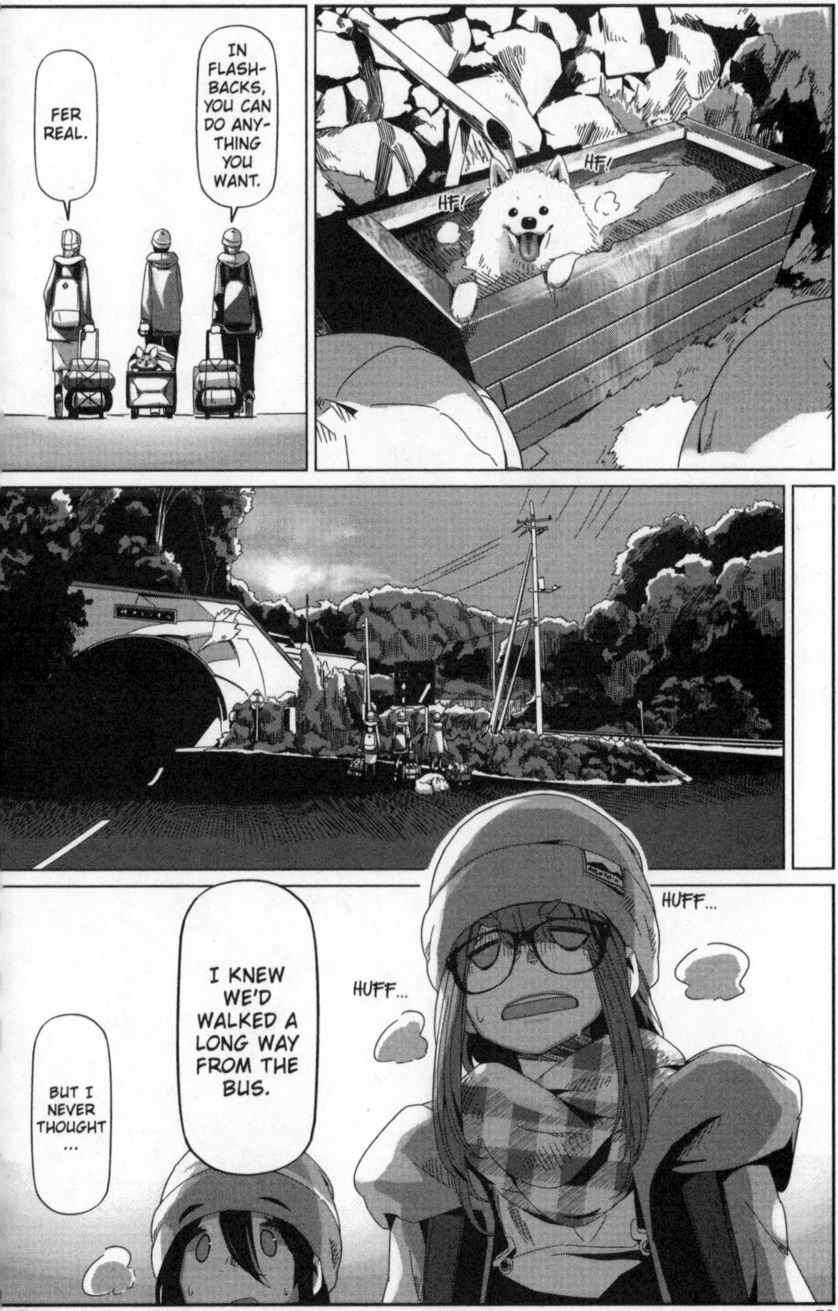
HF!
HF!
IN FLASHBACKS, YOU CAN DO ANYTHING YOU WANT.
FER REAL.
HUFF...
I KNEW WE'D WALKED A LONG WAY FROM THE BUS.
HUFF...
BUT I NEVER THOUGHT ...

IN REAL LIFE, PETS ARE NOT ALLOWED IN YOSHAA SPRING.

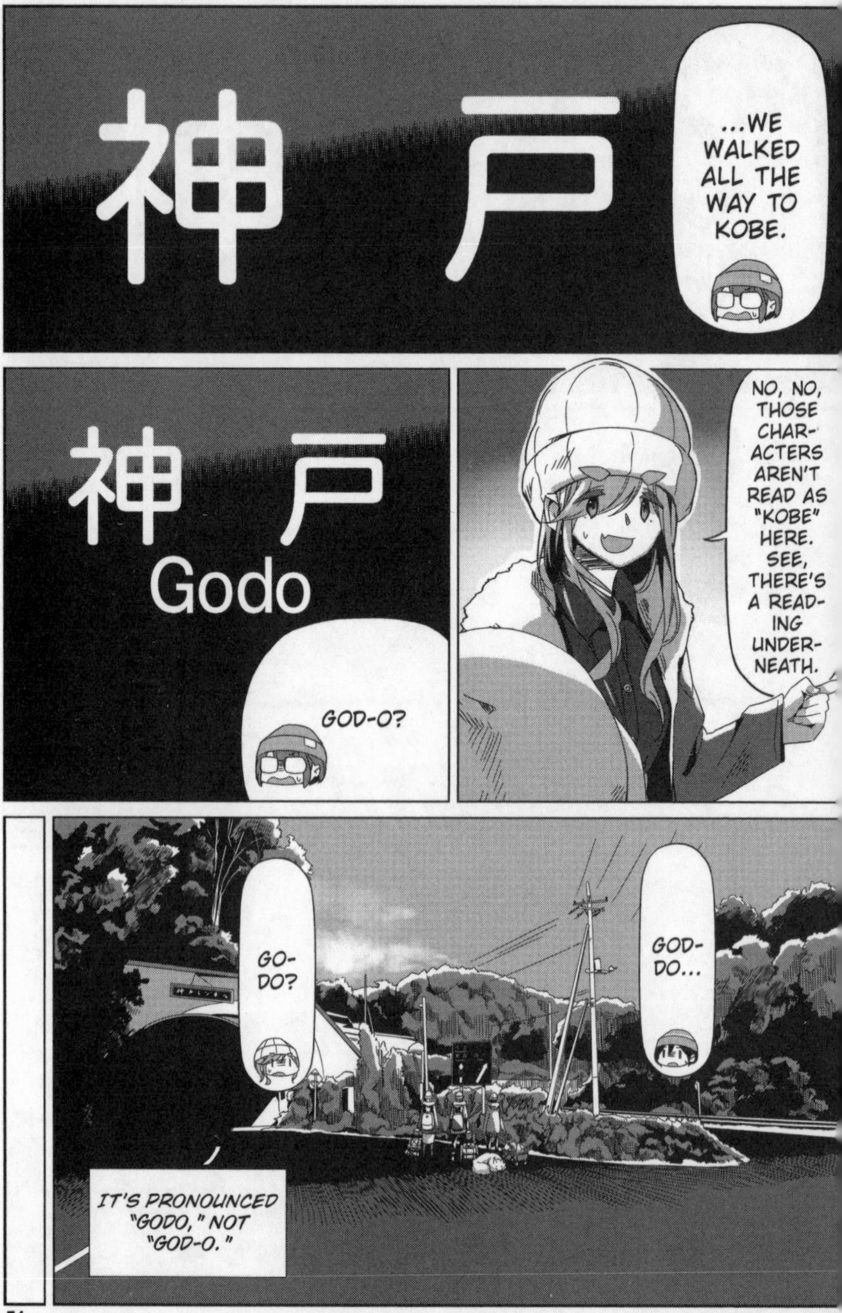
神戸
...WE WALKED ALL THE WAY TO KOBE.
NO, NO, THOSE CHARACTERS AREN'T READ AS "KOBE" HERE. SEE, THERE'S A READING UNDERNEATH.
神戸
Godo
GOD-O?
GOD-DO...
GO-DO?
IT'S PRONOUNCED "GODO," NOT "GOD-O."

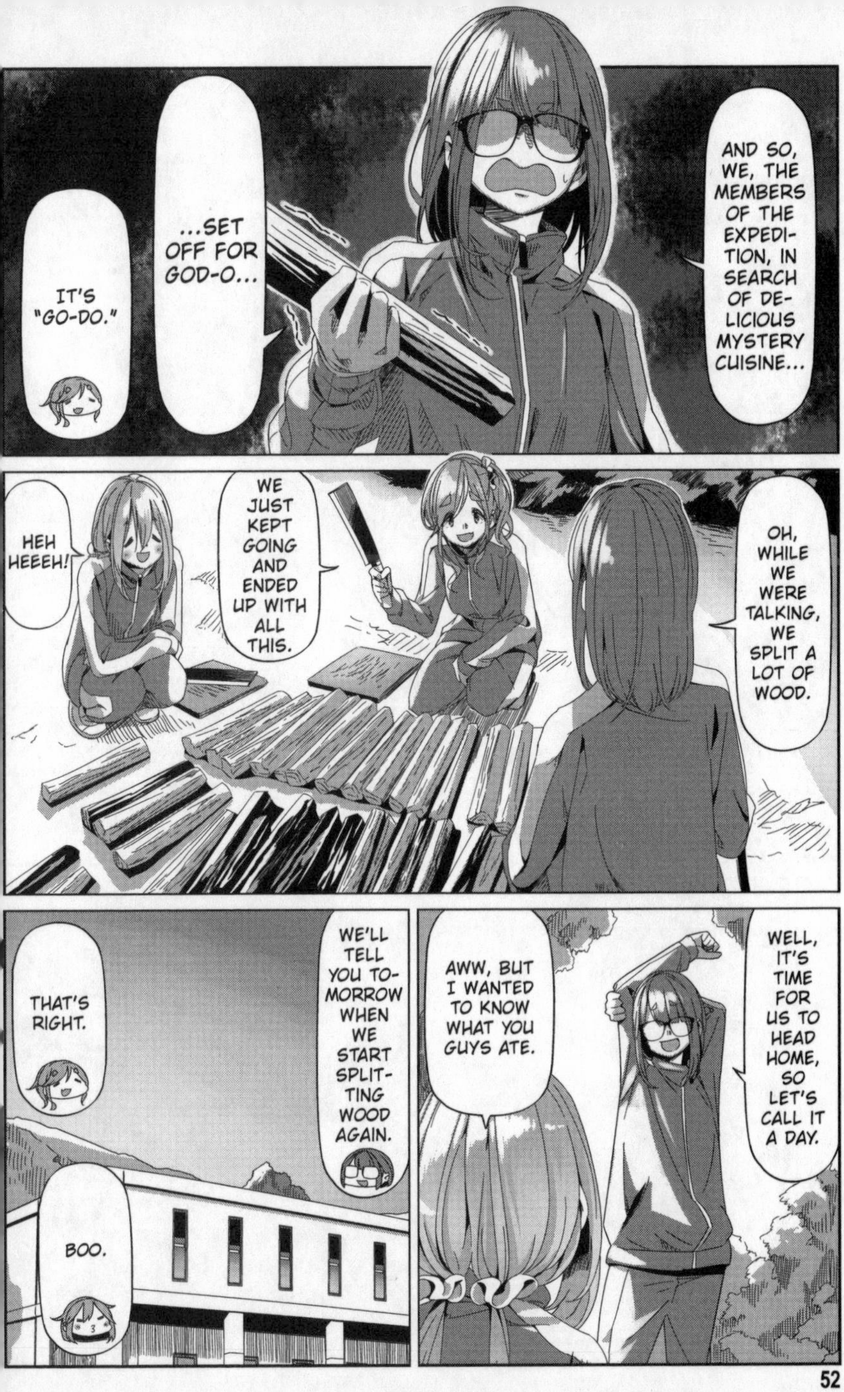
AND SO, WE, THE MEMBERS OF THE EXPEDI-TION, IN SEARCH OF DE-LICIOUS MYSTERY CUISINE...
...SET OFF FOR GOD-O...
IT'S "GO-DO."
OH, WHILE WE WERE TALKING, WE SPLIT A LOT OF WOOD.
WE JUST KEPT GOING AND ENDED UP WITH ALL THIS.
HEH HEEEH!
WELL, IT'S TIME FOR US TO HEAD HOME, SO LET'S CALL IT A DAY.
AWW, BUT I WANTED TO KNOW WHAT YOU GUYS ATE.
WE'LL TELL YOU TO-MORROW WHEN WE START SPLIT-TING WOOD AGAIN.
THAT'S RIGHT.
BOO.

CHIKUWA IN REAL LIFE AT THE TIME...

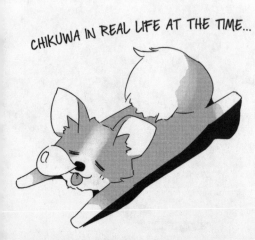

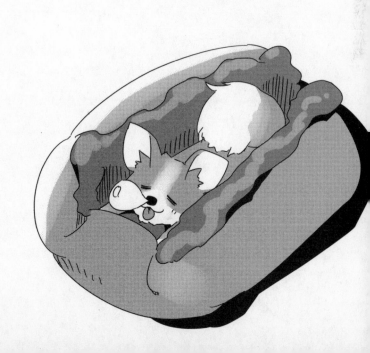

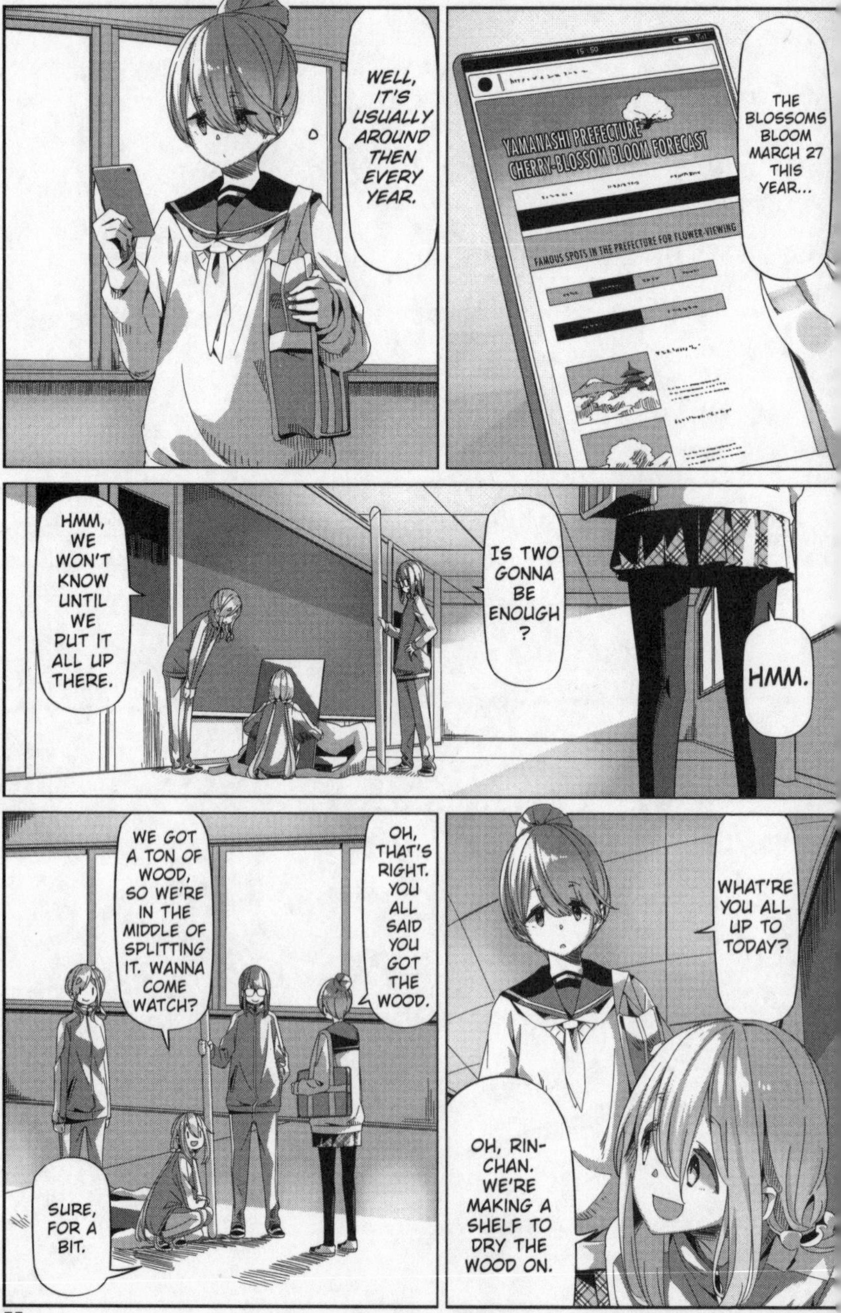
YAMANASHI PREFECTURE CHERRY-BLOSSOM BLOOM FORECAST
FAMOUS SPOTS IN THE PREFECTURE FOR FLOWER-VIEWING
THE BLOSSOMS BLOOM MARCH 27 THIS YEAR...
WELL, IT'S USUALLY AROUND THEN EVERY YEAR.
HMM.
IS TWO GONNA BE ENOUGH?
HMM, WE WON'T KNOW UNTIL WE PUT IT ALL UP THERE.
WHAT'RE YOU ALL UP TO TODAY?
OH, RIN-CHAN. WE'RE MAKING A SHELF TO DRY THE WOOD ON.
OH, THAT'S RIGHT. YOU ALL SAID YOU GOT THE WOOD.
WE GOT A TON OF WOOD, SO WE'RE IN THE MIDDLE OF SPLITTING IT. WANNA COME WATCH?
SURE, FOR A BIT.

Chapter 66 Wood-Splitting Tools and Lake Mizugaki's Mystery Cuisine

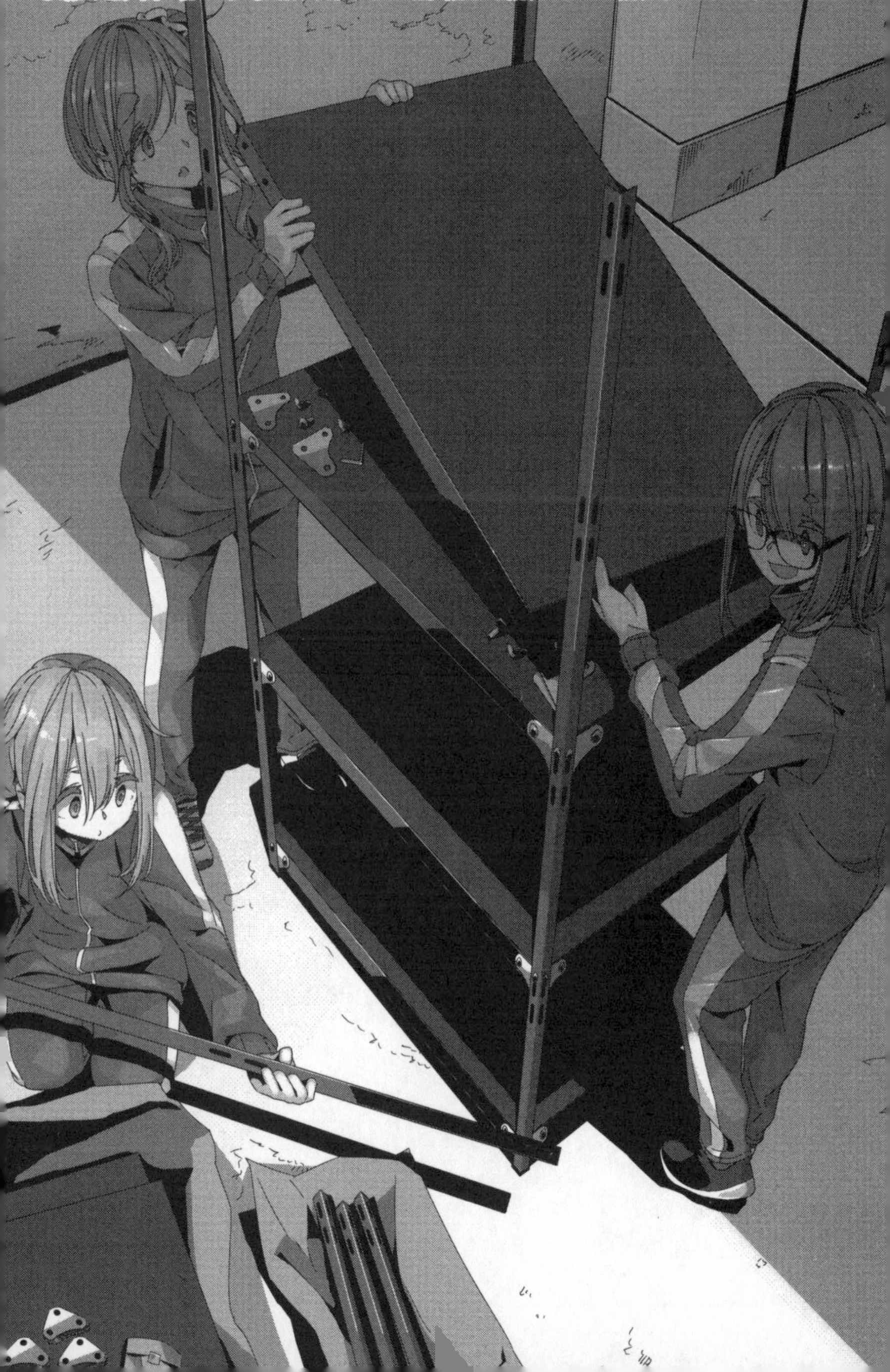

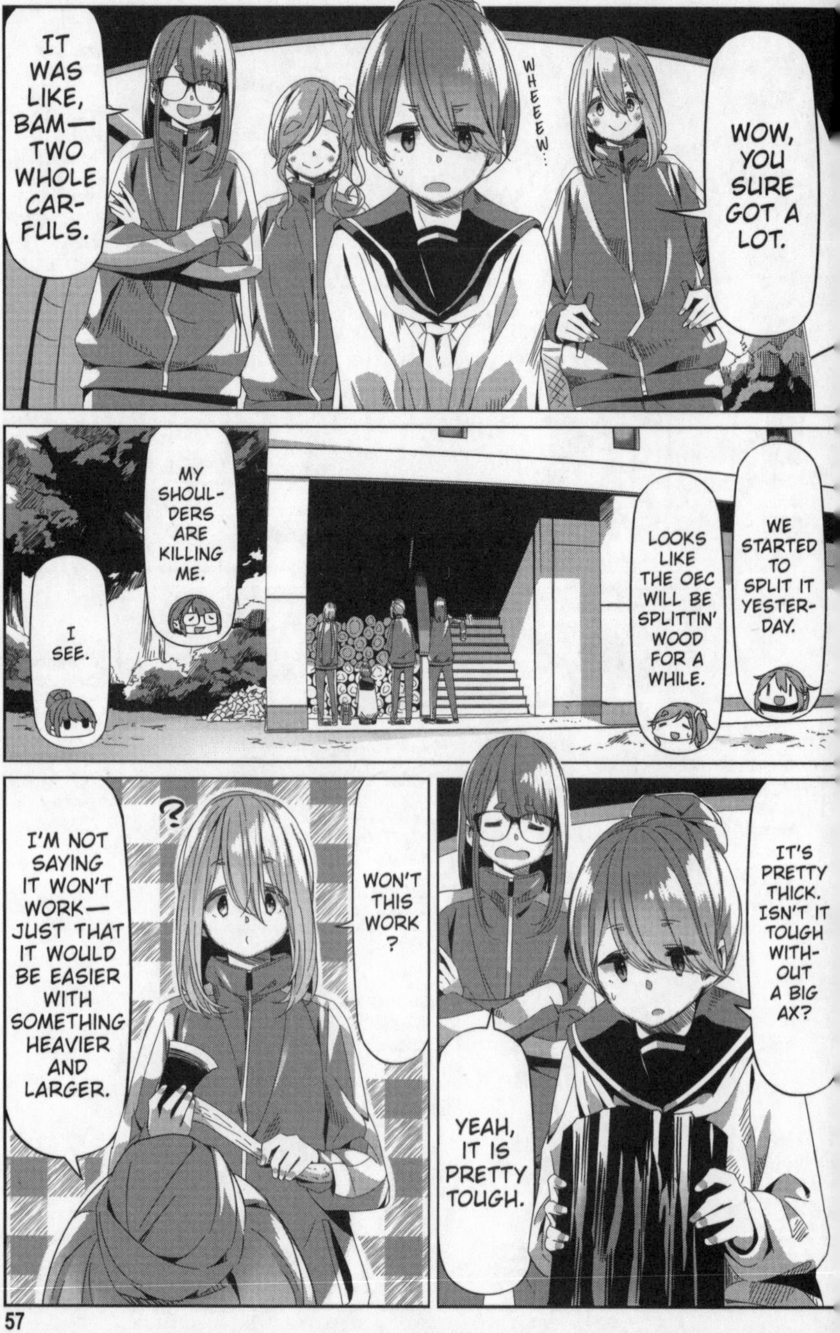
WOW, YOU SURE GOT A LOT.
WHEEEEW...
IT WAS LIKE, BAM—TWO WHOLE CAR-FULS.
WE STARTED TO SPLIT IT YESTER-DAY.
LOOKS LIKE THE OEC WILL BE SPLITTIN' WOOD FOR A WHILE.
MY SHOUL-DERS ARE KILLING ME.
I SEE.
IT'S PRETTY THICK. ISN'T IT TOUGH WITH-OUT A BIG AX?
YEAH, IT IS PRETTY TOUGH.
WON'T THIS WORK?
I'M NOT SAYING IT WON'T WORK—JUST THAT IT WOULD BE EASIER WITH SOMETHING HEAVIER AND LARGER.

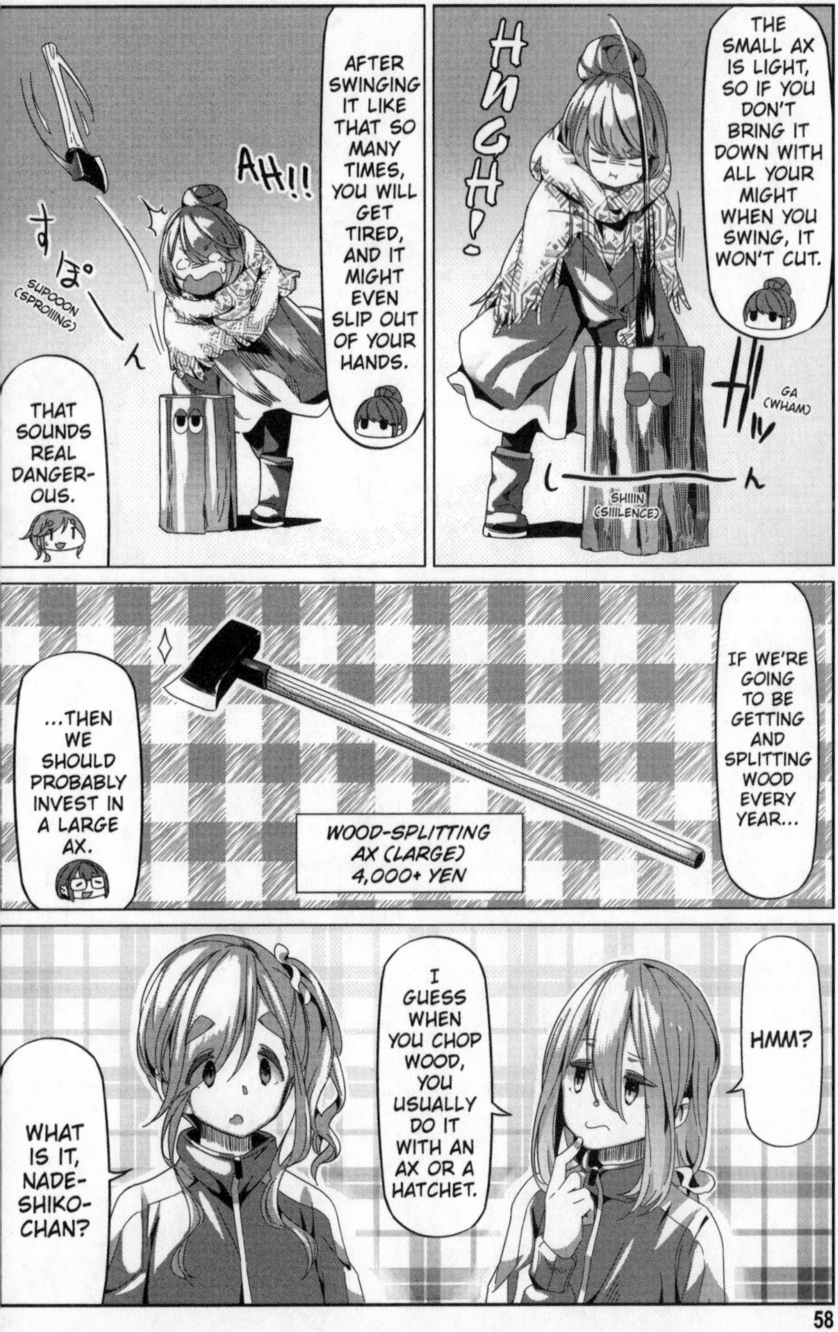
THE SMALL AX IS LIGHT, SO IF YOU DON'T BRING IT DOWN WITH ALL YOUR MIGHT WHEN YOU SWING, IT WON'T CUT.
HNGH!
GA (WHAM)
SHIIIN (SIIILENCE)
AFTER SWINGING IT LIKE THAT SO MANY TIMES, YOU WILL GET TIRED, AND IT MIGHT EVEN SLIP OUT OF YOUR HANDS.
AH!!
SUPOOON (SPROIIING)
THAT SOUNDS REAL DANGER-OUS.
IF WE'RE GOING TO BE GETTING AND SPLITTING WOOD EVERY YEAR...
WOOD-SPLITTING AX (LARGE) 4,000+ YEN
...THEN WE SHOULD PROBABLY INVEST IN A LARGE AX.
HMM?
I GUESS WHEN YOU CHOP WOOD, YOU USUALLY DO IT WITH AN AX OR A HATCHET.
WHAT IS IT, NADE-SHIKO-CHAN?

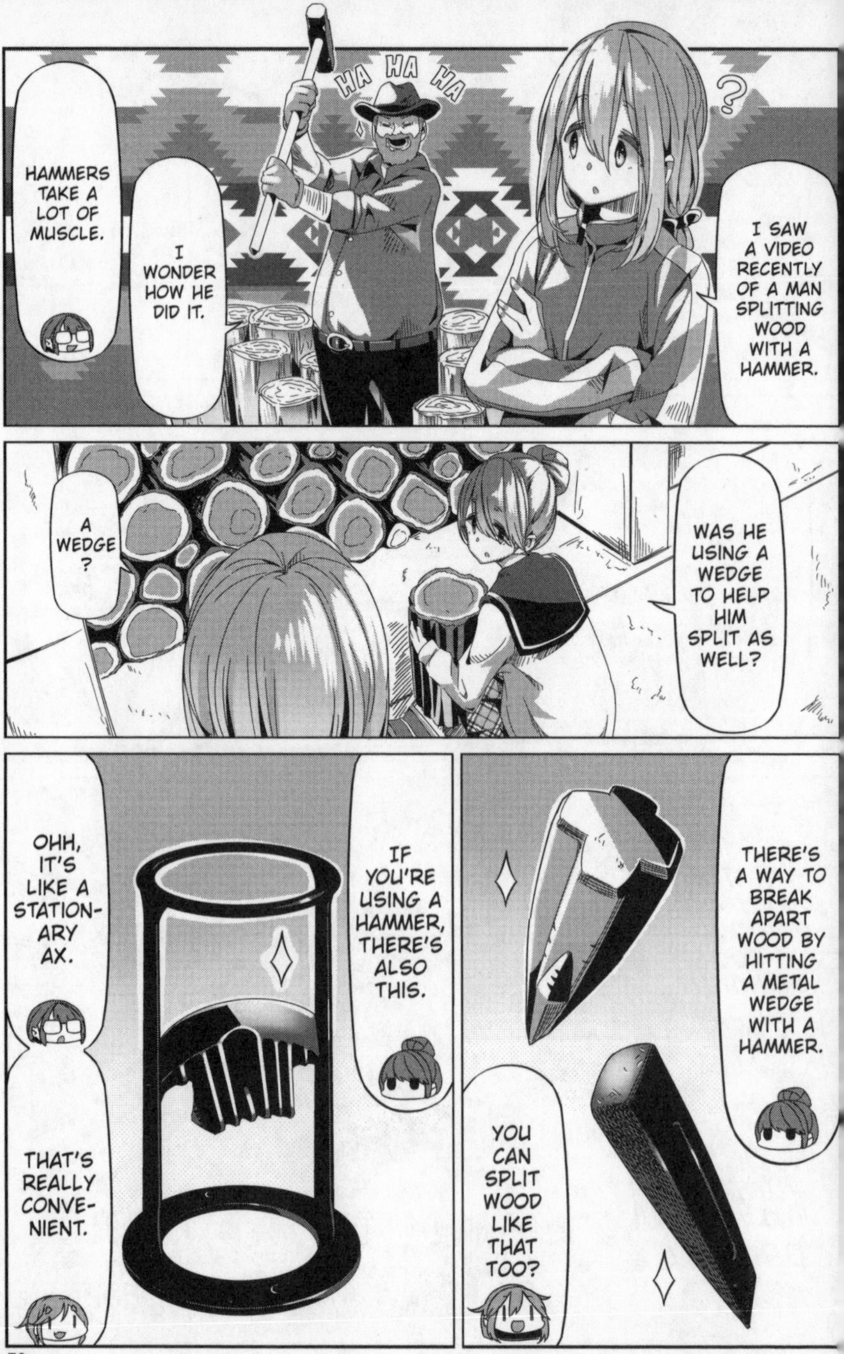
I SAW A VIDEO RECENTLY OF A MAN SPLITTING WOOD WITH A HAMMER.
?
HA HA HA
I WONDER HOW HE DID IT.
HAMMERS TAKE A LOT OF MUSCLE.
WAS HE USING A WEDGE TO HELP HIM SPLIT AS WELL?
A WEDGE?
THERE'S A WAY TO BREAK APART WOOD BY HITTING A METAL WEDGE WITH A HAMMER.
YOU CAN SPLIT WOOD LIKE THAT TOO?
IF YOU'RE USING A HAMMER, THERE'S ALSO THIS.
OHH, IT'S LIKE A STATION-ARY AX.
THAT'S REALLY CONVE-NIENT.

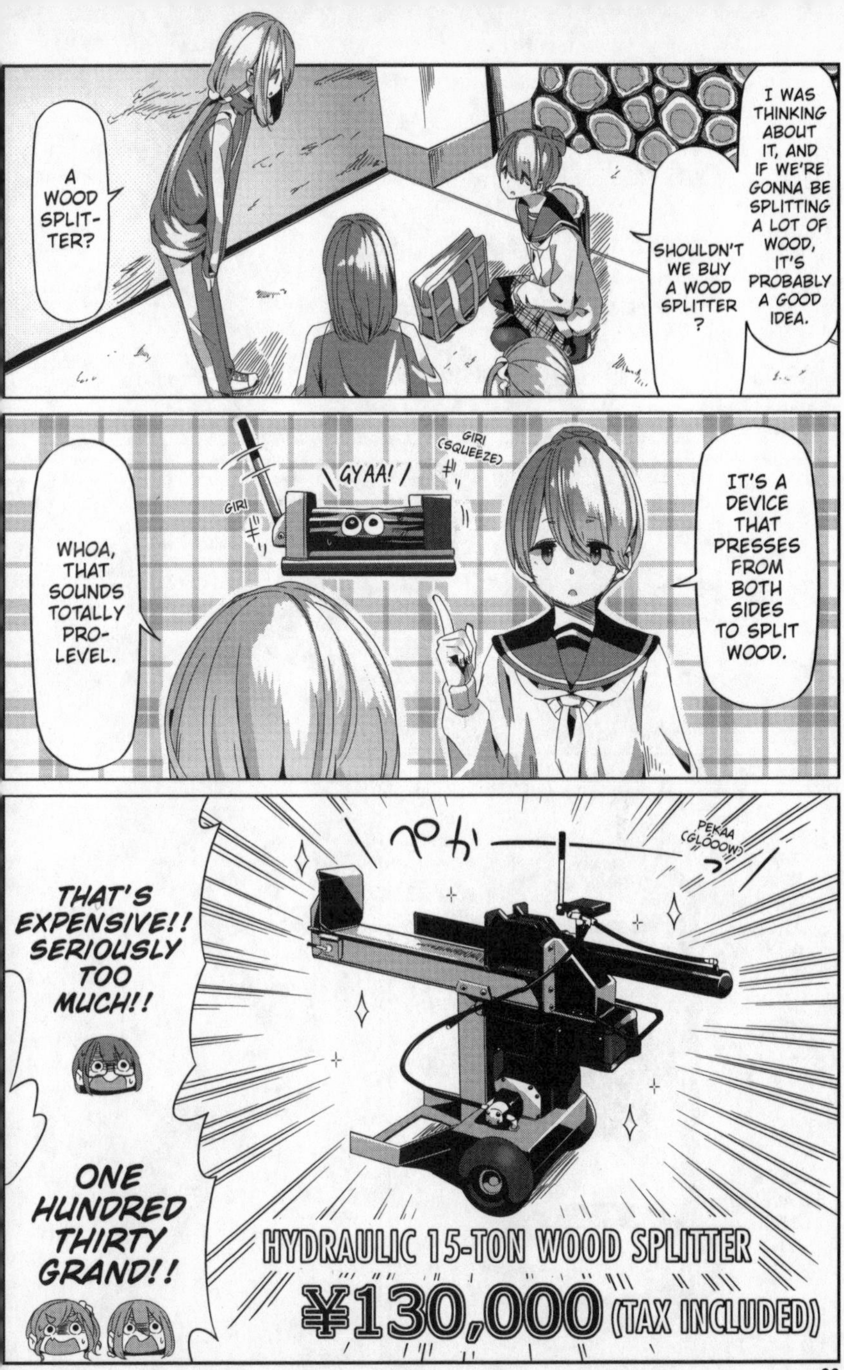
I WAS THINKING ABOUT IT, AND IF WE'RE GONNA BE SPLITTING A LOT OF WOOD, IT'S PROBABLY A GOOD IDEA.
SHOULDN'T WE BUY A WOOD SPLITTER?
A WOOD SPLIT-TER?
IT'S A DEVICE THAT PRESSES FROM BOTH SIDES TO SPLIT WOOD.
GIRI (SQUEEZE)
GYAA!
GIRI
WHOA, THAT SOUNDS TOTALLY PRO-LEVEL.
PEKAA (GLOOOW)
HYDRAULIC 15-TON WOOD SPLITTER
¥130,000 (TAX INCLUDED)
THAT'S EXPENSIVE!! SERIOUSLY TOO MUCH!!
ONE HUNDRED THIRTY GRAND!!

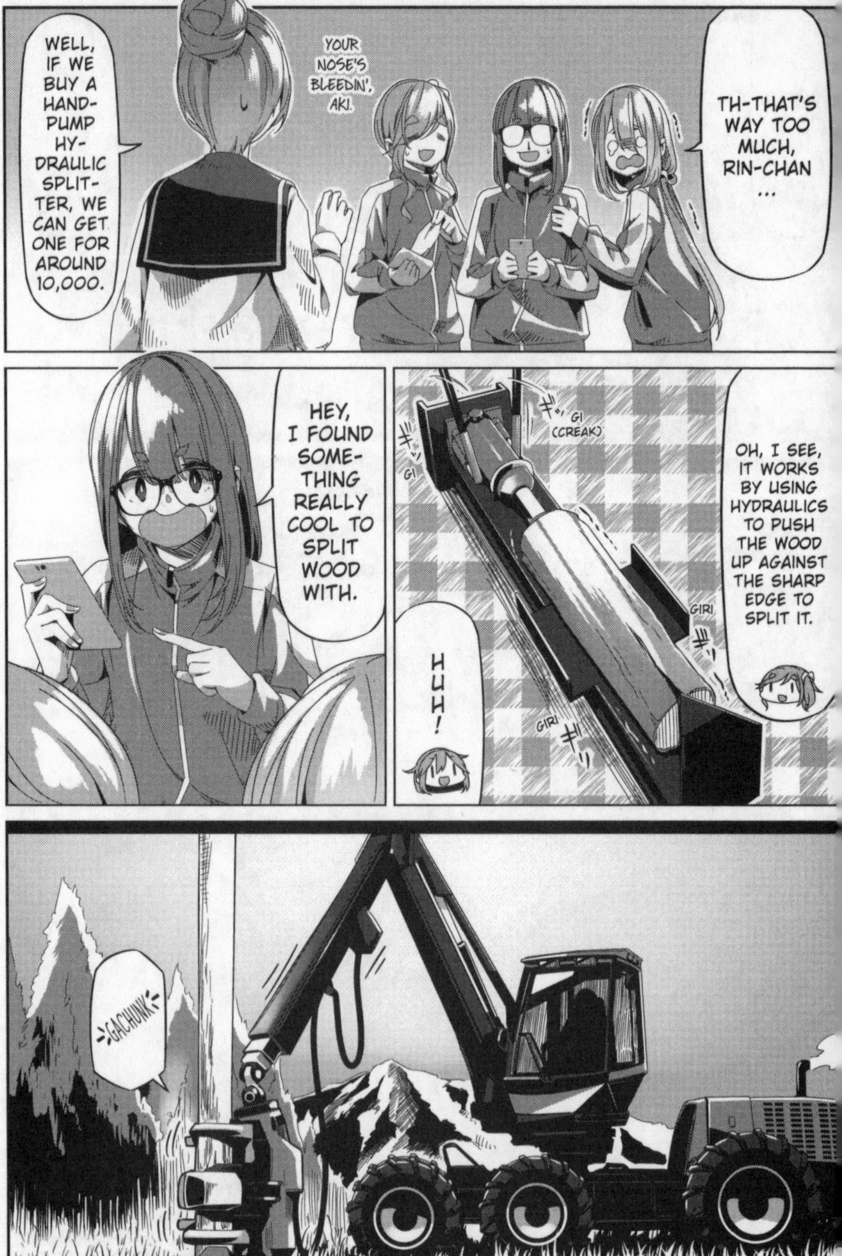
TH-THAT'S WAY TOO MUCH, RIN-CHAN...
YOUR NOSE'S BLEEDIN', AKI.
WELL, IF WE BUY A HAND-PUMP HY-DRAULIC SPLIT-TER, WE CAN GET ONE FOR AROUND 10,000.
OH, I SEE, IT WORKS BY USING HYDRAULICS TO PUSH THE WOOD UP AGAINST THE SHARP EDGE TO SPLIT IT.
GI (CREAK)
GI
GIRI
HUH!
GIRI
HEY, I FOUND SOME-THING REALLY COOL TO SPLIT WOOD WITH.
GACHUNK

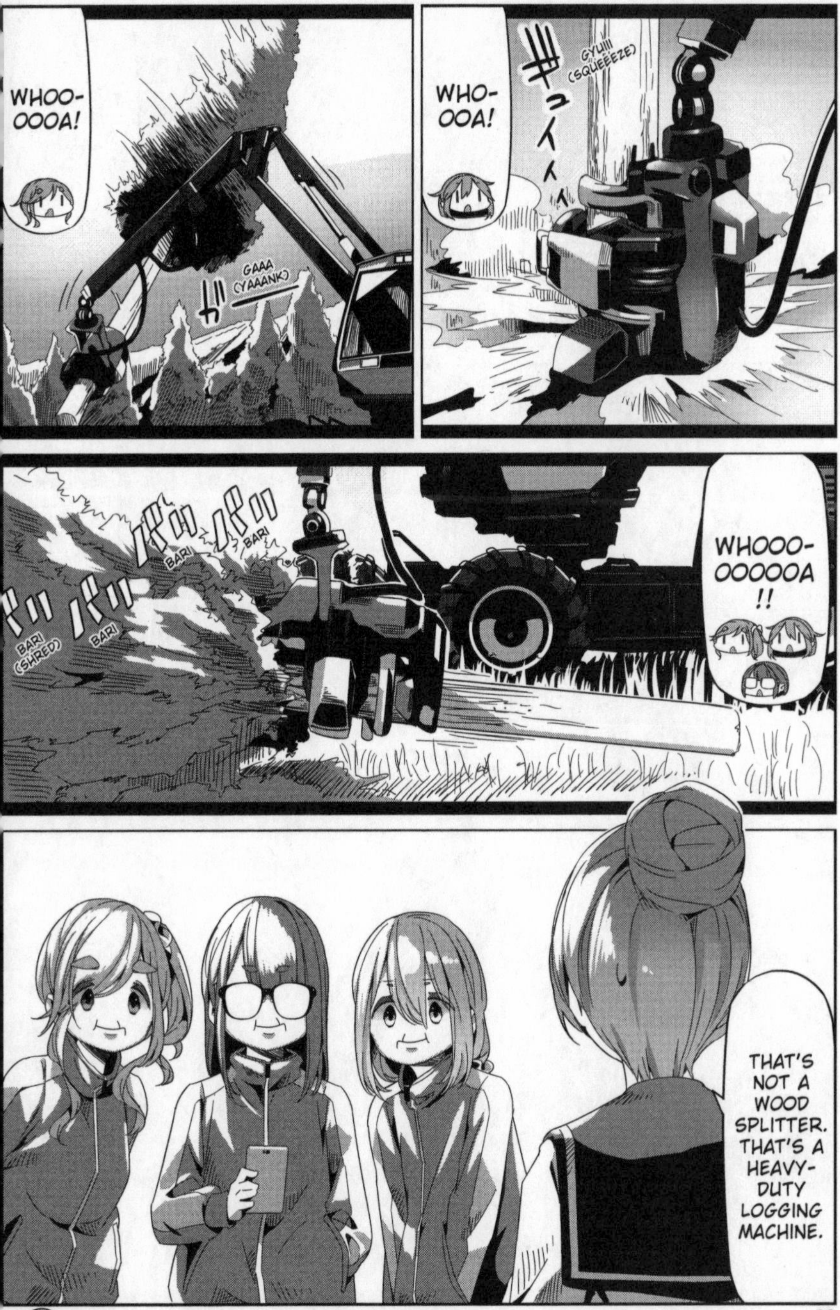
WHO-OOA!
GYUIII (SQUEEEZE)
WHOO-OOOA!
GAAA (YAAANK)
WHOOO-OOOOOA!!
BARI
BARI
BARI (SHRED)
BARI
THAT'S NOT A WOOD SPLITTER. THAT'S A HEAVY-DUTY LOGGING MACHINE.

ACTUALLY, IT'S A LAND-CLEARING EXCAVATOR.

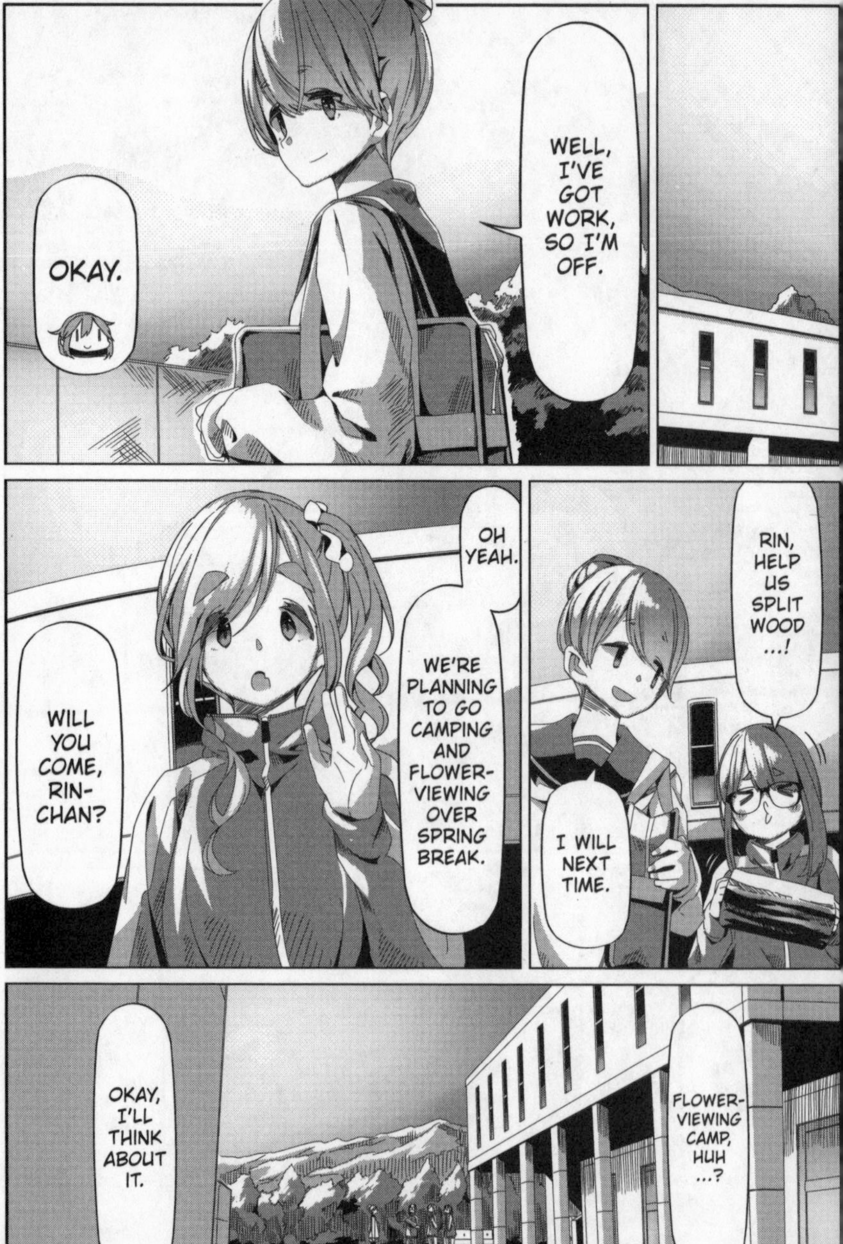
WELL, I'VE GOT WORK, SO I'M OFF.
OKAY.
RIN, HELP US SPLIT WOOD ...!
I WILL NEXT TIME.
OH YEAH.
WE'RE PLANNING TO GO CAMPING AND FLOWER-VIEWING OVER SPRING BREAK.
WILL YOU COME, RIN-CHAN?
FLOWER-VIEWING CAMP, HUH ...?
OKAY, I'LL THINK ABOUT IT.

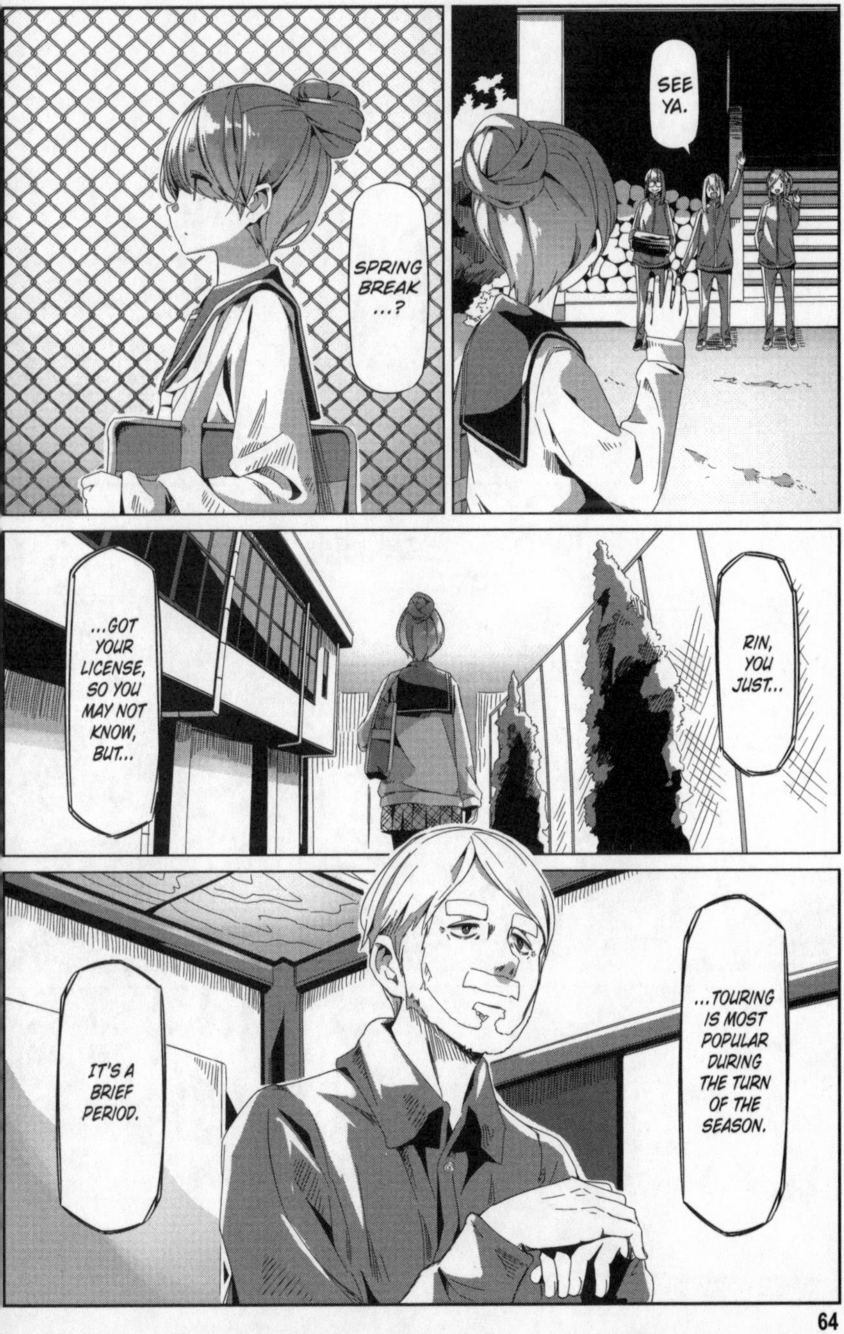
SEE YA.
SPRING BREAK ...?
RIN, YOU JUST...
...GOT YOUR LICENSE, SO YOU MAY NOT KNOW, BUT...
...TOURING IS MOST POPULAR DURING THE TURN OF THE SEASON.
IT'S A BRIEF PERIOD.

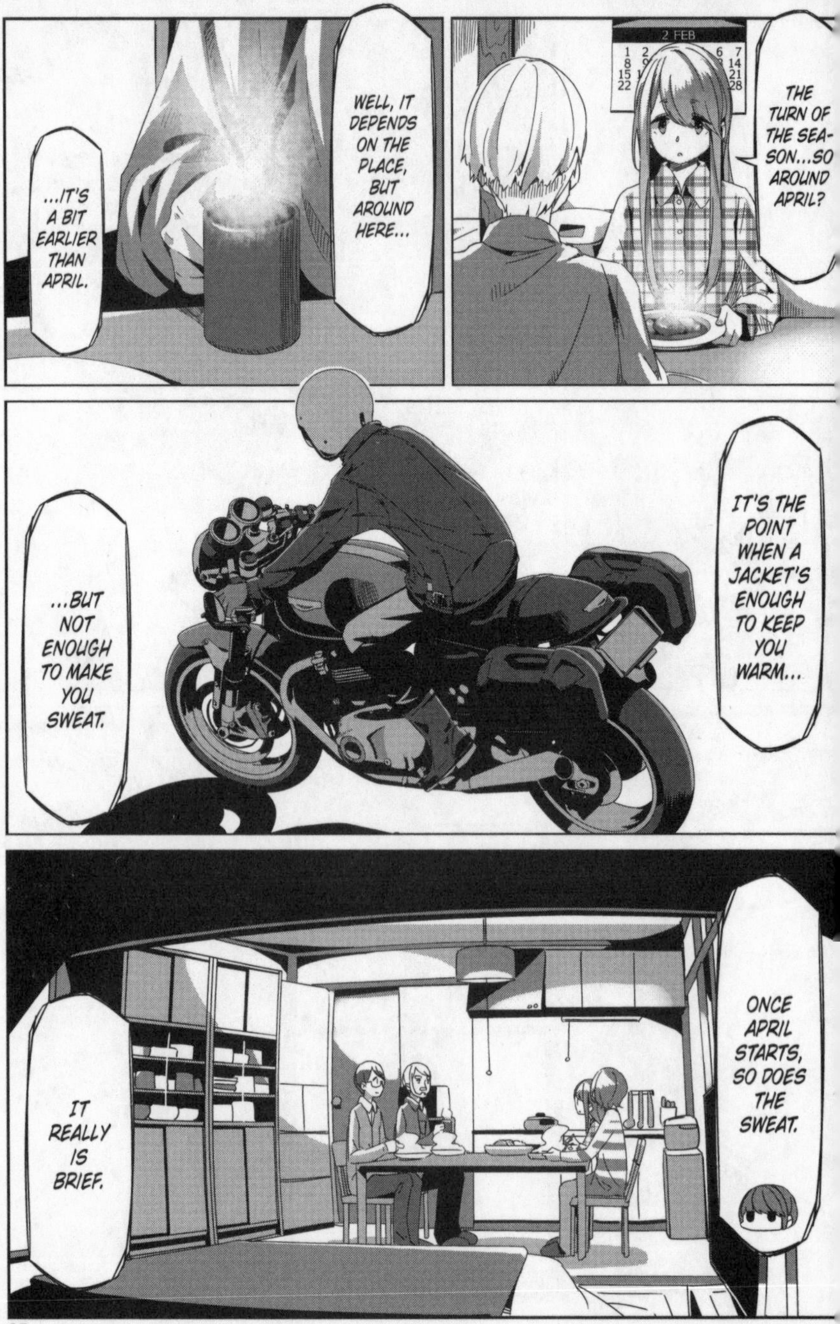
2 FEB
THE TURN OF THE SEA-SON...SO AROUND APRIL?
WELL, IT DEPENDS ON THE PLACE, BUT AROUND HERE...
...IT'S A BIT EARLIER THAN APRIL.
IT'S THE POINT WHEN A JACKET'S ENOUGH TO KEEP YOU WARM...
...BUT NOT ENOUGH TO MAKE YOU SWEAT.
ONCE APRIL STARTS, SO DOES THE SWEAT.
IT REALLY IS BRIEF.

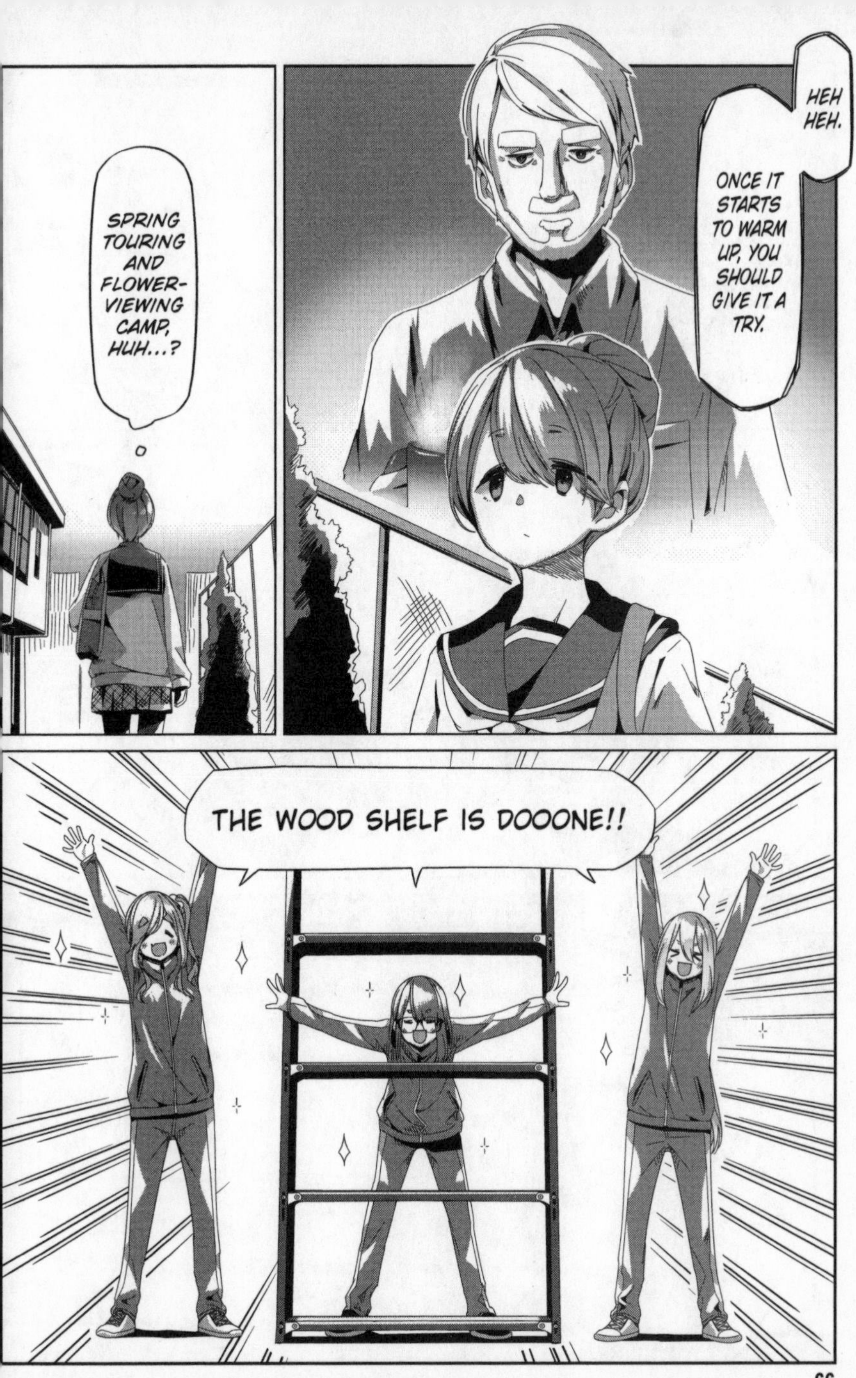
HEH HEH.
ONCE IT STARTS TO WARM UP, YOU SHOULD GIVE IT A TRY.
SPRING TOURING AND FLOWER-VIEWING CAMP, HUH...?
THE WOOD SHELF IS DOOONE!!

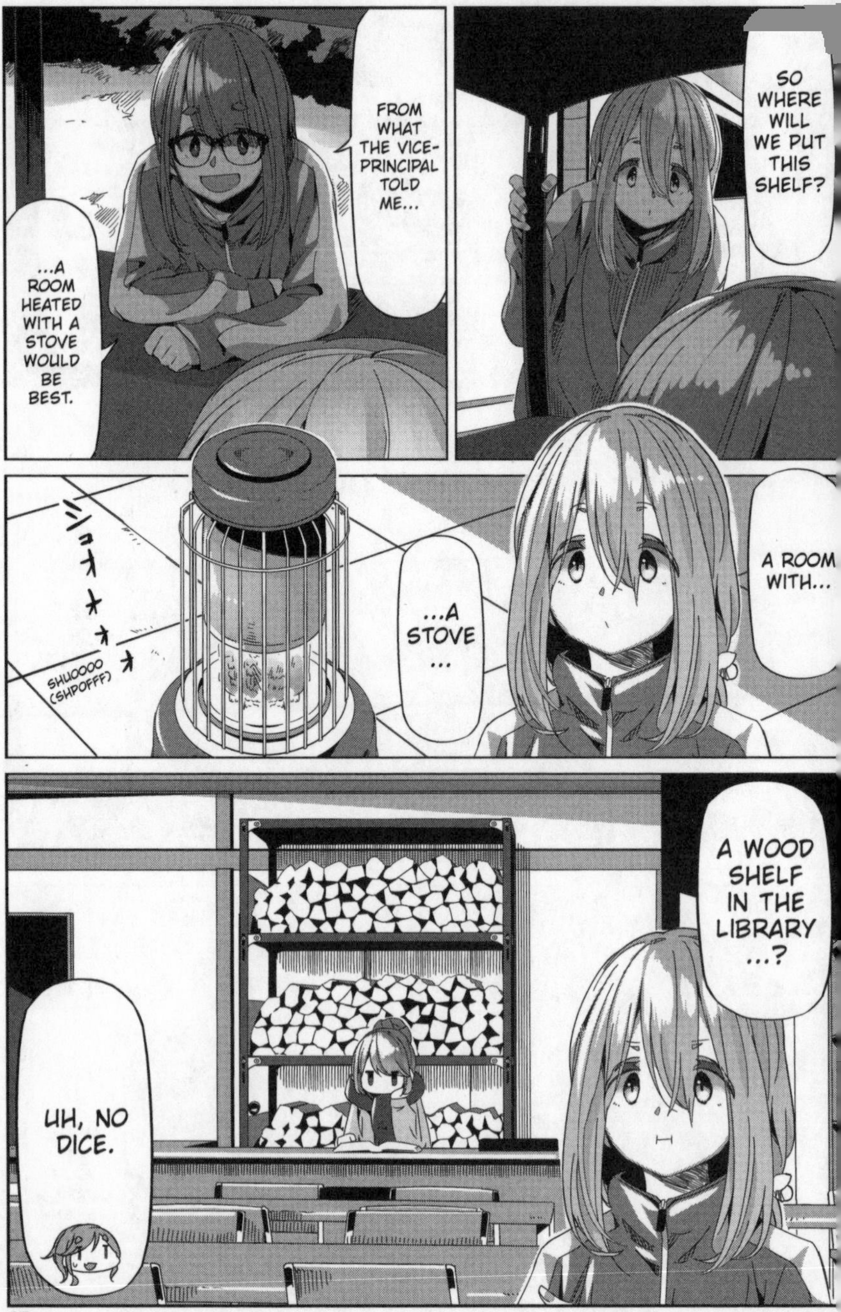
SO WHERE WILL WE PUT THIS SHELF?
FROM WHAT THE VICE-PRINCIPAL TOLD ME...
...A ROOM HEATED WITH A STOVE WOULD BE BEST.
A ROOM WITH...
...A STOVE ...
シュオォォォ
SHUOOOO (SHPOFFF)
A WOOD SHELF IN THE LIBRARY ...?
UH, NO DICE.

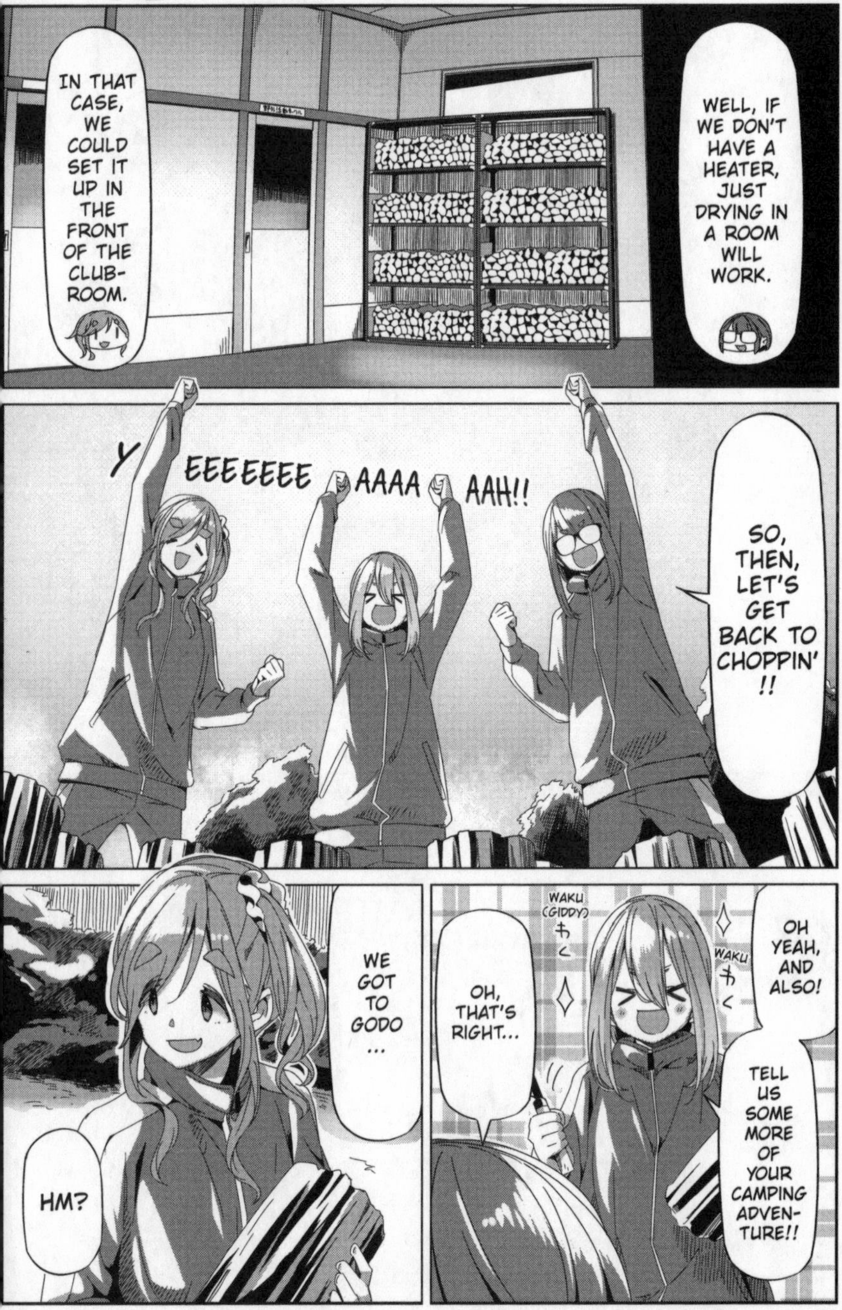
WELL, IF WE DON'T HAVE A HEATER, JUST DRYING IN A ROOM WILL WORK.
IN THAT CASE, WE COULD SET IT UP IN THE FRONT OF THE CLUB-ROOM.
SO, THEN, LET'S GET BACK TO CHOPPIN'!!
YEEEEEEE AAAA AAH!!
OH YEAH, AND ALSO!
TELL US SOME MORE OF YOUR CAMPING ADVEN-TURE!!
WAKU (GIDDY)
WAKU
OH, THAT'S RIGHT...
WE GOT TO GODO...
HM?

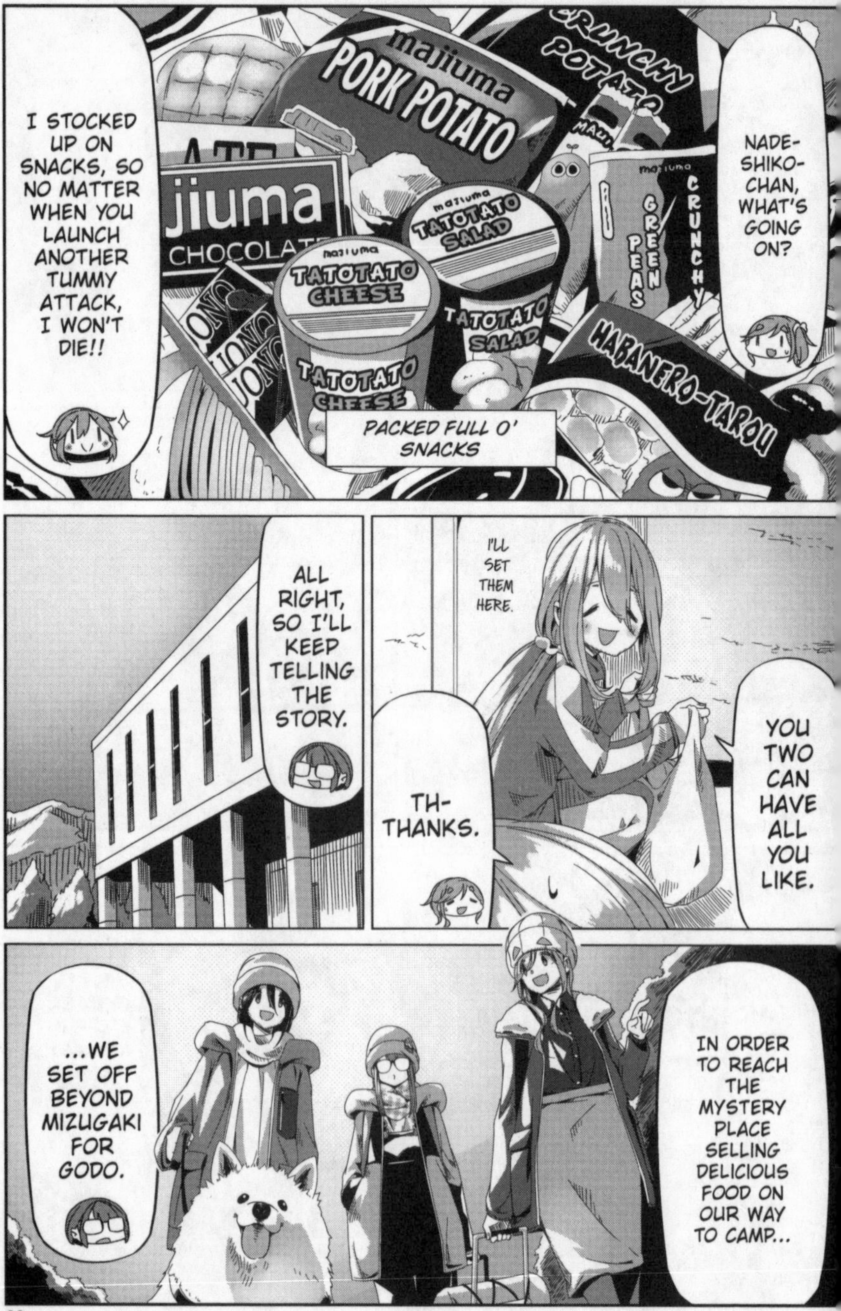
NADE-SHIKO-CHAN, WHAT'S GOING ON?
I STOCKED UP ON SNACKS, SO NO MATTER WHEN YOU LAUNCH ANOTHER TUMMY ATTACK, I WON'T DIE!!
CRUNCHY POTATO
majiuma PORK POTATO
majiuma GREEN PEAS CRUNCHY
majiuma TATOTATO SALAD
jiuma CHOCOLATE
majiuma TATOTATO CHEESE
TATOTATO SALAD
TATOTATO CHEESE
HABANERO-TAROU
PACKED FULL O' SNACKS
I'LL SET THEM HERE.
YOU TWO CAN HAVE ALL YOU LIKE.
TH-THANKS.
ALL RIGHT, SO I'LL KEEP TELLING THE STORY.
IN ORDER TO REACH THE MYSTERY PLACE SELLING DELICIOUS FOOD ON OUR WAY TO CAMP...
...WE SET OFF BEYOND MIZUGAKI FOR GODO.

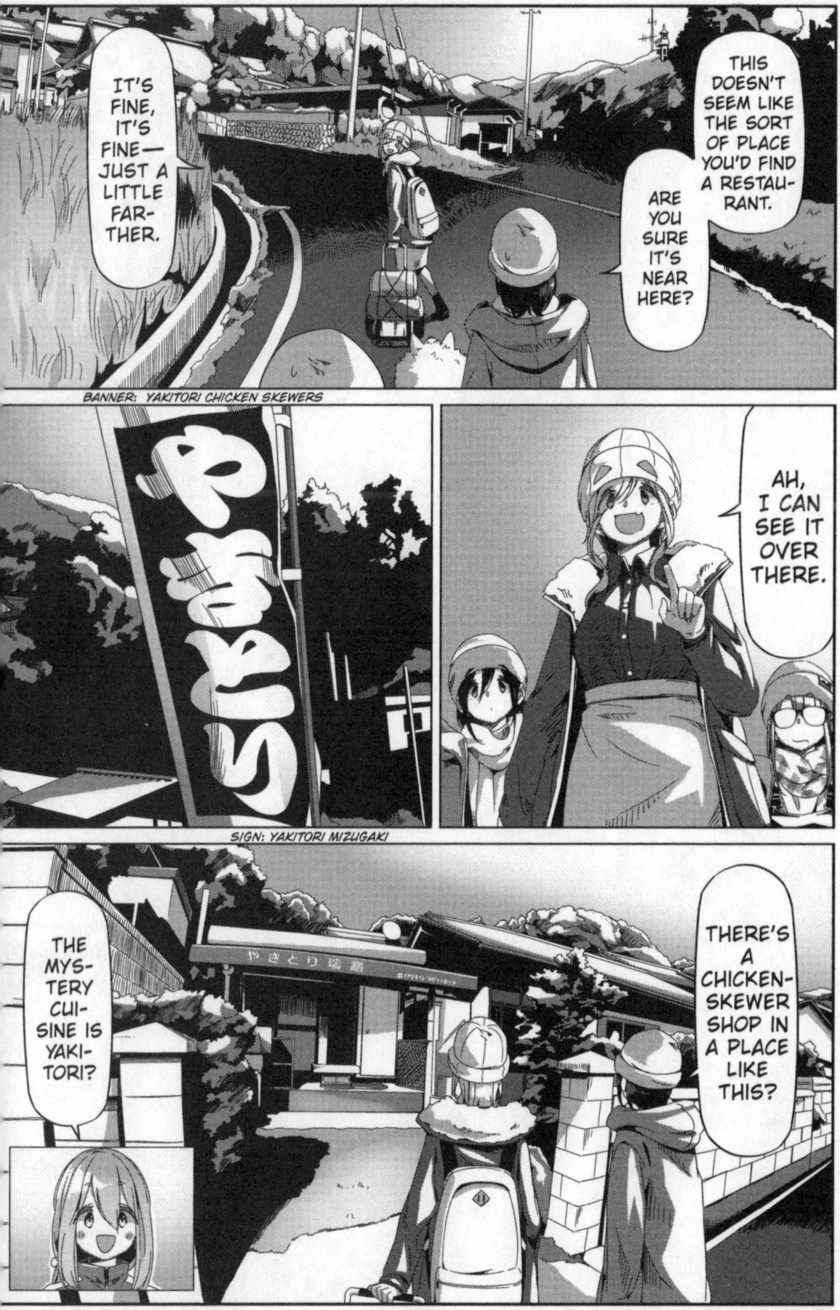
THIS DOESN'T SEEM LIKE THE SORT OF PLACE YOU'D FIND A RESTAURANT.
ARE YOU SURE IT'S NEAR HERE?
IT'S FINE, IT'S FINE—JUST A LITTLE FARTHER.
AH, I CAN SEE IT OVER THERE.
BANNER: YAKITORI CHICKEN SKEWERS
SIGN: YAKITORI MIZUGAKI
THERE'S A CHICKEN-SKEWER SHOP IN A PLACE LIKE THIS?
THE MYSTERY CUISINE IS YAKITORI?

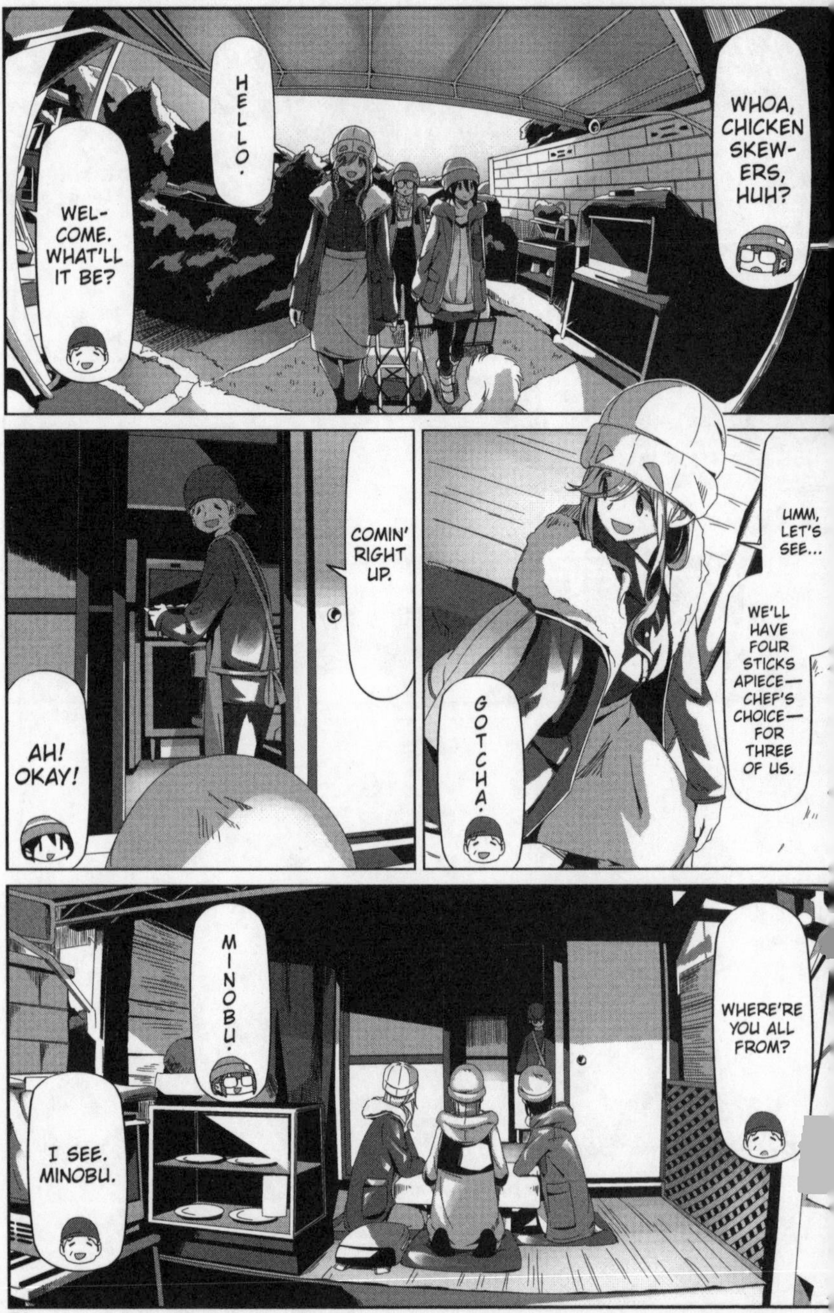
WHOA, CHICKEN SKEWERS, HUH?
HELLO.
WELCOME. WHAT'LL IT BE?
UMM, LET'S SEE...
WE'LL HAVE FOUR STICKS APIECE—CHEF'S CHOICE—FOR THREE OF US.
GOTCHA.
COMIN' RIGHT UP.
AH! OKAY!
WHERE'RE YOU ALL FROM?
MINOBU.
I SEE. MINOBU.

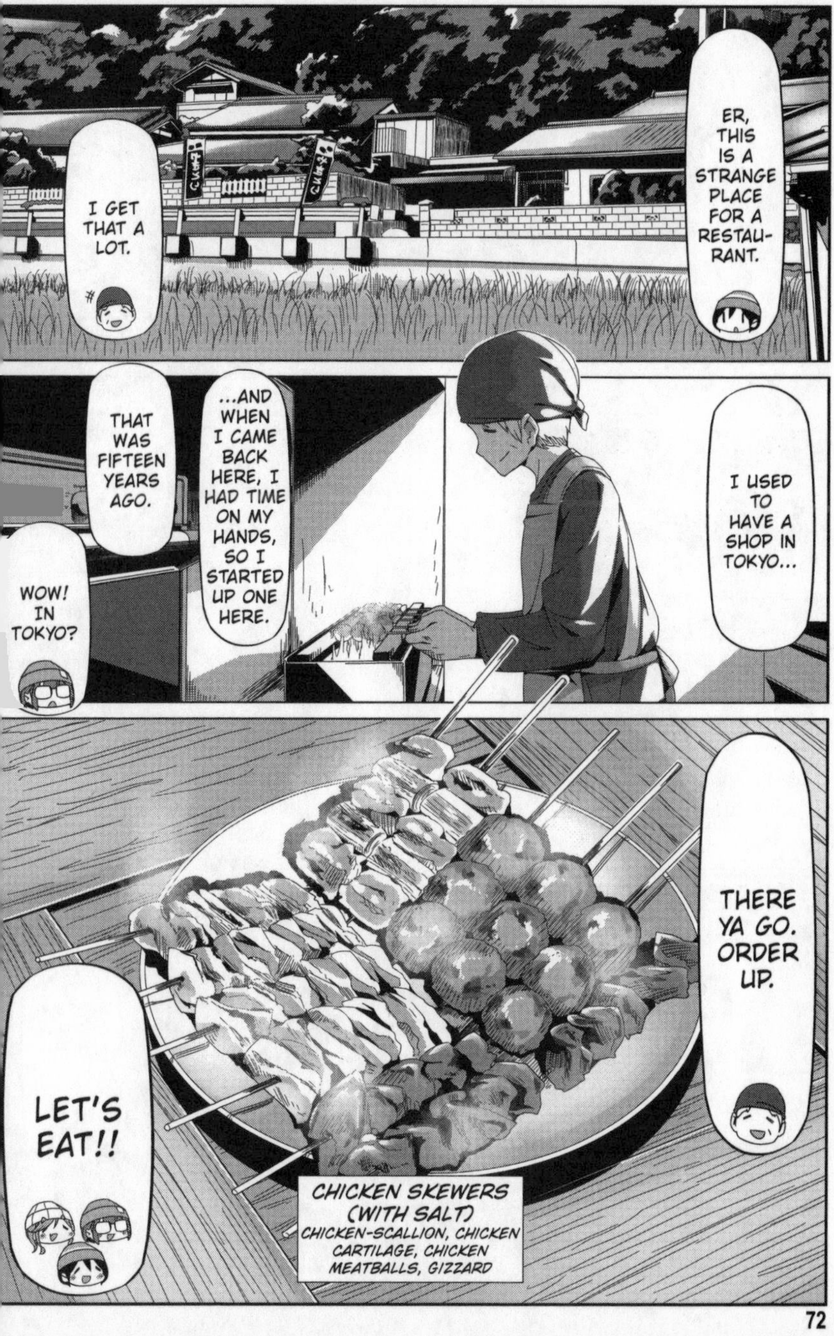
ER, THIS IS A STRANGE PLACE FOR A RESTAU-RANT.
I GET THAT A LOT.
I USED TO HAVE A SHOP IN TOKYO...
...AND WHEN I CAME BACK HERE, I HAD TIME ON MY HANDS, SO I STARTED UP ONE HERE.
THAT WAS FIFTEEN YEARS AGO.
WOW! IN TOKYO?
THERE YA GO. ORDER UP.
CHICKEN SKEWERS (WITH SALT) CHICKEN-SCALLION, CHICKEN CARTILAGE, CHICKEN MEATBALLS, GIZZARD
LET'S EAT!!

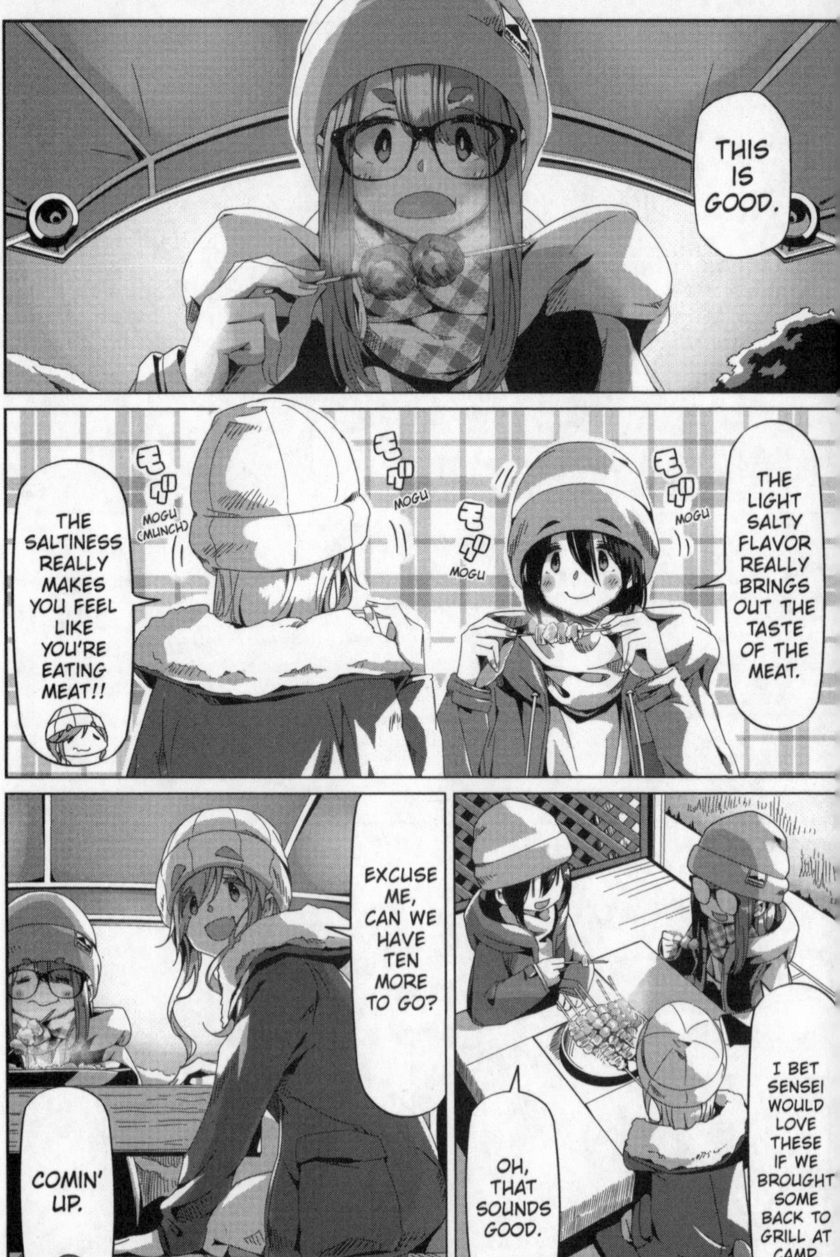
THIS IS GOOD.
モグ
MOGU
THE LIGHT SALTY FLAVOR REALLY BRINGS OUT THE TASTE OF THE MEAT.
モグ
MOGU
モグ
MOGU
モグ
MOGU (MUNCH)
THE SALTINESS REALLY MAKES YOU FEEL LIKE YOU'RE EATING MEAT!!
I BET SENSEI WOULD LOVE THESE IF WE BROUGHT SOME BACK TO GRILL AT CAMP.
OH, THAT SOUNDS GOOD.
EXCUSE ME, CAN WE HAVE TEN MORE TO GO?
COMIN' UP.

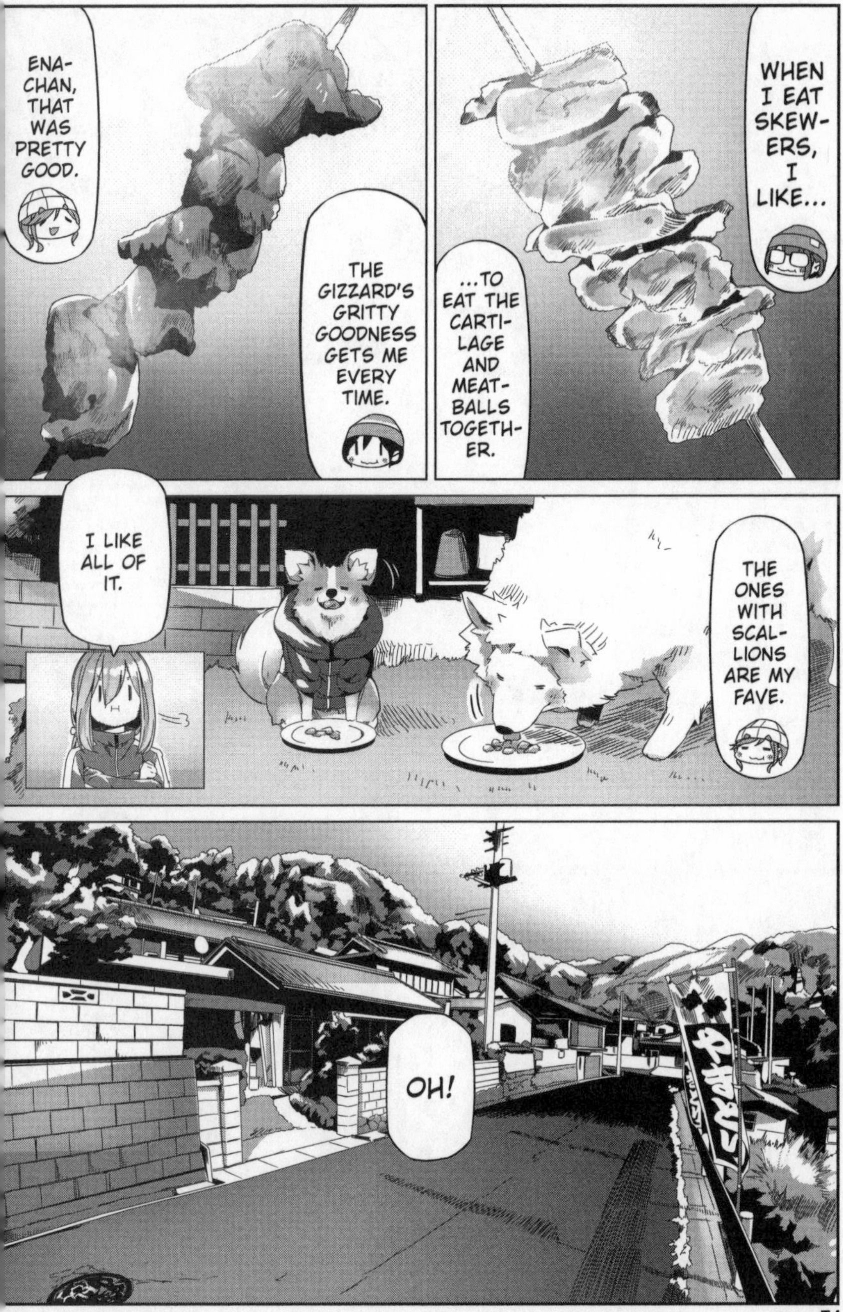
WHEN I EAT SKEW-ERS, I LIKE...
...TO EAT THE CARTI-LAGE AND MEAT-BALLS TOGETH-ER.
ENA-CHAN, THAT WAS PRETTY GOOD.
THE GIZZARD'S GRITTY GOODNESS GETS ME EVERY TIME.
THE ONES WITH SCAL-LIONS ARE MY FAVE.
I LIKE ALL OF IT.
OH!

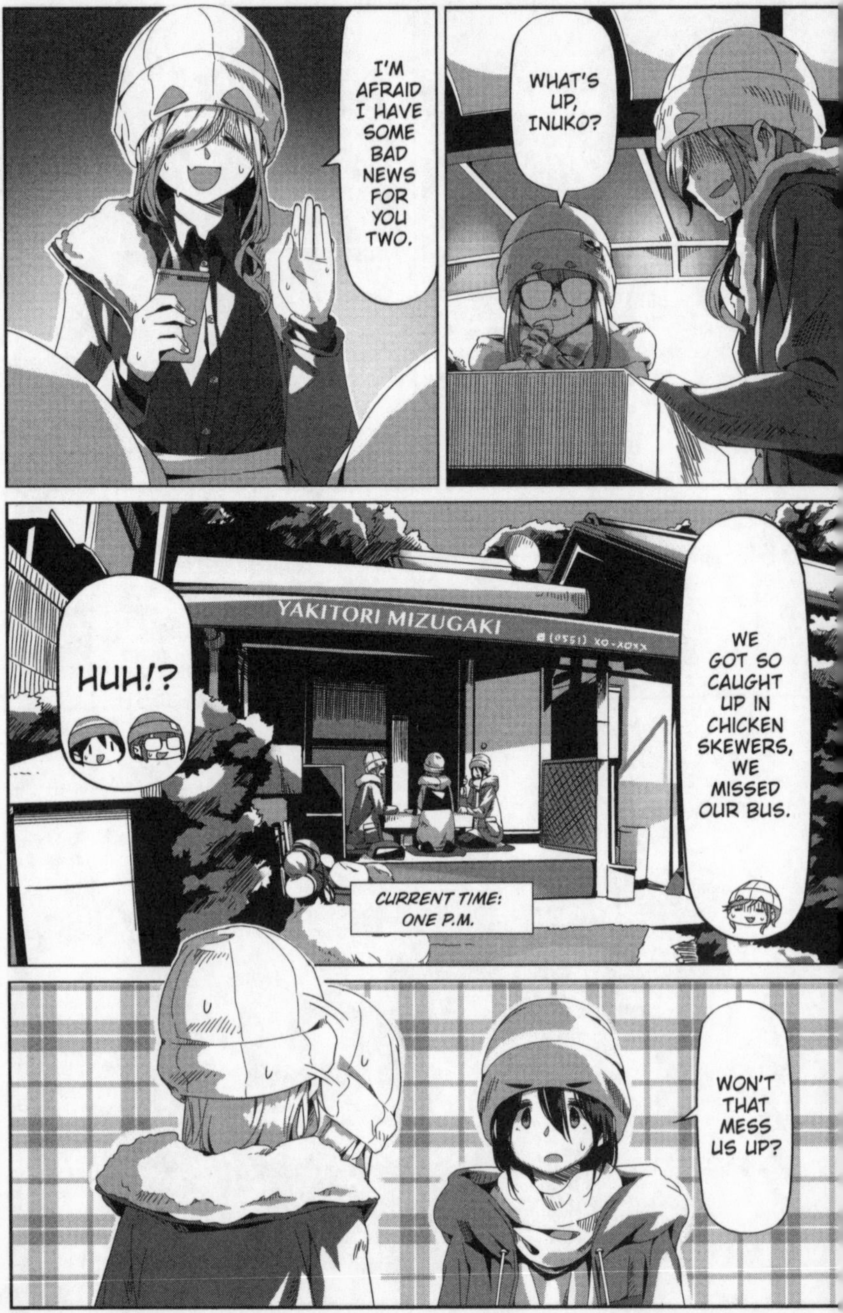
WHAT'S UP, INUKO?
I'M AFRAID I HAVE SOME BAD NEWS FOR YOU TWO.
WE GOT SO CAUGHT UP IN CHICKEN SKEWERS, WE MISSED OUR BUS.
YAKITORI MIZUGAKI
HUH!?
CURRENT TIME: ONE P.M.
WON'T THAT MESS US UP?

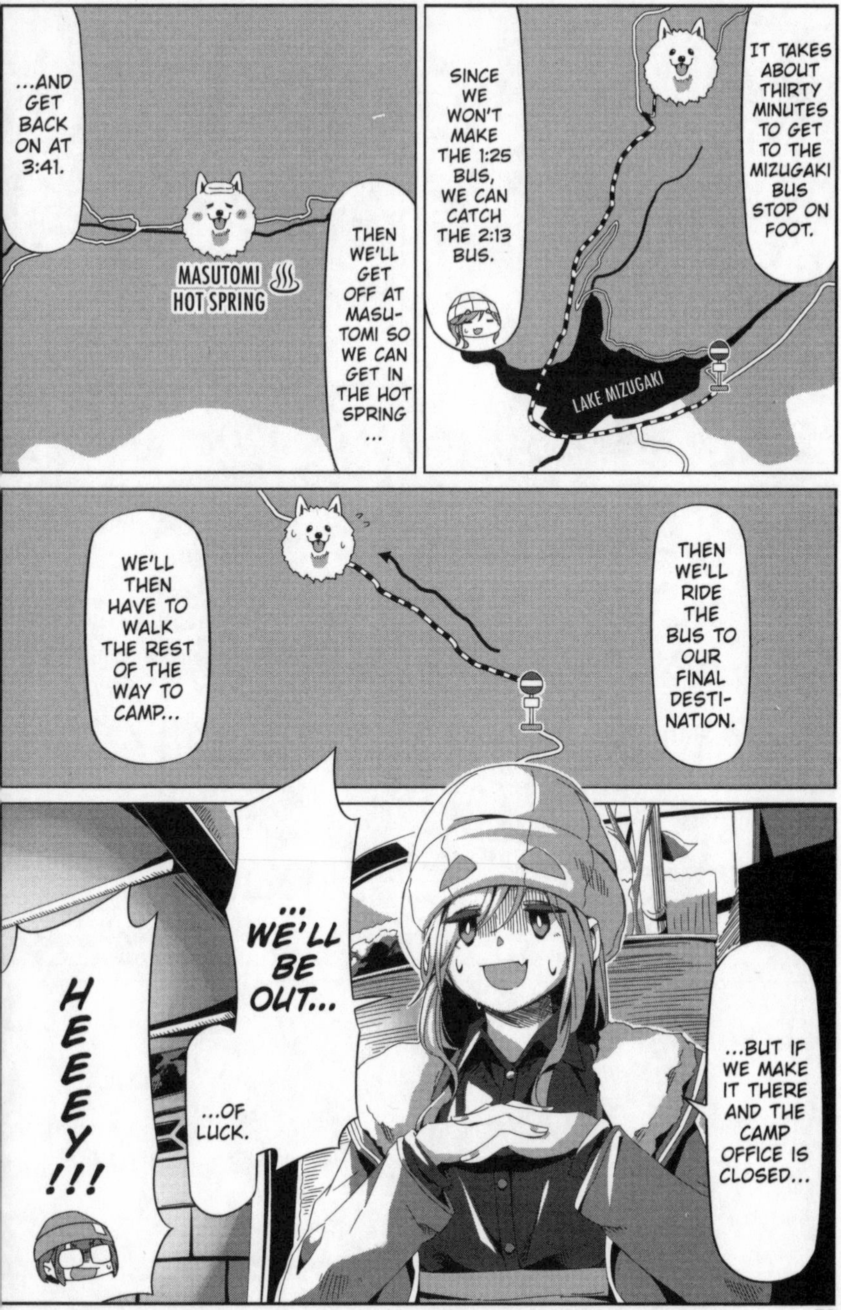

IT TAKES ABOUT THIRTY MINUTES TO GET TO THE MIZUGAKI BUS STOP ON FOOT.
SINCE WE WON'T MAKE THE 1:25 BUS, WE CAN CATCH THE 2:13 BUS.
LAKE MIZUGAKI
THEN WE'LL GET OFF AT MASUTOMI SO WE CAN GET IN THE HOT SPRING...
MASUTOMI HOT SPRING
...AND GET BACK ON AT 3:41.
THEN WE'LL RIDE THE BUS TO OUR FINAL DESTINATION.
WE'LL THEN HAVE TO WALK THE REST OF THE WAY TO CAMP...
...BUT IF WE MAKE IT THERE AND THE CAMP OFFICE IS CLOSED...
...WE'LL BE OUT...
...OF LUCK.
HEEEEY!!!

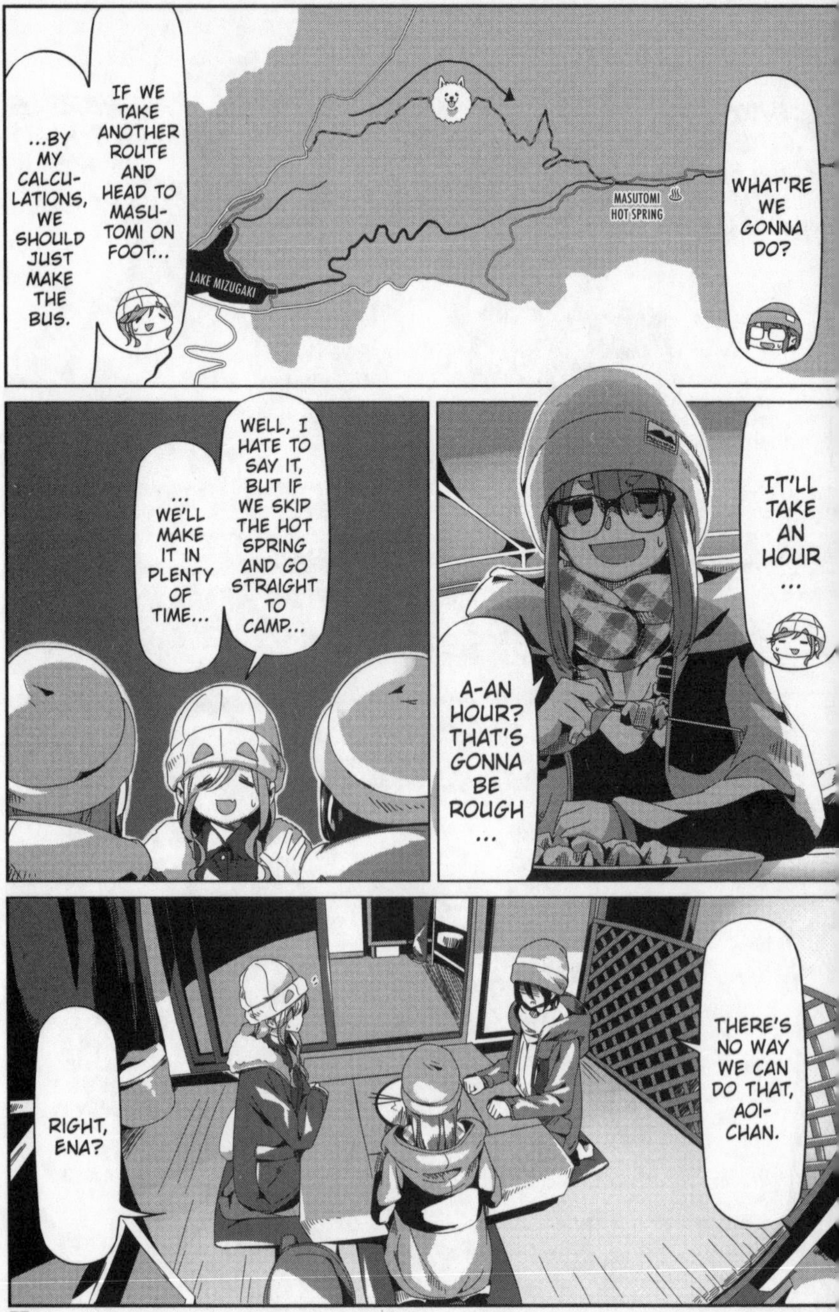
WHAT'RE WE GONNA DO?
MASUTOMI HOT SPRING
IF WE TAKE ANOTHER ROUTE AND HEAD TO MASU-TOMI ON FOOT...
...BY MY CALCU-LATIONS, WE SHOULD JUST MAKE THE BUS.
LAKE MIZUGAKI
IT'LL TAKE AN HOUR ...
A-AN HOUR? THAT'S GONNA BE ROUGH ...
WELL, I HATE TO SAY IT, BUT IF WE SKIP THE HOT SPRING AND GO STRAIGHT TO CAMP...
... WE'LL MAKE IT IN PLENTY OF TIME...
THERE'S NO WAY WE CAN DO THAT, AOI-CHAN.
RIGHT, ENA?

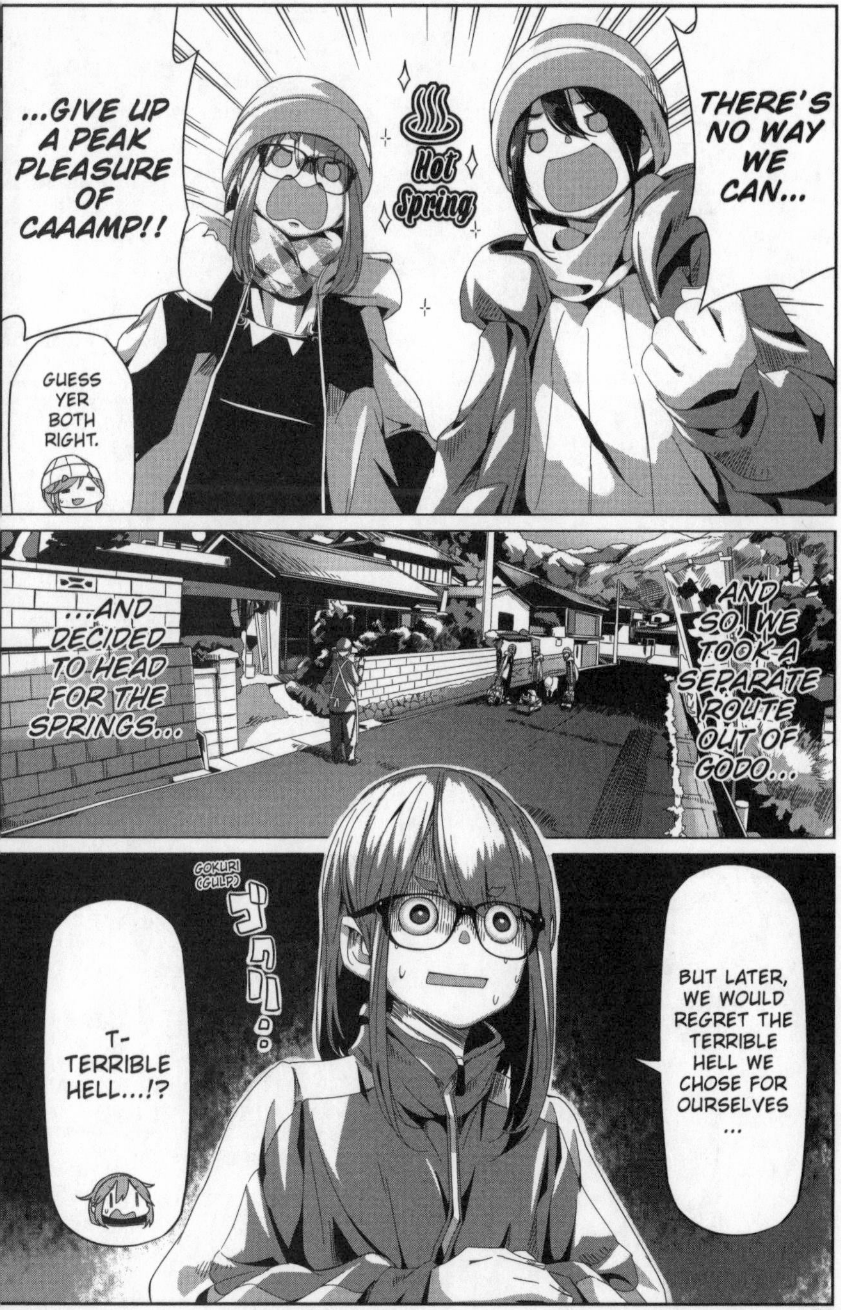
THERE'S NO WAY WE CAN...
Hot Spring
...GIVE UP A PEAK PLEASURE OF CAAAMP!!
GUESS YER BOTH RIGHT.
AND SO, WE TOOK A SEPARATE ROUTE OUT OF GODO...
...AND DECIDED TO HEAD FOR THE SPRINGS...
BUT LATER, WE WOULD REGRET THE TERRIBLE HELL WE CHOSE FOR OURSELVES ...
GOKURI (GULP)
T-TERRIBLE HELL...!?

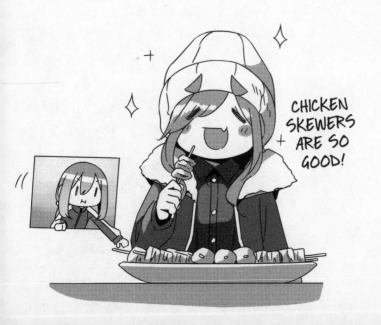

CHICKEN SKEWERS ARE SO GOOD!

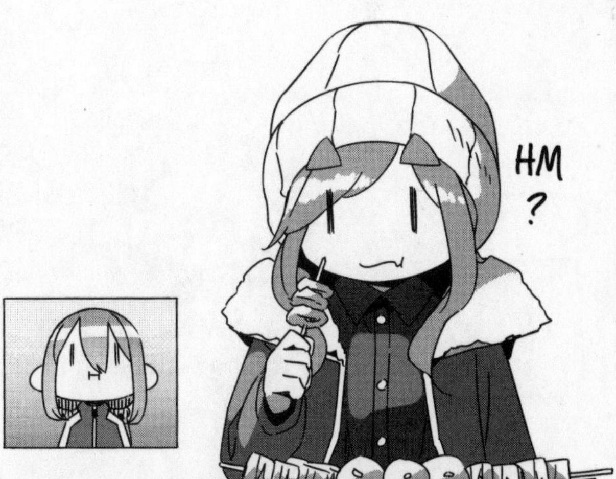
HM
?

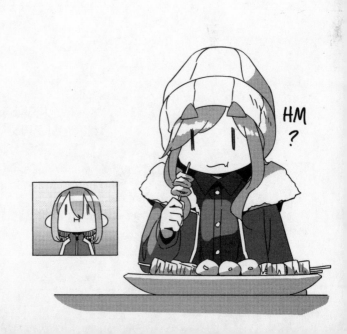

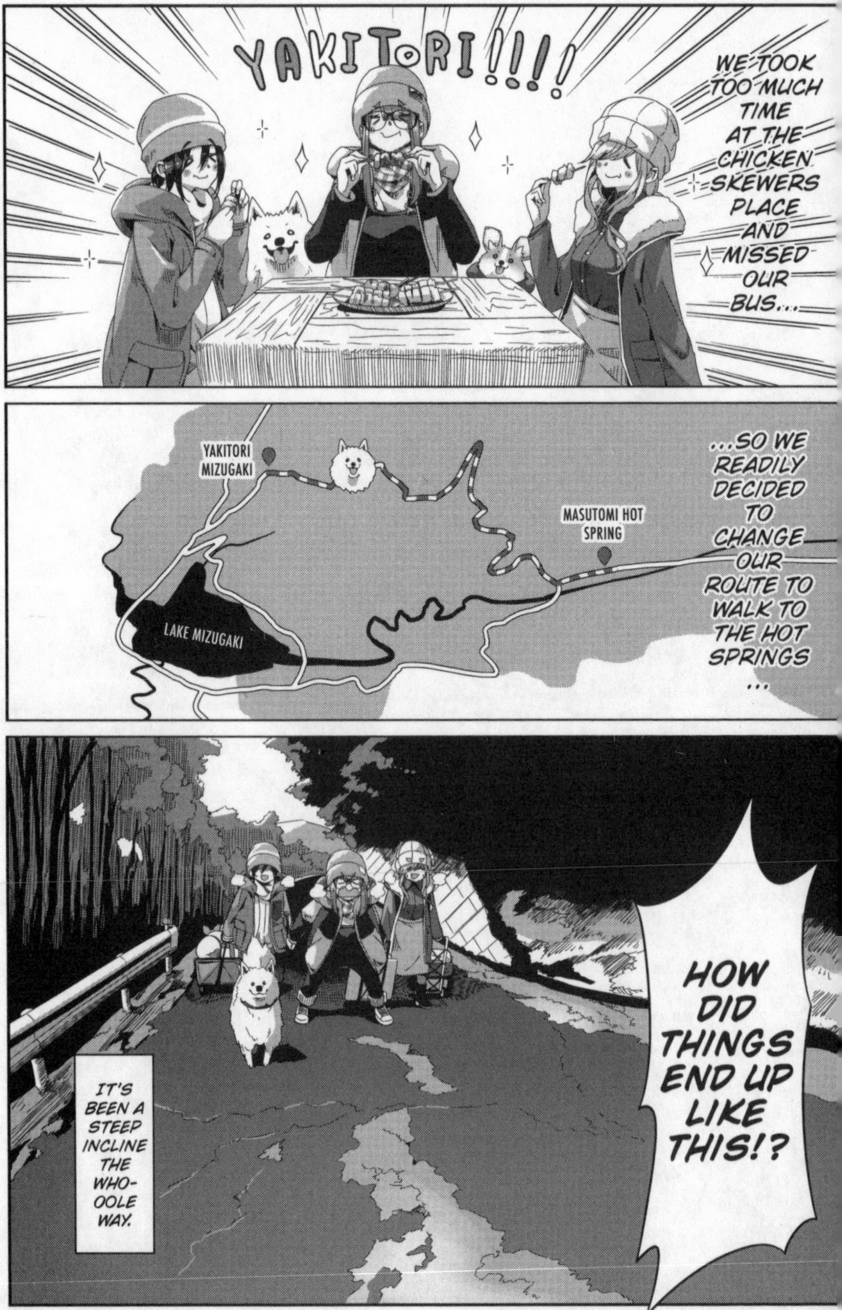
WE TOOK TOO MUCH TIME AT THE CHICKEN SKEWERS PLACE AND MISSED OUR BUS...
YAKITORI!!!!
...SO WE READILY DECIDED TO CHANGE OUR ROUTE TO WALK TO THE HOT SPRINGS...
YAKITORI MIZUGAKI
MASUTOMI HOT SPRING
LAKE MIZUGAKI
HOW DID THINGS END UP LIKE THIS!?
IT'S BEEN A STEEP INCLINE THE WHO-OOLE WAY.

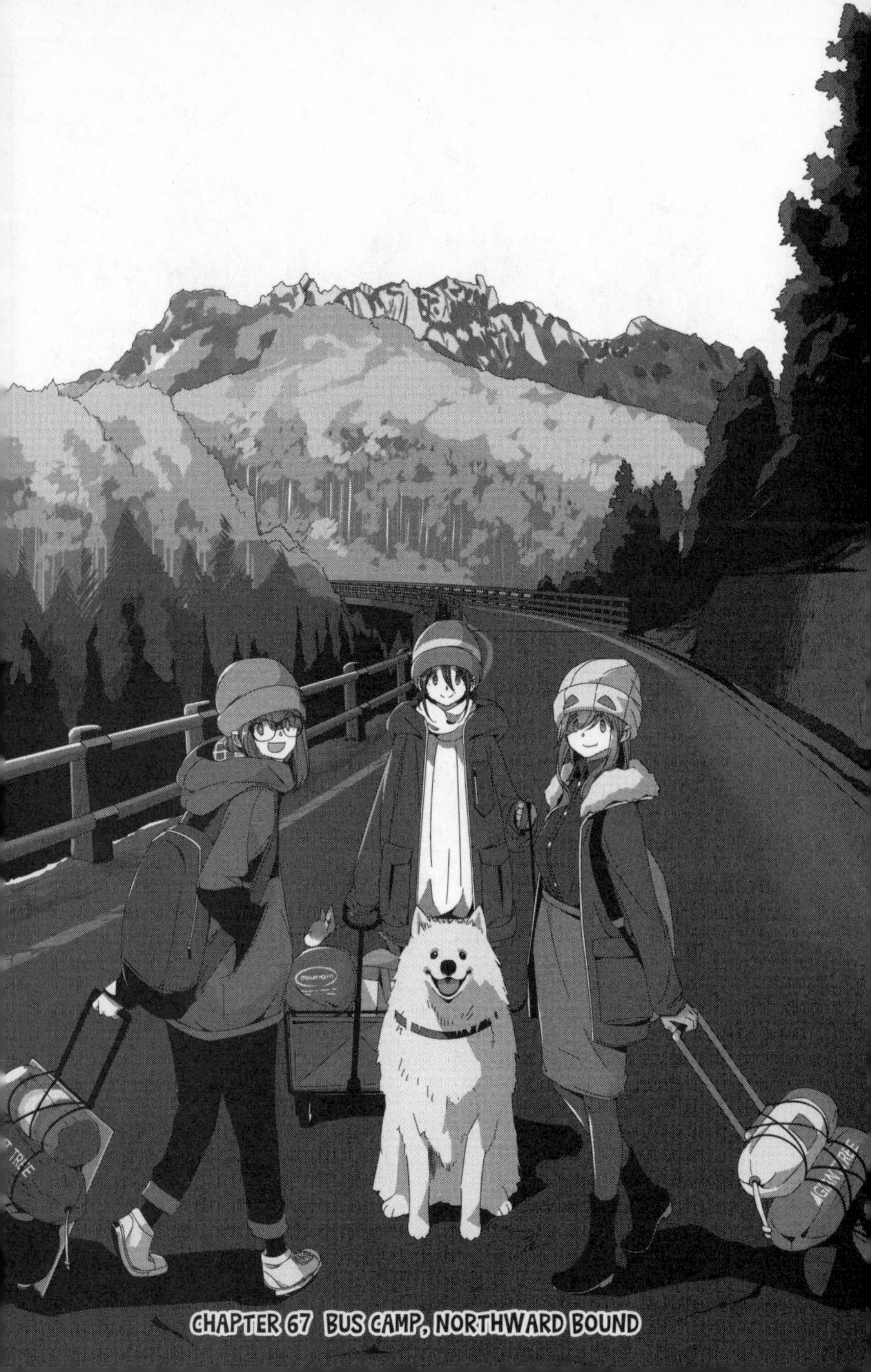

CHAPTER 67 BUS CAMP, NORTHWARD BOUND

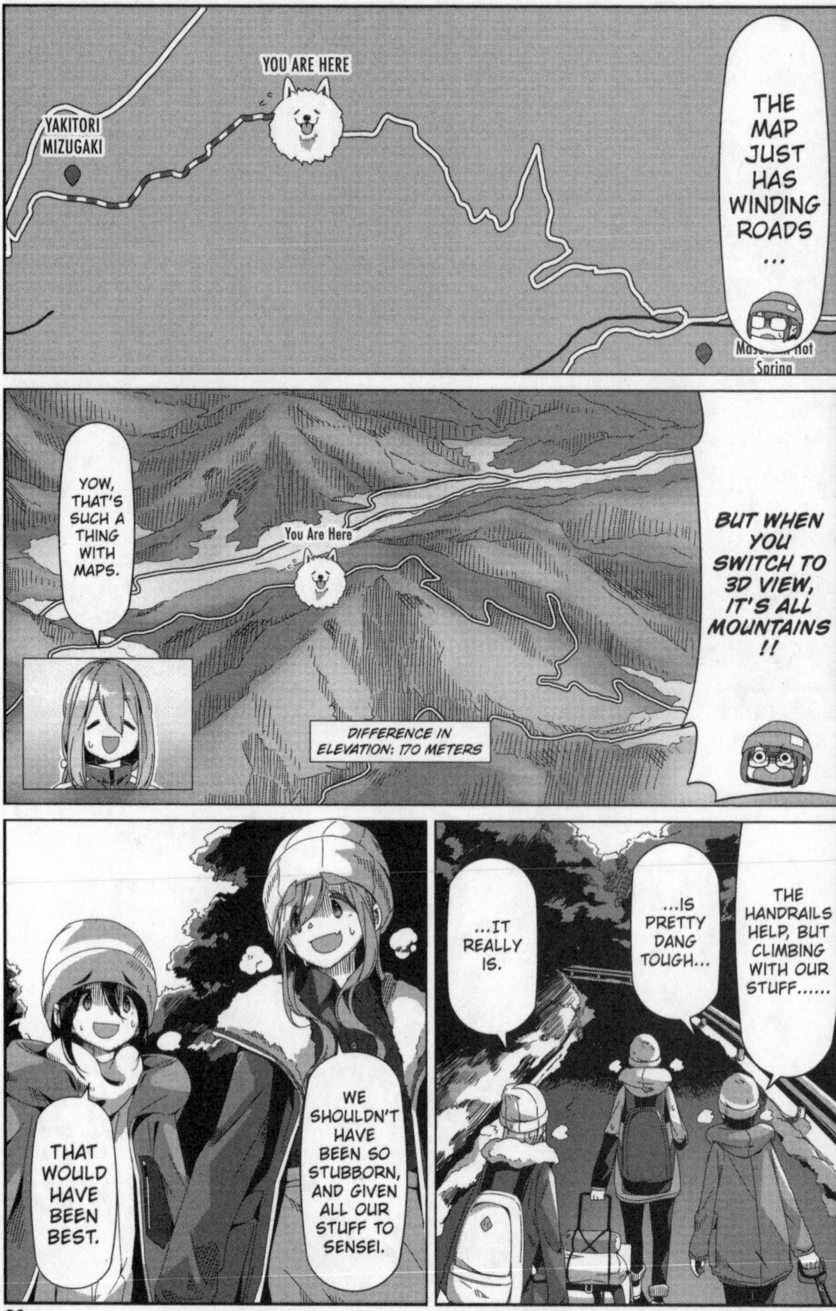
THE MAP JUST HAS WINDING ROADS ...
YOU ARE HERE
YAKITORI MIZUGAKI
BUT WHEN YOU SWITCH TO 3D VIEW, IT'S ALL MOUNTAINS !!
You Are Here
DIFFERENCE IN ELEVATION: 170 METERS
YOW, THAT'S SUCH A THING WITH MAPS.
THE HANDRAILS HELP, BUT CLIMBING WITH OUR STUFF......
...IS PRETTY DANG TOUGH...
...IT REALLY IS.
WE SHOULDN'T HAVE BEEN SO STUBBORN, AND GIVEN ALL OUR STUFF TO SENSEI.
THAT WOULD HAVE BEEN BEST.

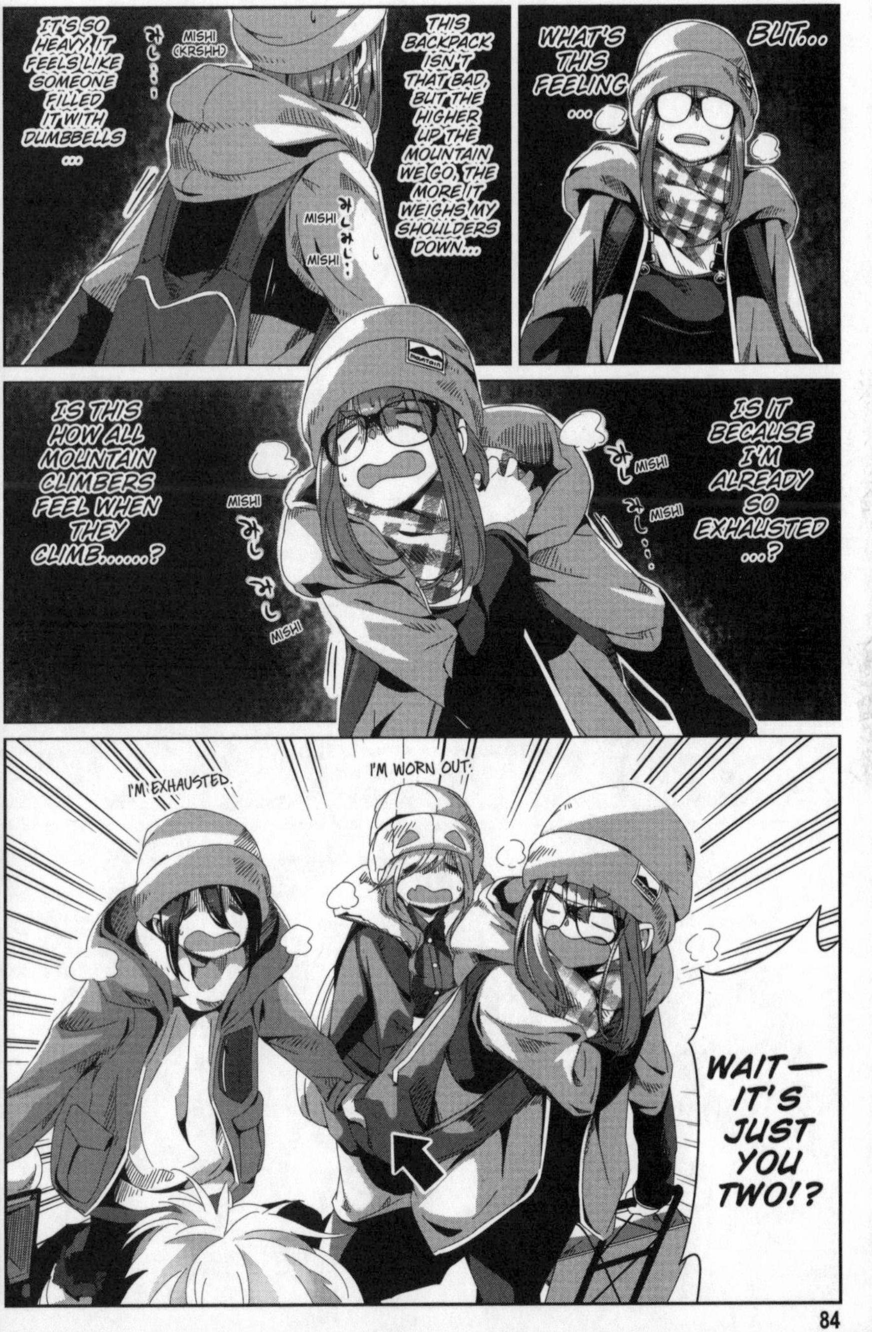
BUT...
WHAT'S THIS FEELING...
THIS BACKPACK ISN'T THAT BAD, BUT THE HIGHER UP THE MOUNTAIN WE GO, THE MORE IT WEIGHS MY SHOULDERS DOWN...
みしみし…
MISHI MISHI
みし…
MISHI (KRSHH)
IT'S SO HEAVY, IT FEELS LIKE SOMEONE FILLED IT WITH DUMBBELLS...
IS IT BECAUSE I'M ALREADY SO EXHAUSTED...?
MISHI MISHI
MISHI MISHI
IS THIS HOW ALL MOUNTAIN CLIMBERS FEEL WHEN THEY CLIMB......?
WAIT— IT'S JUST YOU TWO!?
I'M WORN OUT.
I'M EXHAUSTED.

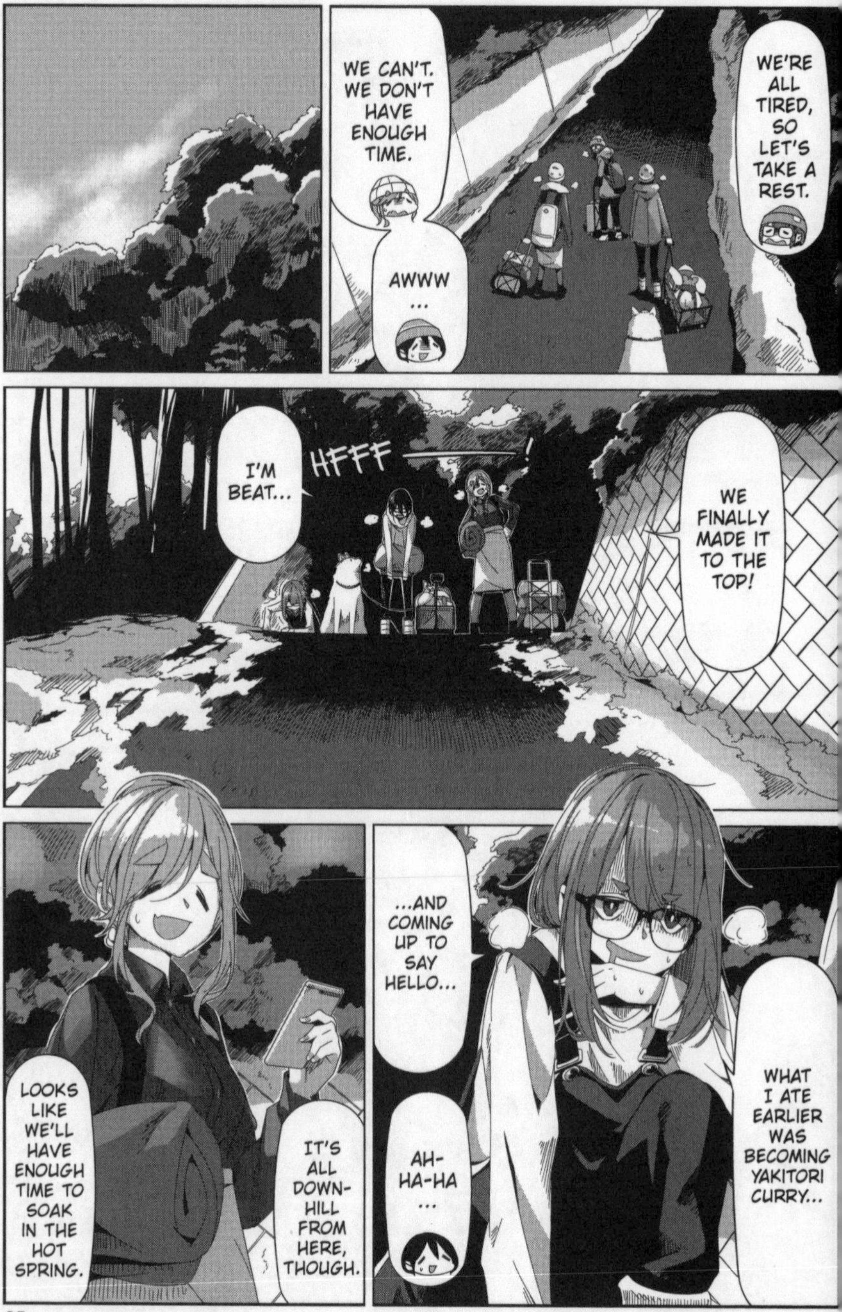
WE'RE ALL TIRED, SO LET'S TAKE A REST.
WE CAN'T. WE DON'T HAVE ENOUGH TIME.
AWWW ...
WE FINALLY MADE IT TO THE TOP!
HFFF
I'M BEAT...
WHAT I ATE EARLIER WAS BECOMING YAKITORI CURRY...
...AND COMING UP TO SAY HELLO...
AH-HA-HA ...
IT'S ALL DOWN-HILL FROM HERE, THOUGH.
LOOKS LIKE WE'LL HAVE ENOUGH TIME TO SOAK IN THE HOT SPRING.

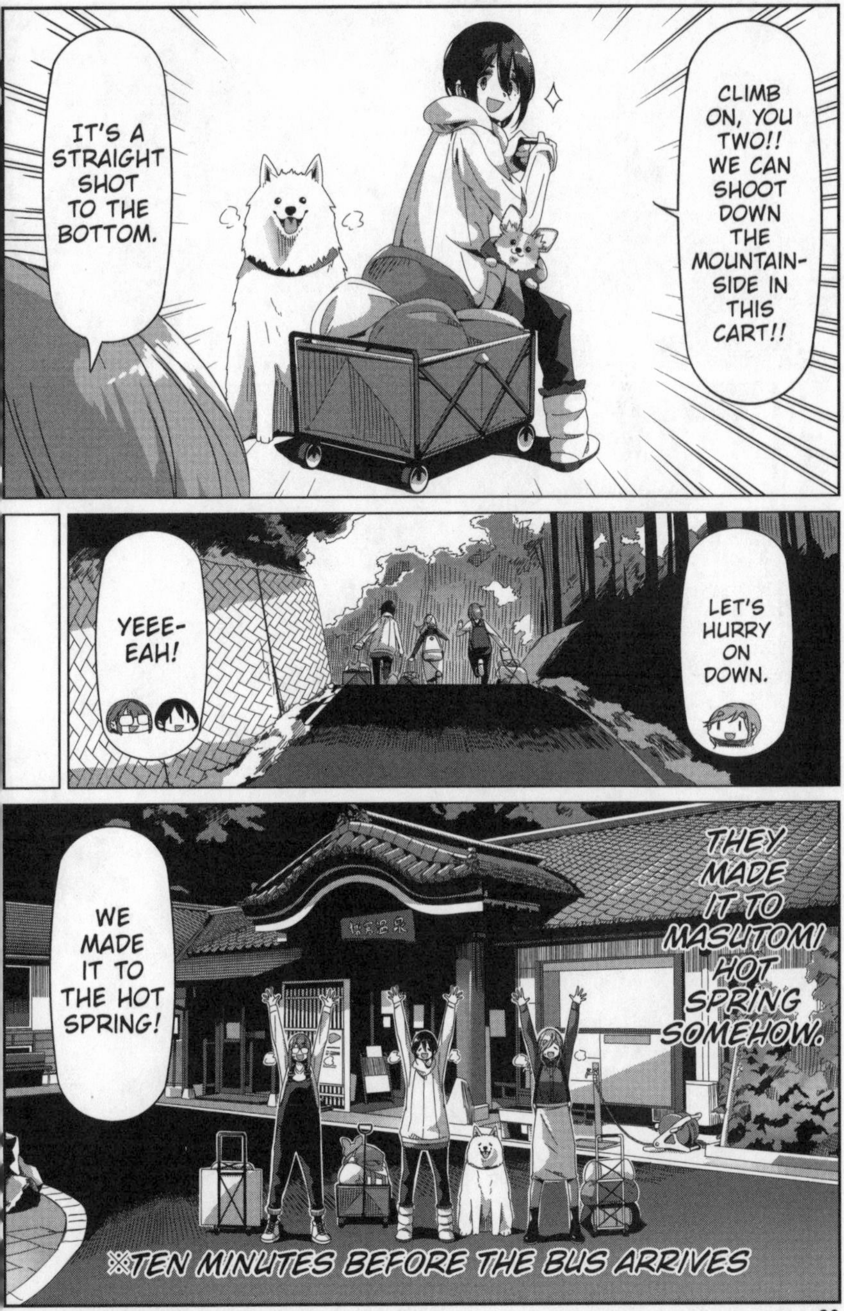
CLIMB ON, YOU TWO!! WE CAN SHOOT DOWN THE MOUNTAIN-SIDE IN THIS CART!!
IT'S A STRAIGHT SHOT TO THE BOTTOM.
LET'S HURRY ON DOWN.
YEEE-EAH!
THEY MADE IT TO MASUTOMI HOT SPRING SOMEHOW.
WE MADE IT TO THE HOT SPRING!
※TEN MINUTES BEFORE THE BUS ARRIVES

SIGN: WOMEN'S BATH

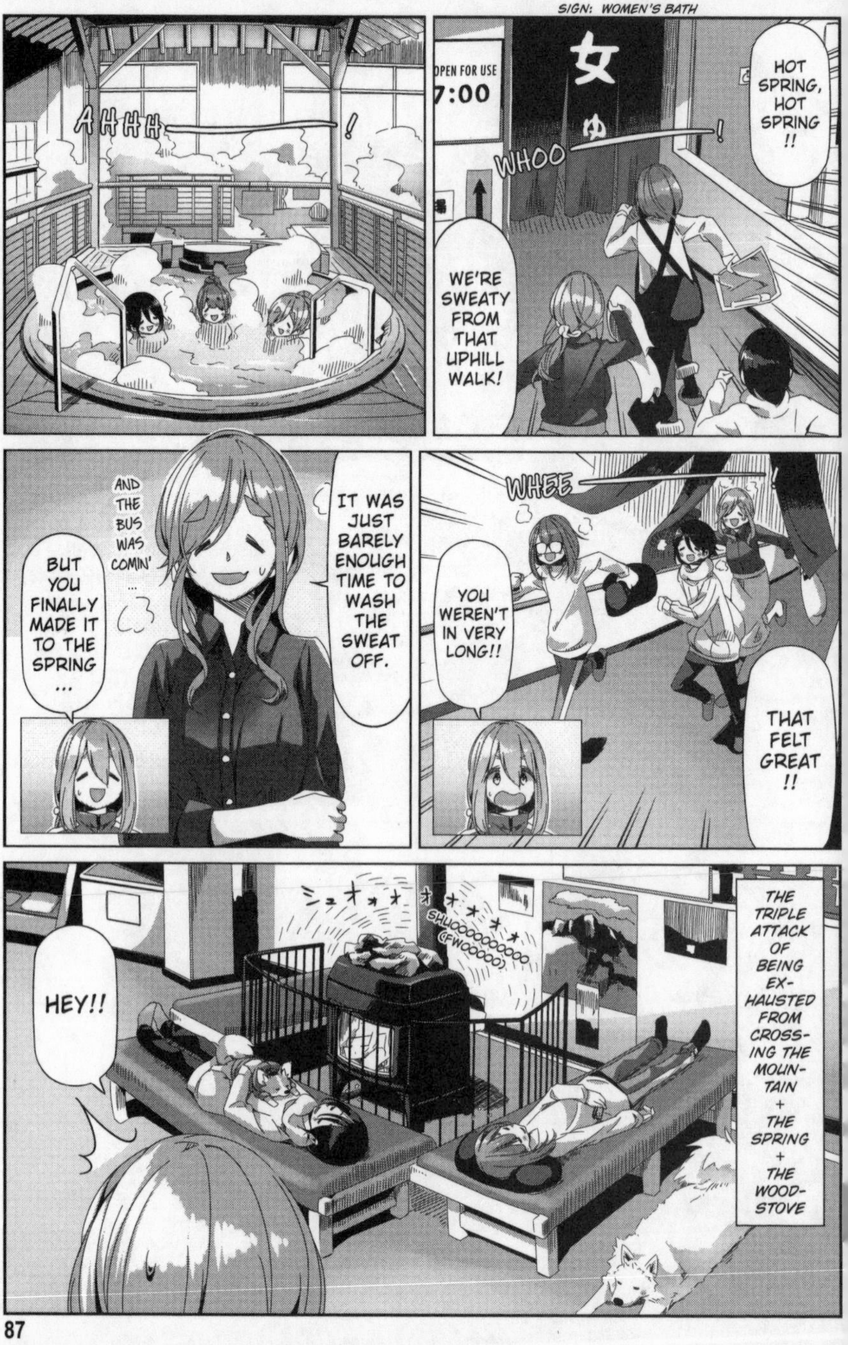

HOT SPRING, HOT SPRING!!
WHOO—!
OPEN FOR USE
7:00
女
WE'RE SWEATY FROM THAT UPHILL WALK!
AHHH—!
WHEE—!
THAT FELT GREAT!!
YOU WEREN'T IN VERY LONG!!
IT WAS JUST BARELY ENOUGH TIME TO WASH THE SWEAT OFF.
AND THE BUS WAS COMIN'...
BUT YOU FINALLY MADE IT TO THE SPRING...
THE TRIPLE ATTACK OF BEING EX-HAUSTED FROM CROSS-ING THE MOUN-TAIN + THE SPRING + THE WOOD-STOVE
シュオオオオオオ
SHUOOOOOOOOOOO (FWOOOOO)
HEY!!

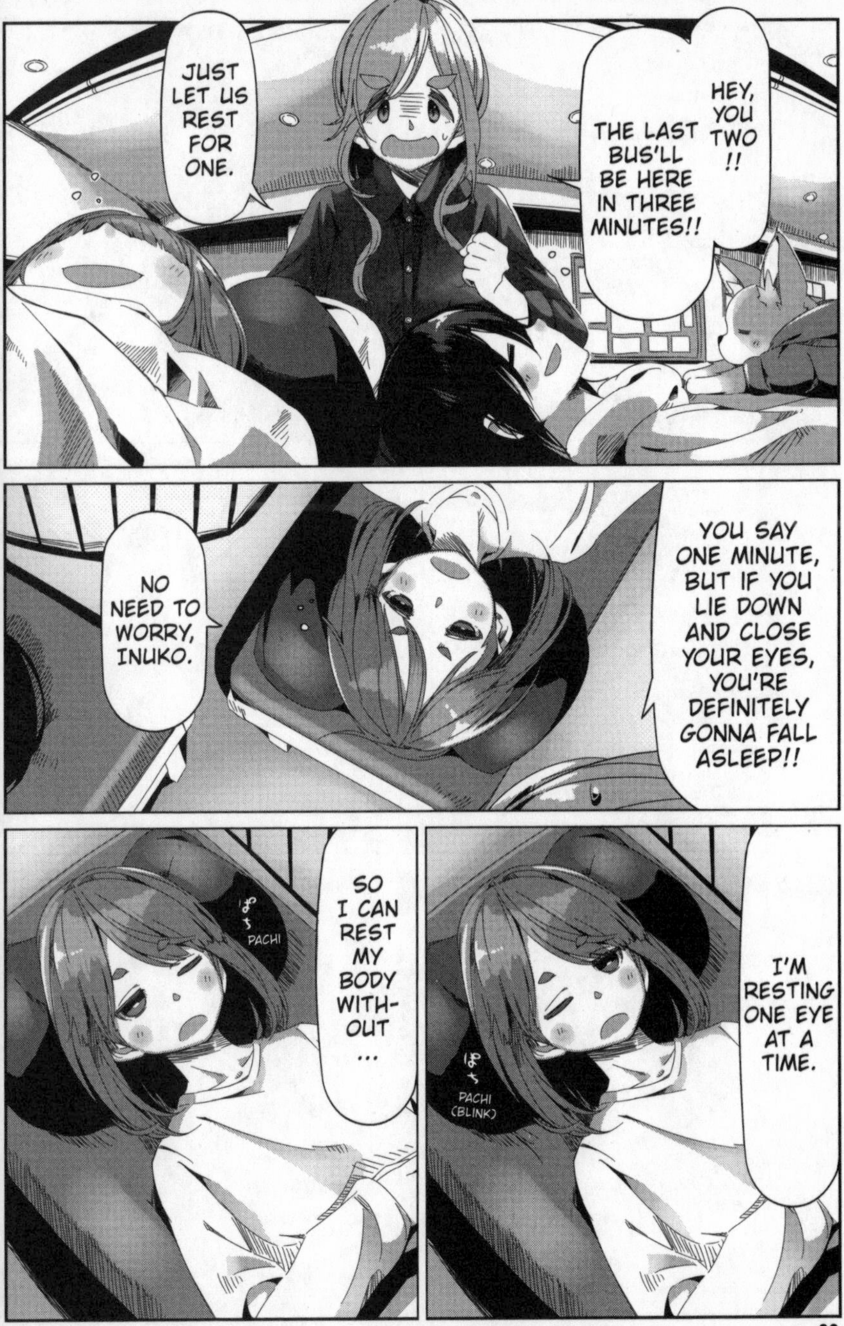
HEY, YOU TWO!!
THE LAST BUS'LL BE HERE IN THREE MINUTES!!
JUST LET US REST FOR ONE.
YOU SAY ONE MINUTE, BUT IF YOU LIE DOWN AND CLOSE YOUR EYES, YOU'RE DEFINITELY GONNA FALL ASLEEP!!
NO NEED TO WORRY, INUKO.
I'M RESTING ONE EYE AT A TIME.
ぱち
PACHI (BLINK)
SO I CAN REST MY BODY WITH-OUT...
ぱち
PACHI

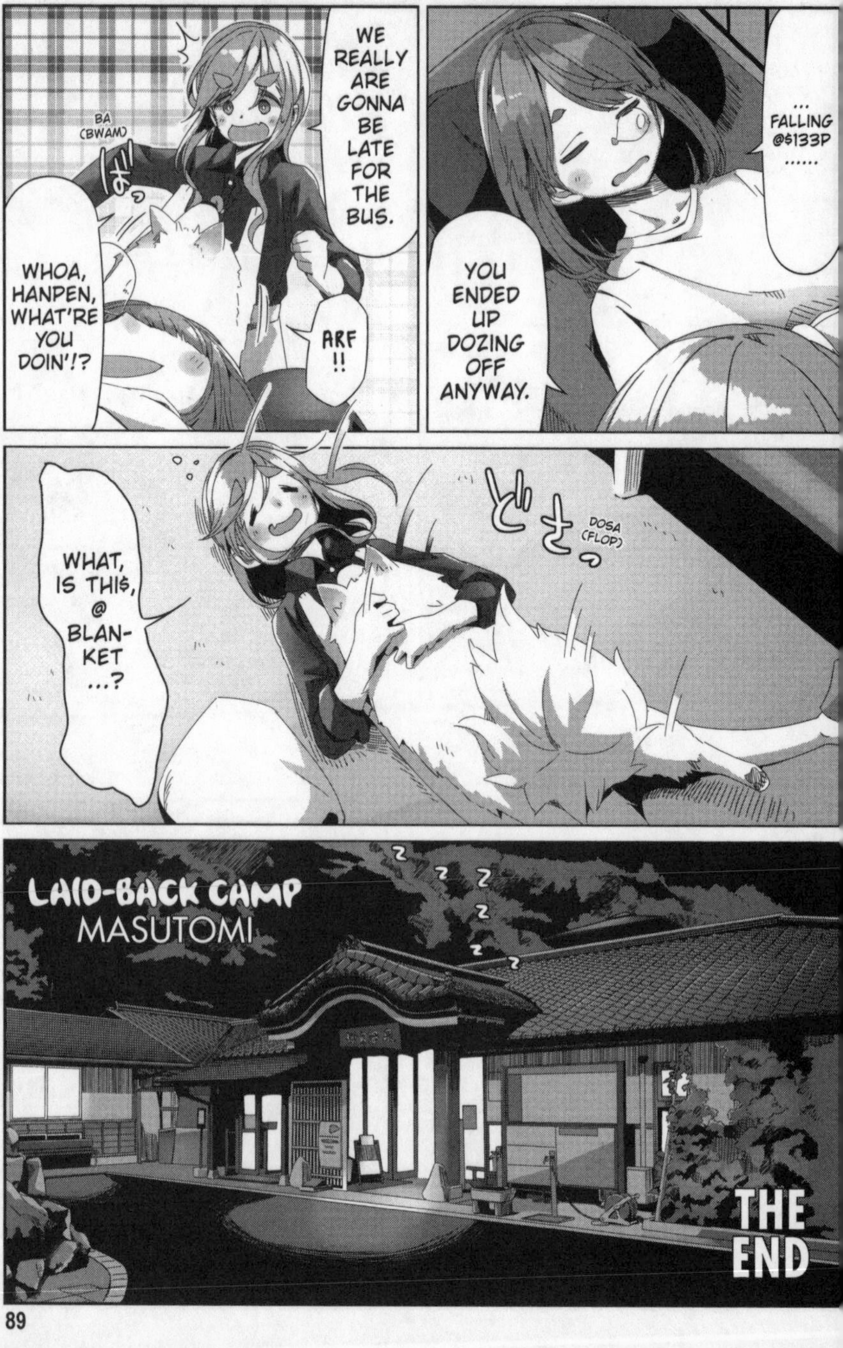
... FALLING @$133P ......
YOU ENDED UP DOZING OFF ANYWAY.
WE REALLY ARE GONNA BE LATE FOR THE BUS.
BA (BWAM)
ARF !!
WHOA, HANPEN, WHAT'RE YOU DOIN'!?
DOSA (FLOP)
WHAT, IS THI$, @ BLANKET ...?
LAID-BACK CAMP
MASUTOMI
THE END

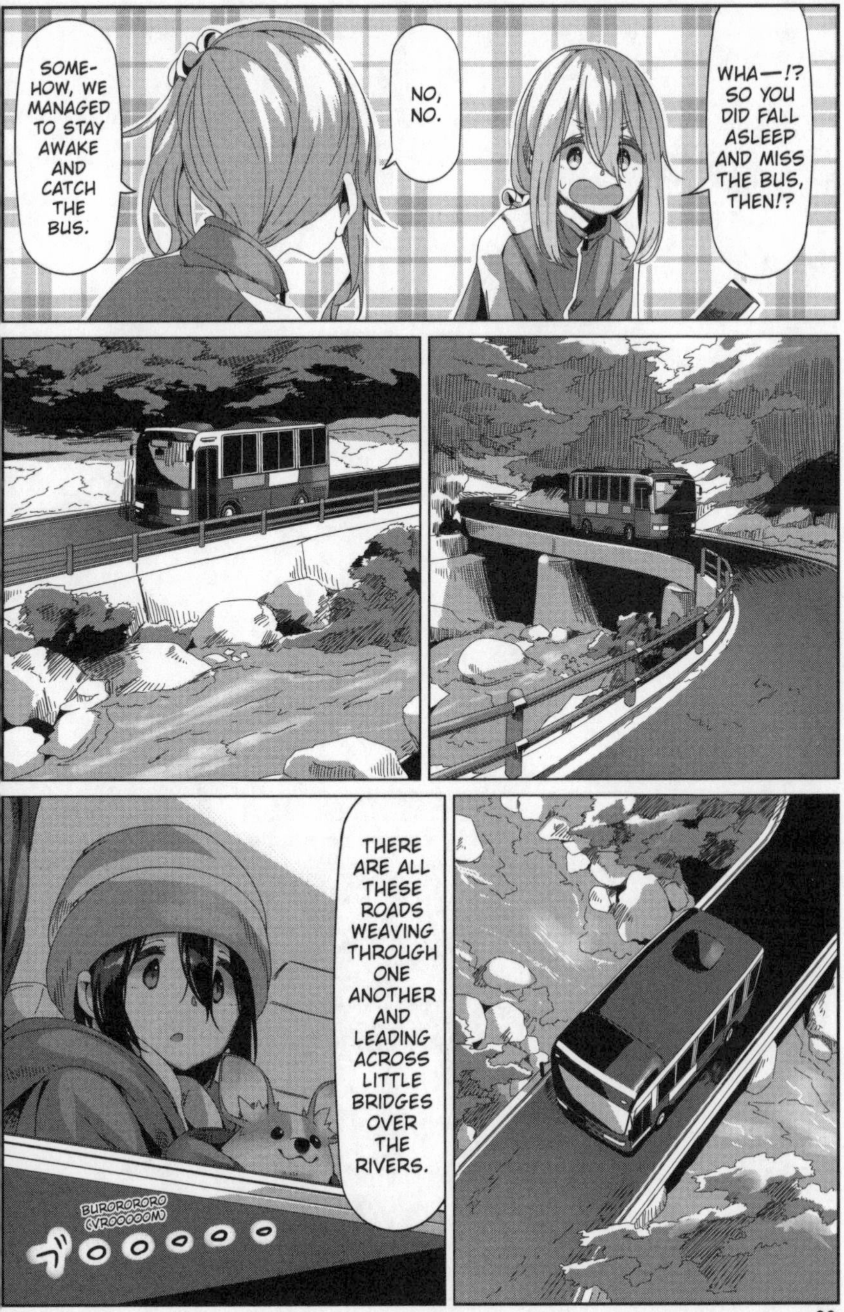
WHA—!? SO YOU DID FALL ASLEEP AND MISS THE BUS, THEN!?
NO, NO.
SOME-HOW, WE MANAGED TO STAY AWAKE AND CATCH THE BUS.
THERE ARE ALL THESE ROADS WEAVING THROUGH ONE ANOTHER AND LEADING ACROSS LITTLE BRIDGES OVER THE RIVERS.
BURORORORO (VROOOOOM)

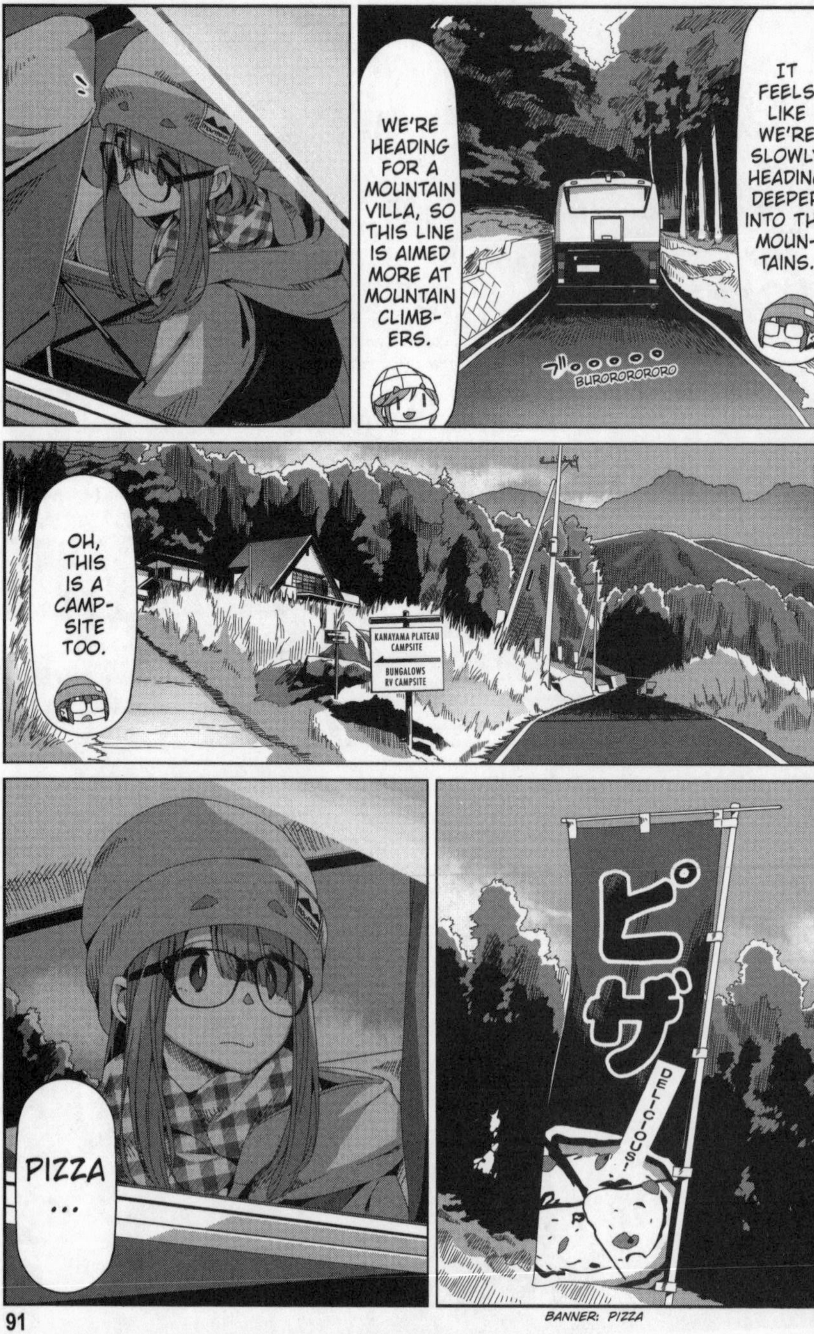
IT FEELS LIKE WE'RE SLOWLY HEADING DEEPER INTO THE MOUN-TAINS.
WE'RE HEADING FOR A MOUNTAIN VILLA, SO THIS LINE IS AIMED MORE AT MOUNTAIN CLIMB-ERS.
BURORORORORO
!
OH, THIS IS A CAMP-SITE TOO.
KANAYAMA PLATEAU CAMPSITE
BUNGALOWS RV CAMPSITE
ピザ
DELICIOUS!
PIZZA ...

BANNER: PIZZA

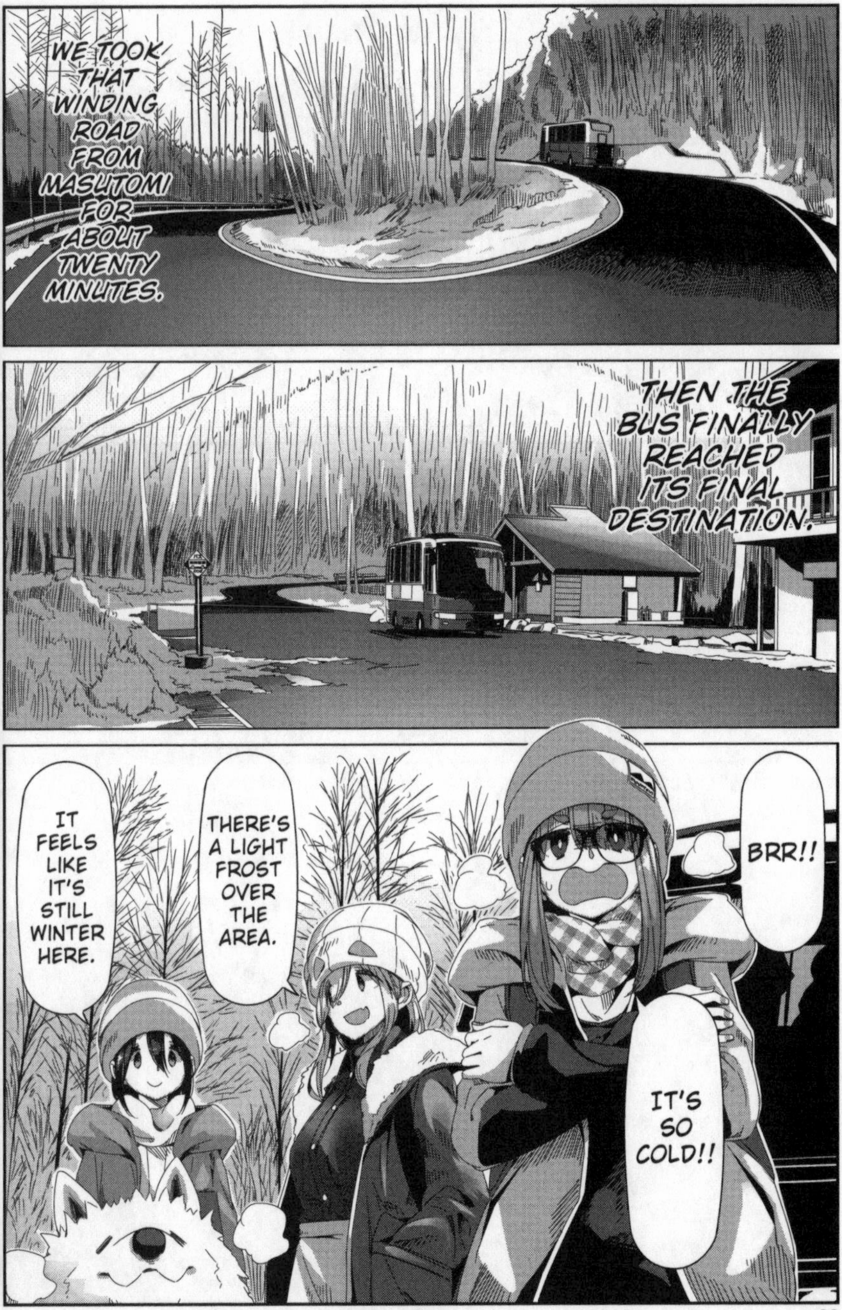
WE TOOK THAT WINDING ROAD FROM MASUTOMI FOR ABOUT TWENTY MINUTES.
THEN THE BUS FINALLY REACHED ITS FINAL DESTINATION.
BRR!!
IT'S SO COLD!!
THERE'S A LIGHT FROST OVER THE AREA.
IT FEELS LIKE IT'S STILL WINTER HERE.

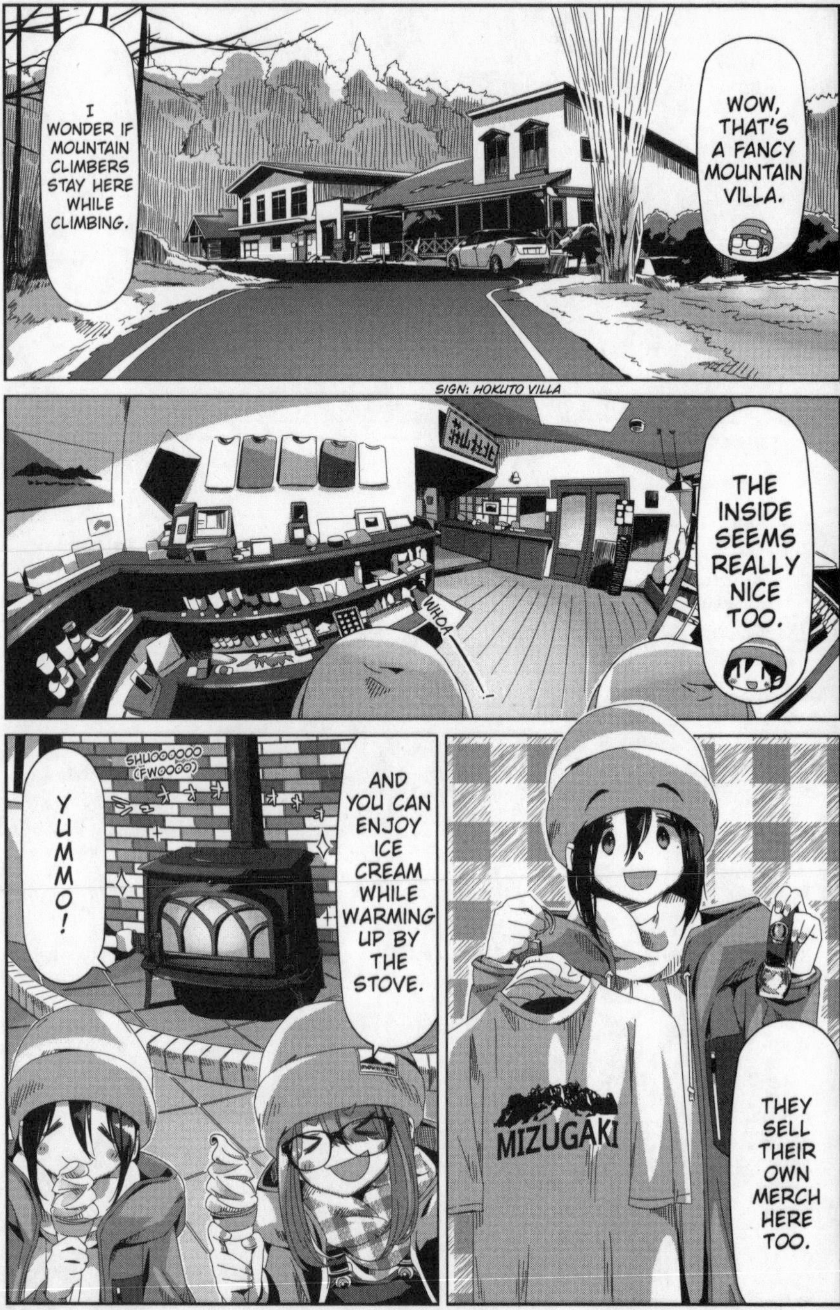
WOW, THAT'S A FANCY MOUNTAIN VILLA.
I WONDER IF MOUNTAIN CLIMBERS STAY HERE WHILE CLIMBING.
SIGN: HOKUTO VILLA
THE INSIDE SEEMS REALLY NICE TOO.
WHOA
THEY SELL THEIR OWN MERCH HERE TOO.
MIZUGAKI
AND YOU CAN ENJOY ICE CREAM WHILE WARMING UP BY THE STOVE.
YUMMO!
SHUOOOOOO (FWOOOO)

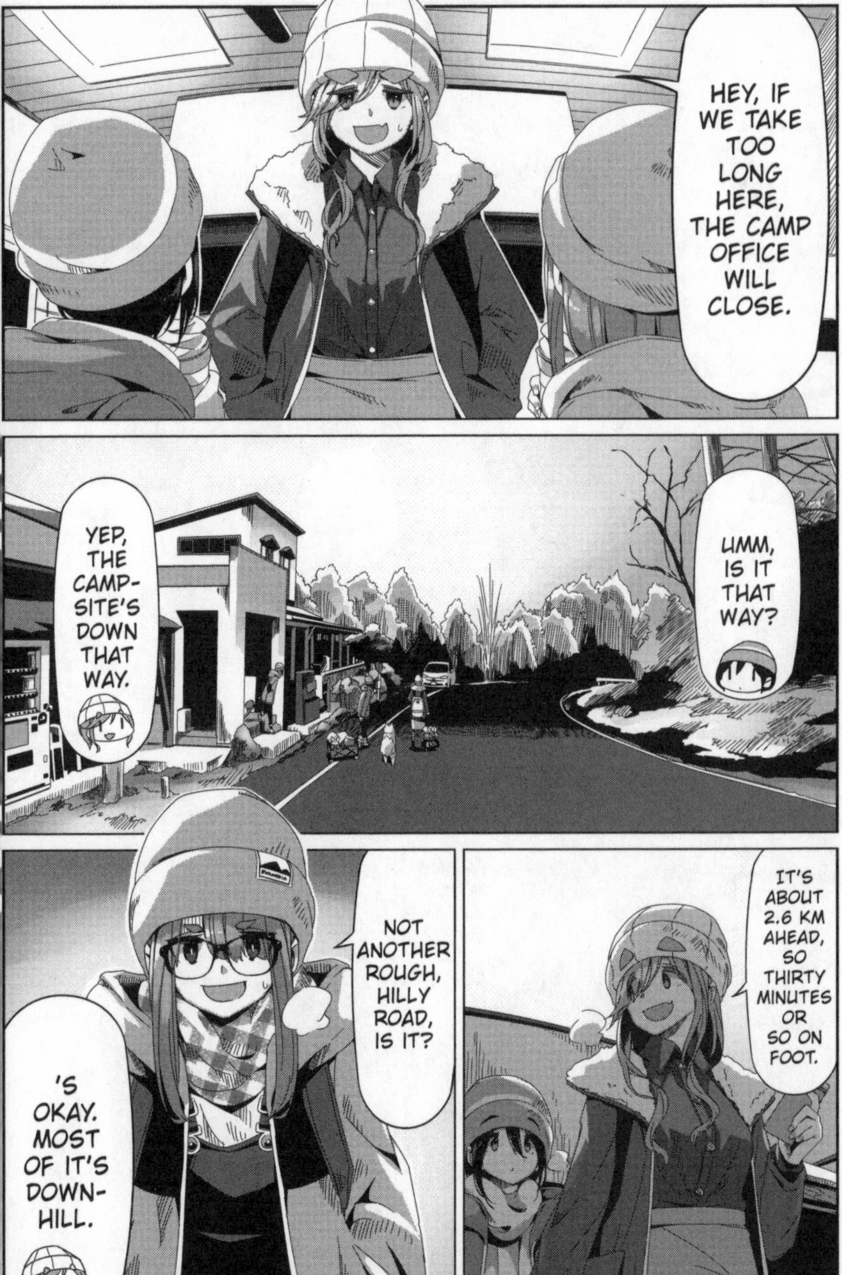
HEY, IF WE TAKE TOO LONG HERE, THE CAMP OFFICE WILL CLOSE.
UMM, IS IT THAT WAY?
YEP, THE CAMP-SITE'S DOWN THAT WAY.
IT'S ABOUT 2.6 KM AHEAD, SO THIRTY MINUTES OR SO ON FOOT.
NOT ANOTHER ROUGH, HILLY ROAD, IS IT?
'S OKAY. MOST OF IT'S DOWN-HILL.

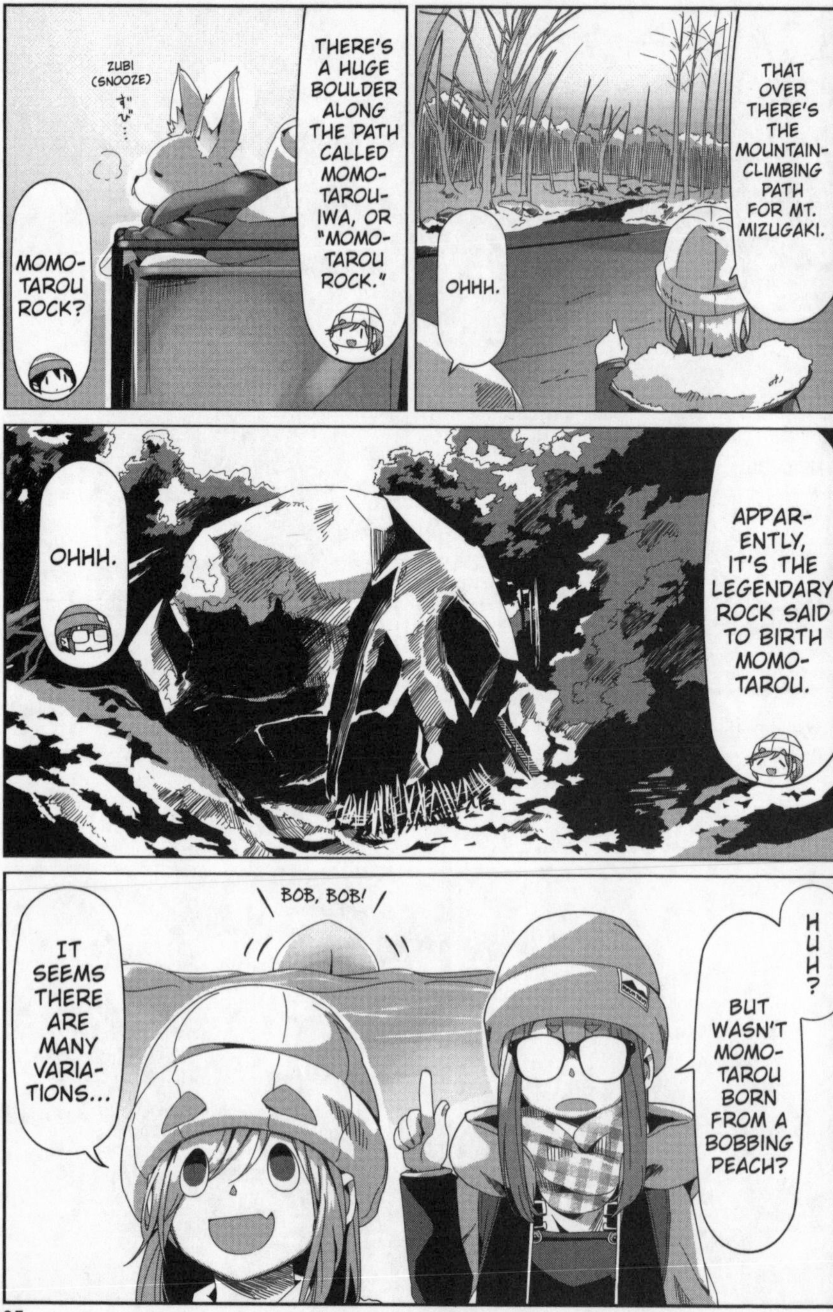
THAT OVER THERE'S THE MOUNTAIN-CLIMBING PATH FOR MT. MIZUGAKI.
OHHH.
THERE'S A HUGE BOULDER ALONG THE PATH CALLED MOMO-TAROU-IWA, OR "MOMO-TAROU ROCK."
ZUBI (SNOOZE)
ずび…
MOMO-TAROU ROCK?
APPAR-ENTLY, IT'S THE LEGENDARY ROCK SAID TO BIRTH MOMO-TAROU.
OHHH.
BOB, BOB!
HUH? BUT WASN'T MOMO-TAROU BORN FROM A BOBBING PEACH?
IT SEEMS THERE ARE MANY VARIA-TIONS...

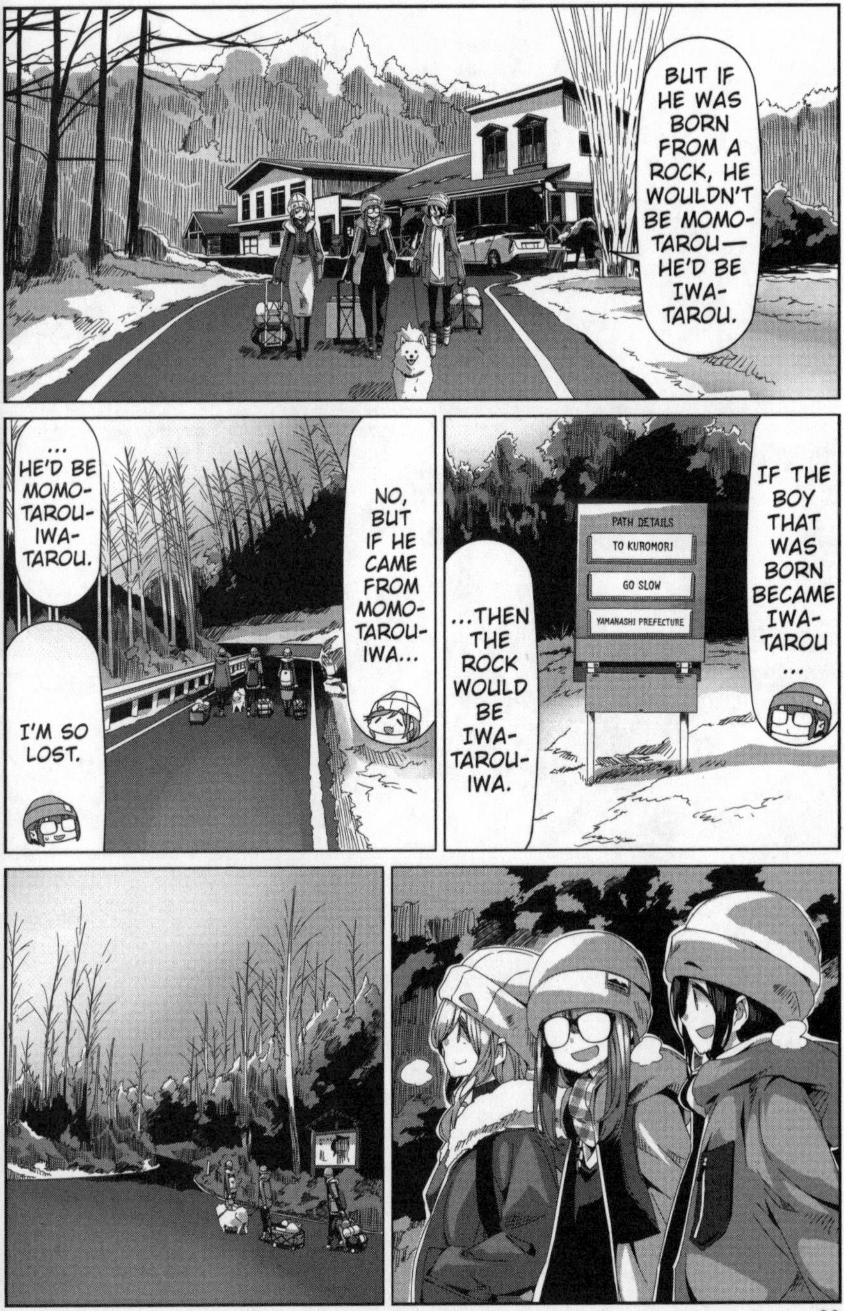
BUT IF HE WAS BORN FROM A ROCK, HE WOULDN'T BE MOMO-TAROU—HE'D BE IWA-TAROU.
IF THE BOY THAT WAS BORN BECAME IWA-TAROU...
PATH DETAILS
TO KUROMORI
GO SLOW
YAMANASHI PREFECTURE
...THEN THE ROCK WOULD BE IWA-TAROU-IWA.
NO, BUT IF HE CAME FROM MOMO-TAROU-IWA...
... HE'D BE MOMO-TAROU-IWA-TAROU.
I'M SO LOST.

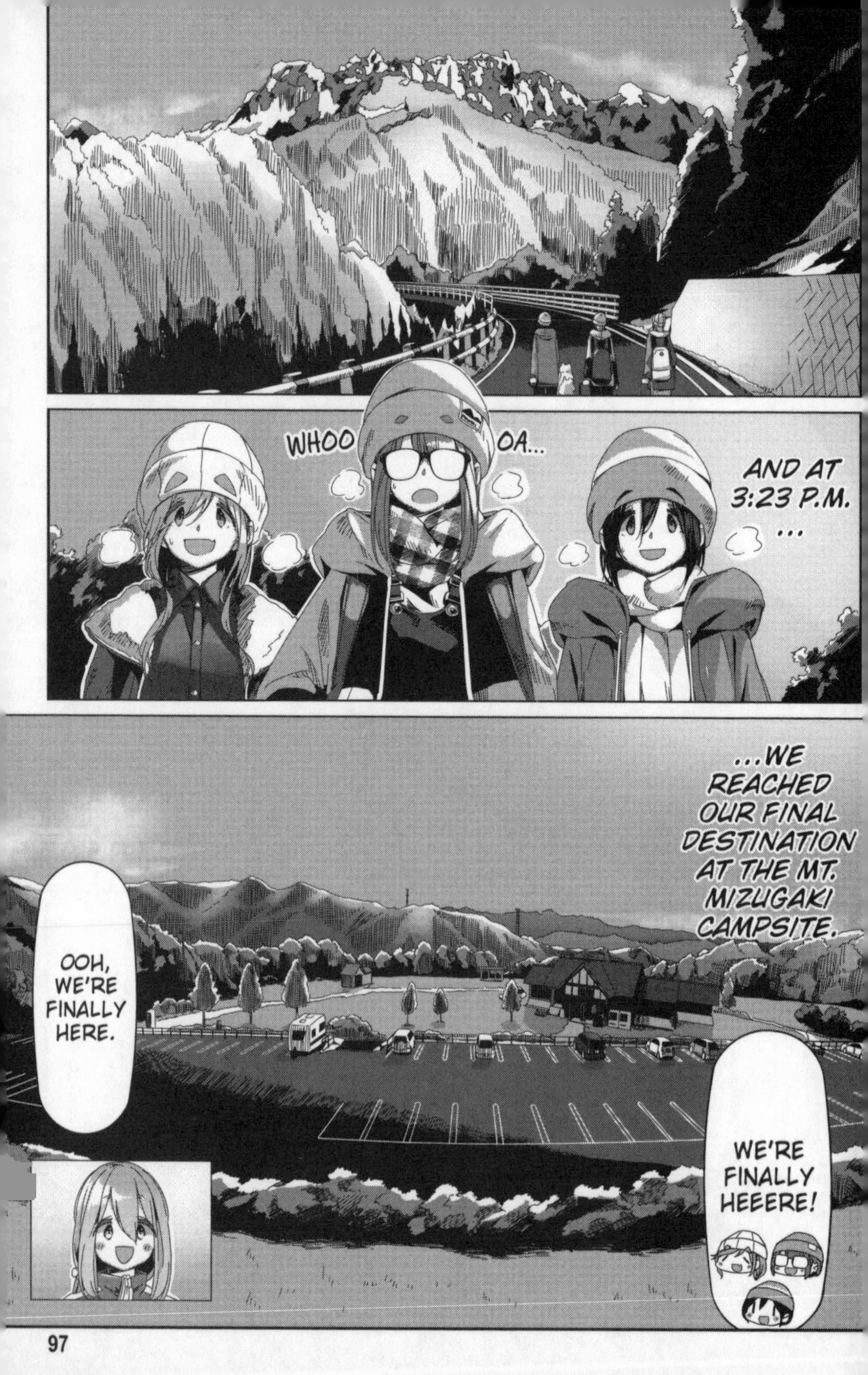
AND AT 3:23 P.M. ...
WHOO OA...
...WE REACHED OUR FINAL DESTINATION AT THE MT. MIZUGAKI CAMPSITE.
WE'RE FINALLY HEEERE!
OOH, WE'RE FINALLY HERE.

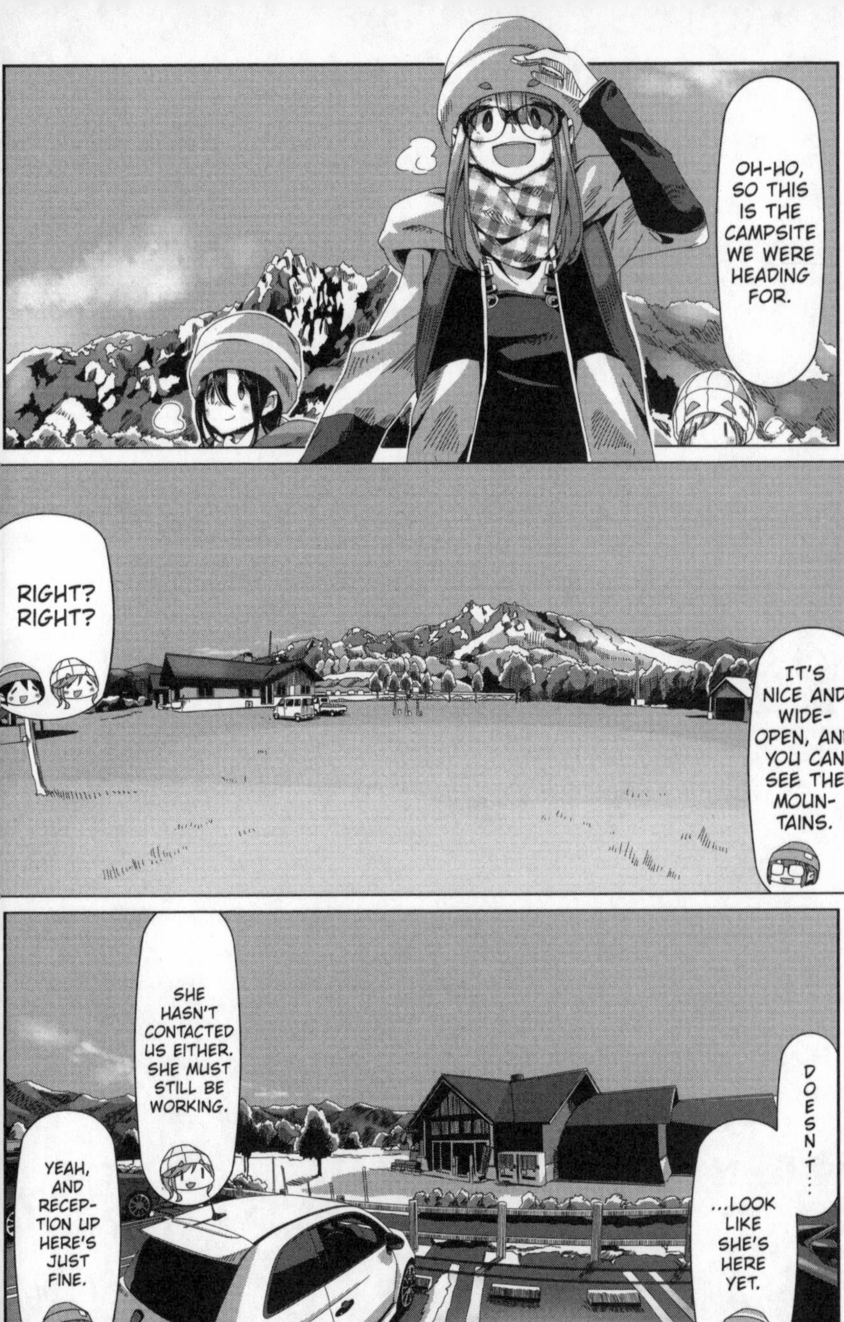
OH-HO, SO THIS IS THE CAMPSITE WE WERE HEADING FOR.
IT'S NICE AND WIDE-OPEN, AND YOU CAN SEE THE MOUN-TAINS.
RIGHT? RIGHT?
DOESN'T...
...LOOK LIKE SHE'S HERE YET.
SHE HASN'T CONTACTED US EITHER. SHE MUST STILL BE WORKING.
YEAH, AND RECEP-TION UP HERE'S JUST FINE.

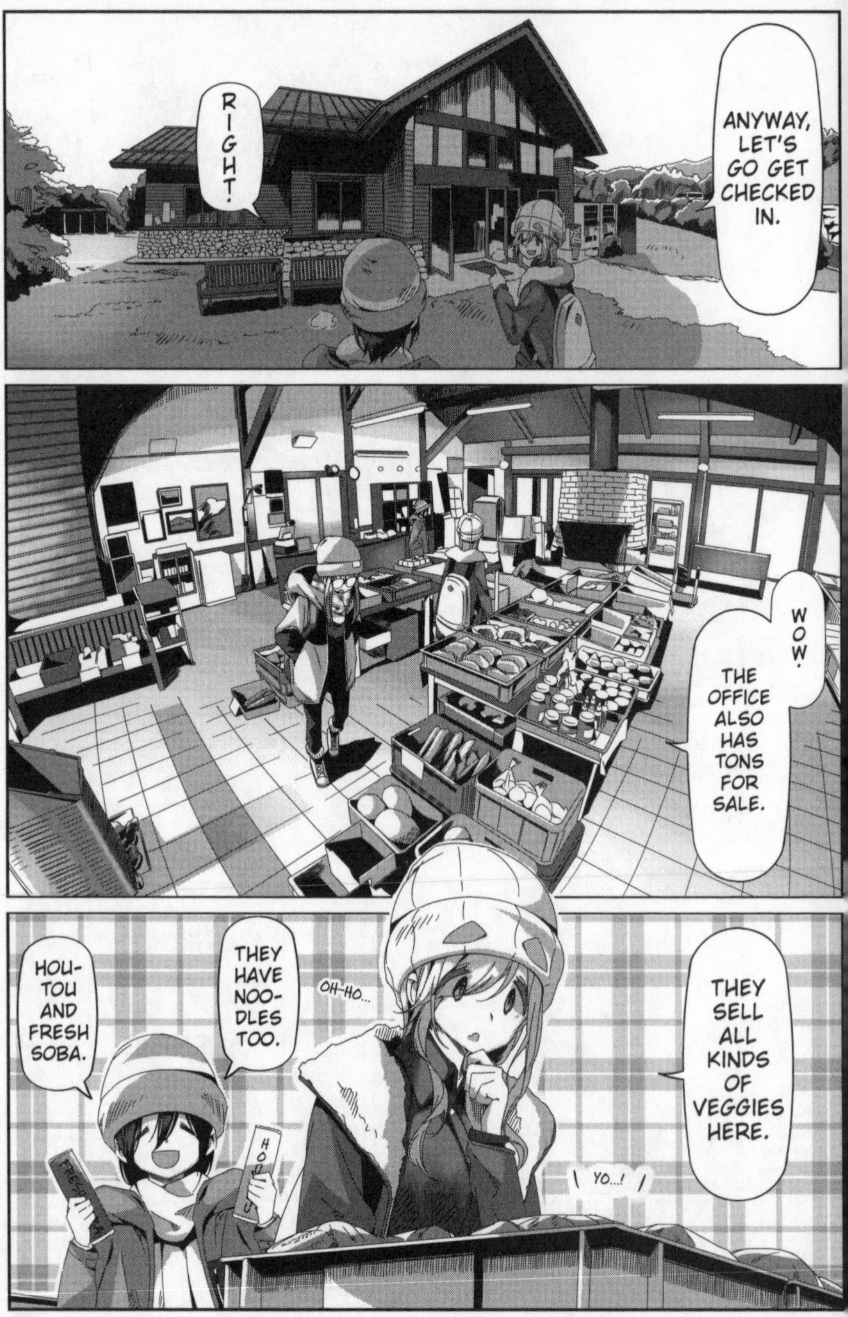
ANYWAY, LET'S GO GET CHECKED IN.
RIGHT!
WOW. THE OFFICE ALSO HAS TONS FOR SALE.
THEY SELL ALL KINDS OF VEGGIES HERE.
YO...!
OH-HO...
THEY HAVE NOODLES TOO.
HOUTOU AND FRESH SOBA.

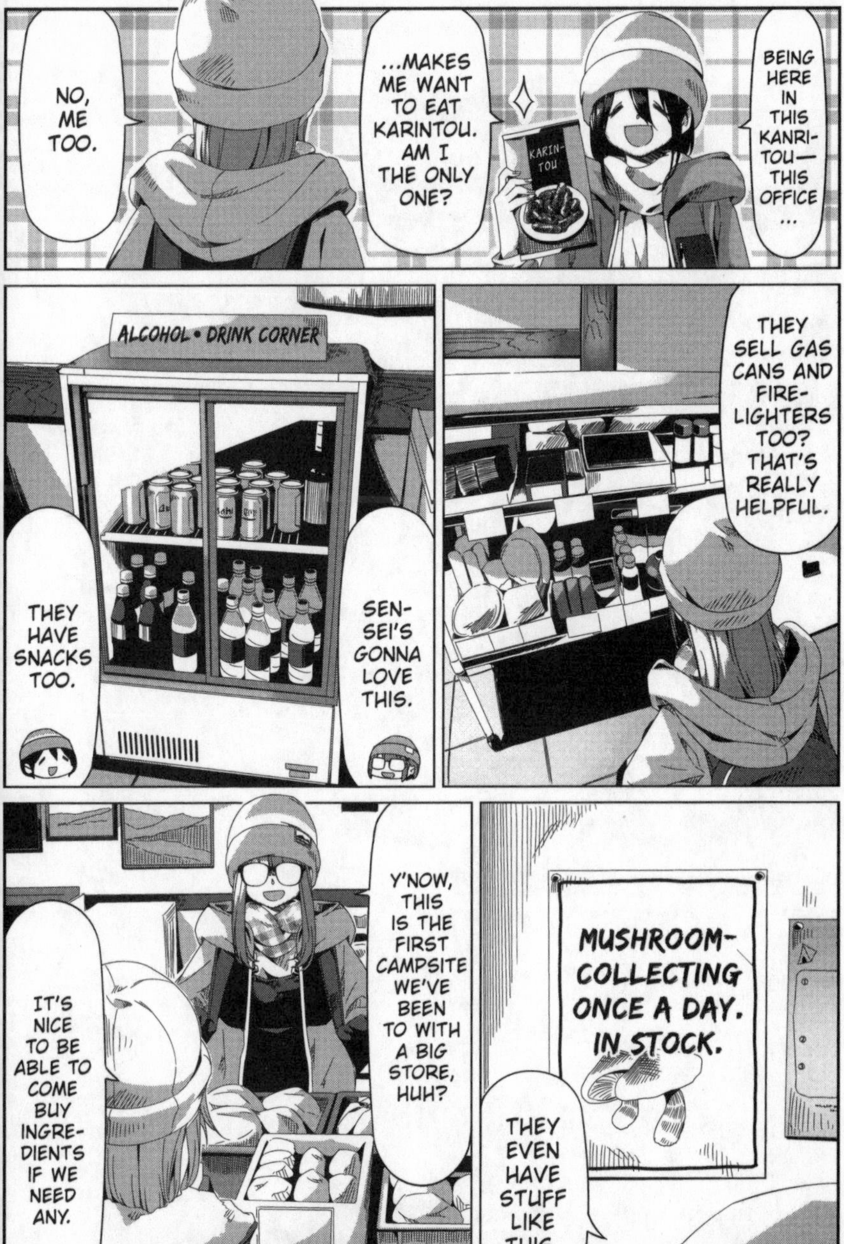
BEING HERE IN THIS KANRI-TOU—THIS OFFICE...
KARIN-TOU
...MAKES ME WANT TO EAT KARINTOU. AM I THE ONLY ONE?
NO, ME TOO.
THEY SELL GAS CANS AND FIRE-LIGHTERS TOO? THAT'S REALLY HELPFUL.
ALCOHOL • DRINK CORNER
SEN-SEI'S GONNA LOVE THIS.
THEY HAVE SNACKS TOO.
MUSHROOM-COLLECTING ONCE A DAY. IN STOCK.
THEY EVEN HAVE STUFF LIKE THIS.
HOW MOUNTAINY.
Y'NOW, THIS IS THE FIRST CAMPSITE WE'VE BEEN TO WITH A BIG STORE, HUH?
IT'S NICE TO BE ABLE TO COME BUY INGRE-DIENTS IF WE NEED ANY.

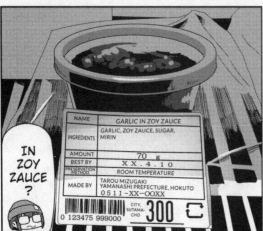

NAME	GARLIC IN ZOY ZAUCE
INGREDIENTS	GARLIC, ZOY ZAUCE, SUGAR, MIRIN
AMOUNT	70 g
BEST BY	XX.4.10
PRESERVATION METHOD	ROOM TEMPERATURE
MADE BY	TAROU MIZUGAKI YAMANASHI PREFECTURE, HOKUTO 0511-XX-OOXX

0 123475 999000   CITY, SUTAMA-CHO   300

IN ZOY ZAUCE?

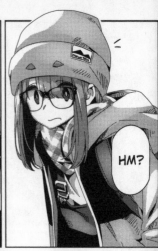

HM?

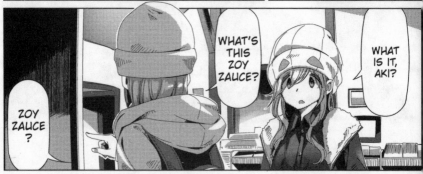

WHAT'S THIS ZOY ZAUCE?

WHAT IS IT, AKI?

ZOY ZAUCE?

TO BE ABLE TO MAKE LABELS BUT NOT KNOW HOW TO WRITE THAT WOULD BE A FEAT.

MAYBE SOMEONE HAD THE WRONG IDEA ABOUT HOW TO SPELL "SOY SAUCE" AND TYPED IT IN A HURRY?

HUH? YER RIGHT.

BUT IT'S EVEN WRITTEN THAT WAY UNDER THE INGREDIENTS.

ISN'T IT JUST A TYPO?

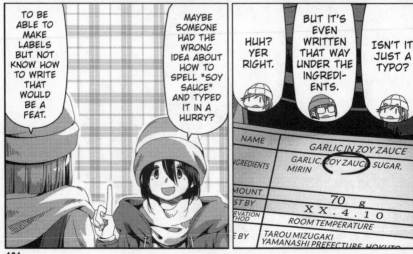

NAME	GARLIC IN ZOY ZAUCE
INGREDIENTS	GARLIC, ZOY ZAUCE, SUGAR, MIRIN
AMOUNT	70 g
BEST BY	XX.4.10
PRESERVATION METHOD	ROOM TEMPERATURE
MADE BY	TAROU MIZUGAKI YAMANASHI PREFECTURE, HOKUTO

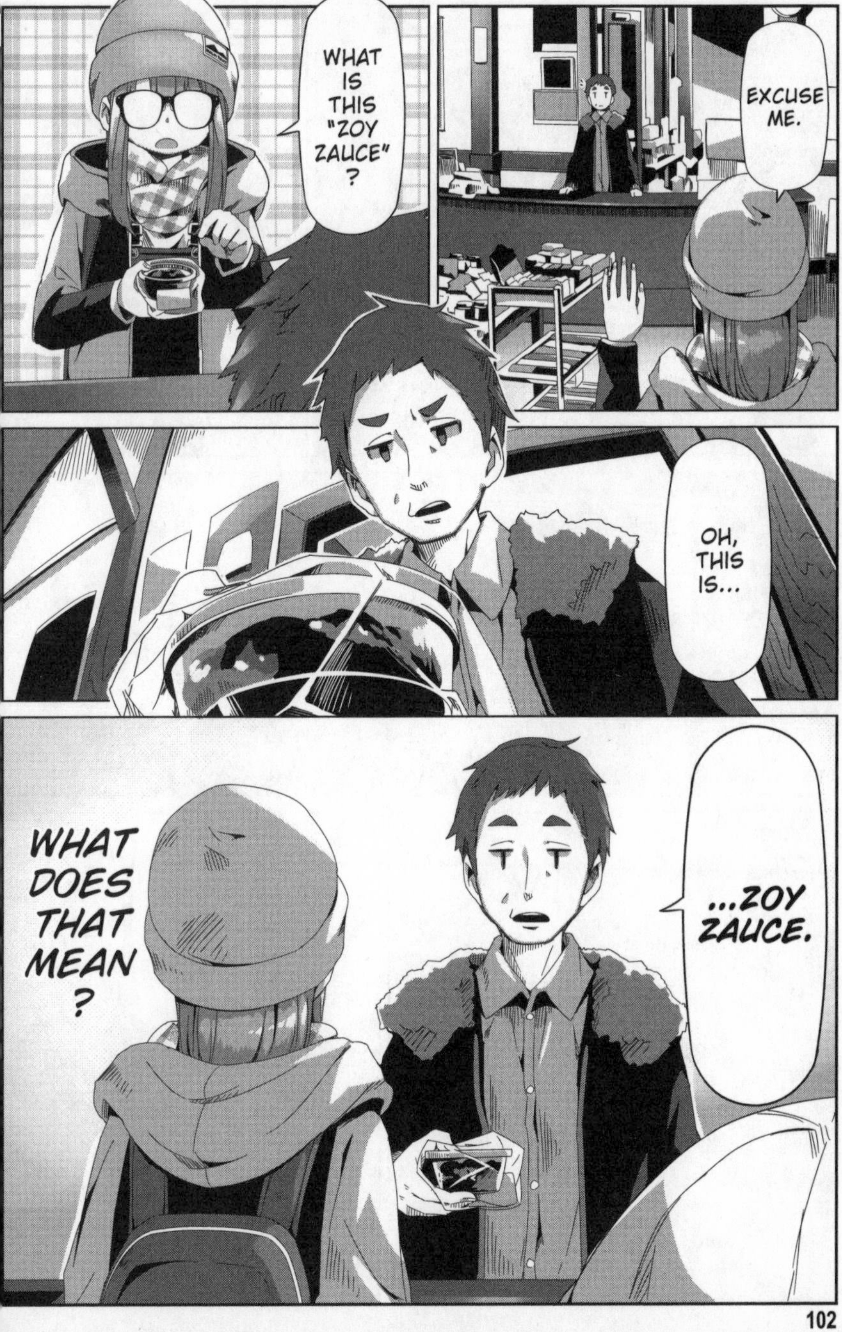
EXCUSE ME.
WHAT IS THIS "ZOY ZAUCE"?
OH, THIS IS...
...ZOY ZAUCE.
WHAT DOES THAT MEAN?

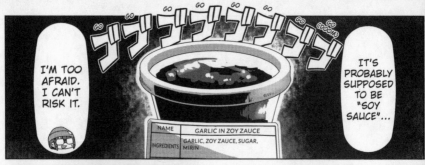

I'M TOO AFRAID. I CAN'T RISK IT.

IT'S PROBABLY SUPPOSED TO BE "SOY SAUCE"...

NAME	GARLIC IN ZOY ZAUCE
INGREDIENTS	GARLIC, ZOY ZAUCE, SUGAR, MIRIN

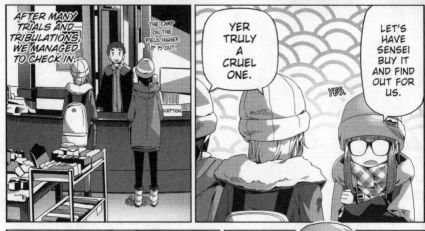

AFTER MANY TRIALS AND TRIBULATIONS, WE MANAGED TO CHECK IN.

THE CAMP ON THE FIELDS HIGHER UP IS OUT.

RECEPTION

YER TRULY A CRUEL ONE.

YES.

LET'S HAVE SENSEI BUY IT AND FIND OUT FOR US.

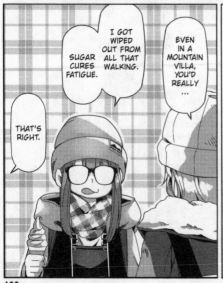

SUGAR CURES FATIGUE.

I GOT WIPED OUT FROM ALL THAT WALKING.

EVEN IN A MOUNTAIN VILLA, YOU'D REALLY...

THAT'S RIGHT.

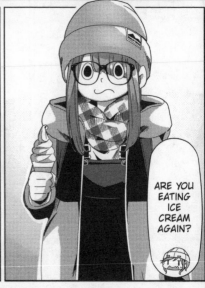

ARE YOU EATING ICE CREAM AGAIN?

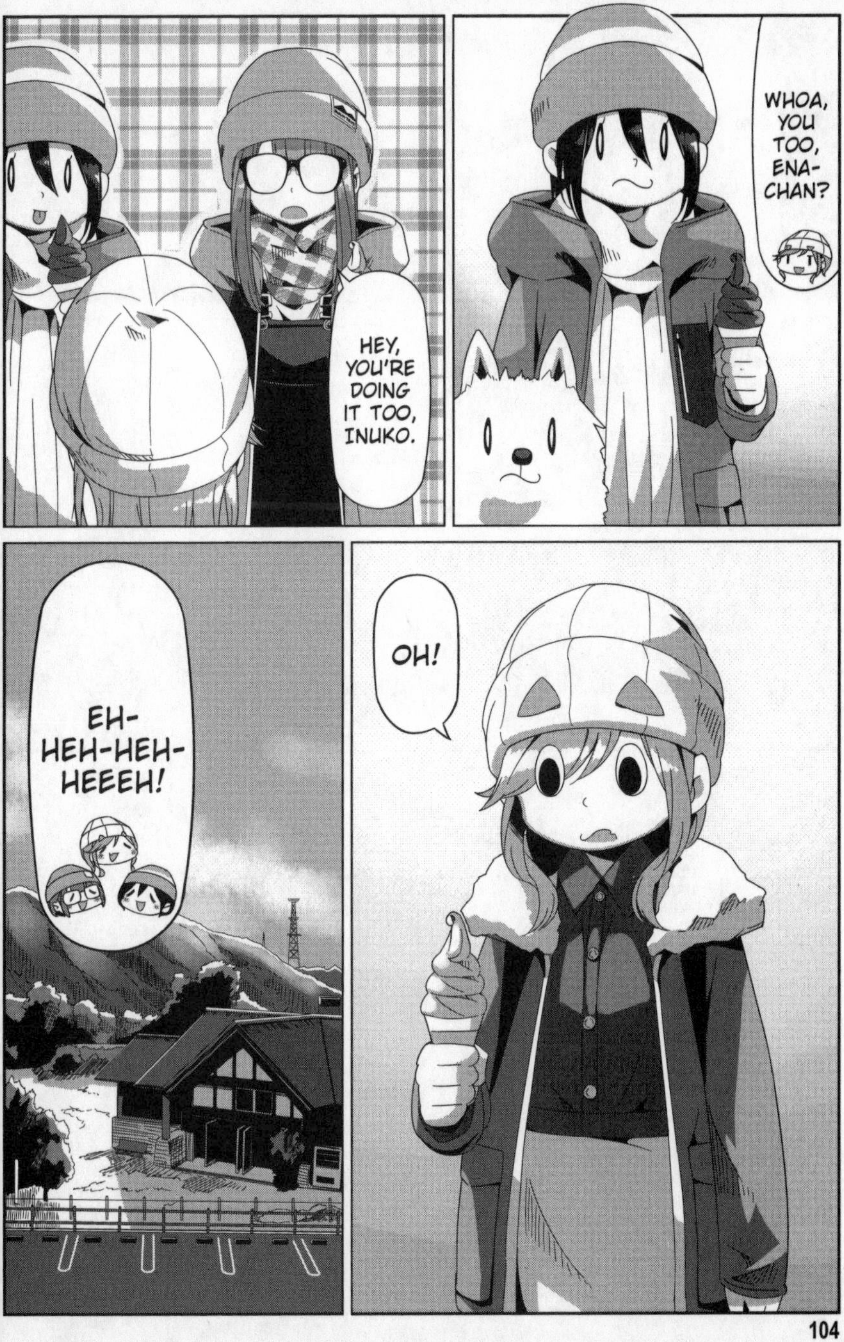
WHOA, YOU TOO, ENA-CHAN?
HEY, YOU'RE DOING IT TOO, INUKO.
OH!
EH-HEH-HEH-HEEEH!

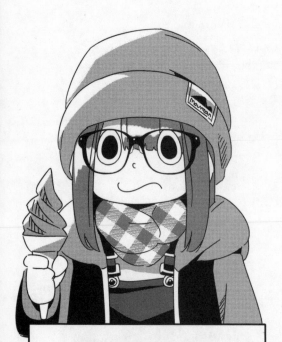

ICE-CREAM FACE

WHEN YOU GET CARELESS AND BELIEVE
GROSS ICE CREAM COULDN'T EXIST.
EATING A NASTY FLAVOR AT EXACTLY
SUCH A MOMENT IS INSTANT DEATH.

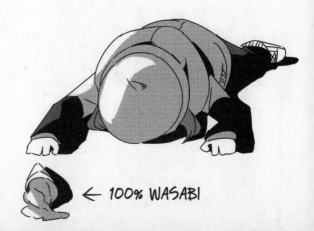

← 100% WASABI

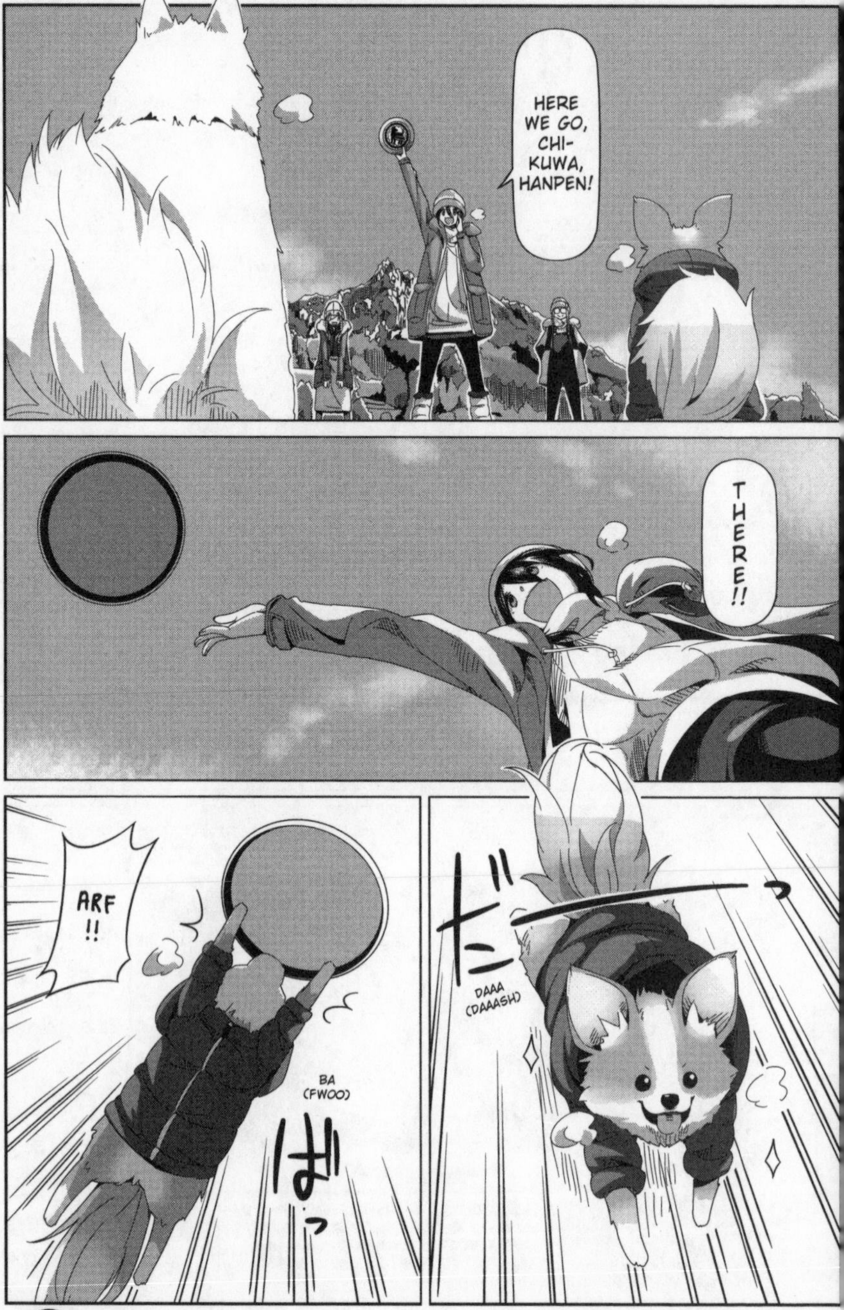
HERE WE GO, CHI-KUWA, HANPEN!
THERE!!
だーっ
DAAA (DAAASH)
ARF !!
BA (FWOO)
ぱっ

IN REAL LIFE, PLEASE ONLY PLAY FRISBEE WITH YOUR DOGS AT DOG PARKS.

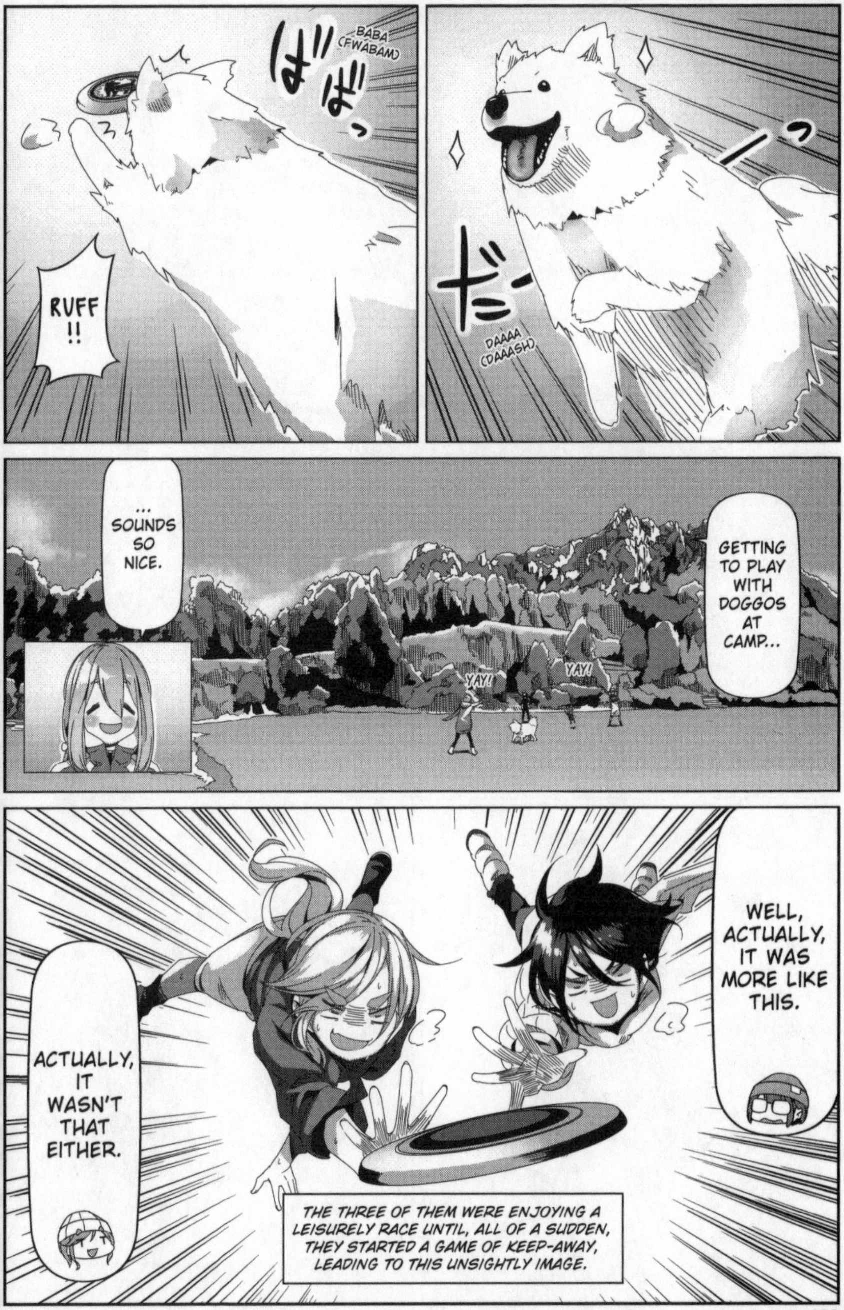
だーっ
DAAAA (DAAASH)
ばばっ
BABA (FWABAM)
RUFF!!
GETTING TO PLAY WITH DOGGOS AT CAMP...
YAY!
YAY!
...SOUNDS SO NICE.
WELL, ACTUALLY, IT WAS MORE LIKE THIS.
ACTUALLY, IT WASN'T THAT EITHER.
THE THREE OF THEM WERE ENJOYING A LEISURELY RACE UNTIL, ALL OF A SUDDEN, THEY STARTED A GAME OF KEEP-AWAY, LEADING TO THIS UNSIGHTLY IMAGE.

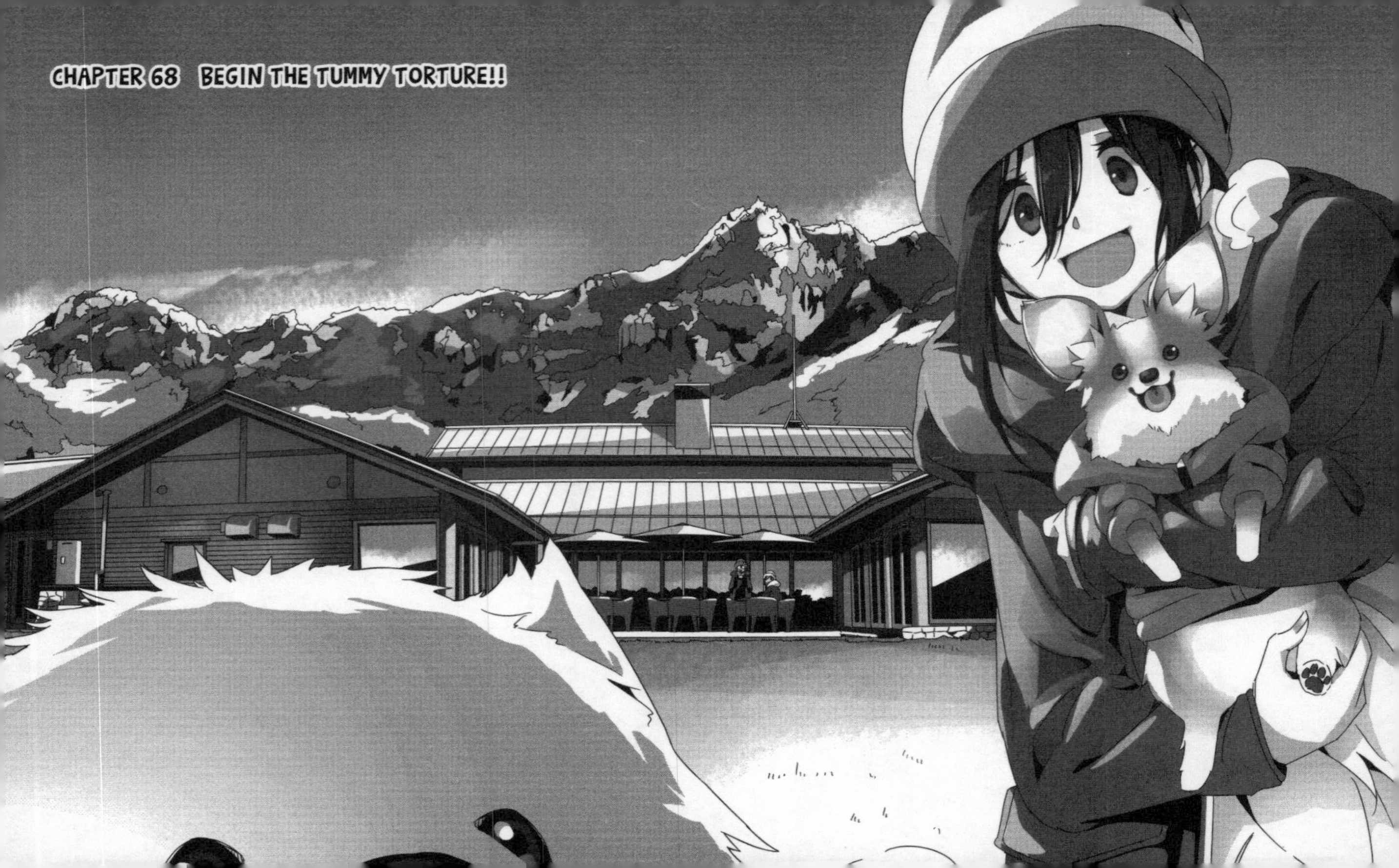
CHAPTER 68 BEGIN THE TUMMY TORTURE!!

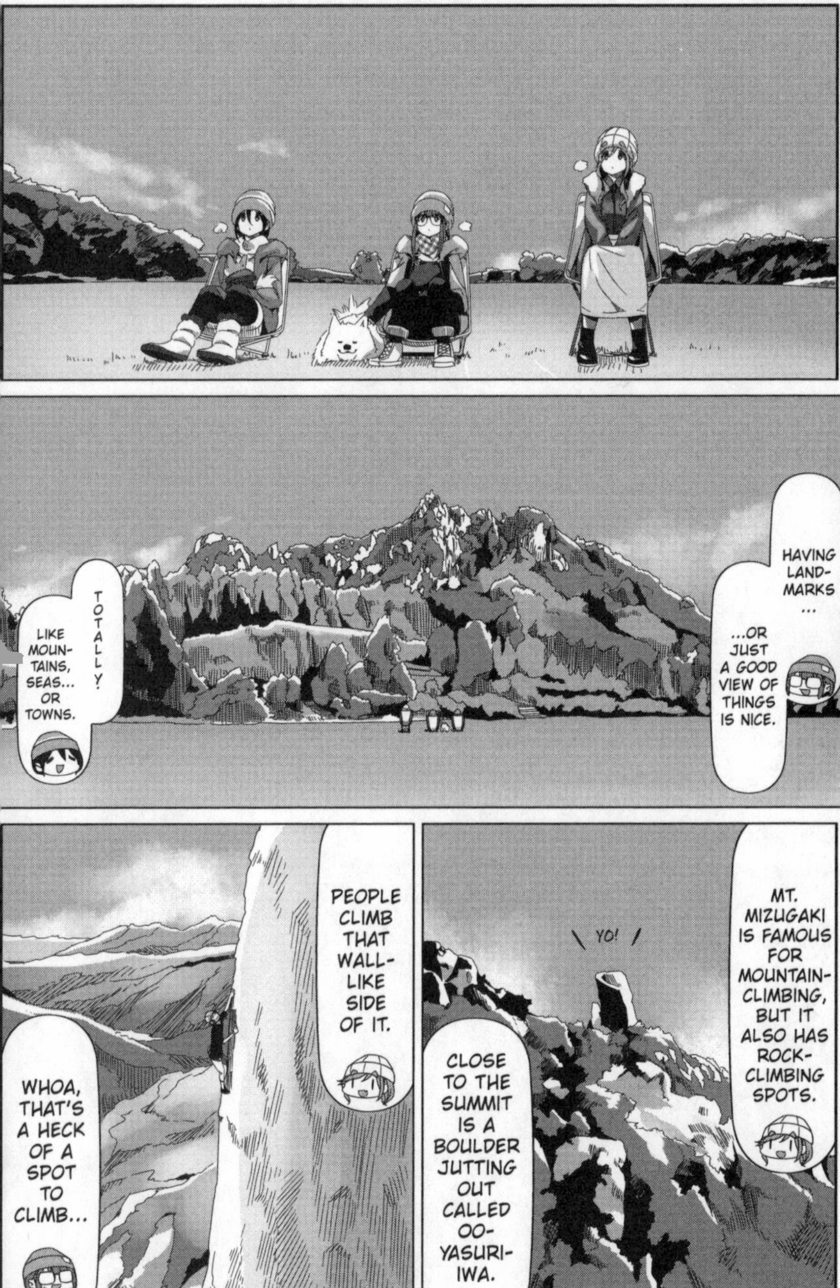
HAVING LANDMARKS...
...OR JUST A GOOD VIEW OF THINGS IS NICE.
TOTALLY.
LIKE MOUNTAINS, SEAS... OR TOWNS.
MT. MIZUGAKI IS FAMOUS FOR MOUNTAIN-CLIMBING, BUT IT ALSO HAS ROCK-CLIMBING SPOTS.
YO!
CLOSE TO THE SUMMIT IS A BOULDER JUTTING OUT CALLED OO-YASURI-IWA.
PEOPLE CLIMB THAT WALL-LIKE SIDE OF IT.
WHOA, THAT'S A HECK OF A SPOT TO CLIMB...

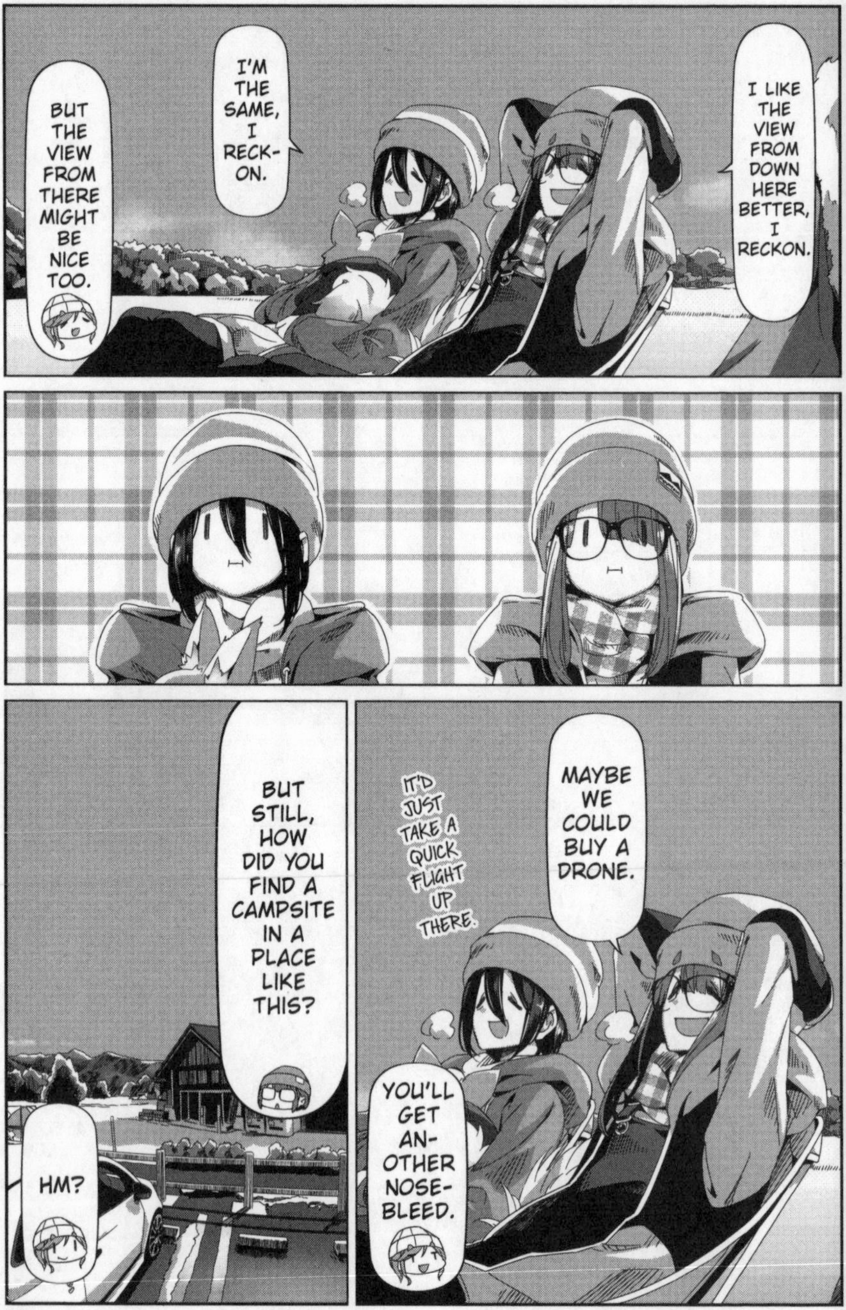
I LIKE THE VIEW FROM DOWN HERE BETTER, I RECKON.
I'M THE SAME, I RECKON.
BUT THE VIEW FROM THERE MIGHT BE NICE TOO.
MAYBE WE COULD BUY A DRONE.
IT'D JUST TAKE A QUICK FLIGHT UP THERE.
YOU'LL GET AN-OTHER NOSE-BLEED.
BUT STILL, HOW DID YOU FIND A CAMPSITE IN A PLACE LIKE THIS?
HM?

※ *A MASSIVE NATIONAL PARK THAT SPANS SAITAMA PREFECTURE, TOKYO PREFECTURE, YAMANASHI PREFECTURE, AND NAGANO PREFECTURE*

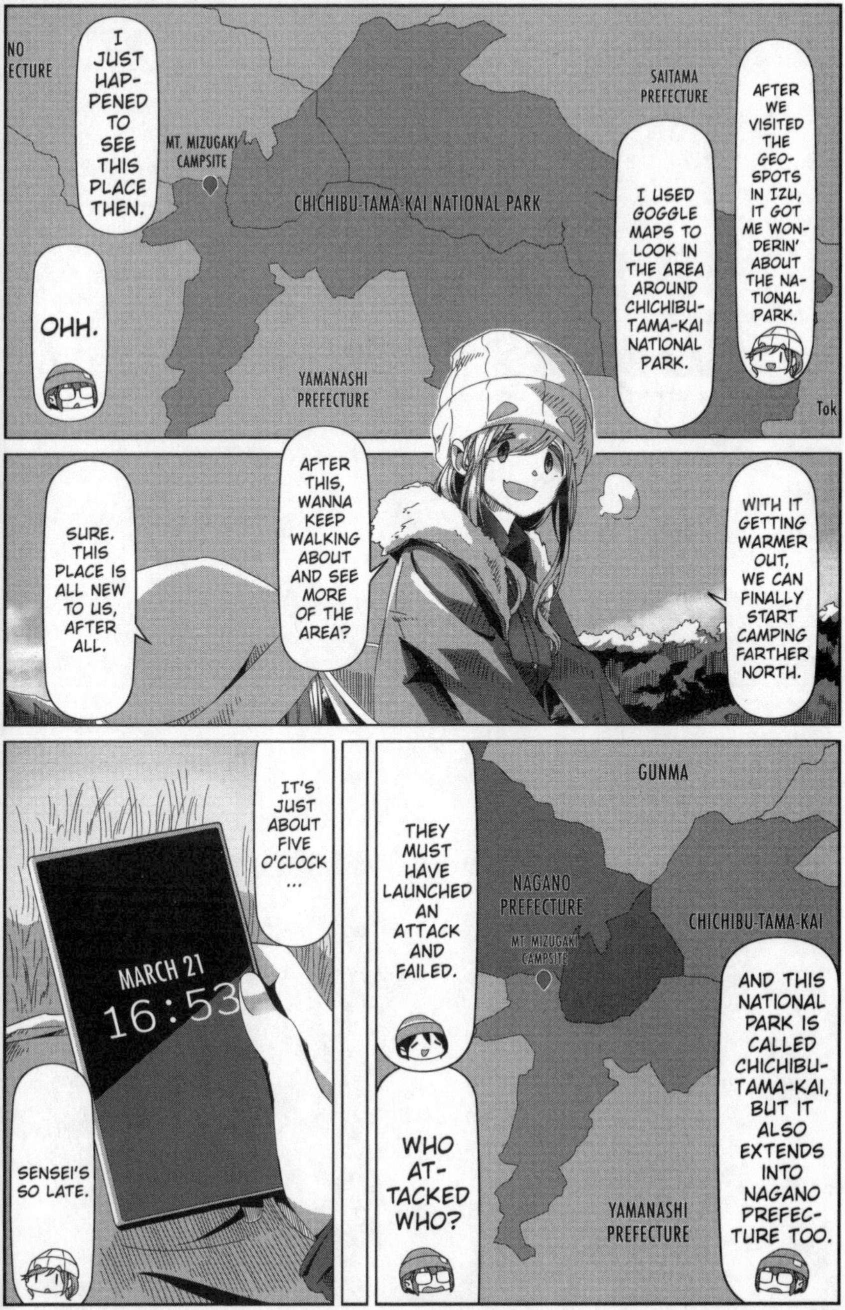
AFTER WE VISITED THE GEO-SPOTS IN IZU, IT GOT ME WONDERIN' ABOUT THE NATIONAL PARK.
I USED GOGGLE MAPS TO LOOK IN THE AREA AROUND CHICHIBU-TAMA-KAI NATIONAL PARK.
SAITAMA PREFECTURE
CHICHIBU-TAMA-KAI NATIONAL PARK
MT. MIZUGAKI CAMPSITE
YAMANASHI PREFECTURE
I JUST HAPPENED TO SEE THIS PLACE THEN.
OHH.
WITH IT GETTING WARMER OUT, WE CAN FINALLY START CAMPING FARTHER NORTH.
AFTER THIS, WANNA KEEP WALKING ABOUT AND SEE MORE OF THE AREA?
SURE. THIS PLACE IS ALL NEW TO US, AFTER ALL.
GUNMA
NAGANO PREFECTURE
CHICHIBU-TAMA-KAI
MT. MIZUGAKI CAMPSITE
YAMANASHI PREFECTURE
AND THIS NATIONAL PARK IS CALLED CHICHIBU-TAMA-KAI, BUT IT ALSO EXTENDS INTO NAGANO PREFECTURE TOO.
THEY MUST HAVE LAUNCHED AN ATTACK AND FAILED.
WHO ATTACKED WHO?
IT'S JUST ABOUT FIVE O'CLOCK...
MARCH 21
16:53
SENSEI'S SO LATE.

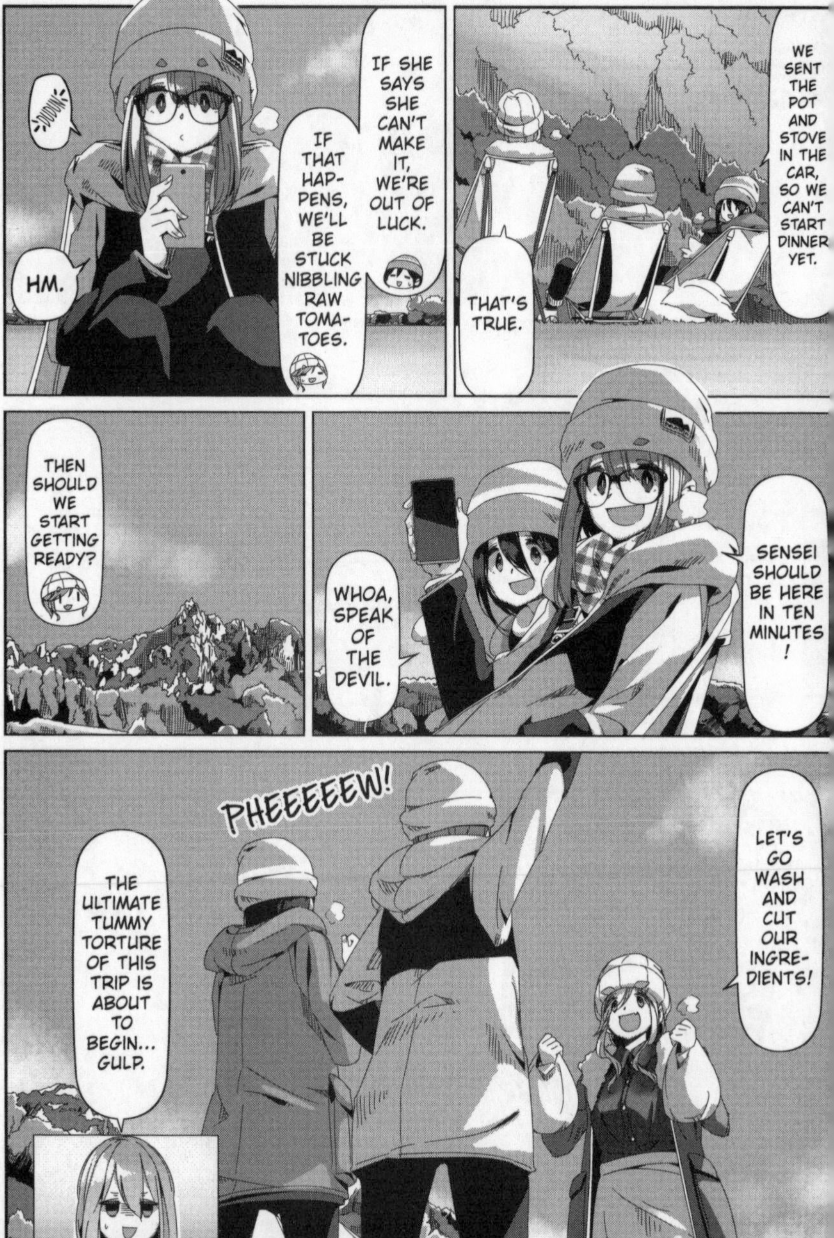
WE SENT THE POT AND STOVE IN THE CAR, SO WE CAN'T START DINNER YET.
THAT'S TRUE.
IF SHE SAYS SHE CAN'T MAKE IT, WE'RE OUT OF LUCK.
IF THAT HAP-PENS, WE'LL BE STUCK NIBBLING RAW TOMA-TOES.
DUDUN
HM.
SENSEI SHOULD BE HERE IN TEN MINUTES!
WHOA, SPEAK OF THE DEVIL.
THEN SHOULD WE START GETTING READY?
LET'S GO WASH AND CUT OUR INGRE-DIENTS!
PHEEEEEW!
THE ULTIMATE TUMMY TORTURE OF THIS TRIP IS ABOUT TO BEGIN... GULP.

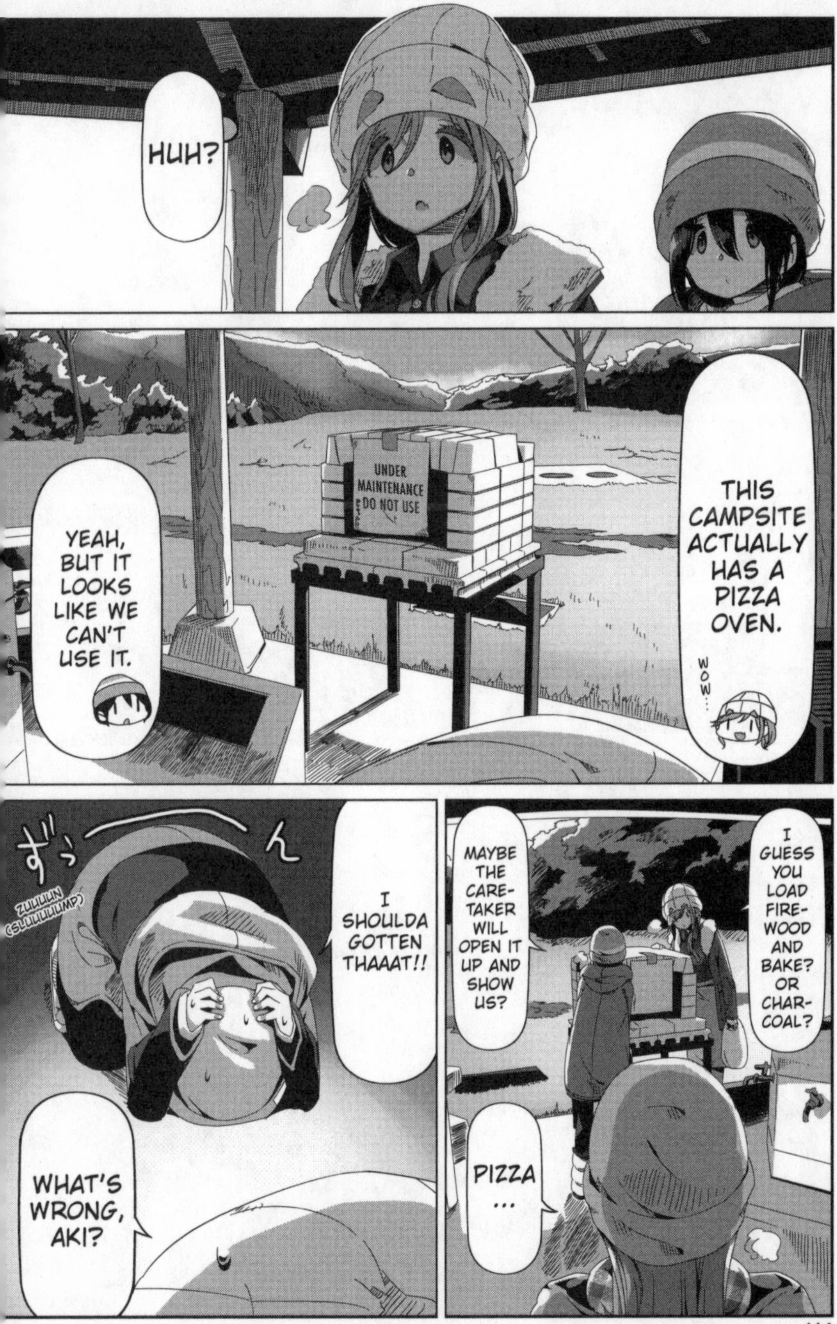
HUH?
THIS CAMPSITE ACTUALLY HAS A PIZZA OVEN.
WOW...
UNDER MAINTENANCE DO NOT USE
YEAH, BUT IT LOOKS LIKE WE CAN'T USE IT.
I GUESS YOU LOAD FIRE-WOOD AND BAKE? OR CHAR-COAL?
MAYBE THE CARE-TAKER WILL OPEN IT UP AND SHOW US?
PIZZA ...
ずぅーーん
ZULULULN (SLULULULUMP)
I SHOULDA GOTTEN THAAAT!!
WHAT'S WRONG, AKI?

SIGN: HOKUTO PRODUCE MARKET

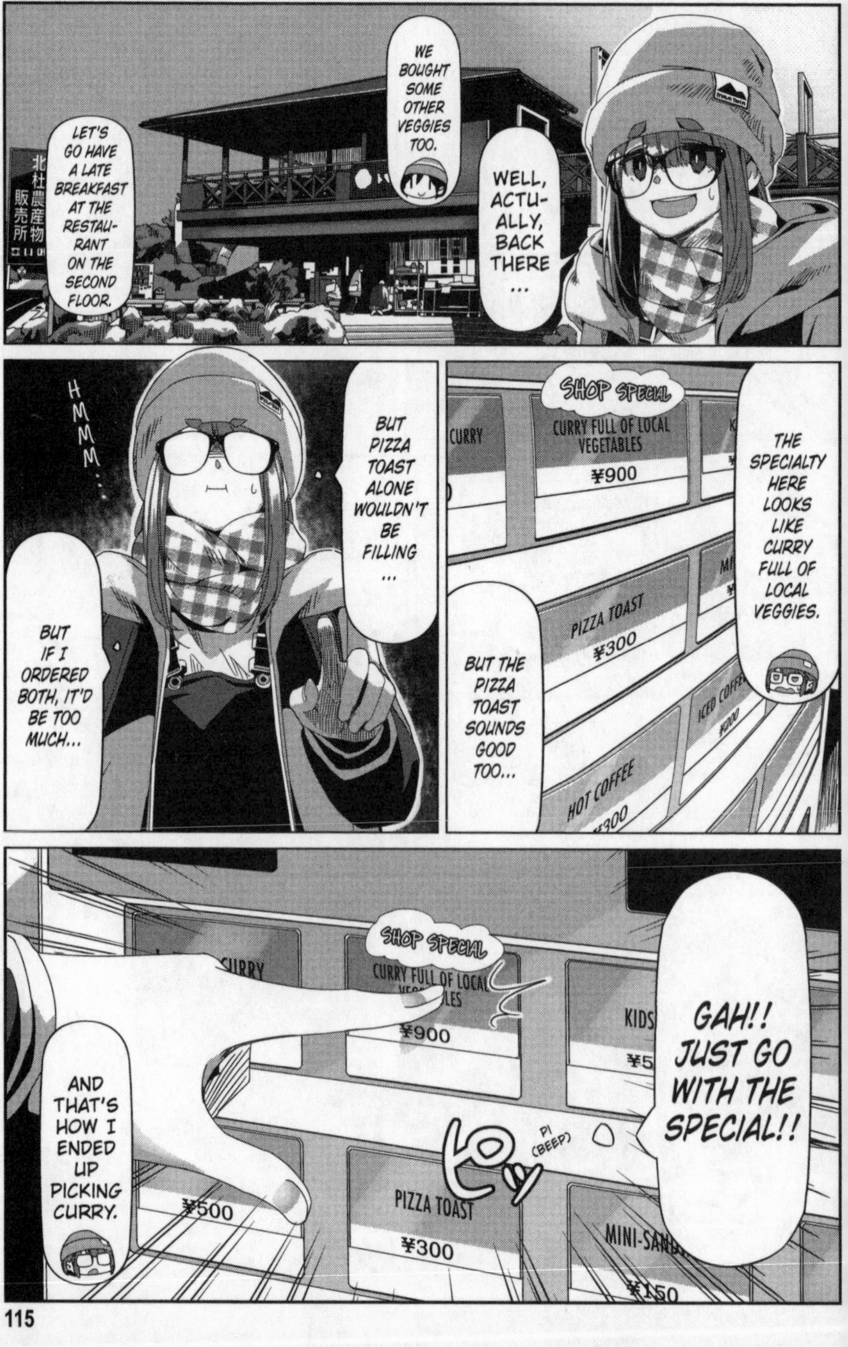
WELL, ACTUALLY, BACK THERE...
WE BOUGHT SOME OTHER VEGGIES TOO.
LET'S GO HAVE A LATE BREAKFAST AT THE RESTAURANT ON THE SECOND FLOOR.
北杜農産物販売所
SHOP SPECIAL
CURRY FULL OF LOCAL VEGETABLES
¥900
PIZZA TOAST
¥300
HOT COFFEE
ICED COFFEE
¥200
THE SPECIALTY HERE LOOKS LIKE CURRY FULL OF LOCAL VEGGIES.
BUT THE PIZZA TOAST SOUNDS GOOD TOO...
BUT PIZZA TOAST ALONE WOULDN'T BE FILLING...
HMMM...
BUT IF I ORDERED BOTH, IT'D BE TOO MUCH...
GAH!! JUST GO WITH THE SPECIAL!!
SHOP SPECIAL
CURRY FULL OF LOCAL VEGETABLES
¥900
PI (BEEP)
PIZZA TOAST
¥300
¥500
¥150
AND THAT'S HOW I ENDED UP PICKING CURRY.

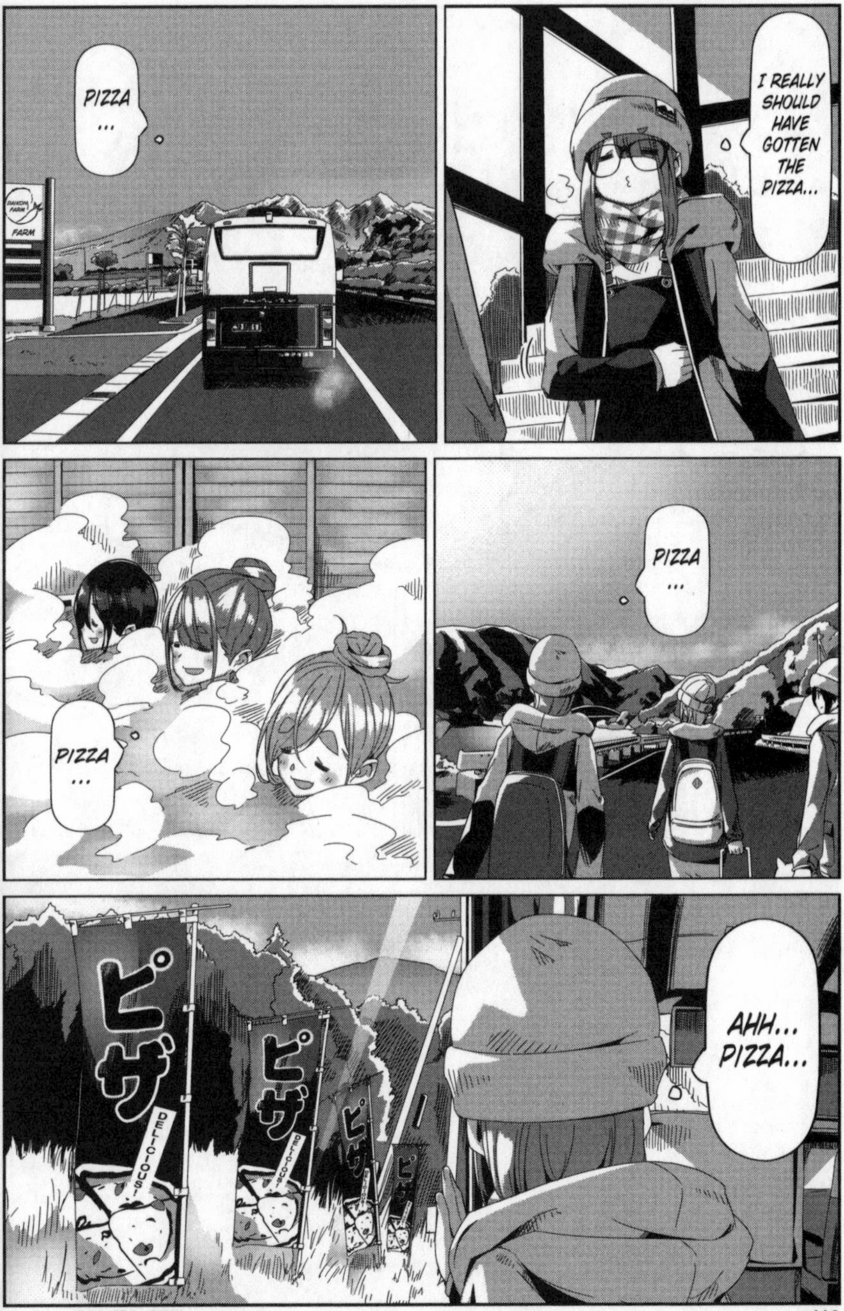
I REALLY SHOULD HAVE GOTTEN THE PIZZA...
PIZZA ...
PIZZA ...
PIZZA ...
AHH... PIZZA...
ピザ
DELICIOUS!
ピザ
DELICIOUS!
ピザ
ピザ

BANNERS: PIZZA

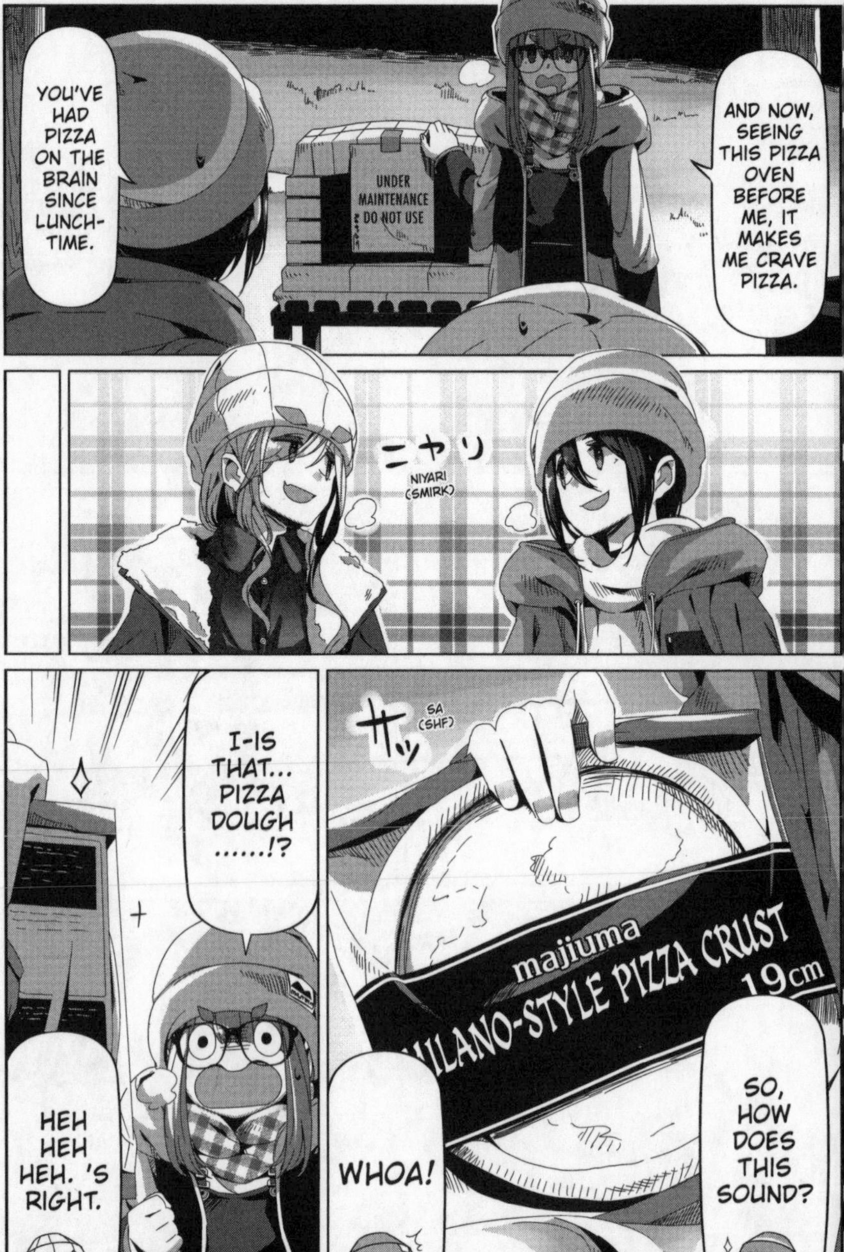
YOU'VE HAD PIZZA ON THE BRAIN SINCE LUNCH-TIME.
AND NOW, SEEING THIS PIZZA OVEN BEFORE ME, IT MAKES ME CRAVE PIZZA.
UNDER MAINTENANCE DO NOT USE
ニヤリ
NIYARI (SMIRK)
サッ
SA (SHF)
majiuma
ILANO-STYLE PIZZA CRUST
19cm
SO, HOW DOES THIS SOUND?
WHOA!
I-IS THAT... PIZZA DOUGH ......!?
HEH HEH HEH. 'S RIGHT.

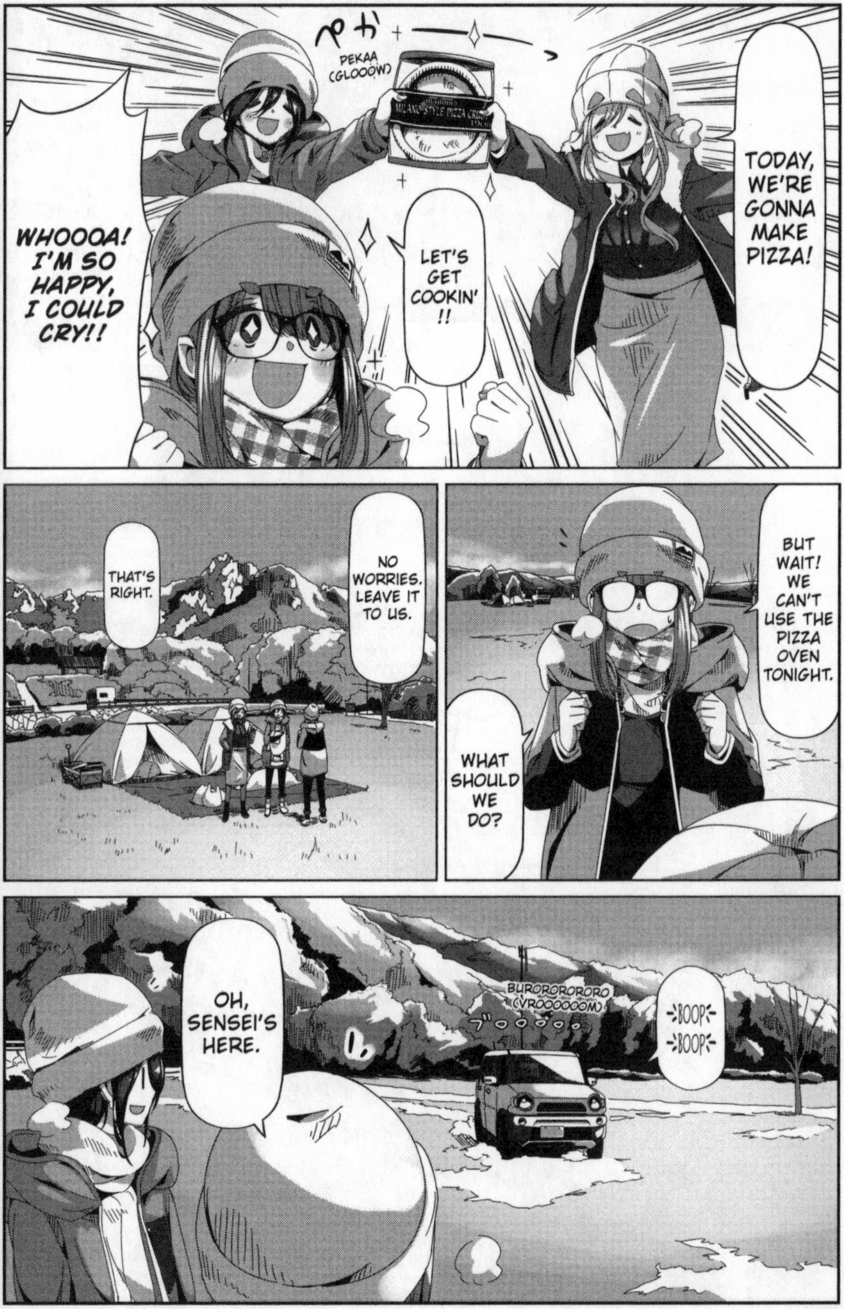
TODAY, WE'RE GONNA MAKE PIZZA!
PEKAA (GLOOOW)
MILANO STYLE PIZZA CRUST
LET'S GET COOKIN' !!
WHOOOA! I'M SO HAPPY, I COULD CRY!!
BUT WAIT! WE CAN'T USE THE PIZZA OVEN TONIGHT.
WHAT SHOULD WE DO?
NO WORRIES. LEAVE IT TO US.
THAT'S RIGHT.
BOOP BOOP
BURORORORORO (VROOOOOOM)
OH, SENSEI'S HERE.

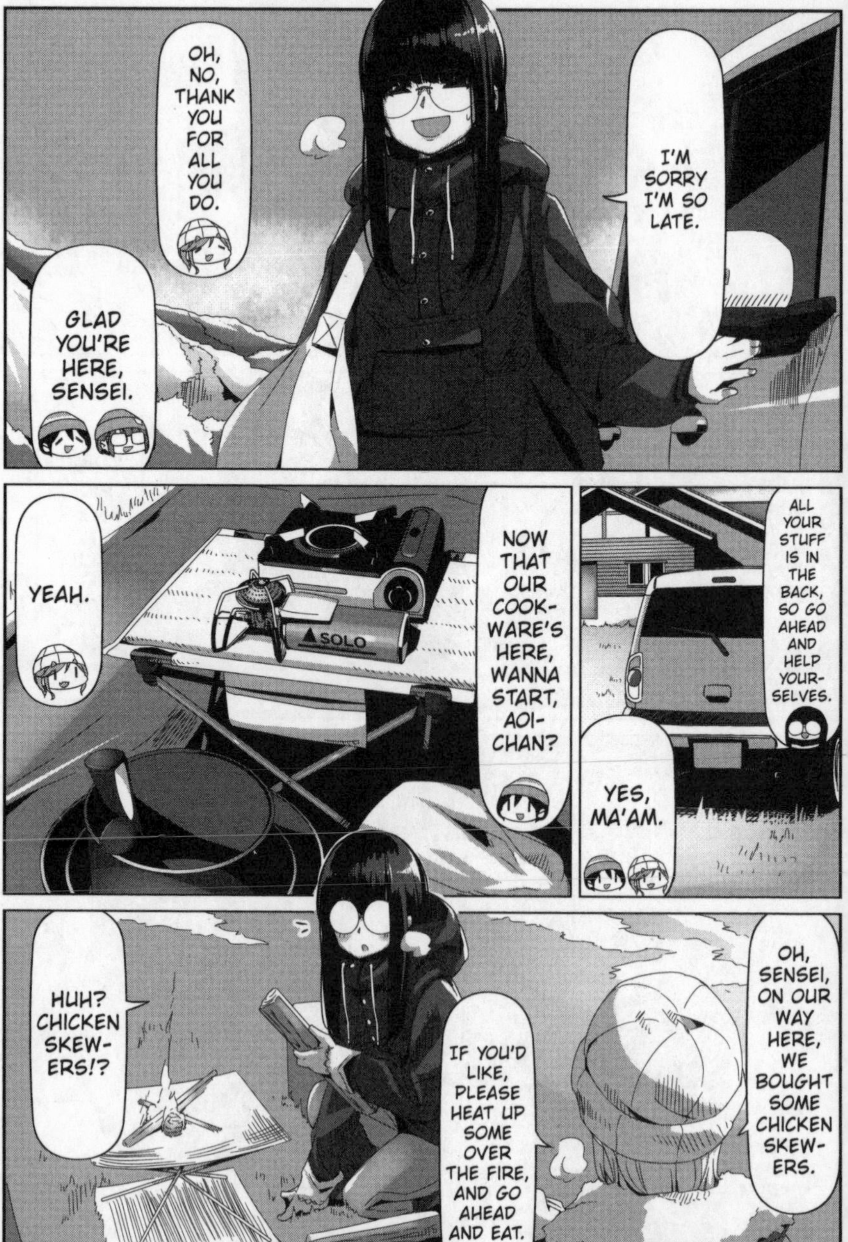
I'M SORRY I'M SO LATE.
OH, NO, THANK YOU FOR ALL YOU DO.
GLAD YOU'RE HERE, SENSEI.
ALL YOUR STUFF IS IN THE BACK, SO GO AHEAD AND HELP YOURSELVES.
YES, MA'AM.
NOW THAT OUR COOKWARE'S HERE, WANNA START, AOI-CHAN?
YEAH.
SOLO
OH, SENSEI, ON OUR WAY HERE, WE BOUGHT SOME CHICKEN SKEWERS.
HUH? CHICKEN SKEWERS!?
IF YOU'D LIKE, PLEASE HEAT UP SOME OVER THE FIRE, AND GO AHEAD AND EAT.

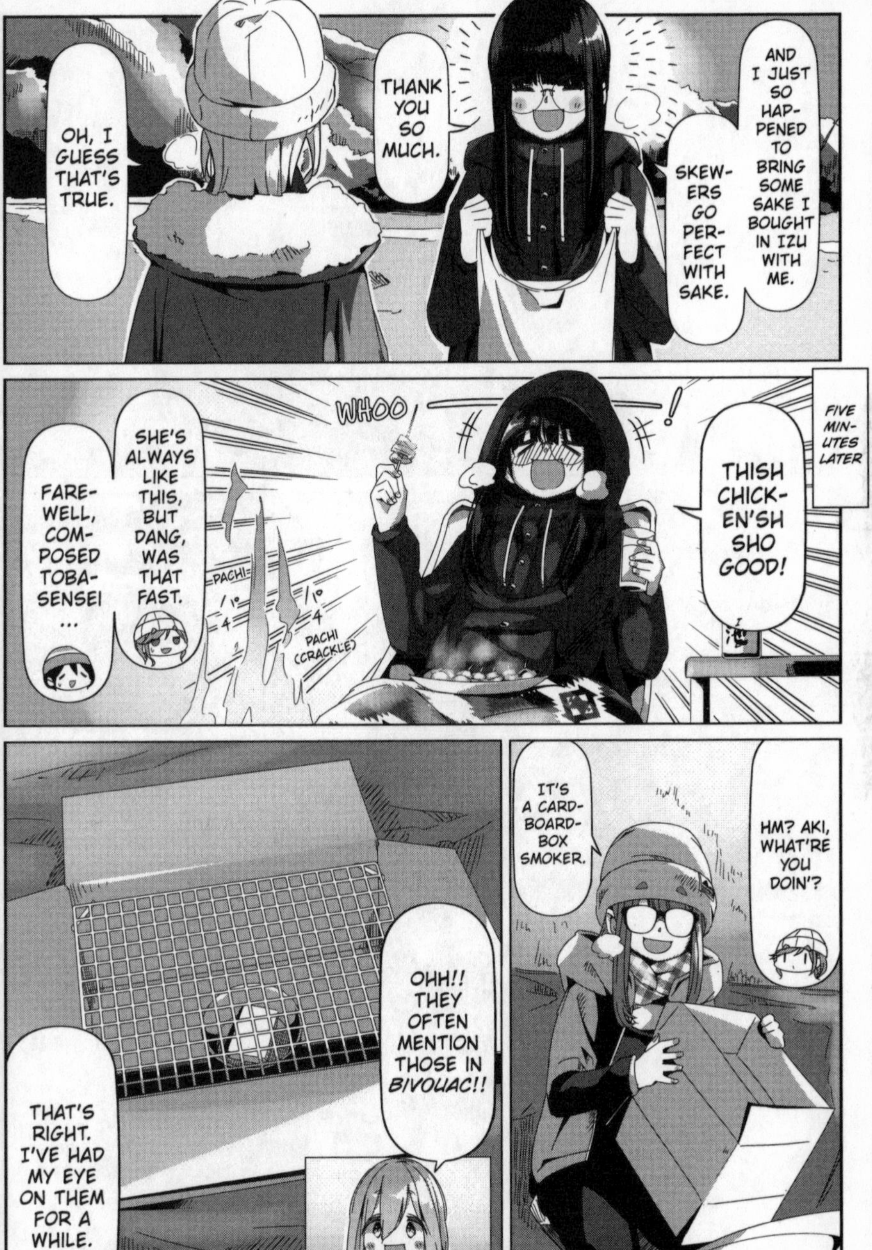
AND I JUST SO HAPPENED TO BRING SOME SAKE I BOUGHT IN IZU WITH ME.
SKEWERS GO PERFECT WITH SAKE.
THANK YOU SO MUCH.
OH, I GUESS THAT'S TRUE.
FIVE MINUTES LATER
THISH CHICKEN'SH SHO GOOD!
WHOO
PACHI
PACHI (CRACKLE)
SHE'S ALWAYS LIKE THIS, BUT DANG, WAS THAT FAST.
FAREWELL, COMPOSED TOBA-SENSEI...
HM? AKI, WHAT'RE YOU DOIN'?
IT'S A CARDBOARD-BOX SMOKER.
OHH!! THEY OFTEN MENTION THOSE IN *BIVOUAC*!!
THAT'S RIGHT. I'VE HAD MY EYE ON THEM FOR A WHILE.

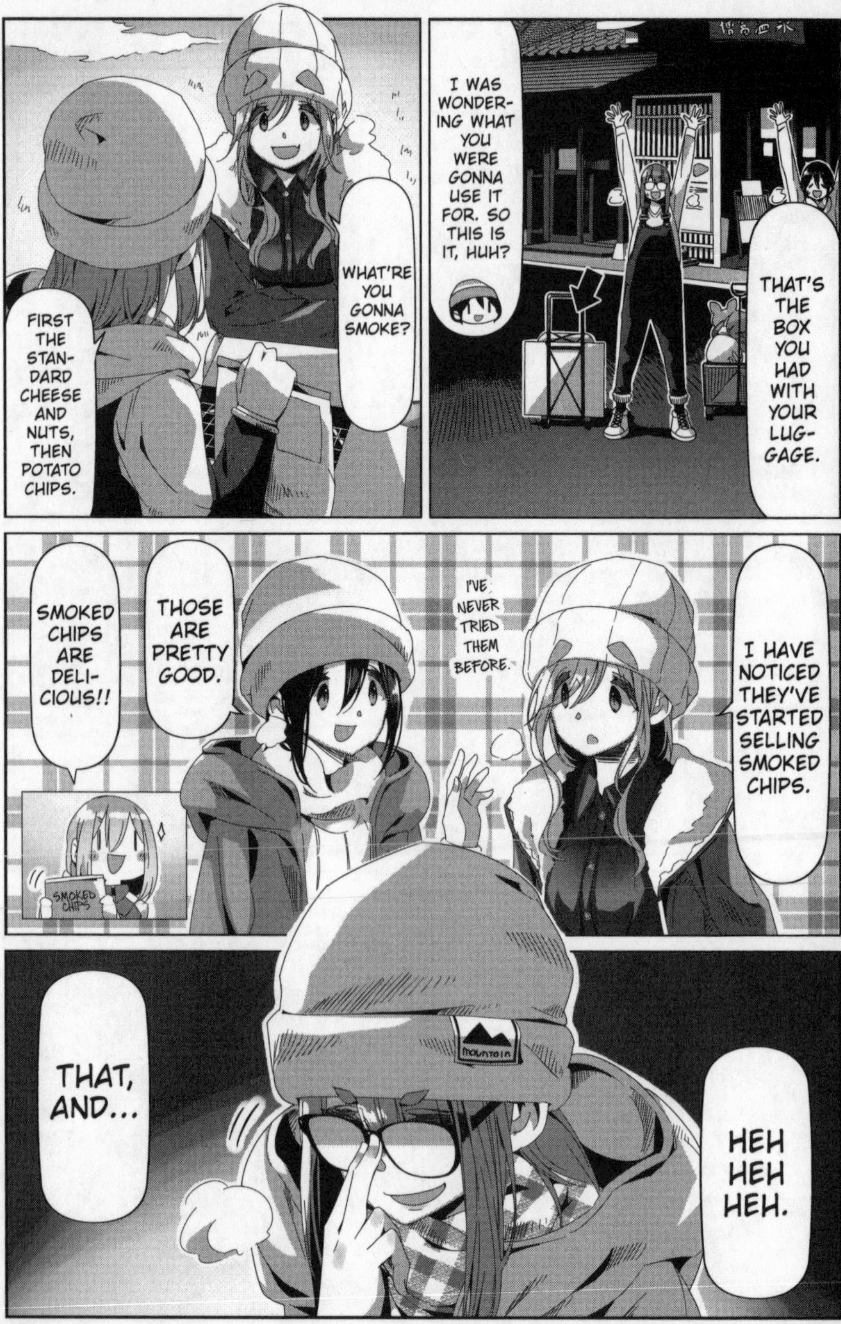
THAT'S THE BOX YOU HAD WITH YOUR LUG-GAGE.
I WAS WONDER-ING WHAT YOU WERE GONNA USE IT FOR. SO THIS IS IT, HUH?
WHAT'RE YOU GONNA SMOKE?
FIRST THE STAN-DARD CHEESE AND NUTS, THEN POTATO CHIPS.
I HAVE NOTICED THEY'VE STARTED SELLING SMOKED CHIPS.
I'VE NEVER TRIED THEM BEFORE.
THOSE ARE PRETTY GOOD.
SMOKED CHIPS ARE DELI-CIOUS!!
SMOKED CHIPS
HEH HEH HEH.
THAT, AND...

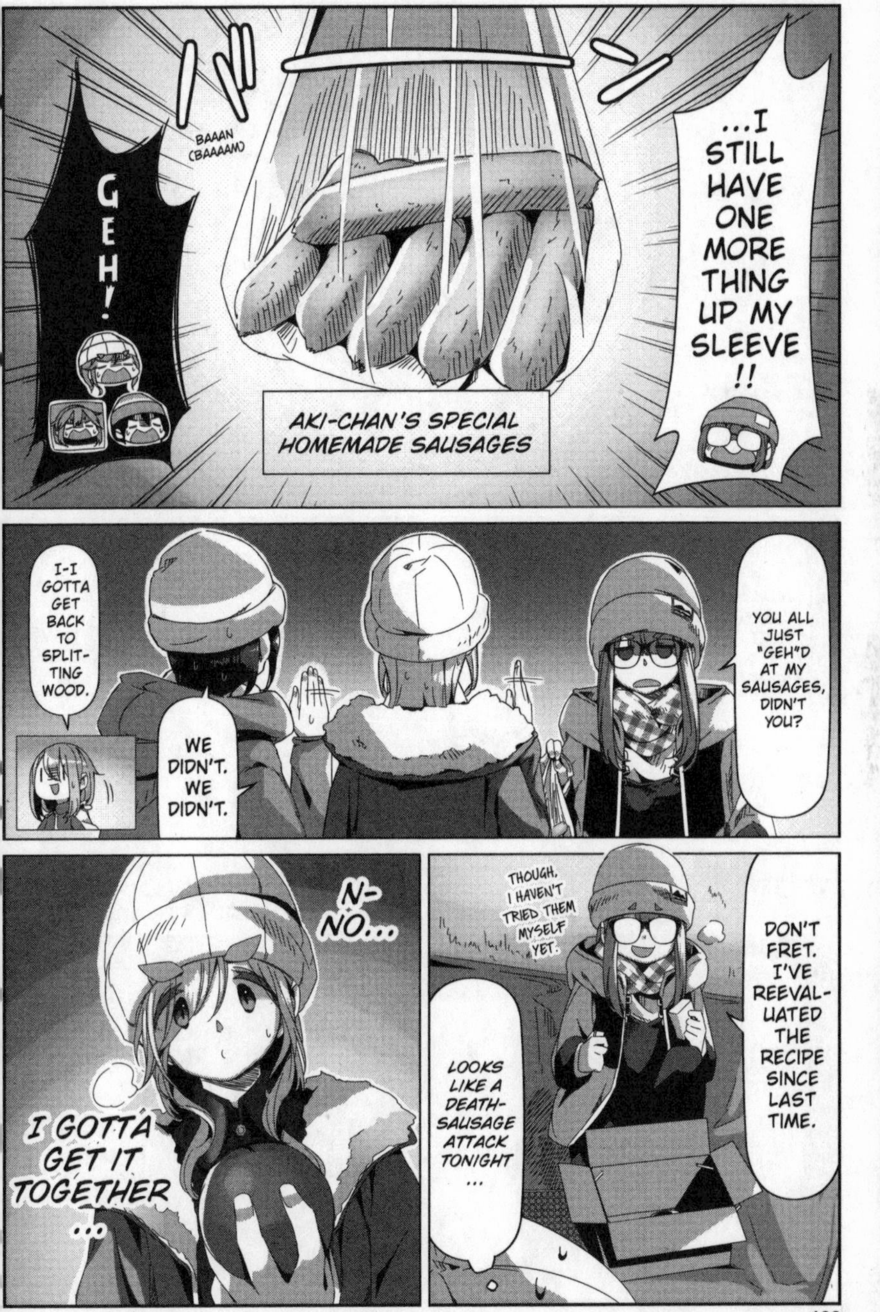
...I STILL HAVE ONE MORE THING UP MY SLEEVE!!
BAAAN (BAAAAM)
GEH!
AKI-CHAN'S SPECIAL HOMEMADE SAUSAGES
YOU ALL JUST "GEH"D AT MY SAUSAGES, DIDN'T YOU?
WE DIDN'T. WE DIDN'T.
I-I GOTTA GET BACK TO SPLIT-TING WOOD.
DON'T FRET. I'VE REEVAL-UATED THE RECIPE SINCE LAST TIME.
THOUGH, I HAVEN'T TRIED THEM MYSELF YET.
LOOKS LIKE A DEATH-SAUSAGE ATTACK TONIGHT...
N-NO...
I GOTTA GET IT TOGETHER...

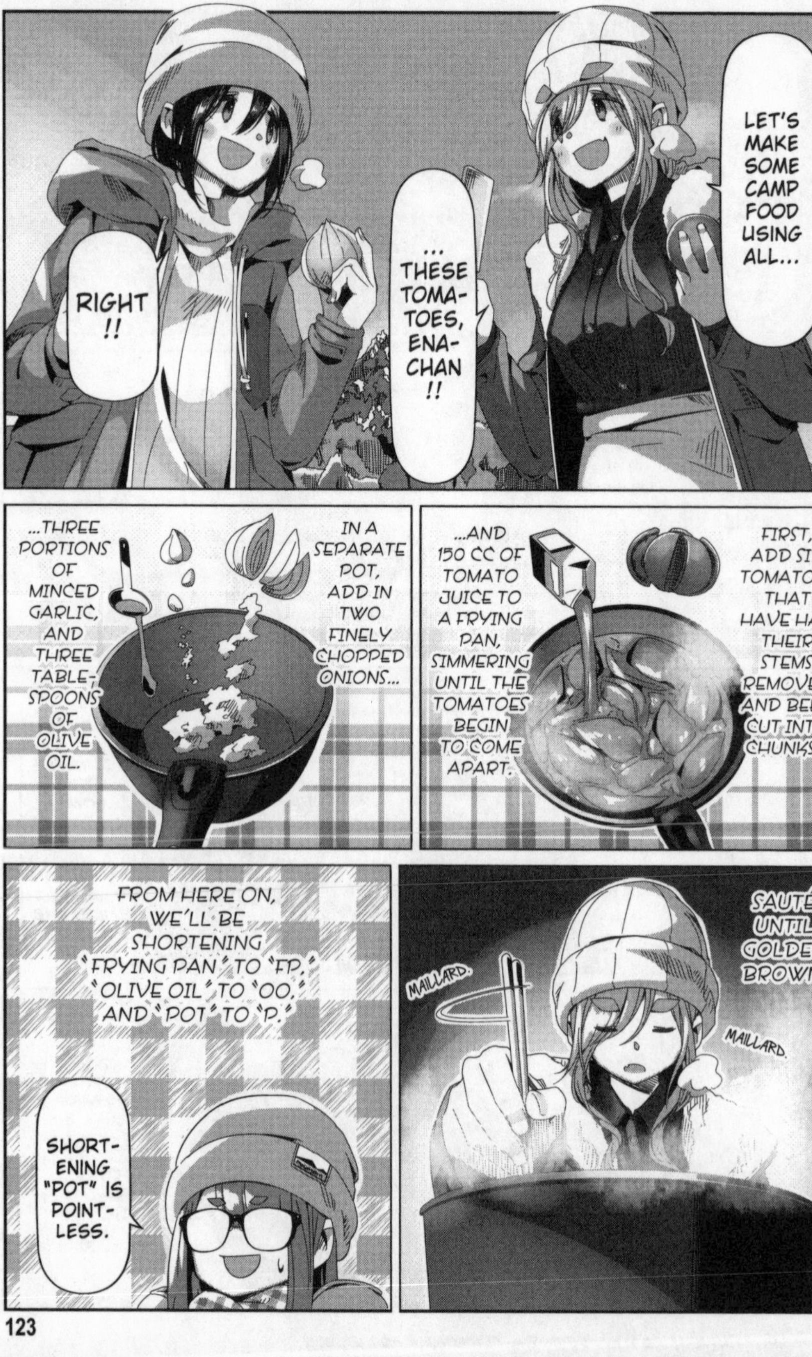
LET'S MAKE SOME CAMP FOOD USING ALL...
... THESE TOMATOES, ENA-CHAN!!
RIGHT!!
FIRST, ADD SIX TOMATOES THAT HAVE HAD THEIR STEMS REMOVED AND BEEN CUT INTO CHUNKS...
...AND 150 CC OF TOMATO JUICE TO A FRYING PAN, SIMMERING UNTIL THE TOMATOES BEGIN TO COME APART.
IN A SEPARATE POT, ADD IN TWO FINELY CHOPPED ONIONS...
...THREE PORTIONS OF MINCED GARLIC, AND THREE TABLESPOONS OF OLIVE OIL.
SAUTÉ UNTIL GOLDEN BROWN.
MAILLARD.
MAILLARD.
FROM HERE ON, WE'LL BE SHORTENING "FRYING PAN" TO "FP," "OLIVE OIL" TO "OO," AND "POT" TO "P."
SHORTENING "POT" IS POINTLESS.

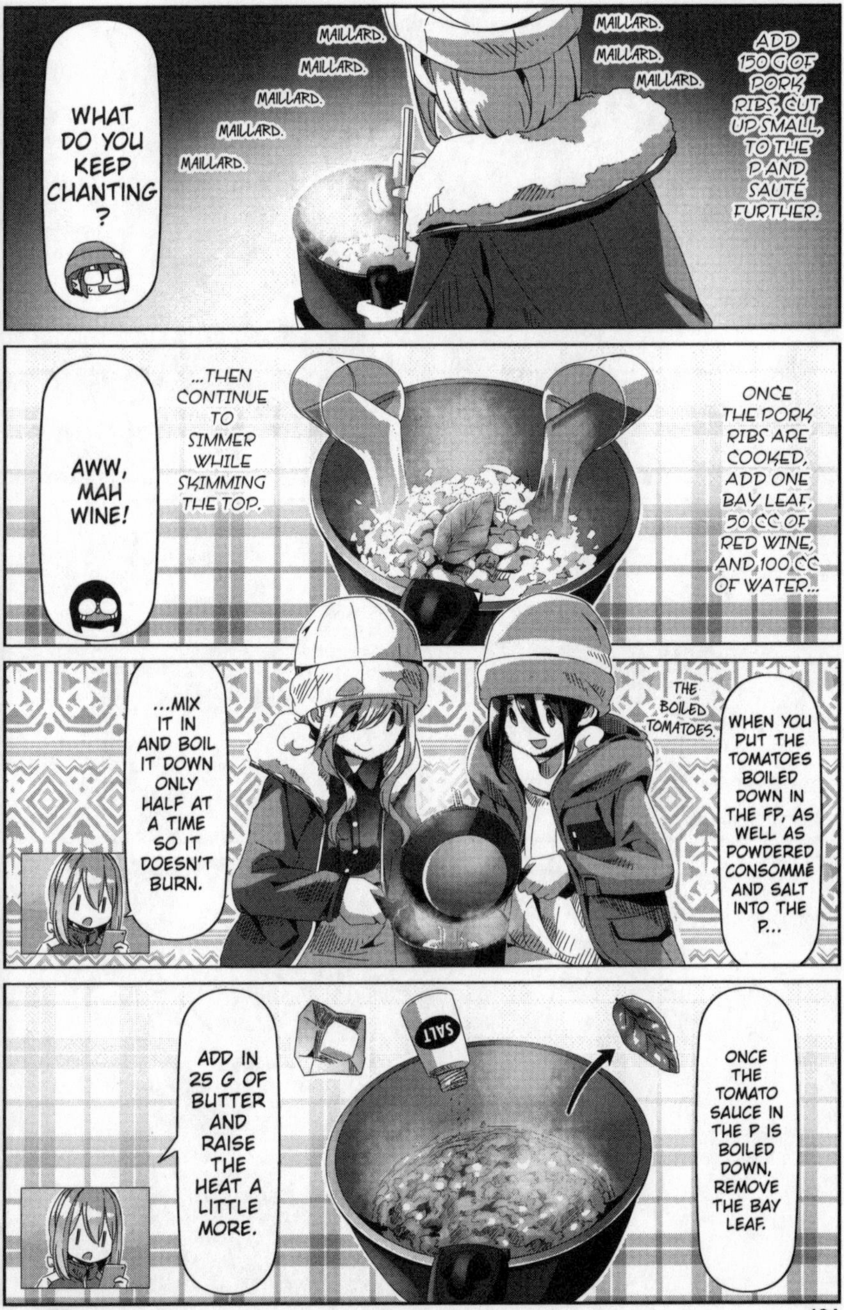
ADD 150 G OF PORK RIBS, CUT UP SMALL, TO THE P AND SAUTÉ FURTHER.
MAILLARD.
MAILLARD.
MAILLARD.
MAILLARD.
MAILLARD.
MAILLARD.
MAILLARD.
MAILLARD.
WHAT DO YOU KEEP CHANTING?
ONCE THE PORK RIBS ARE COOKED, ADD ONE BAY LEAF, 50 CC OF RED WINE, AND 100 CC OF WATER...
...THEN CONTINUE TO SIMMER WHILE SKIMMING THE TOP.
AWW, MAH WINE!
WHEN YOU PUT THE TOMATOES BOILED DOWN IN THE FP, AS WELL AS POWDERED CONSOMMÉ AND SALT INTO THE P...
THE BOILED TOMATOES.
...MIX IT IN AND BOIL IT DOWN ONLY HALF AT A TIME SO IT DOESN'T BURN.
ONCE THE TOMATO SAUCE IN THE P IS BOILED DOWN, REMOVE THE BAY LEAF.
SALT
ADD IN 25 G OF BUTTER AND RAISE THE HEAT A LITTLE MORE.

TASTE IT AS YOU ADD IN THE CONSOMMÉ AND SALT.

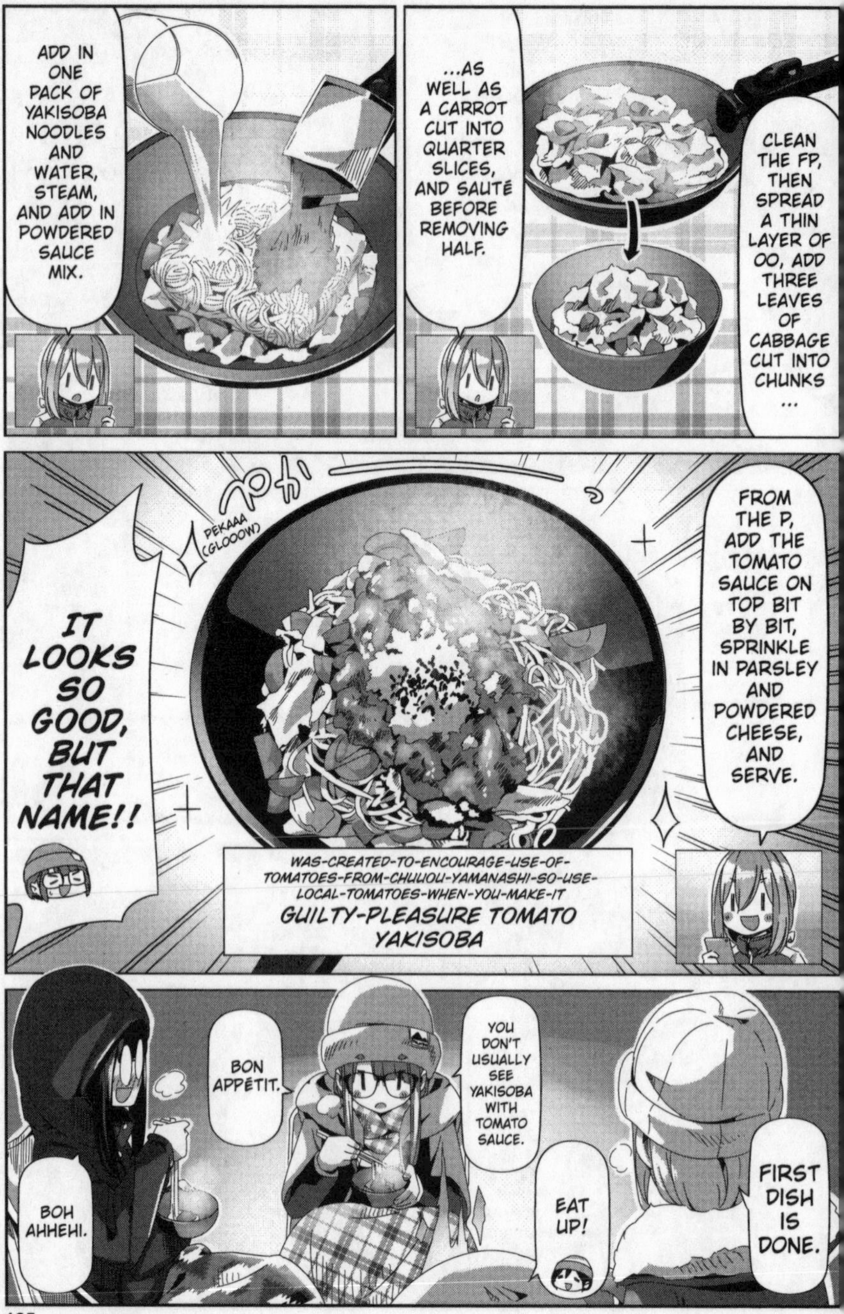
CLEAN THE FP, THEN SPREAD A THIN LAYER OF OO, ADD THREE LEAVES OF CABBAGE CUT INTO CHUNKS ...
...AS WELL AS A CARROT CUT INTO QUARTER SLICES, AND SAUTÉ BEFORE REMOVING HALF.
ADD IN ONE PACK OF YAKISOBA NOODLES AND WATER, STEAM, AND ADD IN POWDERED SAUCE MIX.
FROM THE P, ADD THE TOMATO SAUCE ON TOP BIT BY BIT, SPRINKLE IN PARSLEY AND POWDERED CHEESE, AND SERVE.
PEKAAA (GLOOOW)
IT LOOKS SO GOOD, BUT THAT NAME!!
WAS-CREATED-TO-ENCOURAGE-USE-OF-TOMATOES-FROM-CHUUOU-YAMANASHI-SO-USE-LOCAL-TOMATOES-WHEN-YOU-MAKE-IT
GUILTY-PLEASURE TOMATO YAKISOBA
FIRST DISH IS DONE.
EAT UP!
YOU DON'T USUALLY SEE YAKISOBA WITH TOMATO SAUCE.
BON APPÉTIT.
BOH AHHEHI.

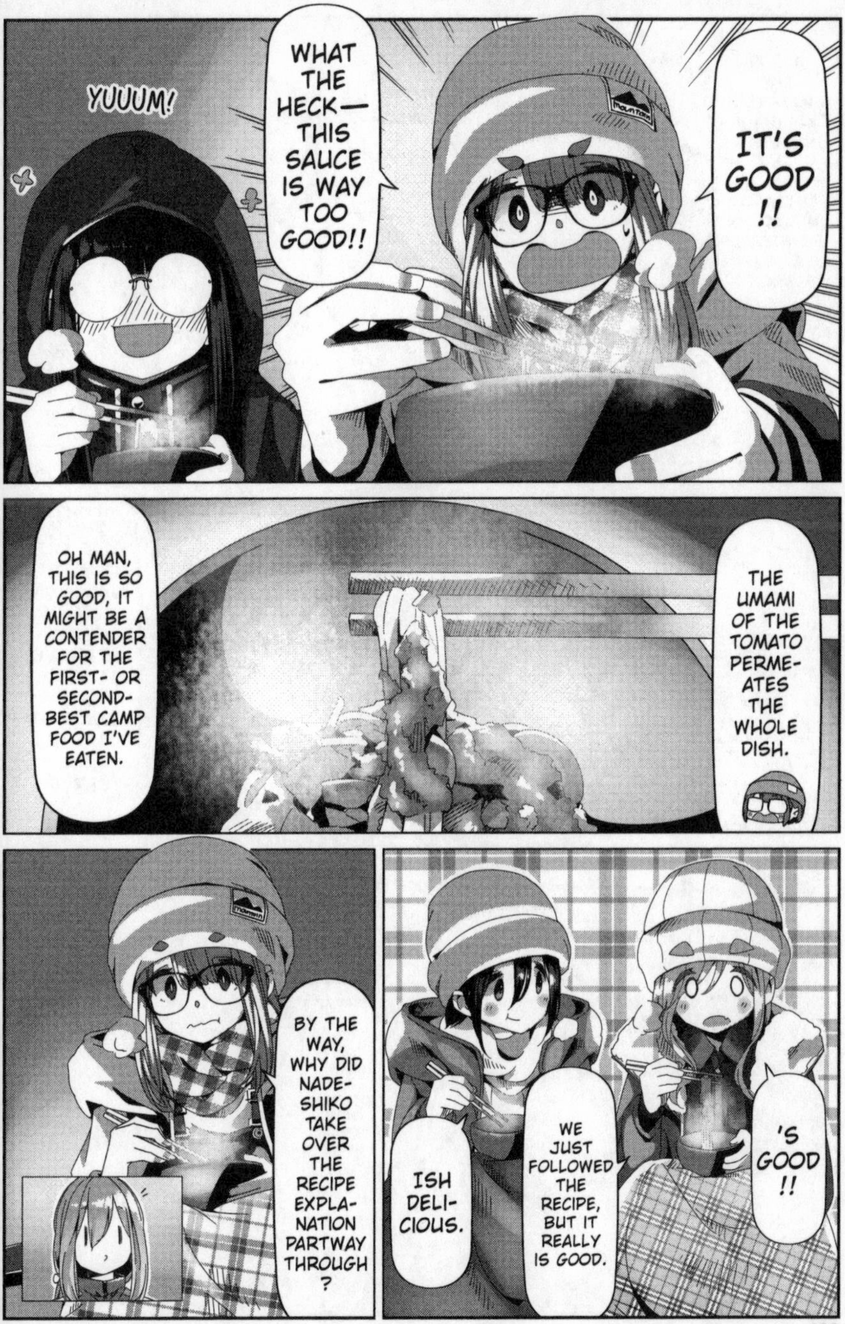
IT'S GOOD!!
WHAT THE HECK—THIS SAUCE IS WAY TOO GOOD!!
YUUUM!
THE UMAMI OF THE TOMATO PERMEATES THE WHOLE DISH.
OH MAN, THIS IS SO GOOD, IT MIGHT BE A CONTENDER FOR THE FIRST- OR SECOND-BEST CAMP FOOD I'VE EATEN.
'S GOOD!!
WE JUST FOLLOWED THE RECIPE, BUT IT REALLY IS GOOD.
ISH DELICIOUS.
BY THE WAY, WHY DID NADESHIKO TAKE OVER THE RECIPE EXPLANATION PARTWAY THROUGH?

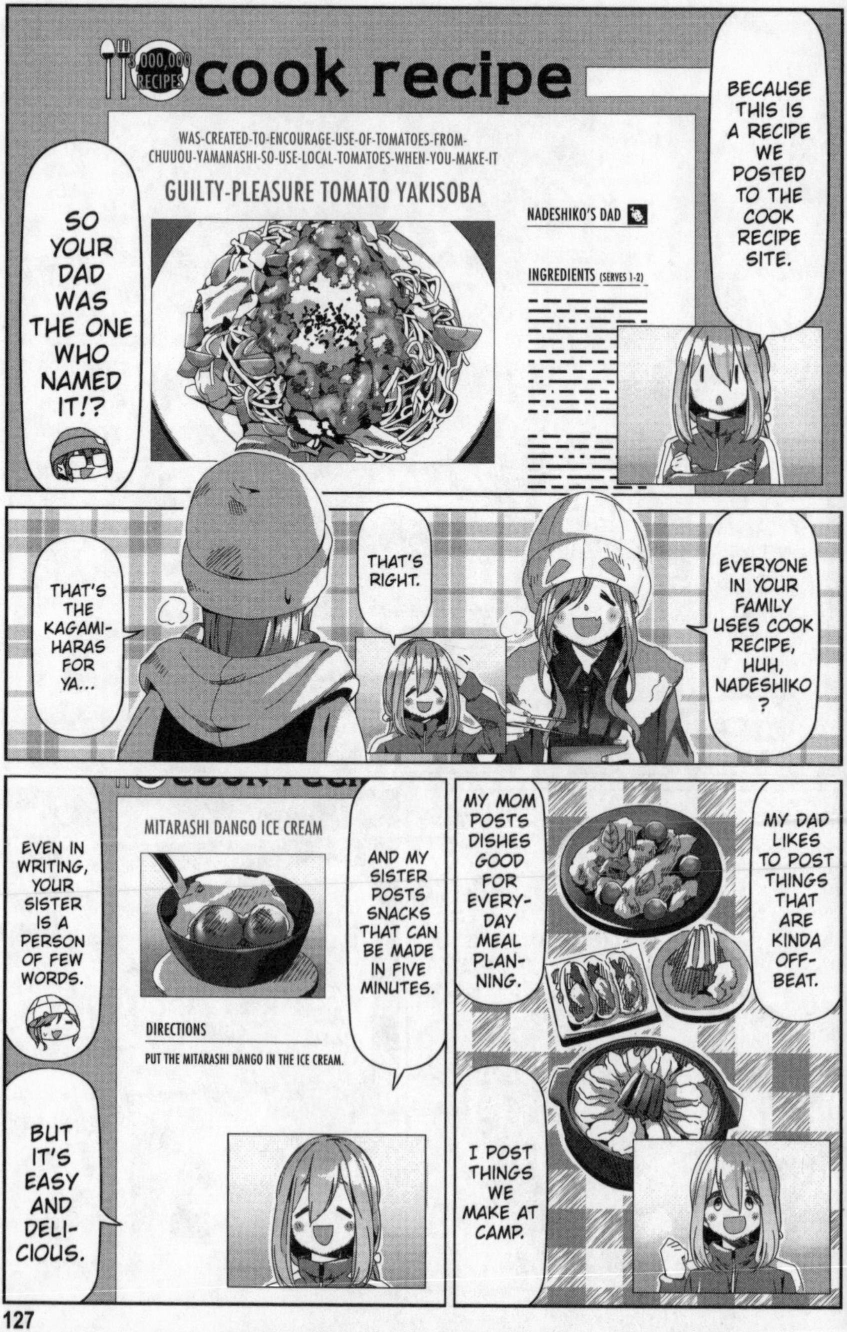
BECAUSE THIS IS A RECIPE WE POSTED TO THE COOK RECIPE SITE.
3,000,000 RECIPES
cook recipe
WAS-CREATED-TO-ENCOURAGE-USE-OF-TOMATOES-FROM-CHUUOU-YAMANASHI-SO-USE-LOCAL-TOMATOES-WHEN-YOU-MAKE-IT
GUILTY-PLEASURE TOMATO YAKISOBA
NADESHIKO'S DAD
INGREDIENTS (SERVES 1-2)
SO YOUR DAD WAS THE ONE WHO NAMED IT!?
EVERYONE IN YOUR FAMILY USES COOK RECIPE, HUH, NADESHIKO?
THAT'S RIGHT.
THAT'S THE KAGAMIHARAS FOR YA...
MY DAD LIKES TO POST THINGS THAT ARE KINDA OFF-BEAT.
MY MOM POSTS DISHES GOOD FOR EVERY-DAY MEAL PLAN-NING.
I POST THINGS WE MAKE AT CAMP.
AND MY SISTER POSTS SNACKS THAT CAN BE MADE IN FIVE MINUTES.
MITARASHI DANGO ICE CREAM
DIRECTIONS
PUT THE MITARASHI DANGO IN THE ICE CREAM.
EVEN IN WRITING, YOUR SISTER IS A PERSON OF FEW WORDS.
BUT IT'S EASY AND DELI-CIOUS.

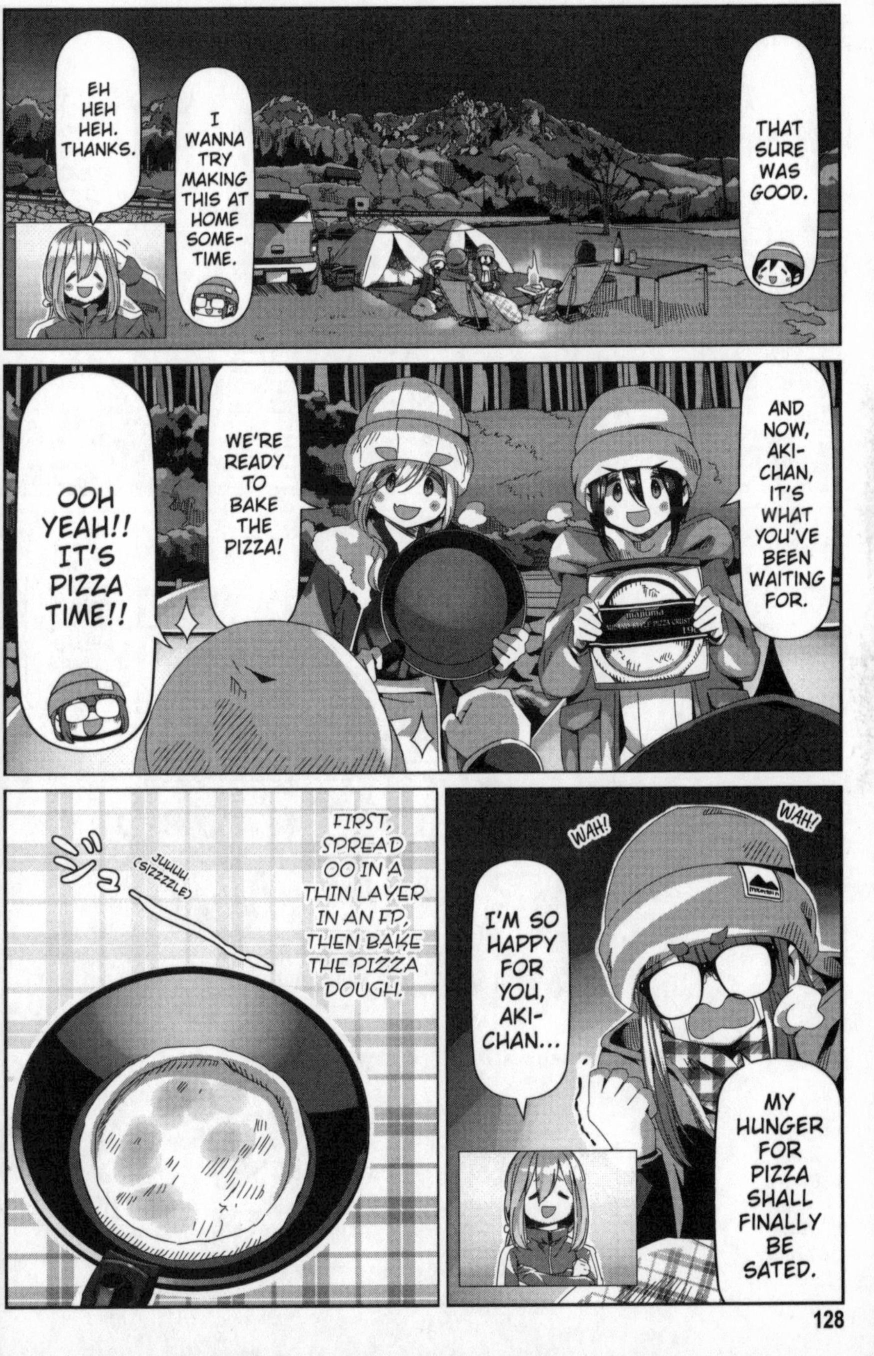
THAT SURE WAS GOOD.
I WANNA TRY MAKING THIS AT HOME SOMETIME.
EH HEH HEH. THANKS.
AND NOW, AKI-CHAN, IT'S WHAT YOU'VE BEEN WAITING FOR.
WE'RE READY TO BAKE THE PIZZA!
OOH YEAH!! IT'S PIZZA TIME!!
WAH!
WAH!
MY HUNGER FOR PIZZA SHALL FINALLY BE SATED.
I'M SO HAPPY FOR YOU, AKI-CHAN...
FIRST, SPREAD OO IN A THIN LAYER IN AN FP, THEN BAKE THE PIZZA DOUGH.
JUUUU (SIZZZZLE)

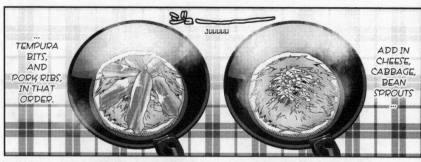

ADD IN CHEESE, CABBAGE, BEAN SPROUTS ...
JUUUUU
... TEMPURA BITS, AND PORK RIBS, IN THAT ORDER.
THEN ADD IN WHEAT FLOUR, BLENDED WITH WATER, FROM ABOVE.
JUJUUUUU
IN A SEPARATE FP, FRY UP YAKISOBA AND EGGS.
ONCE THE FLOUR HARDENS, PUT THE DOUGH ON TOP OF THE YAKISOBA AND PRESS DOWN WITH A SPATULA.
GYUUU (PRESSS)
THEN PUT ALL OF THAT ON THE EGG AND FLATTEN FURTHER.
GYUGYUUU

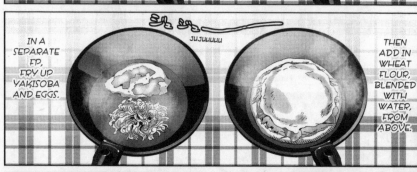

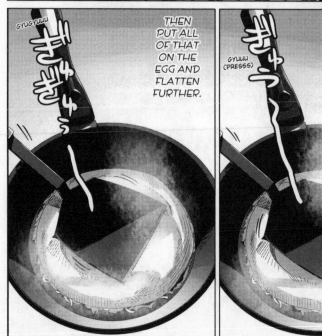

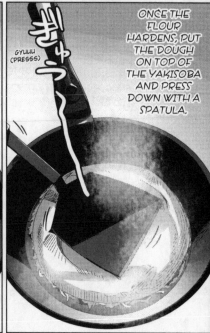

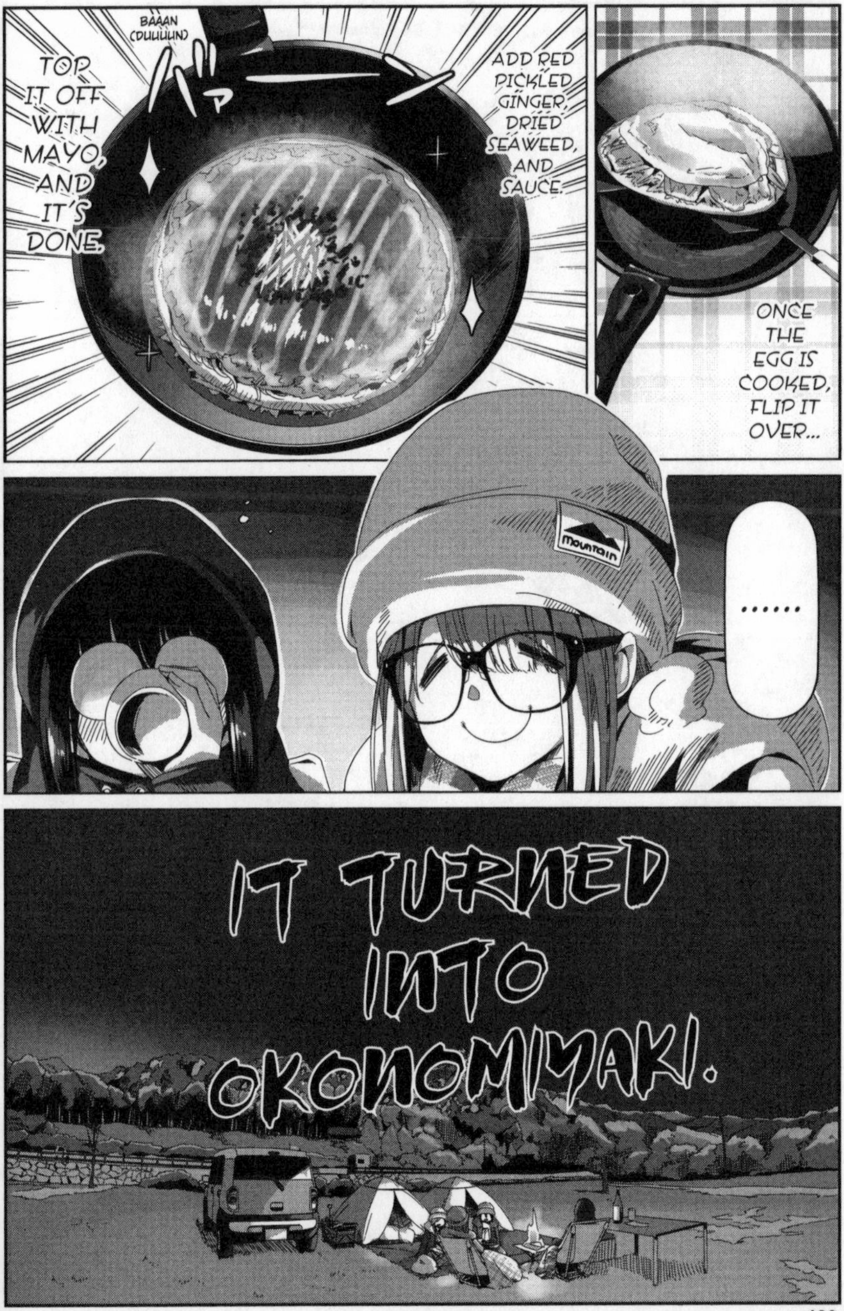
ONCE THE EGG IS COOKED, FLIP IT OVER...
ADD RED PICKLED GINGER, DRIED SEAWEED, AND SAUCE.
TOP IT OFF WITH MAYO, AND IT'S DONE.
BAAAN (DUUUUUN)
......
IT TURNED INTO OKONOMIYAKI.

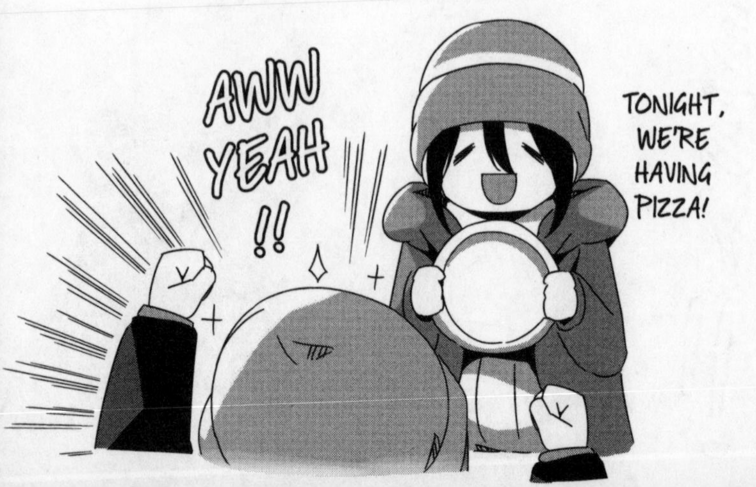
TONIGHT, WE'RE HAVING PIZZA!
AWW YEAH !!

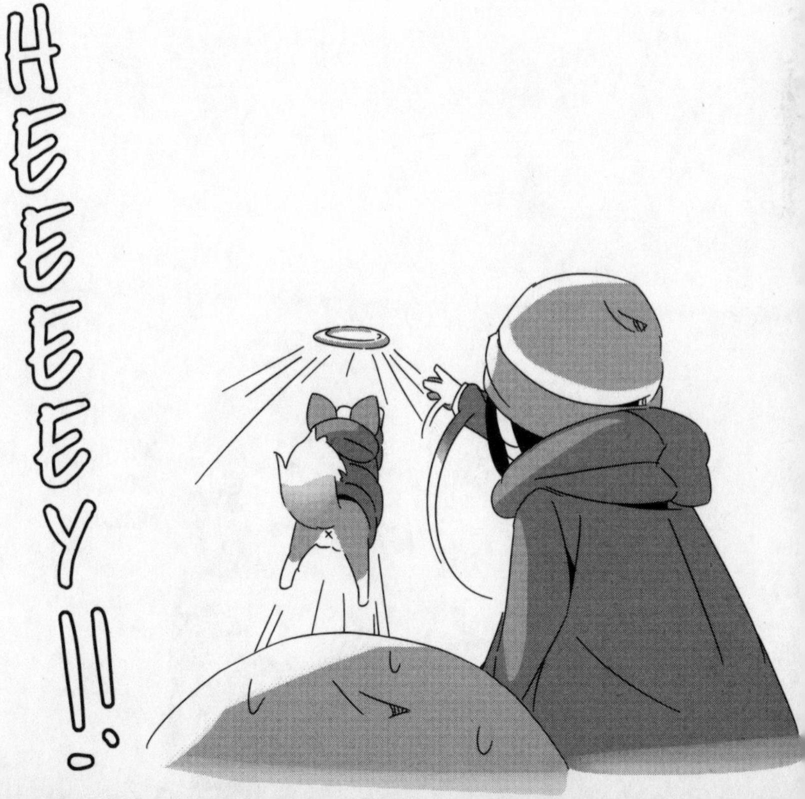
HEEEEY!!

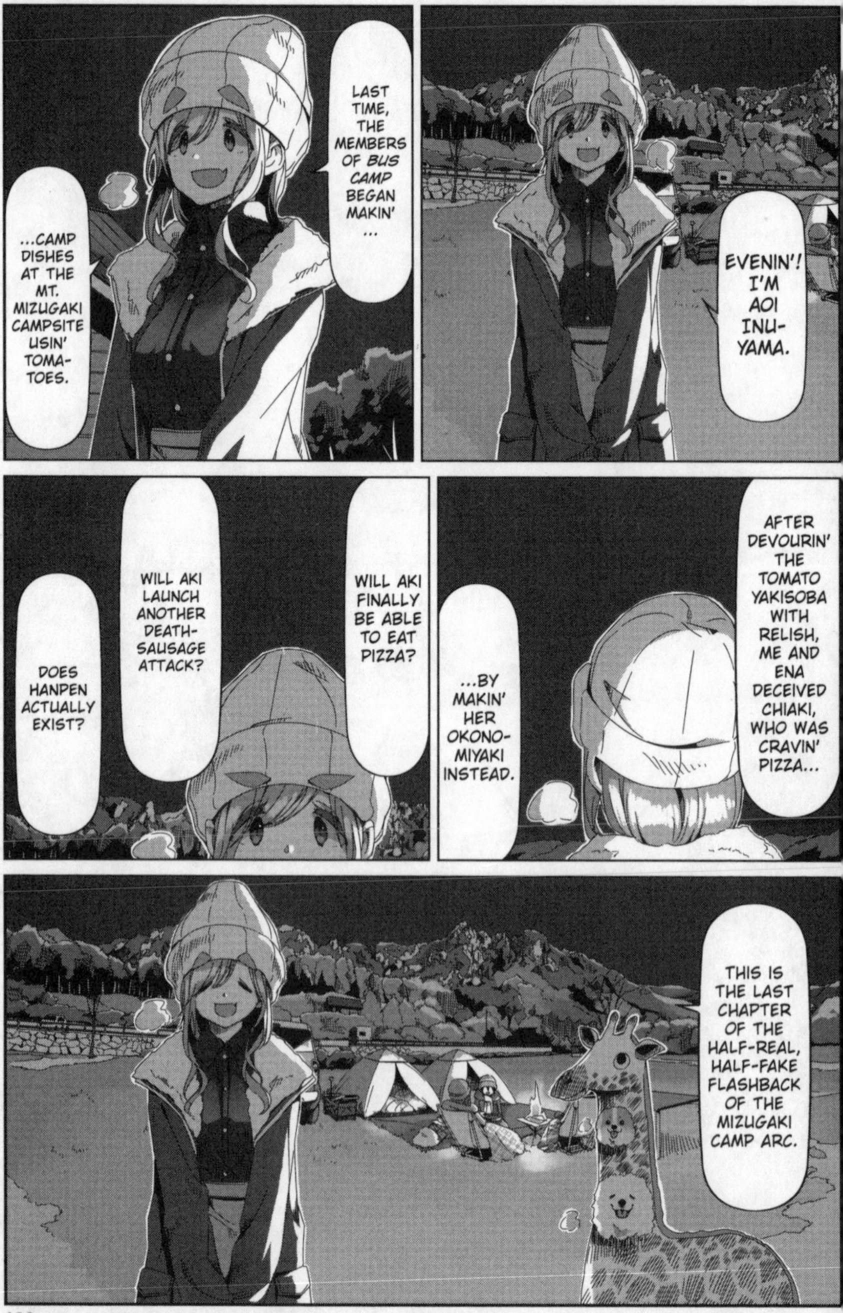
EVENIN'! I'M AOI INU-YAMA.
LAST TIME, THE MEMBERS OF BUS CAMP BEGAN MAKIN' ...
...CAMP DISHES AT THE MT. MIZUGAKI CAMPSITE USIN' TOMA-TOES.
AFTER DEVOURIN' THE TOMATO YAKISOBA WITH RELISH, ME AND ENA DECEIVED CHIAKI, WHO WAS CRAVIN' PIZZA...
...BY MAKIN' HER OKONO-MIYAKI INSTEAD.
WILL AKI FINALLY BE ABLE TO EAT PIZZA?
WILL AKI LAUNCH ANOTHER DEATH-SAUSAGE ATTACK?
DOES HANPEN ACTUALLY EXIST?
THIS IS THE LAST CHAPTER OF THE HALF-REAL, HALF-FAKE FLASHBACK OF THE MIZUGAKI CAMP ARC.

CHAPTER 64 SPRINGTIME MIZUGAKI WINTER CAMP

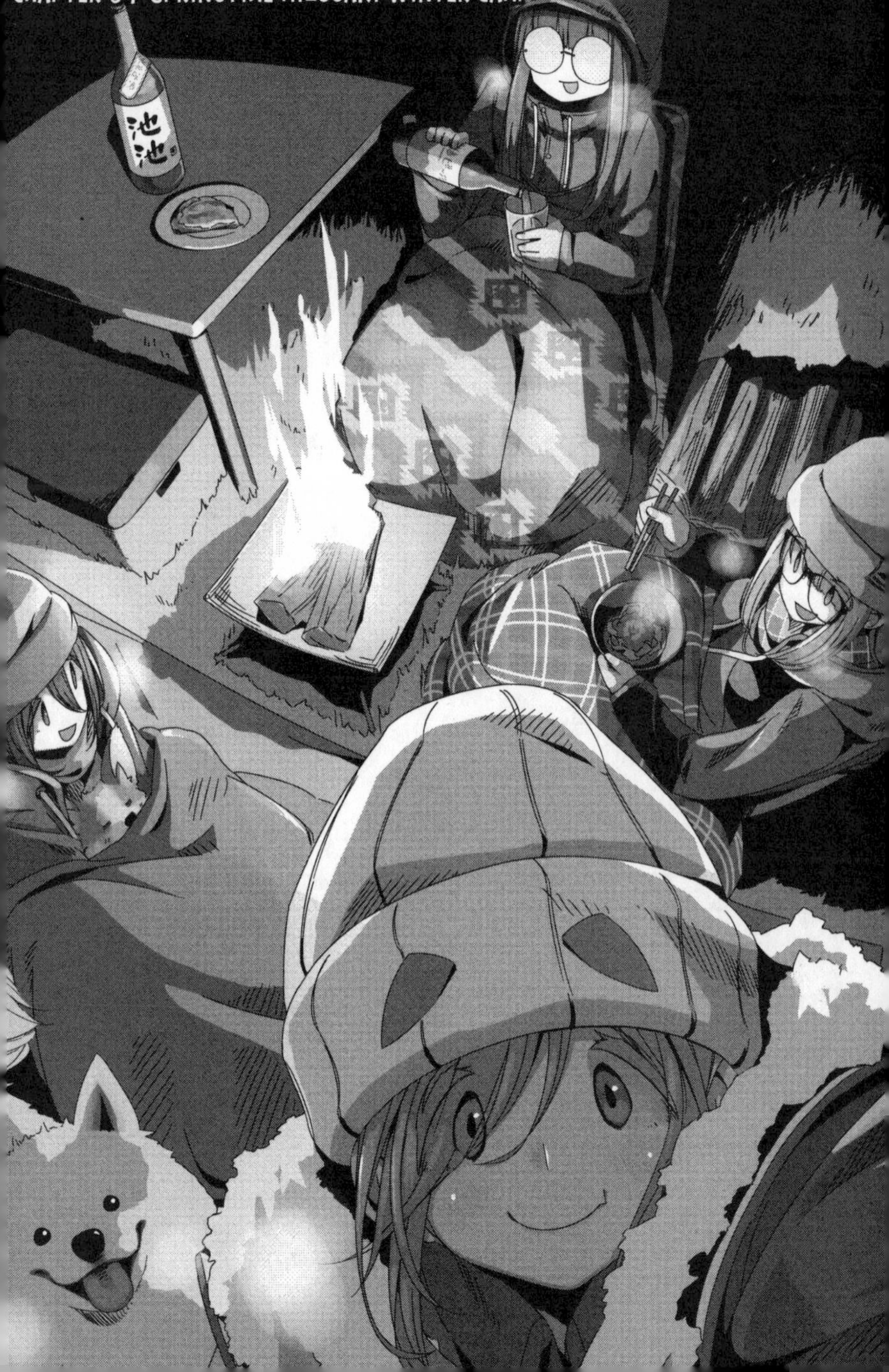
池池

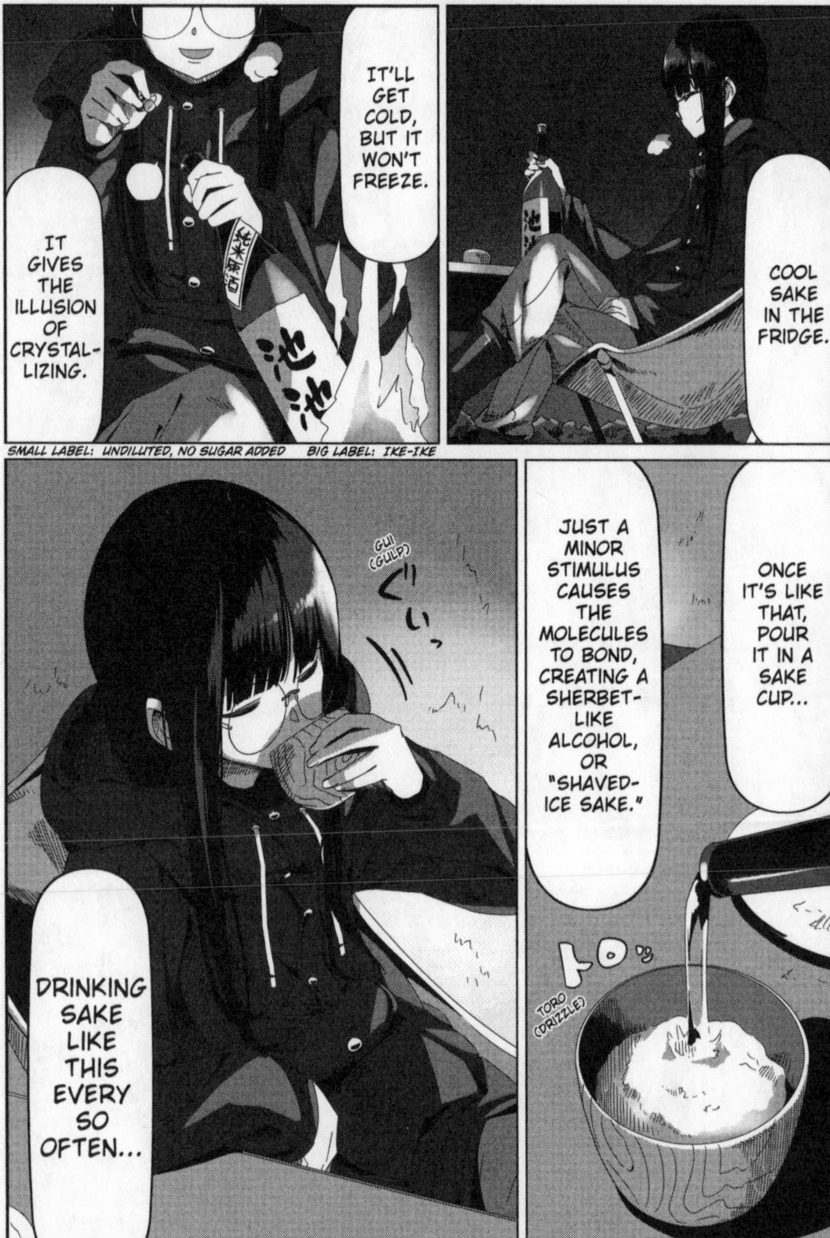

COOL SAKE IN THE FRIDGE.
IT'LL GET COLD, BUT IT WON'T FREEZE.
IT GIVES THE ILLUSION OF CRYSTAL-LIZING.
SMALL LABEL: UNDILUTED, NO SUGAR ADDED BIG LABEL: IKE-IKE
ONCE IT'S LIKE THAT, POUR IT IN A SAKE CUP...
JUST A MINOR STIMULUS CAUSES THE MOLECULES TO BOND, CREATING A SHERBET-LIKE ALCOHOL, OR "SHAVED-ICE SAKE."
TORO (DRIZZLE)
GUI (GULP)
DRINKING SAKE LIKE THIS EVERY SO OFTEN...

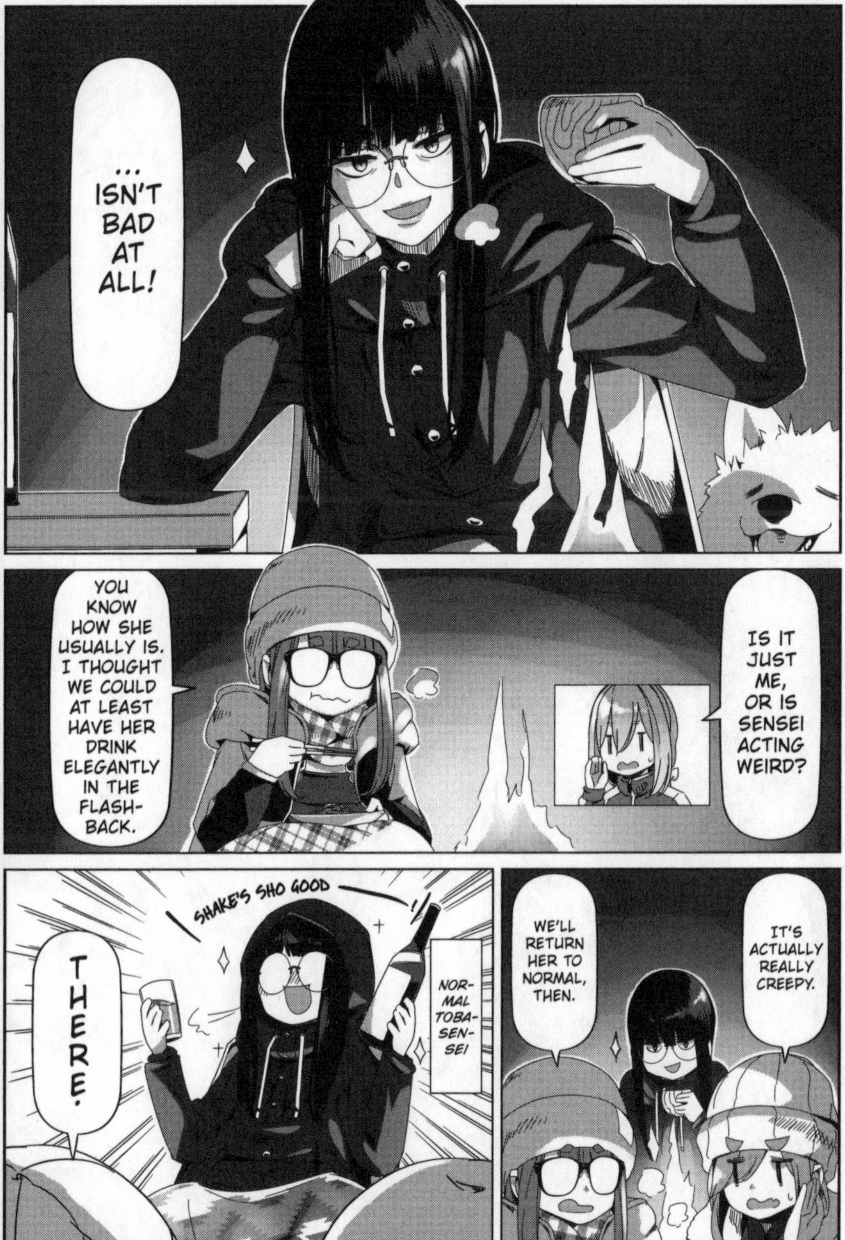
... ISN'T BAD AT ALL!
IS IT JUST ME, OR IS SENSEI ACTING WEIRD?
YOU KNOW HOW SHE USUALLY IS. I THOUGHT WE COULD AT LEAST HAVE HER DRINK ELEGANTLY IN THE FLASH-BACK.
IT'S ACTUALLY REALLY CREEPY.
WE'LL RETURN HER TO NORMAL, THEN.
SHAKE'S SHO GOOD
NOR-MAL TOBA-SEN-SEI
THERE.

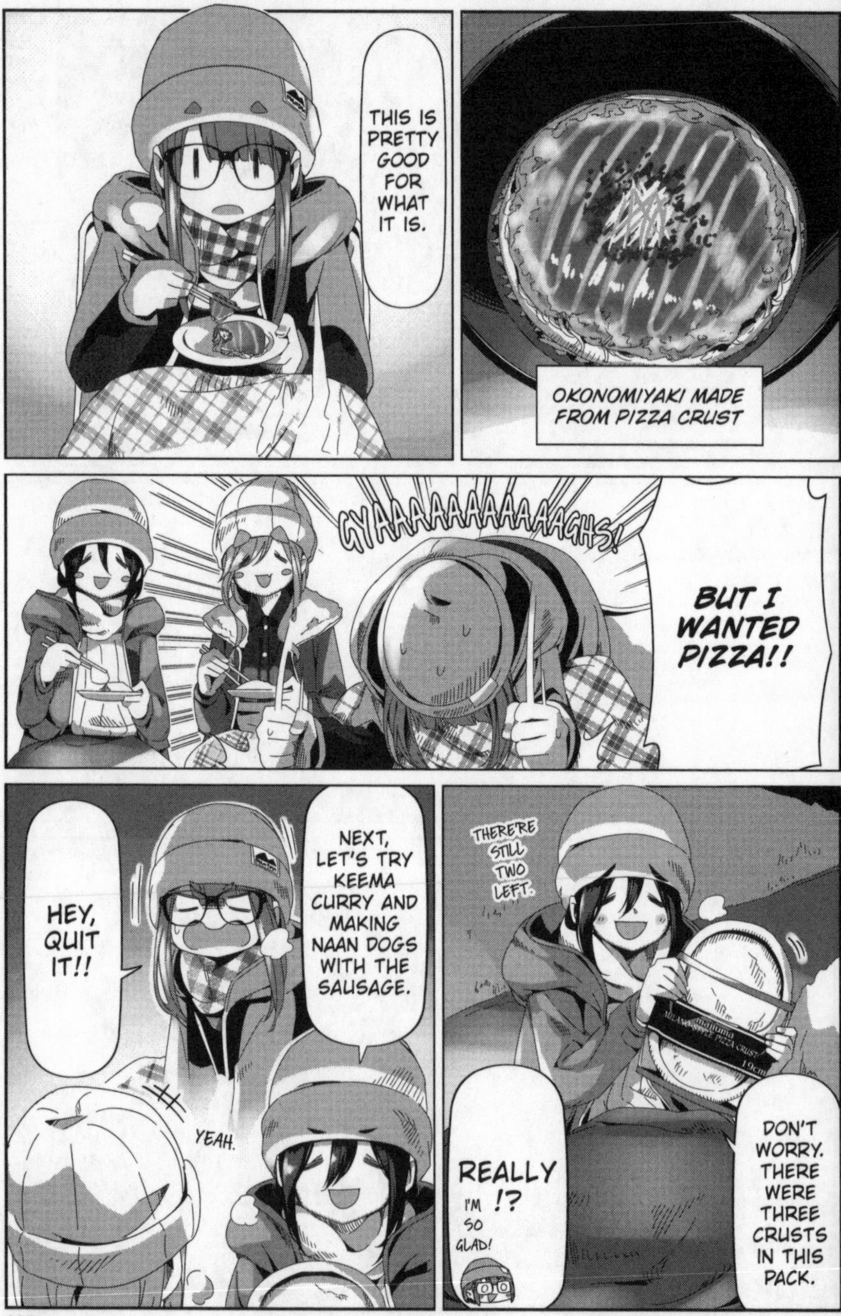
OKONOMIYAKI MADE FROM PIZZA CRUST
THIS IS PRETTY GOOD FOR WHAT IT IS.
BUT I WANTED PIZZA!!
GYAAAAAAAAAAAGHS!
DON'T WORRY. THERE WERE THREE CRUSTS IN THIS PACK.
THERE'RE STILL TWO LEFT.
REALLY !?
I'M SO GLAD!
NEXT, LET'S TRY KEEMA CURRY AND MAKING NAAN DOGS WITH THE SAUSAGE.
HEY, QUIT IT!!
YEAH.

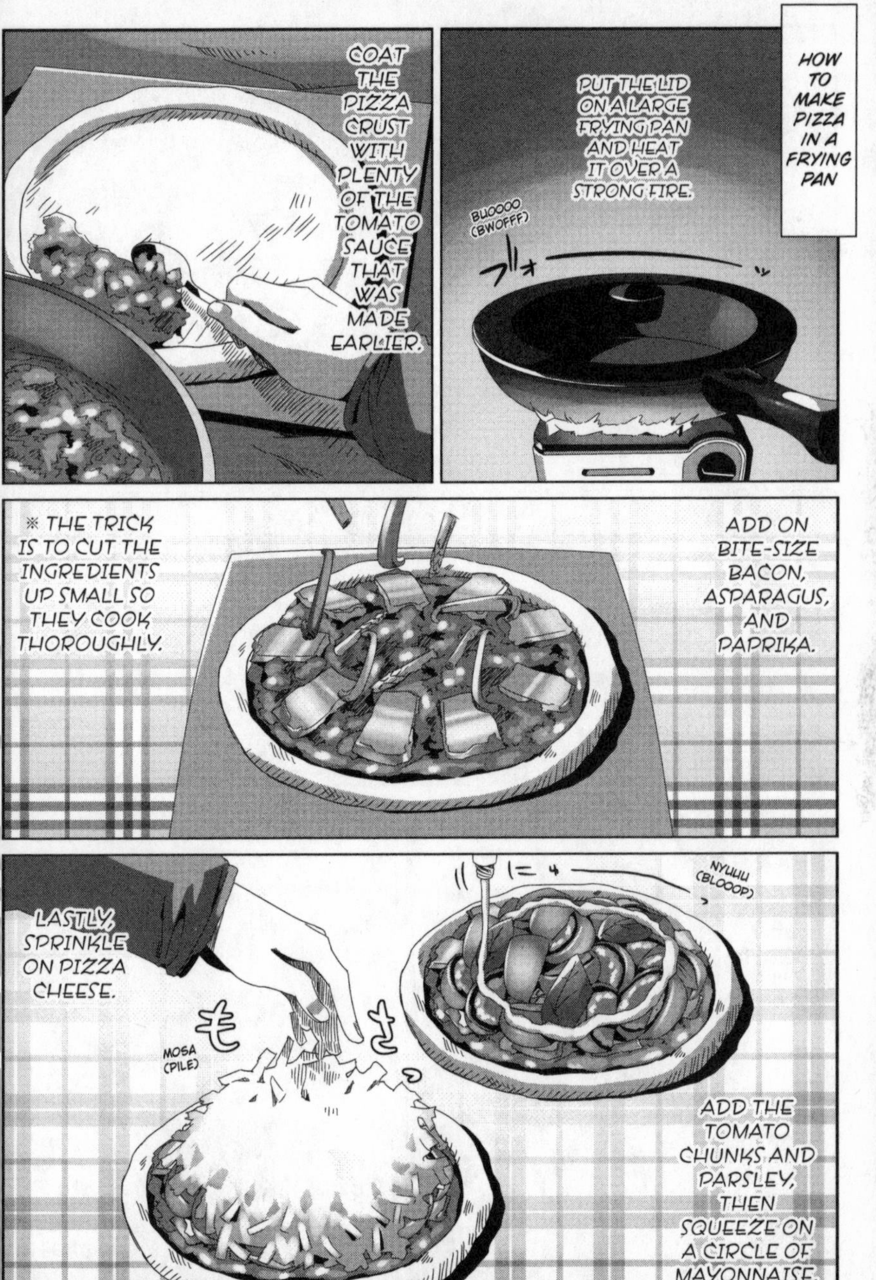
HOW TO MAKE PIZZA IN A FRYING PAN
PUT THE LID ON A LARGE FRYING PAN AND HEAT IT OVER A STRONG FIRE.
BUOOOO (BWOFFF)
COAT THE PIZZA CRUST WITH PLENTY OF THE TOMATO SAUCE THAT WAS MADE EARLIER.
ADD ON BITE-SIZE BACON, ASPARAGUS, AND PAPRIKA.
※ THE TRICK IS TO CUT THE INGREDIENTS UP SMALL SO THEY COOK THOROUGHLY.
NYUUU (BLOOOP)
ADD THE TOMATO CHUNKS AND PARSLEY, THEN SQUEEZE ON A CIRCLE OF MAYONNAISE.
LASTLY, SPRINKLE ON PIZZA CHEESE.
MOSA (PILE)

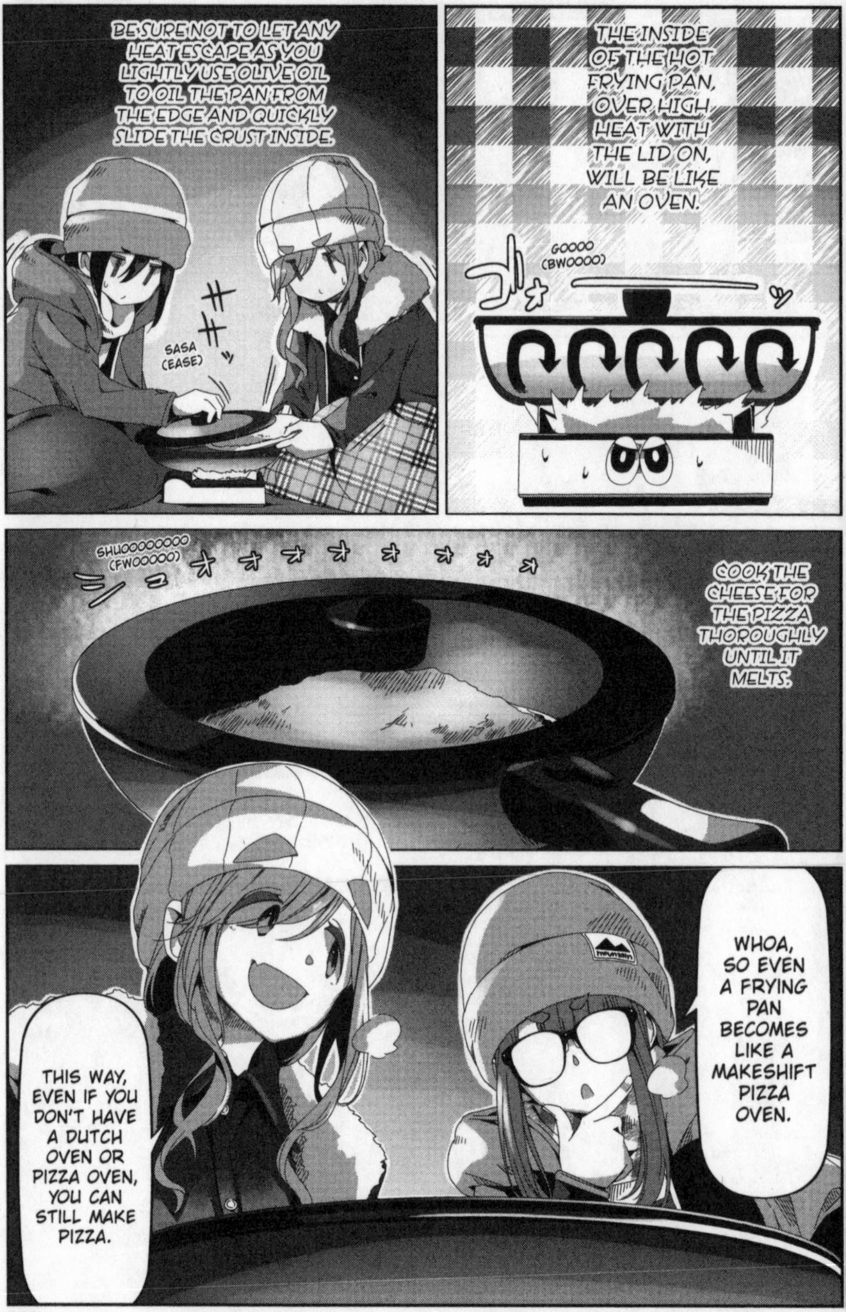
THE INSIDE OF THE HOT FRYING PAN, OVER HIGH HEAT WITH THE LID ON, WILL BE LIKE AN OVEN.
GOOOO (BWOOOO)
BE SURE NOT TO LET ANY HEAT ESCAPE AS YOU LIGHTLY USE OLIVE OIL TO OIL THE PAN FROM THE EDGE AND QUICKLY SLIDE THE CRUST INSIDE.
SASA (EASE)
COOK THE CHEESE FOR THE PIZZA THOROUGHLY UNTIL IT MELTS.
SHUOOOOOOOO (FWOOOOO)
WHOA, SO EVEN A FRYING PAN BECOMES LIKE A MAKESHIFT PIZZA OVEN.
THIS WAY, EVEN IF YOU DON'T HAVE A DUTCH OVEN OR PIZZA OVEN, YOU CAN STILL MAKE PIZZA.

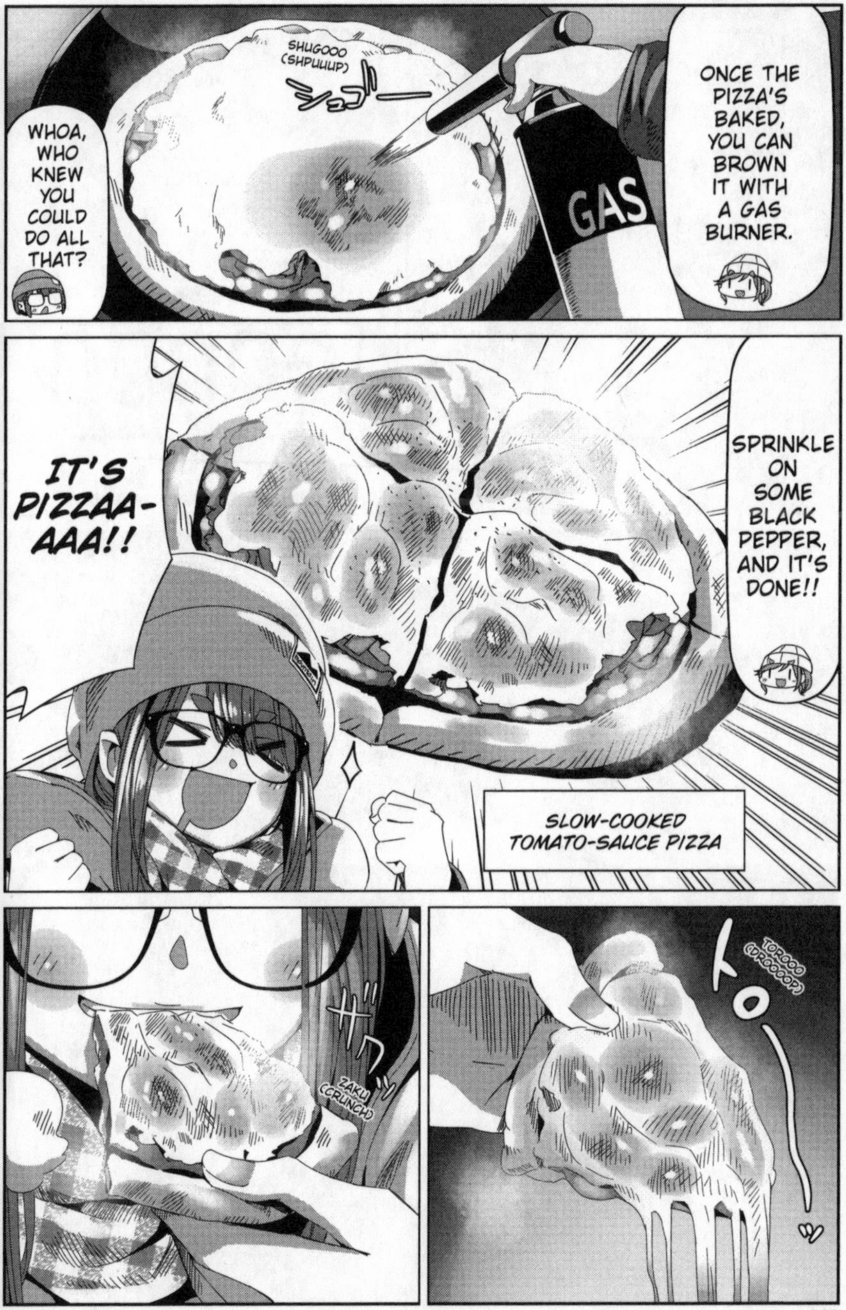
ONCE THE PIZZA'S BAKED, YOU CAN BROWN IT WITH A GAS BURNER.
SHUGOOO (SHPUUUP)
GAS
WHOA, WHO KNEW YOU COULD DO ALL THAT?
SPRINKLE ON SOME BLACK PEPPER, AND IT'S DONE!!
IT'S PIZZAA-AAA!!
SLOW-COOKED TOMATO-SAUCE PIZZA
TOROOO (DROOOOP)
ZAKU (CRUNCH)

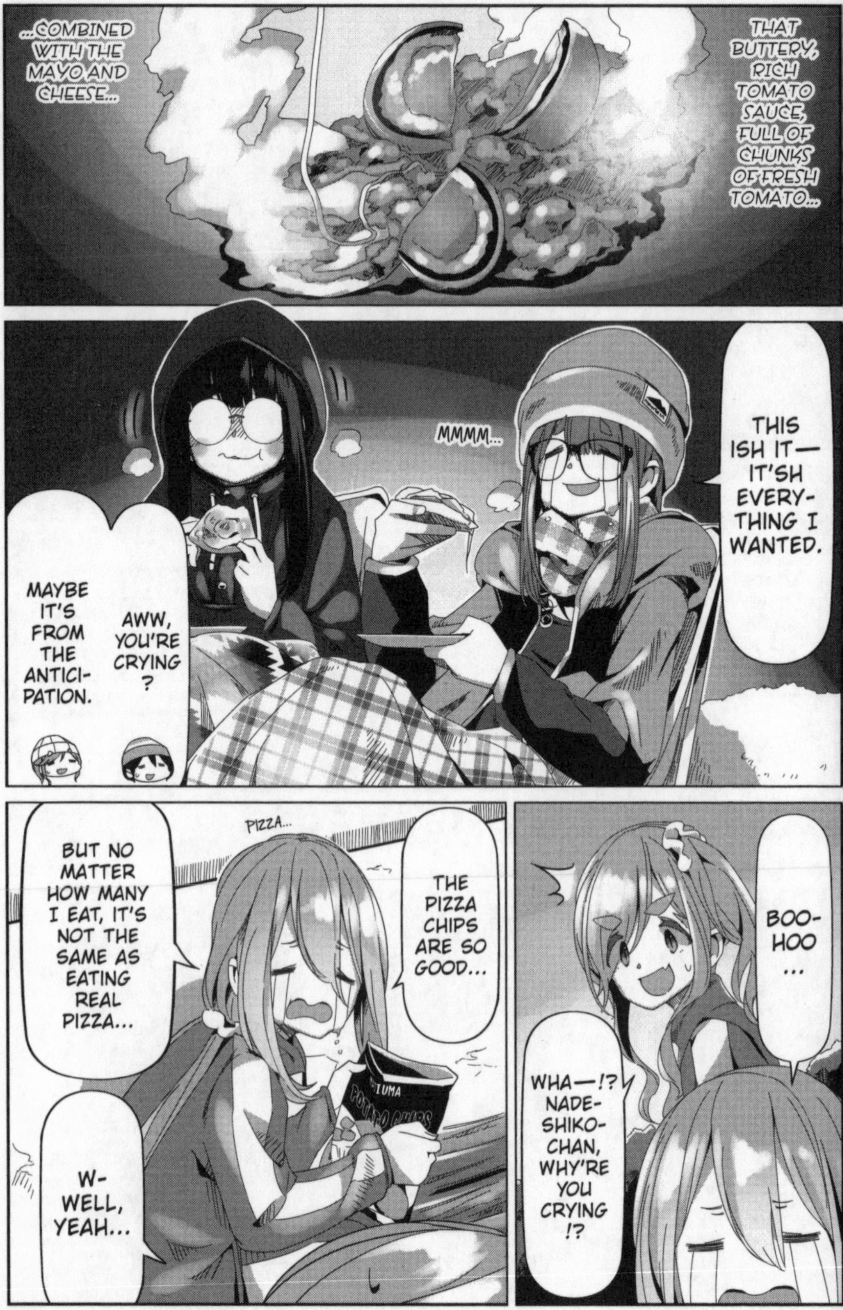
THAT BUTTERY, RICH TOMATO SAUCE, FULL OF CHUNKS OF FRESH TOMATO...
...COMBINED WITH THE MAYO AND CHEESE...
THIS ISH IT—IT'SH EVERYTHING I WANTED.
MMMM...
AWW, YOU'RE CRYING?
MAYBE IT'S FROM THE ANTICIPATION.
BOO-HOO...
WHA—!? NADESHIKO-CHAN, WHY'RE YOU CRYING!?
PIZZA...
THE PIZZA CHIPS ARE SO GOOD...
BUT NO MATTER HOW MANY I EAT, IT'S NOT THE SAME AS EATING REAL PIZZA...
W-WELL, YEAH...

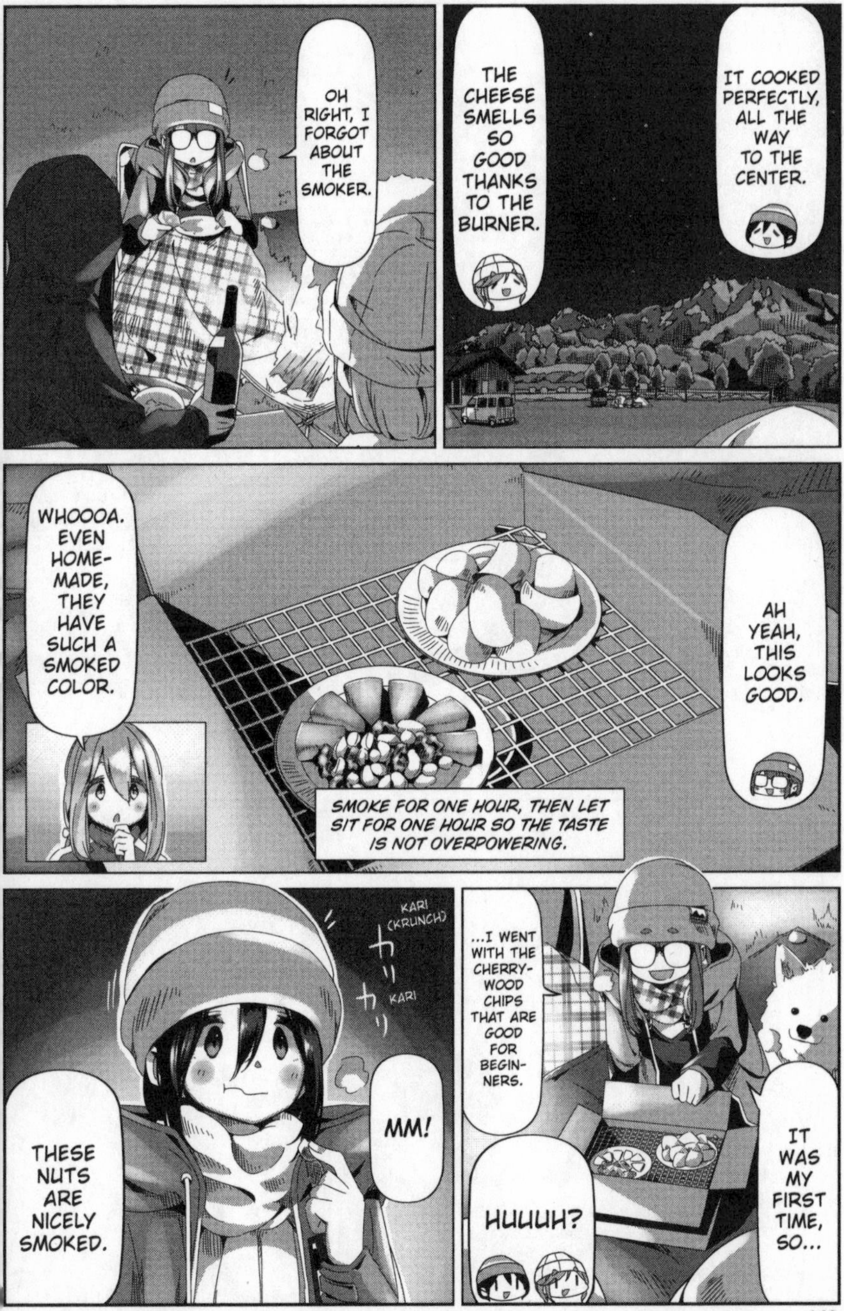
IT COOKED PERFECTLY, ALL THE WAY TO THE CENTER.
THE CHEESE SMELLS SO GOOD THANKS TO THE BURNER.
OH RIGHT, I FORGOT ABOUT THE SMOKER.
AH YEAH, THIS LOOKS GOOD.
WHOOOA. EVEN HOME-MADE, THEY HAVE SUCH A SMOKED COLOR.
SMOKE FOR ONE HOUR, THEN LET SIT FOR ONE HOUR SO THE TASTE IS NOT OVERPOWERING.
IT WAS MY FIRST TIME, SO...
...I WENT WITH THE CHERRY-WOOD CHIPS THAT ARE GOOD FOR BEGIN-NERS.
HUUUH?
KARI (KRUNCH)
KARI
MM!
THESE NUTS ARE NICELY SMOKED.

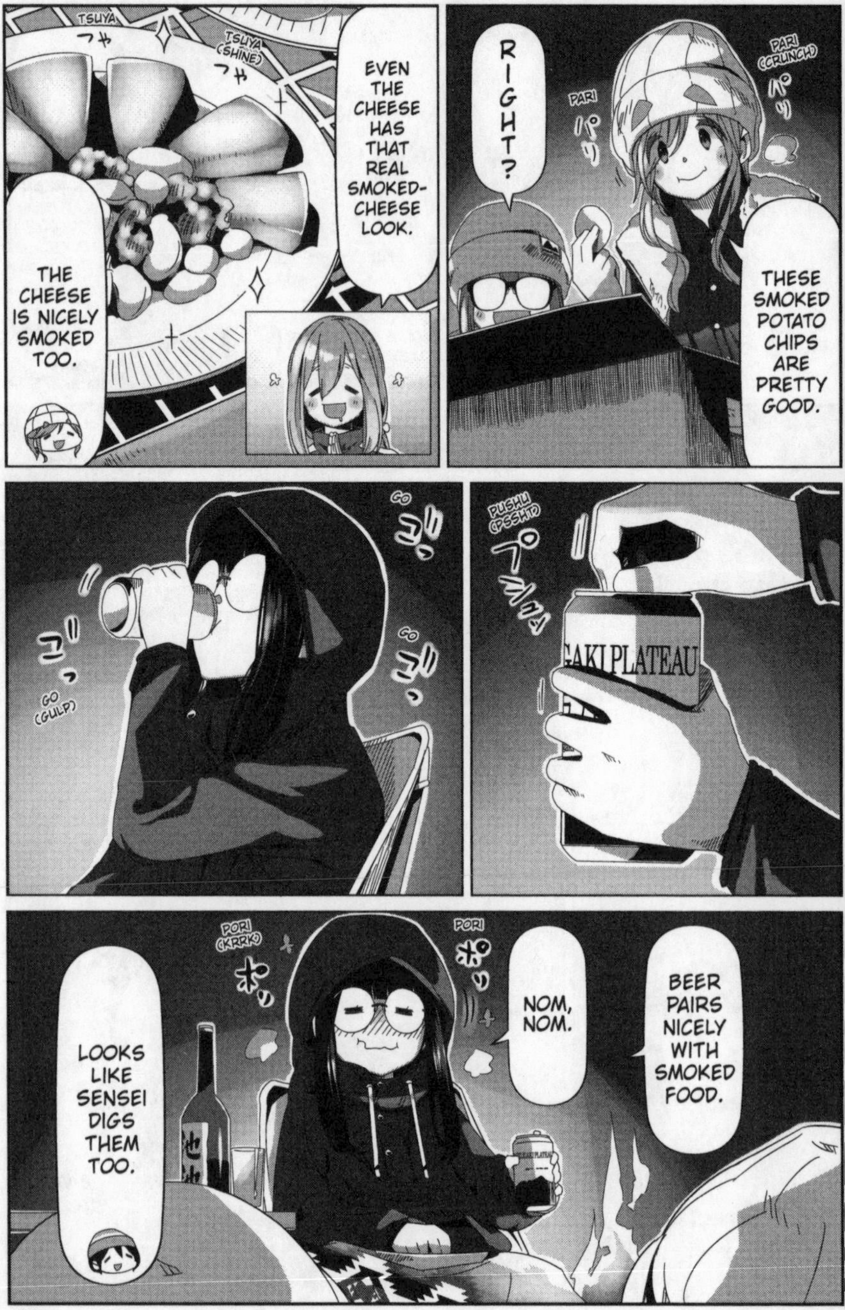
PARI (CRUNCH)
PARI
THESE SMOKED POTATO CHIPS ARE PRETTY GOOD.
RIGHT?
TSUYA
TSUYA (SHINE)
EVEN THE CHEESE HAS THAT REAL SMOKED-CHEESE LOOK.
THE CHEESE IS NICELY SMOKED TOO.
PUSHU (PSSHT)
AKI PLATEAU
GO
GO
GO (GULP)
PORI
BEER PAIRS NICELY WITH SMOKED FOOD.
NOM, NOM.
PORI (KRRK)
LOOKS LIKE SENSEI DIGS THEM TOO.

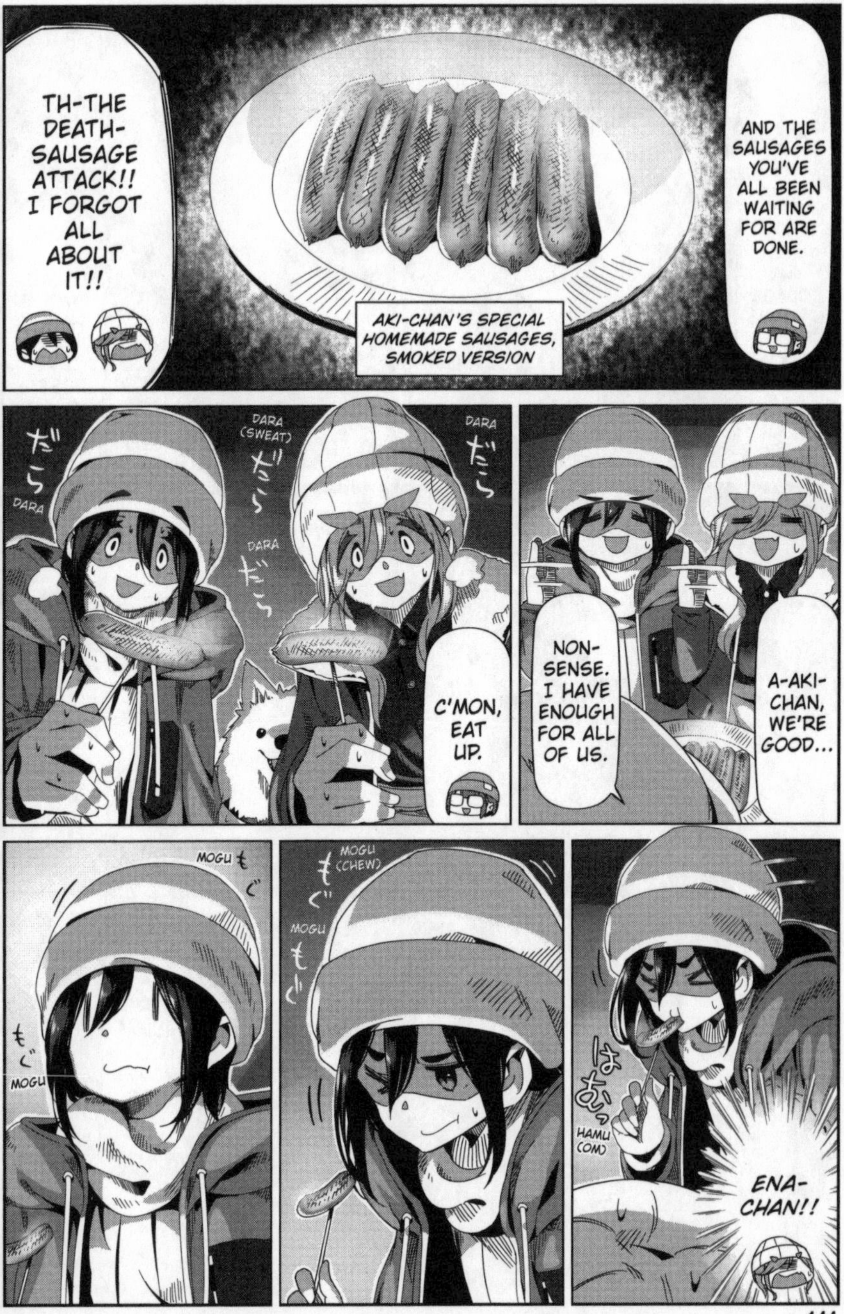
AND THE SAUSAGES YOU'VE ALL BEEN WAITING FOR ARE DONE.
AKI-CHAN'S SPECIAL HOMEMADE SAUSAGES, SMOKED VERSION
TH-THE DEATH-SAUSAGE ATTACK!! I FORGOT ALL ABOUT IT!!
A-AKI-CHAN, WE'RE GOOD...
NON-SENSE. I HAVE ENOUGH FOR ALL OF US.
DARA だら
DARA (SWEAT) だら
DARA だら
C'MON, EAT UP.
DARA だら
HAMU (OM) はむっ
ENA-CHAN!!
MOGU (CHEW) もぐ
MOGU もぐ
MOGU もぐ
MOGU もぐ

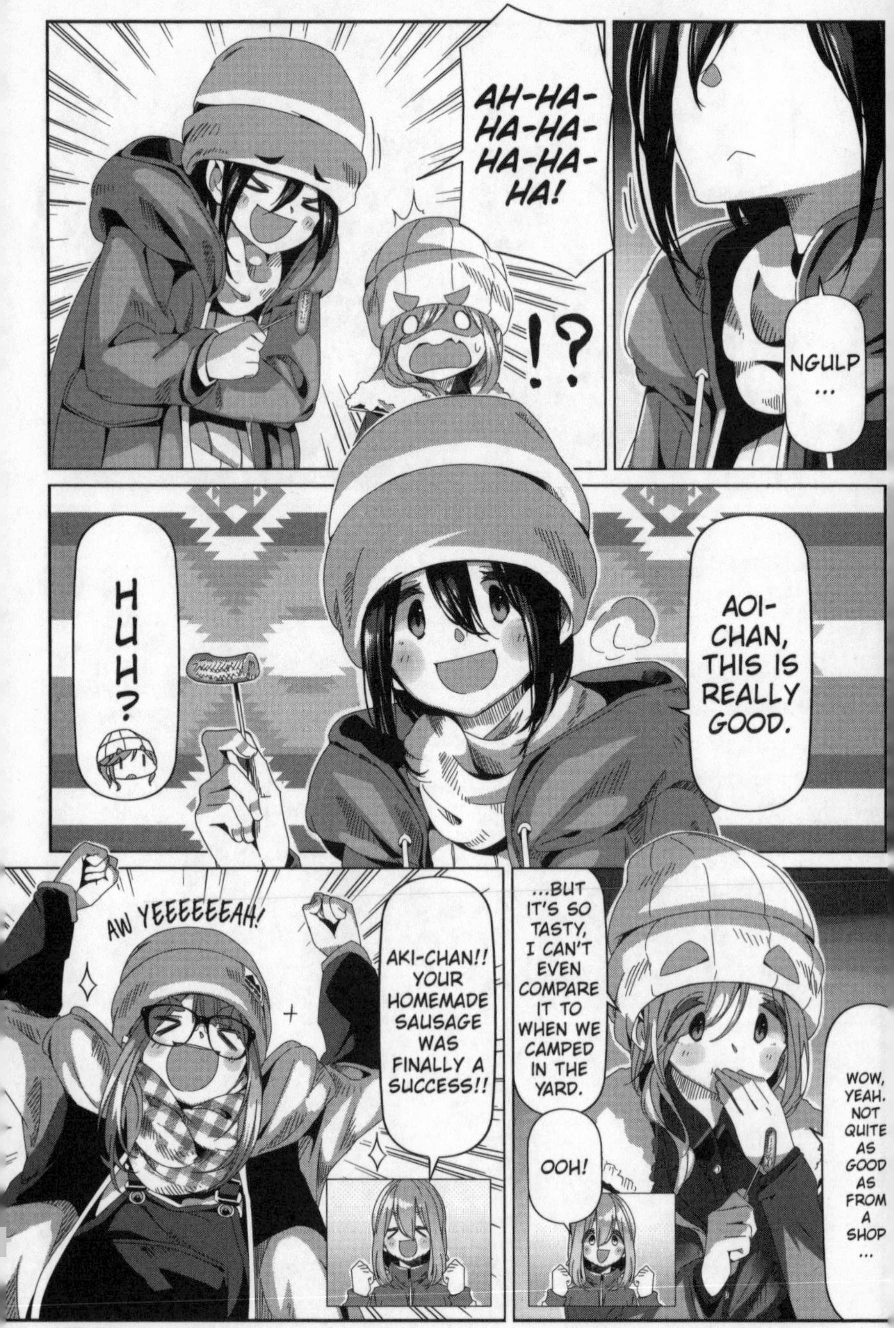
NGULP ...
AH-HA-HA-HA-HA-HA-HA!
!?
AOI-CHAN, THIS IS REALLY GOOD.
HUH?
WOW, YEAH. NOT QUITE AS GOOD AS FROM A SHOP ...
...BUT IT'S SO TASTY, I CAN'T EVEN COMPARE IT TO WHEN WE CAMPED IN THE YARD.
OOH!
AKI-CHAN!! YOUR HOMEMADE SAUSAGE WAS FINALLY A SUCCESS!!
AW YEEEEEEAH!

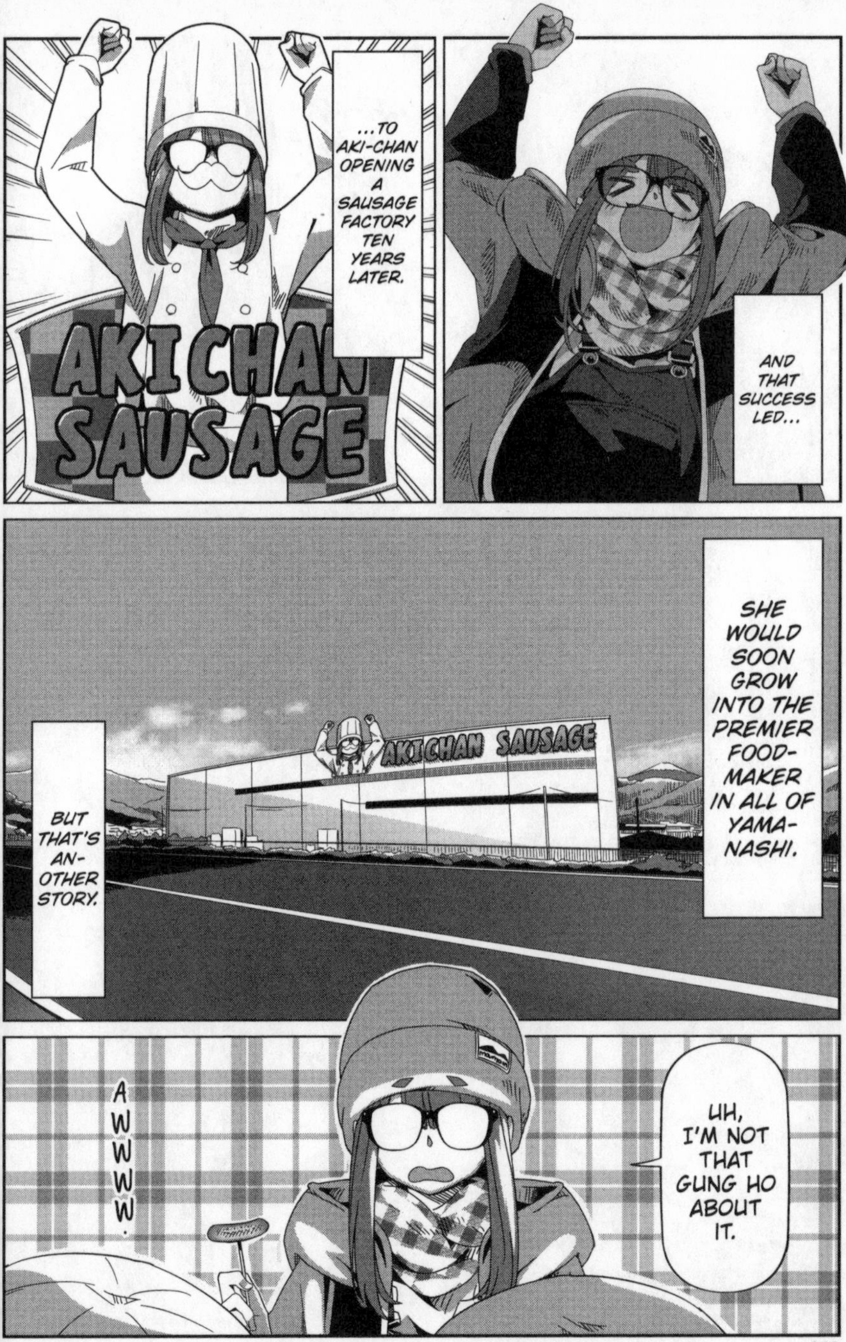
AND THAT SUCCESS LED...
...TO AKI-CHAN OPENING A SAUSAGE FACTORY TEN YEARS LATER.
AKICHAN SAUSAGE
SHE WOULD SOON GROW INTO THE PREMIER FOOD-MAKER IN ALL OF YAMA-NASHI.
AKICHAN SAUSAGE
BUT THAT'S AN-OTHER STORY.
UH, I'M NOT THAT GUNG HO ABOUT IT.
AWWWWW.

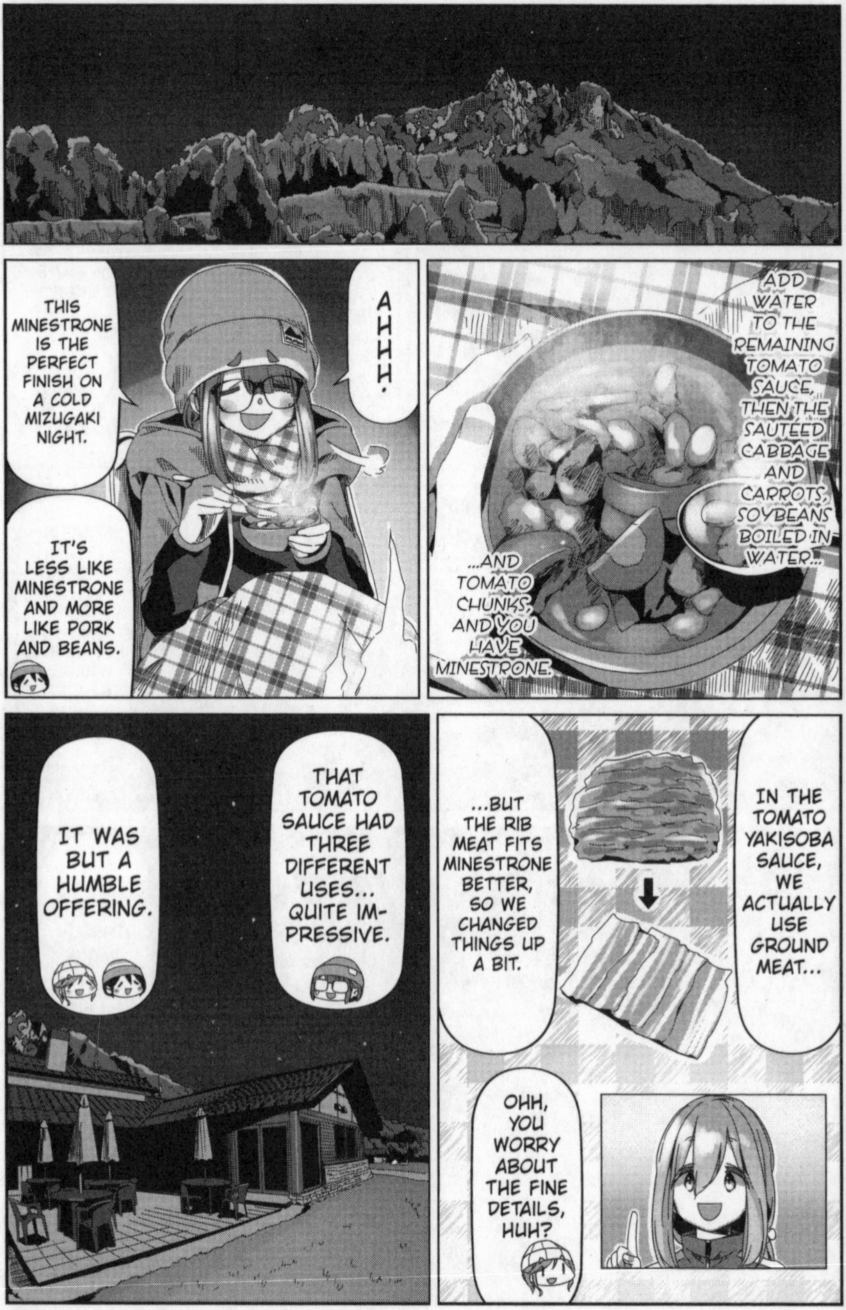
ADD WATER TO THE REMAINING TOMATO SAUCE, THEN THE SAUTÉED CABBAGE AND CARROTS, SOYBEANS BOILED IN WATER...
...AND TOMATO CHUNKS, AND YOU HAVE MINESTRONE.
AHHH.
THIS MINESTRONE IS THE PERFECT FINISH ON A COLD MIZUGAKI NIGHT.
IT'S LESS LIKE MINESTRONE AND MORE LIKE PORK AND BEANS.
IN THE TOMATO YAKISOBA SAUCE, WE ACTUALLY USE GROUND MEAT...
...BUT THE RIB MEAT FITS MINESTRONE BETTER, SO WE CHANGED THINGS UP A BIT.
OHH, YOU WORRY ABOUT THE FINE DETAILS, HUH?
THAT TOMATO SAUCE HAD THREE DIFFERENT USES... QUITE IMPRESSIVE.
IT WAS BUT A HUMBLE OFFERING.

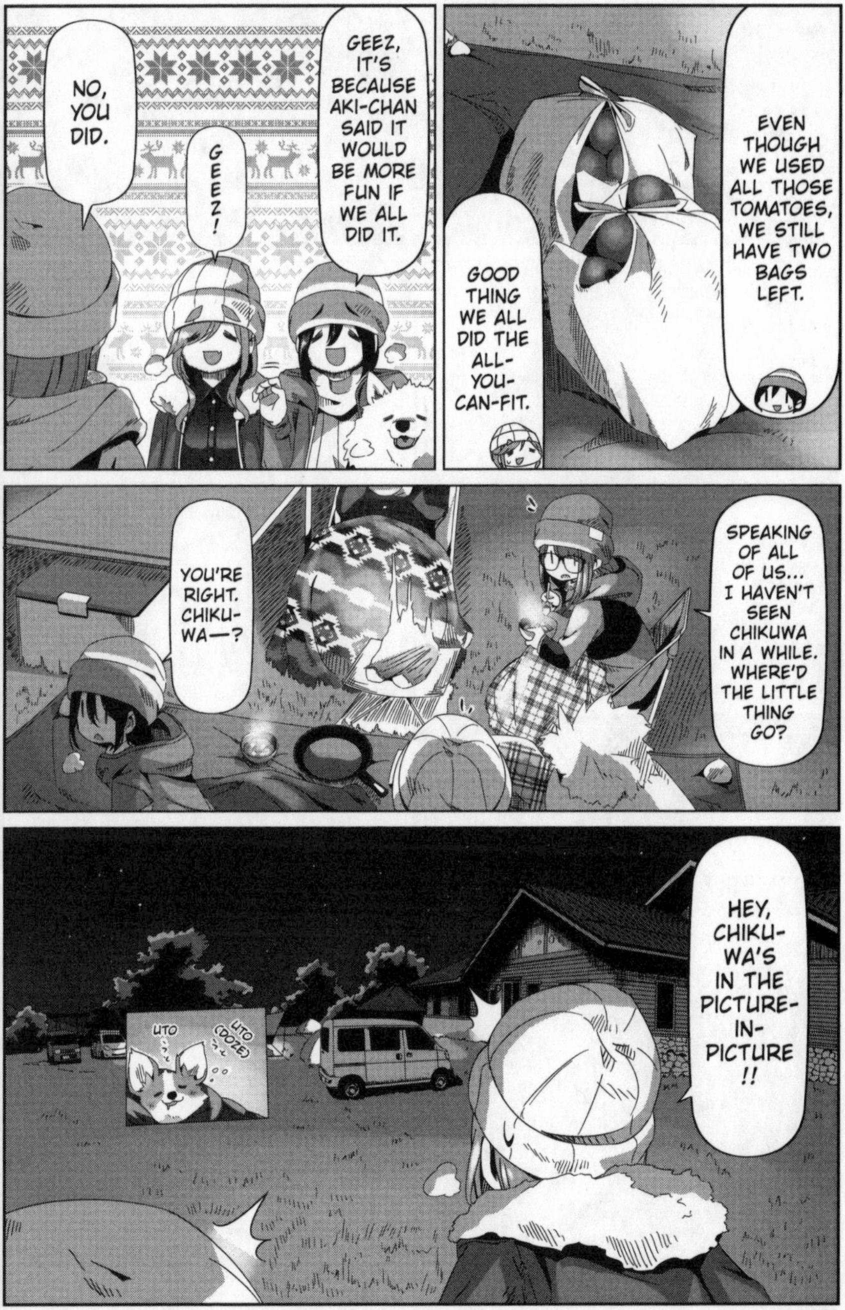
EVEN THOUGH WE USED ALL THOSE TOMATOES, WE STILL HAVE TWO BAGS LEFT.
GOOD THING WE ALL DID THE ALL-YOU-CAN-FIT.
GEEZ, IT'S BECAUSE AKI-CHAN SAID IT WOULD BE MORE FUN IF WE ALL DID IT.
GEEZ!
NO, YOU DID.
SPEAKING OF ALL OF US... I HAVEN'T SEEN CHIKUWA IN A WHILE. WHERE'D THE LITTLE THING GO?
YOU'RE RIGHT. CHIKUWA—?
HEY, CHIKUWA'S IN THE PICTURE-IN-PICTURE!!
UTO (DOZE)
UTO

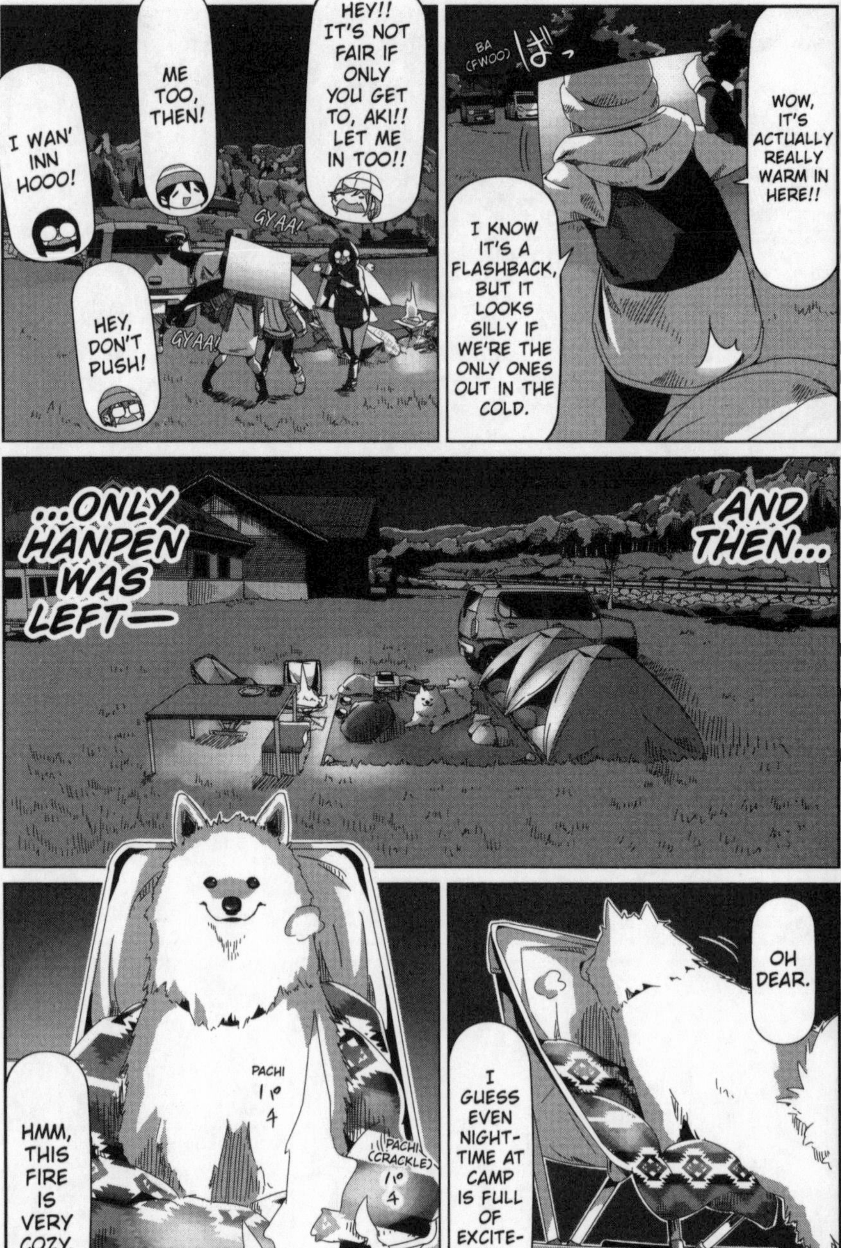
BA (FWOO)
ぱっ
WOW, IT'S ACTUALLY REALLY WARM IN HERE!!
I KNOW IT'S A FLASHBACK, BUT IT LOOKS SILLY IF WE'RE THE ONLY ONES OUT IN THE COLD.
HEY!! IT'S NOT FAIR IF ONLY YOU GET TO, AKI!! LET ME IN TOO!!
ME TOO, THEN!
I WAN' INN HOOO!
GYAA!
HEY, DON'T PUSH!
GYAA!
AND THEN...
...ONLY HANPEN WAS LEFT—
OH DEAR.
I GUESS EVEN NIGHT-TIME AT CAMP IS FULL OF EXCITE-MENT.
PACHI
PACHI (CRACKLE)
HMM, THIS FIRE IS VERY COZY.

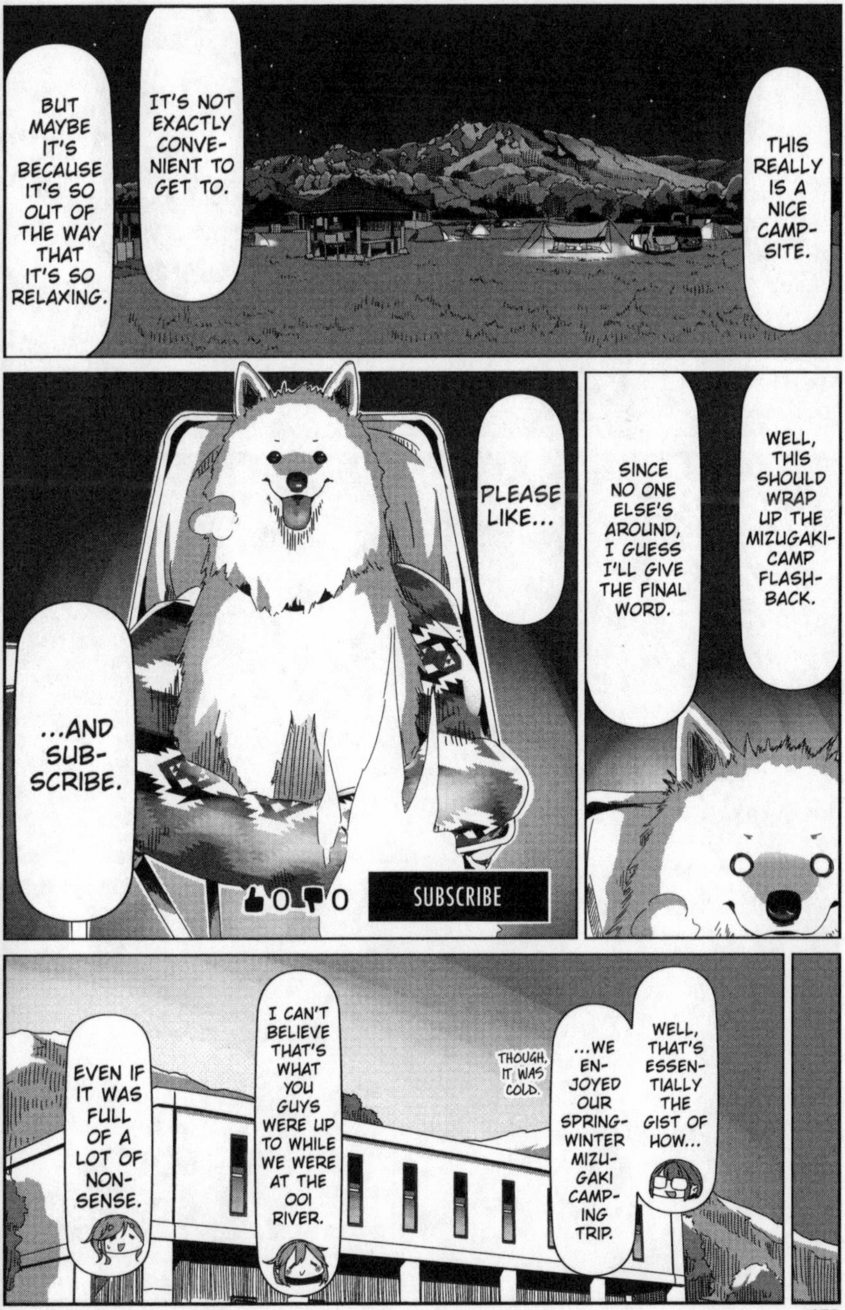
THIS REALLY IS A NICE CAMPSITE.
IT'S NOT EXACTLY CONVENIENT TO GET TO.
BUT MAYBE IT'S BECAUSE IT'S SO OUT OF THE WAY THAT IT'S SO RELAXING.
WELL, THIS SHOULD WRAP UP THE MIZUGAKI-CAMP FLASHBACK.
SINCE NO ONE ELSE'S AROUND, I GUESS I'LL GIVE THE FINAL WORD.
PLEASE LIKE...
...AND SUBSCRIBE.
0 0
SUBSCRIBE
WELL, THAT'S ESSENTIALLY THE GIST OF HOW...
...WE ENJOYED OUR SPRING-WINTER MIZUGAKI CAMPING TRIP.
THOUGH, IT WAS COLD.
I CAN'T BELIEVE THAT'S WHAT YOU GUYS WERE UP TO WHILE WE WERE AT THE OOI RIVER.
EVEN IF IT WAS FULL OF A LOT OF NONSENSE.

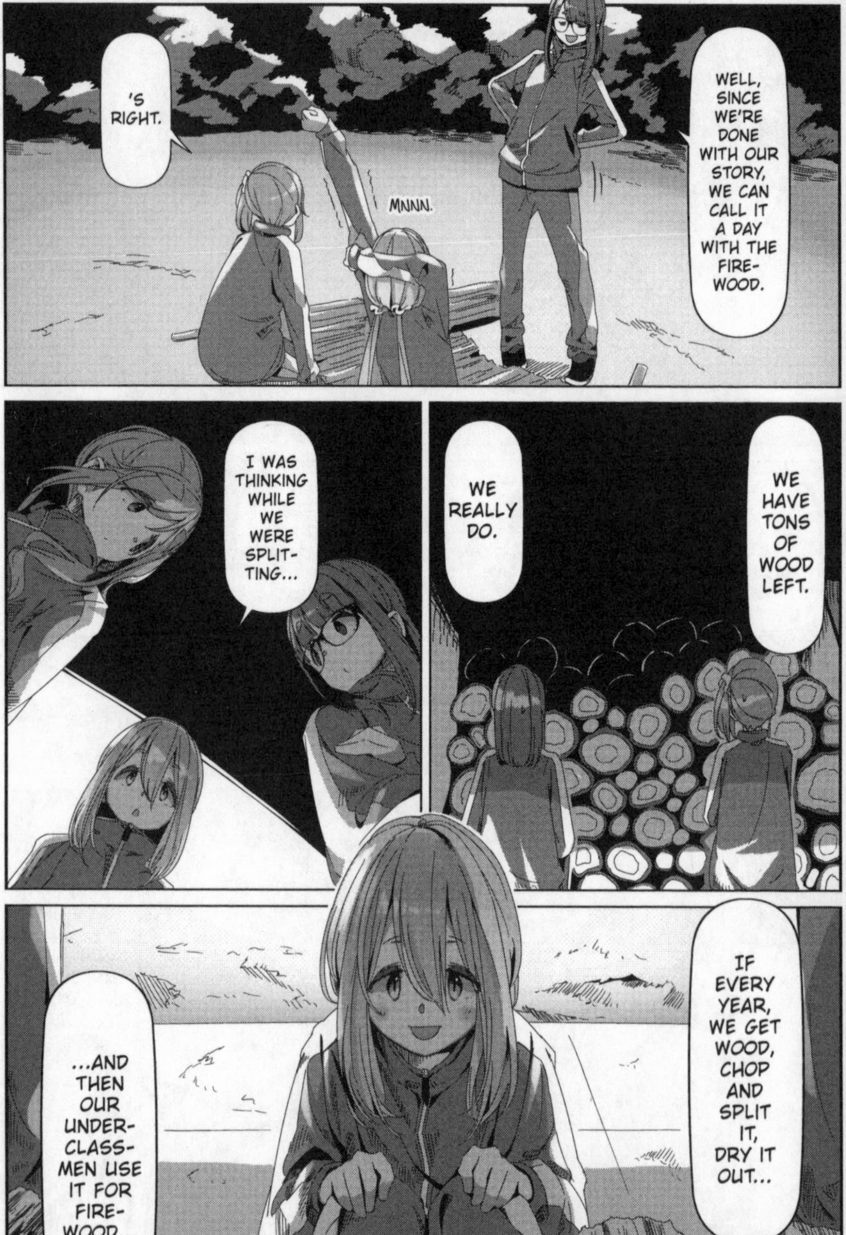
WELL, SINCE WE'RE DONE WITH OUR STORY, WE CAN CALL IT A DAY WITH THE FIRE-WOOD.
'S RIGHT.
MNNN.
WE HAVE TONS OF WOOD LEFT.
WE REALLY DO.
I WAS THINKING WHILE WE WERE SPLIT-TING...
IF EVERY YEAR, WE GET WOOD, CHOP AND SPLIT IT, DRY IT OUT...
...AND THEN OUR UNDER-CLASS-MEN USE IT FOR FIRE-WOOD...

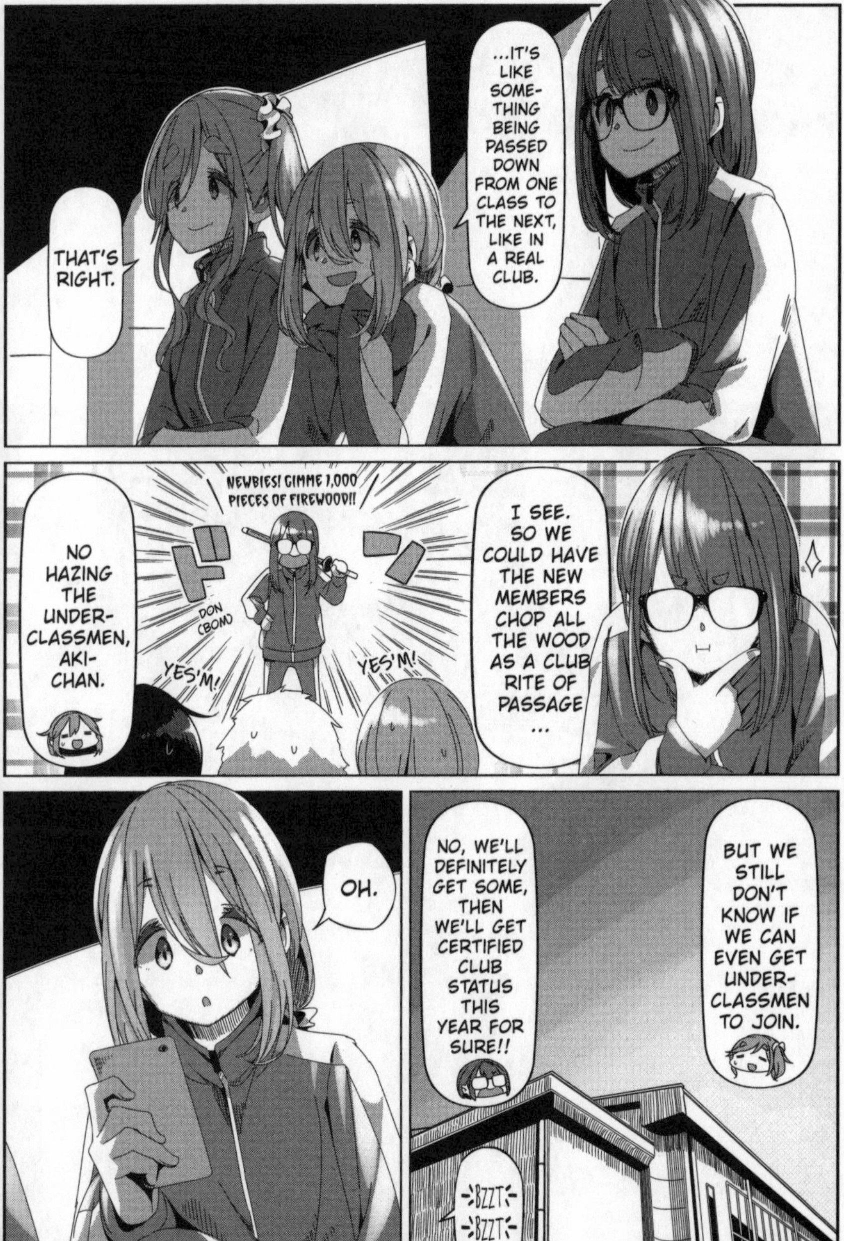
...IT'S LIKE SOMETHING BEING PASSED DOWN FROM ONE CLASS TO THE NEXT, LIKE IN A REAL CLUB.
THAT'S RIGHT.
I SEE. SO WE COULD HAVE THE NEW MEMBERS CHOP ALL THE WOOD AS A CLUB RITE OF PASSAGE...
NEWBIES! GIMME 1,000 PIECES OF FIREWOOD!!
DON (BOM)
YES'M!
YES'M!
NO HAZING THE UNDERCLASSMEN, AKI-CHAN.
BUT WE STILL DON'T KNOW IF WE CAN EVEN GET UNDERCLASSMEN TO JOIN.
NO, WE'LL DEFINITELY GET SOME, THEN WE'LL GET CERTIFIED CLUB STATUS THIS YEAR FOR SURE!!
BZZT
BZZT
OH.

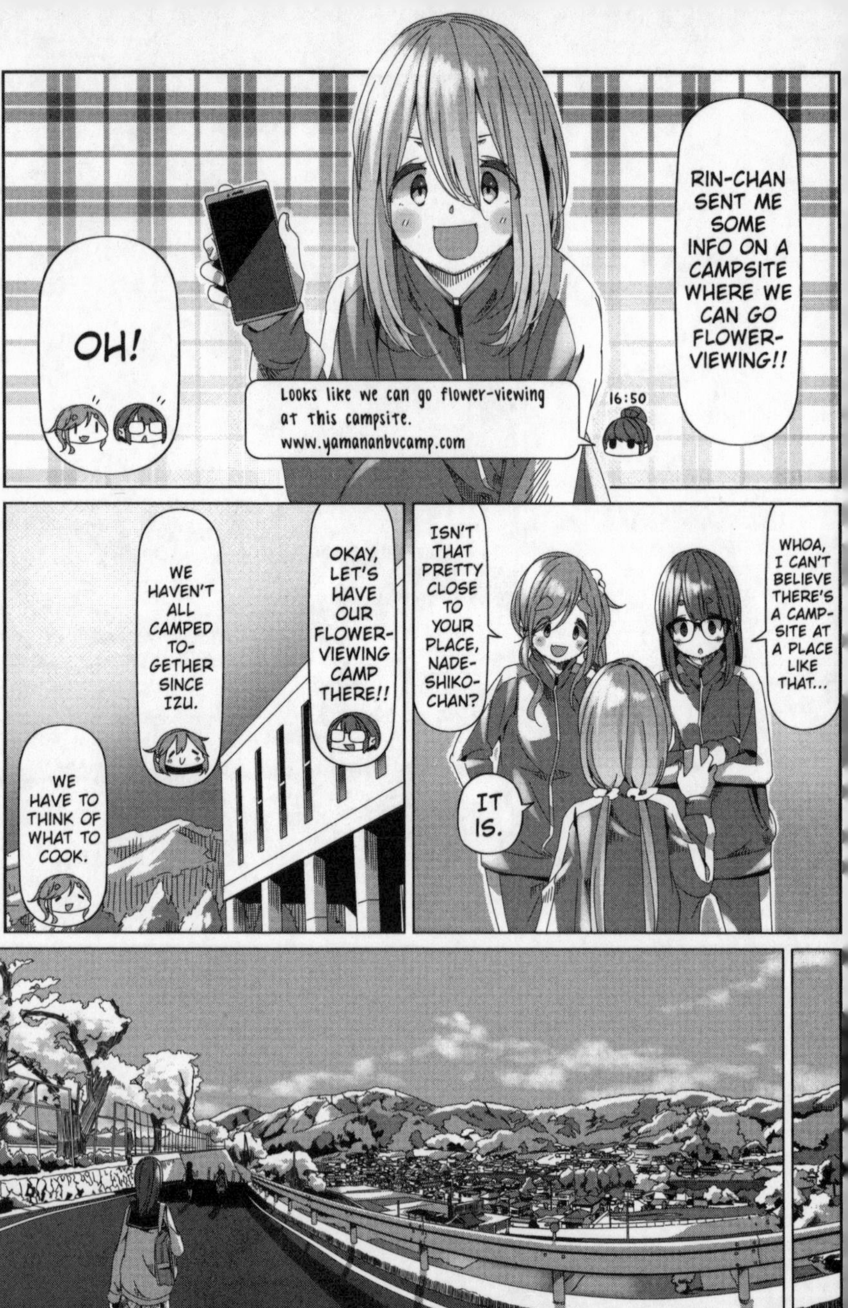
RIN-CHAN SENT ME SOME INFO ON A CAMPSITE WHERE WE CAN GO FLOWER-VIEWING!!
Looks like we can go flower-viewing at this campsite. www.yamananbvcamp.com
16:50
OH!
WHOA, I CAN'T BELIEVE THERE'S A CAMPSITE AT A PLACE LIKE THAT...
ISN'T THAT PRETTY CLOSE TO YOUR PLACE, NADESHIKO-CHAN?
IT IS.
OKAY, LET'S HAVE OUR FLOWER-VIEWING CAMP THERE!!
WE HAVEN'T ALL CAMPED TOGETHER SINCE IZU.
WE HAVE TO THINK OF WHAT TO COOK.

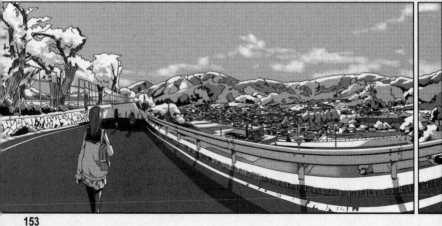

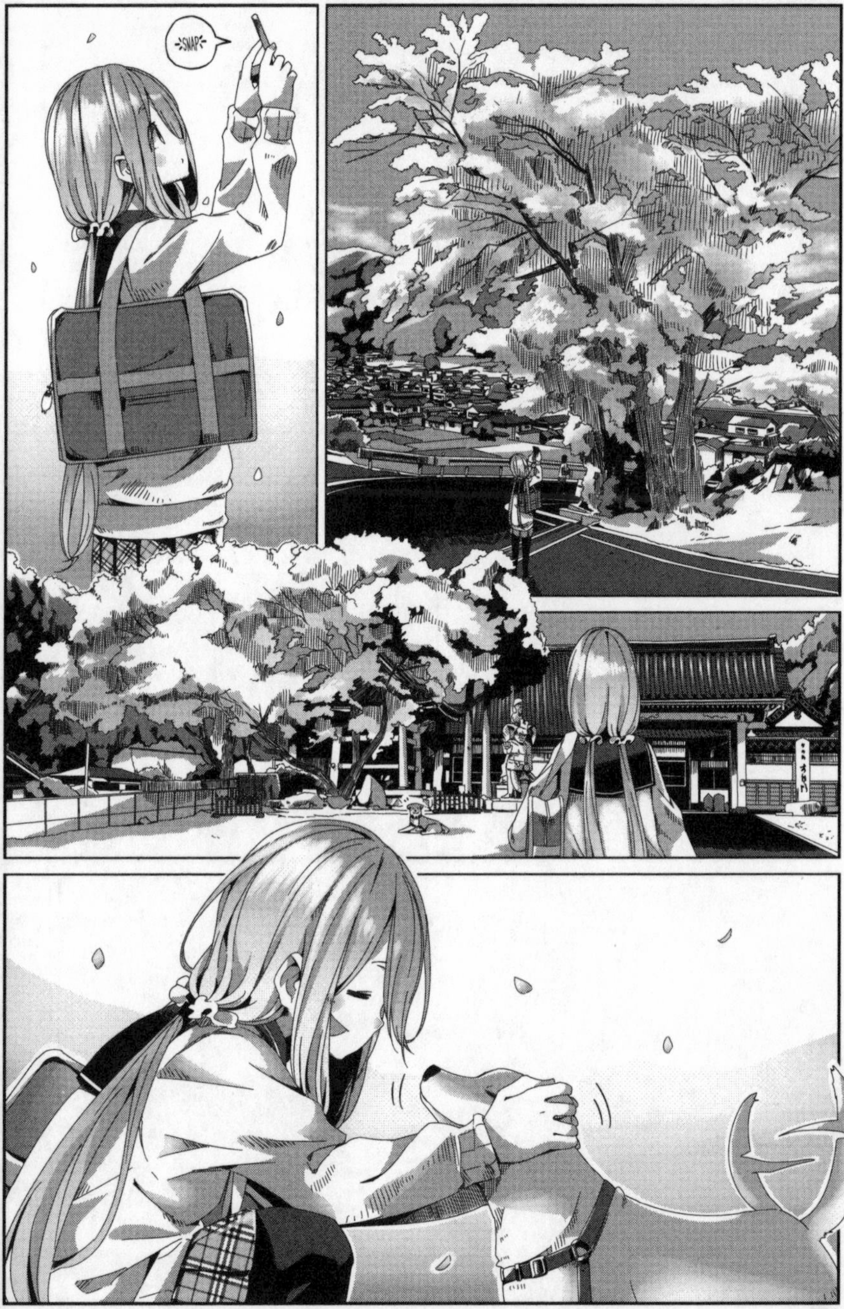
SNAP

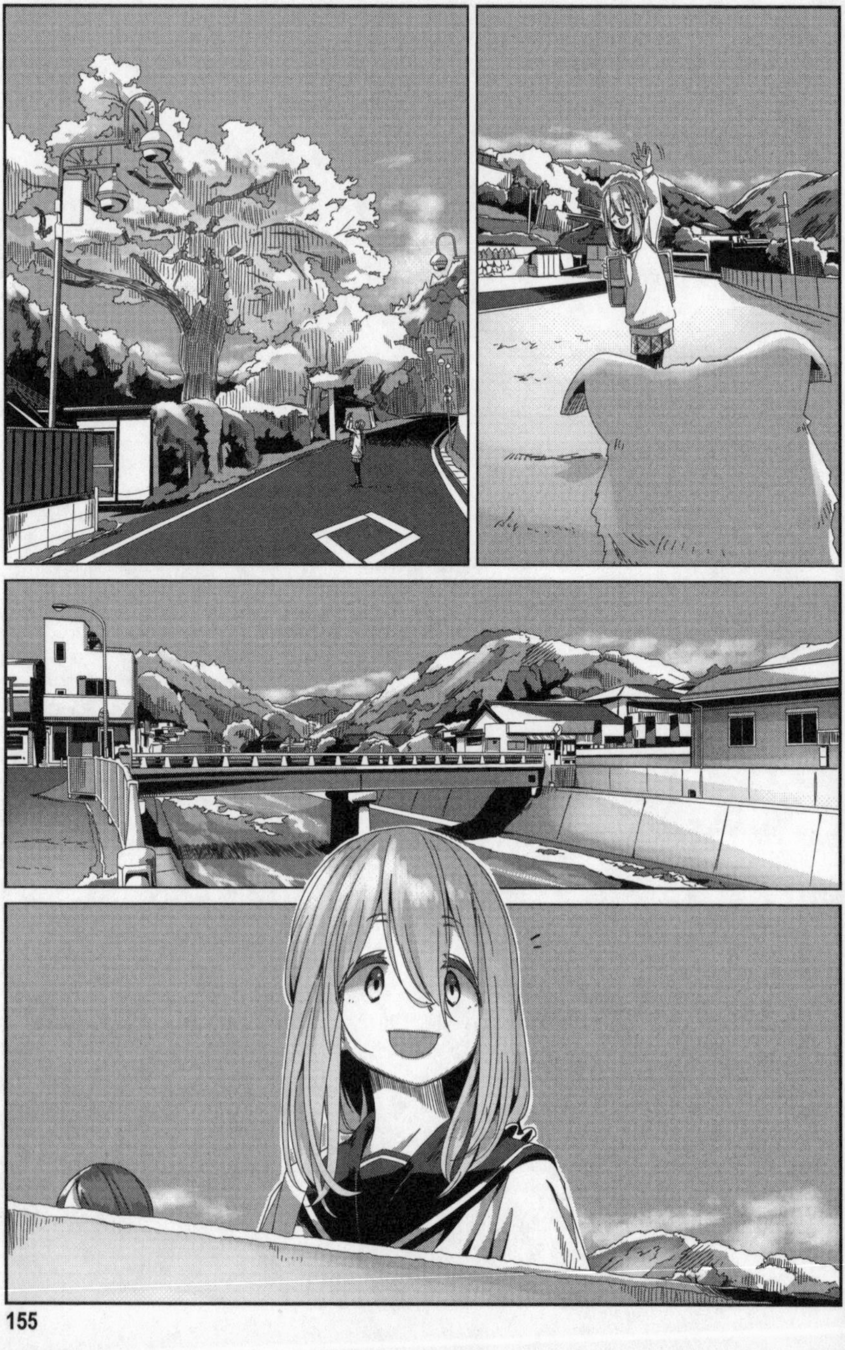

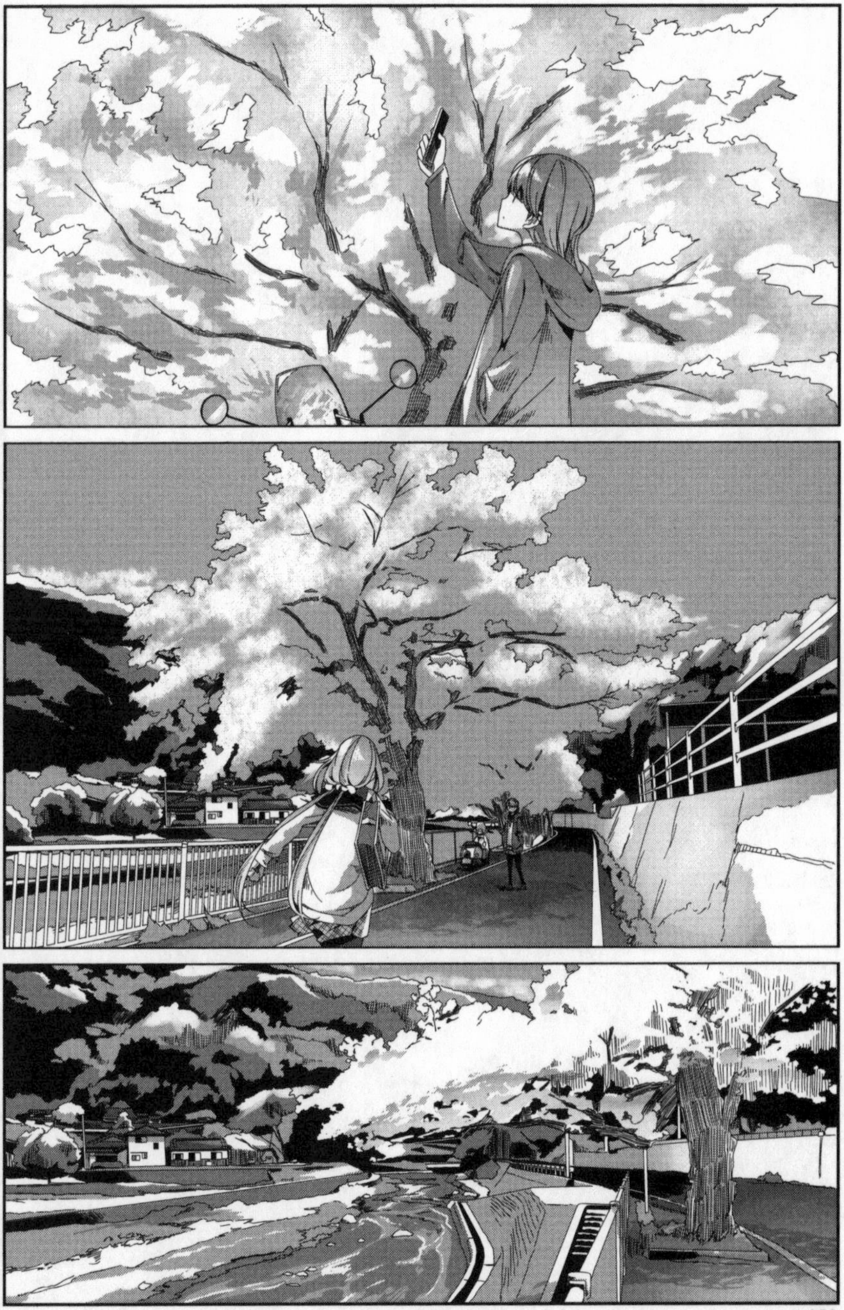

TRANSLATION NOTES

COMMON HONORIFICS

no honorific: Indicates familiarity or closeness; if used without permission or reason, addressing someone in this manner would constitute an insult.

-san: The Japanese equivalent of Mr./Mrs./Miss. If a situation calls for politeness, this is the fail-safe honorific.

-kun: Used most often when referring to boys, this indicates affection or familiarity. Occasionally used by older men among their peers, but it may also be used by anyone referring to a person of lower standing.

-chan: An affectionate honorific indicating familiarity used mostly in reference to girls; also used in reference to cute persons or animals regardless of gender.

-sensei: A respectful term for teachers, artists, or high-level professionals.

(o)nee: Japanese equivalent to "older sis."

(o)nii: Japanese equivalent to "older bro."

100 yen is approximately 1 USD.

1 centimeter is approximately 0.39 inches. 1 kilometer is approximately 0.621 miles.

PAGE 3

Okaki: A type of Japanese rice crackers.

PAGE 4

Cross counter: This is a type of counterpunch in boxing, but also the signature move of the hero in the famous boxing manga *Ashita no Joe*. It's of the most referenced attacks in all of manga.

PAGE 32

Nirasaki Heiwa Kannon Statue: A statue of Kannon, a bodhisattva and figure of compassion, mercy, and peace.

PAGE 42

Tummy torture: The original Japanese term is *meshi tero*, or "food terrorism." It's internet slang for sharing indulgent pictures of food to people and making them hungry.

PAGE 51

Kobe, Godo: In Japanese, both these places are written with the same characters but have different readings.

PAGE 70

Yakitori: A Japanese style of grilled chicken, typically served on skewers. As shown, *yakitori* shops serve different types of chicken meat—and even some non-chicken-based skewers.

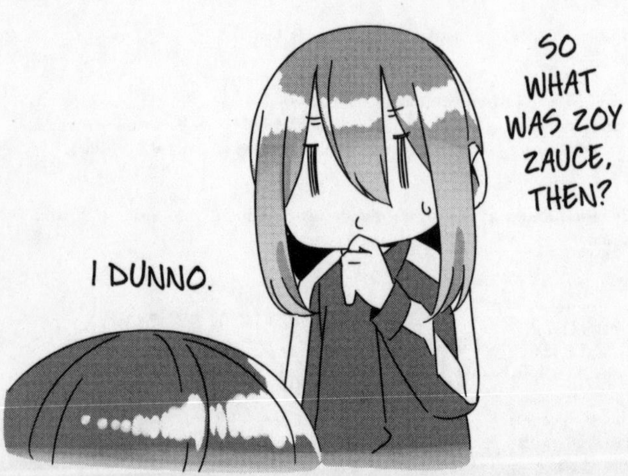
SO WHAT WAS ZOY ZAUCE, THEN?
I DUNNO.

TRANSLATION NOTES (continued)

PAGE 95
"Momotarou": A fairy tale about a boy born to a childless couple from a peach floating down a river. The boy grows to defeat a band of ogres, or *oni*, wreaking havoc on the land.

PAGE 99
Soba, houtou: Buckwheat noodles and flat wheat noodles used for a soup dish, respectively.

PAGE 100
Karintou: A deep-fried brown-sugar snack made with flour and yeast.

PAGE 101
Zoy zauce: In the Japanese, the label lists *shiyoyu* instead of *shoyu* ("soy sauce"). Ena speculates that the seeming error stems from not knowing how to type small characters—the difference between writing *sho* and *shiyo*. It's a simple but vital aspect of typing in Japanese.

PAGE 124
Maillard: This is a reference to the Maillard reaction, the complex chemical processes by which food becomes browned and more aromatic (and thus delicious).

PAGE 127
Mitarashi dango: Chewy, glutinous rice dumplings in a soy-sauce glaze.

PAGE 129
Tempura **bits**: Called *tenkasu* in Japanese, these are pieces of broken *tempura* batter that are commonly used as a topping for noodles.

PAGE 130
Okonomiyaki: A pan-fried cabbage pancake commonly served with various savory toppings.

PAGE 135
Ike-Ike: A parody of an actual brand called Ike.

PAGE 137
Keema **curry**: Indian minced-meat curry.

PAGE 165
Kotatsu: A heated table that can be found in Japanese homes. It's notorious for being so comfortable, it lulls people into not wanting to do anything except relax in it.

PAGE 166
Himono: A traditional Japanese method of preserving fish through drying.

PAGE 172
Tiun (bloop): This is a reference to the Mega Man video games. When defeated, Mega Man and the enemy Robot Masters explode into circles while making this sound. Robot Masters have weapons they're extra-vulnerable to, and the poor diner's weakness is apparently metal spoons scraping against china.

PAGE 176
Steamed chicken in spicy sauce: Known as *yodaredori* ("mouth-watering chicken") in Japanese, this dish is inspired by Sichuan cuisine.

INSIDE COVER (FRONT)
"...Dondoko?": This is a reference to an old TV commercial for DonDon, a Shizuoka-based food chain that sells prepared meals. In it, a game show asks, "Where's the happy gourmet box meal everyone's been talking about?" The sole girl contestant answers quizzically with "...DonDon?" and wins the whole thing.

◁ SIDE STORIES BEGIN ON THE NEXT PAGE ◁

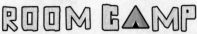

AFTER-SCHOOL 99 NIGHTMARES

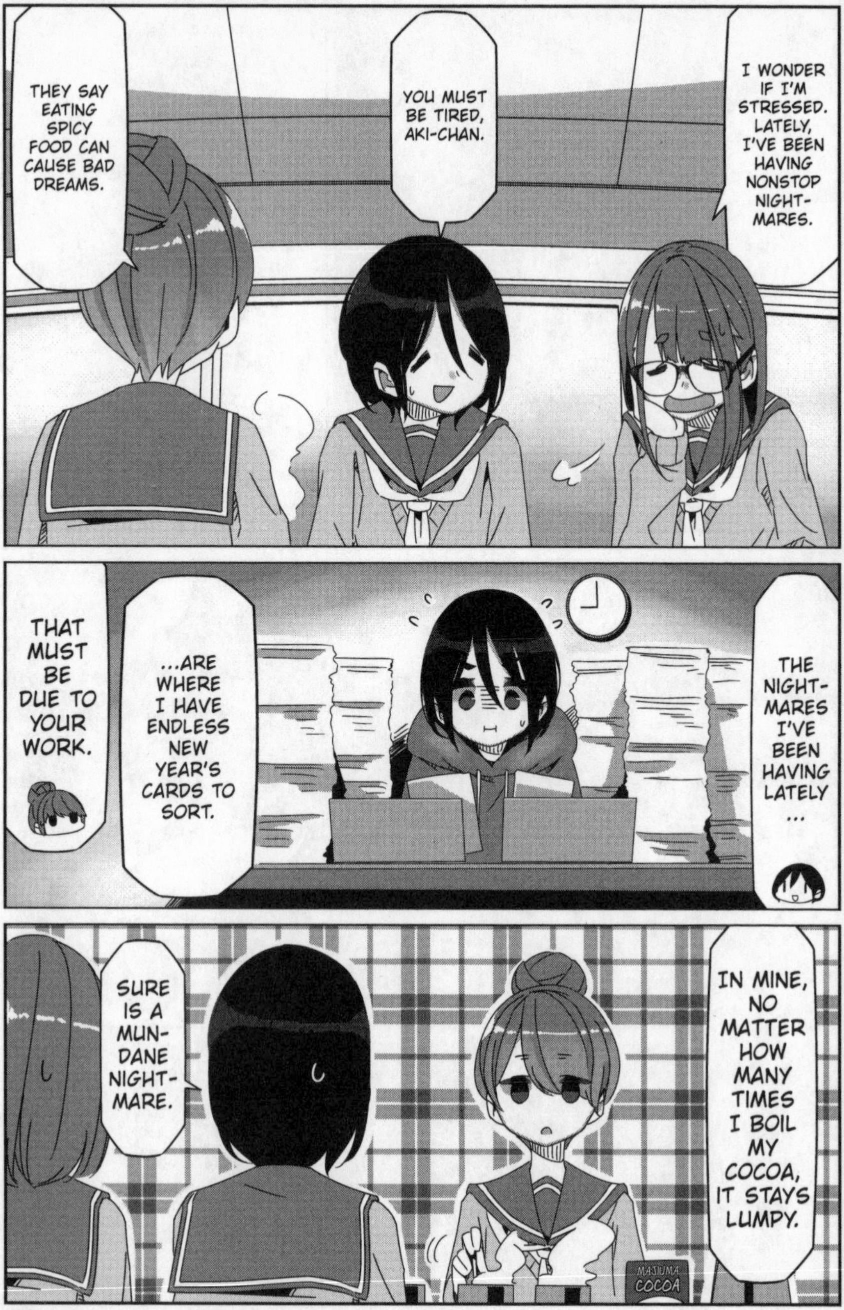
I WONDER IF I'M STRESSED. LATELY, I'VE BEEN HAVING NONSTOP NIGHT-MARES.
YOU MUST BE TIRED, AKI-CHAN.
THEY SAY EATING SPICY FOOD CAN CAUSE BAD DREAMS.
THE NIGHT-MARES I'VE BEEN HAVING LATELY...
...ARE WHERE I HAVE ENDLESS NEW YEAR'S CARDS TO SORT.
THAT MUST BE DUE TO YOUR WORK.
IN MINE, NO MATTER HOW MANY TIMES I BOIL MY COCOA, IT STAYS LUMPY.
MAJIUMA COCOA
SURE IS A MUN-DANE NIGHT-MARE.

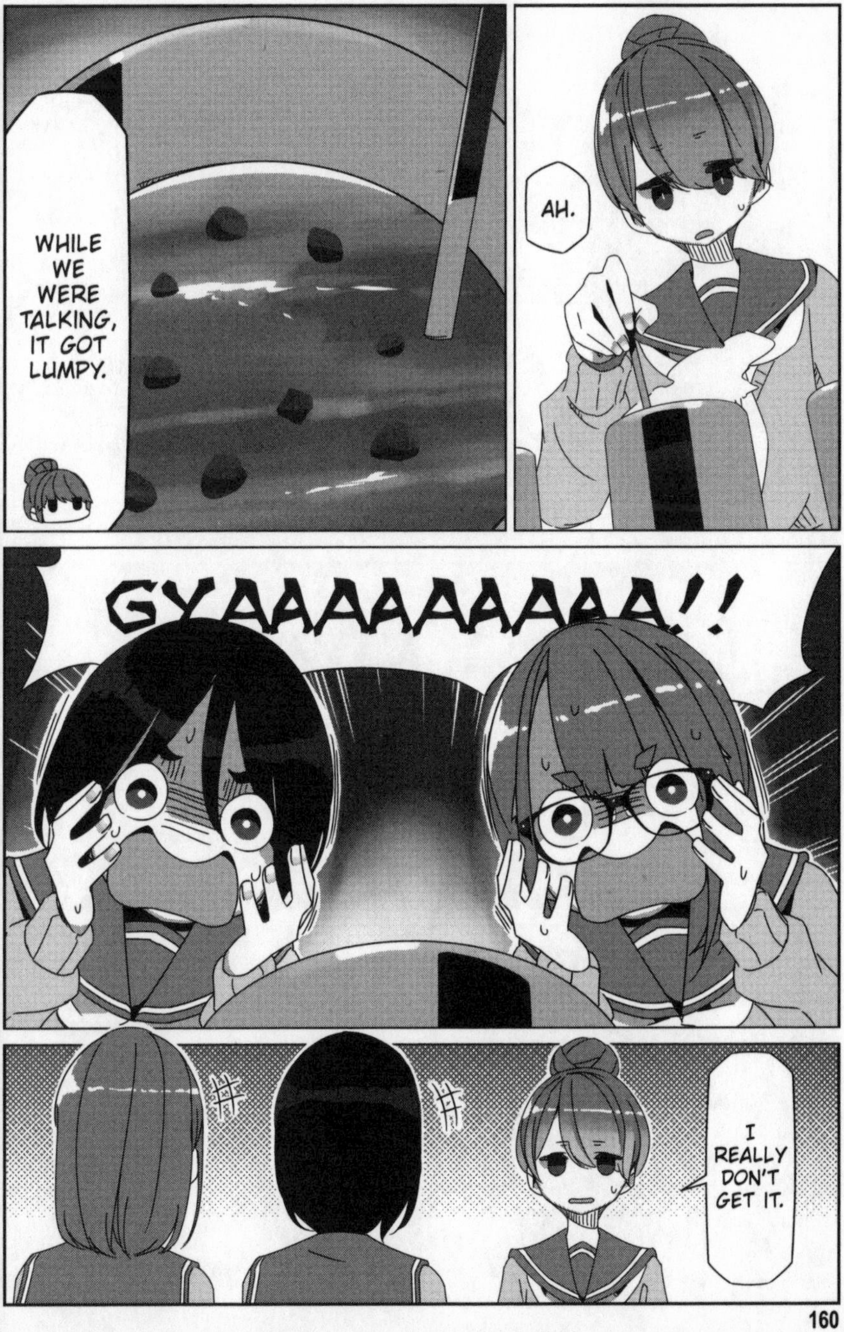
AH.
WHILE WE WERE TALKING, IT GOT LUMPY.
GYAAAAAAAAAA!!
I REALLY DON'T GET IT.

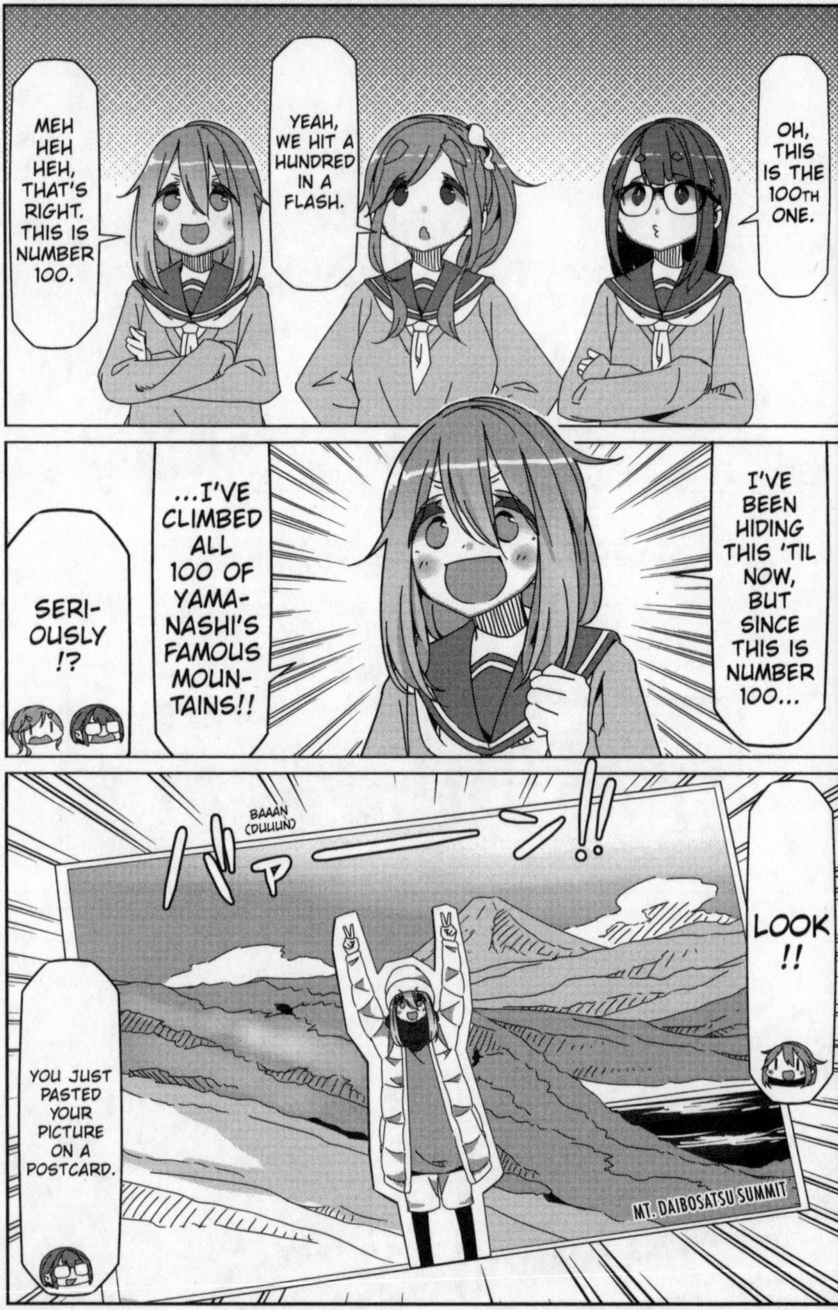
OH, THIS IS THE 100TH ONE.
YEAH, WE HIT A HUNDRED IN A FLASH.
MEH HEH HEH, THAT'S RIGHT. THIS IS NUMBER 100.
I'VE BEEN HIDING THIS 'TIL NOW, BUT SINCE THIS IS NUMBER 100...
...I'VE CLIMBED ALL 100 OF YAMANASHI'S FAMOUS MOUNTAINS!!
SERIOUSLY!?
LOOK!!
BAAAN (DUUUN)
MT. DAIBOSATSU SUMMIT
YOU JUST PASTED YOUR PICTURE ON A POSTCARD.

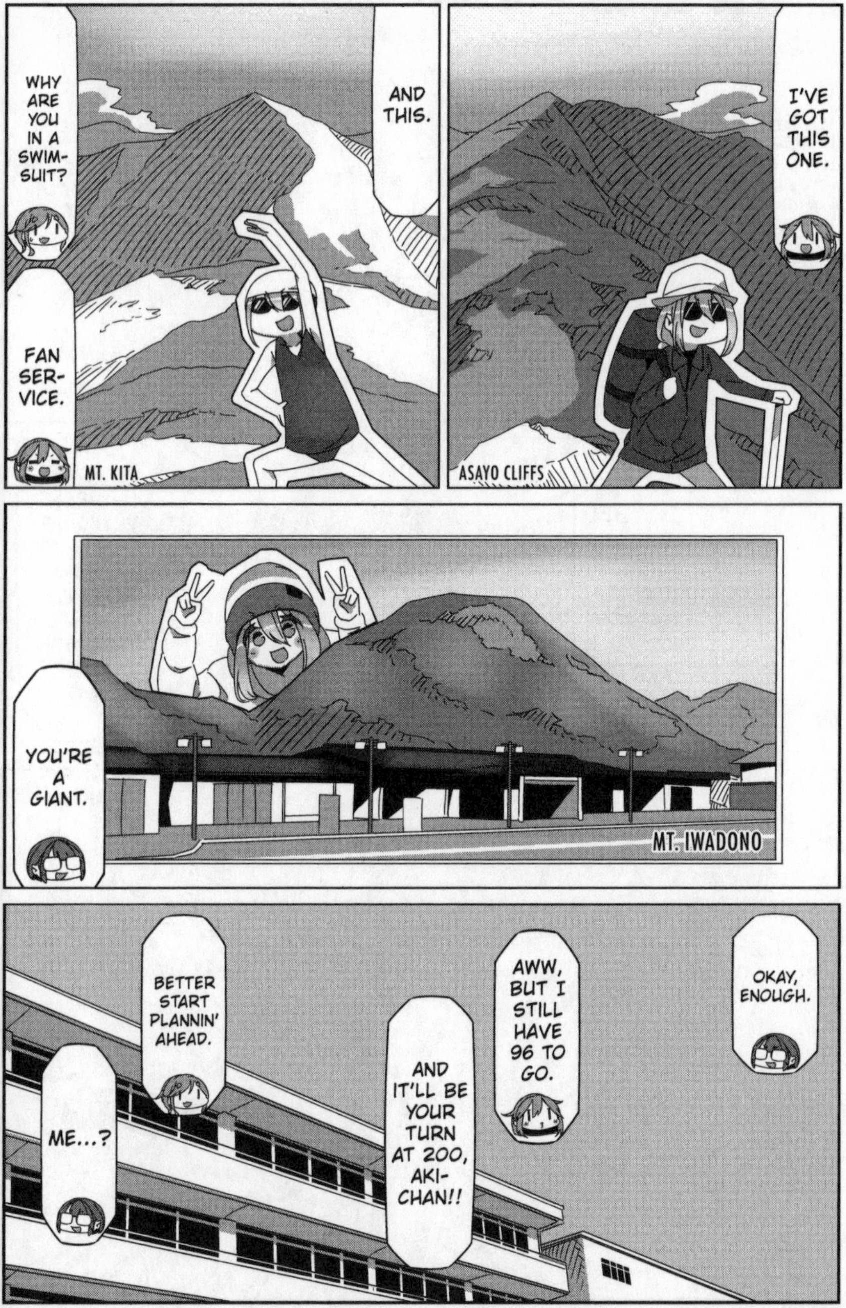
I'VE GOT THIS ONE.
ASAYO CLIFFS
AND THIS.
WHY ARE YOU IN A SWIMSUIT?
FAN SERVICE.
MT. KITA
YOU'RE A GIANT.
MT. IWADONO
OKAY, ENOUGH.
AWW, BUT I STILL HAVE 96 TO GO.
AND IT'LL BE YOUR TURN AT 200, AKI-CHAN!!
BETTER START PLANNIN' AHEAD.
ME...?

AFTER-SCHOOL 101 HOW ENA AND RIN MET

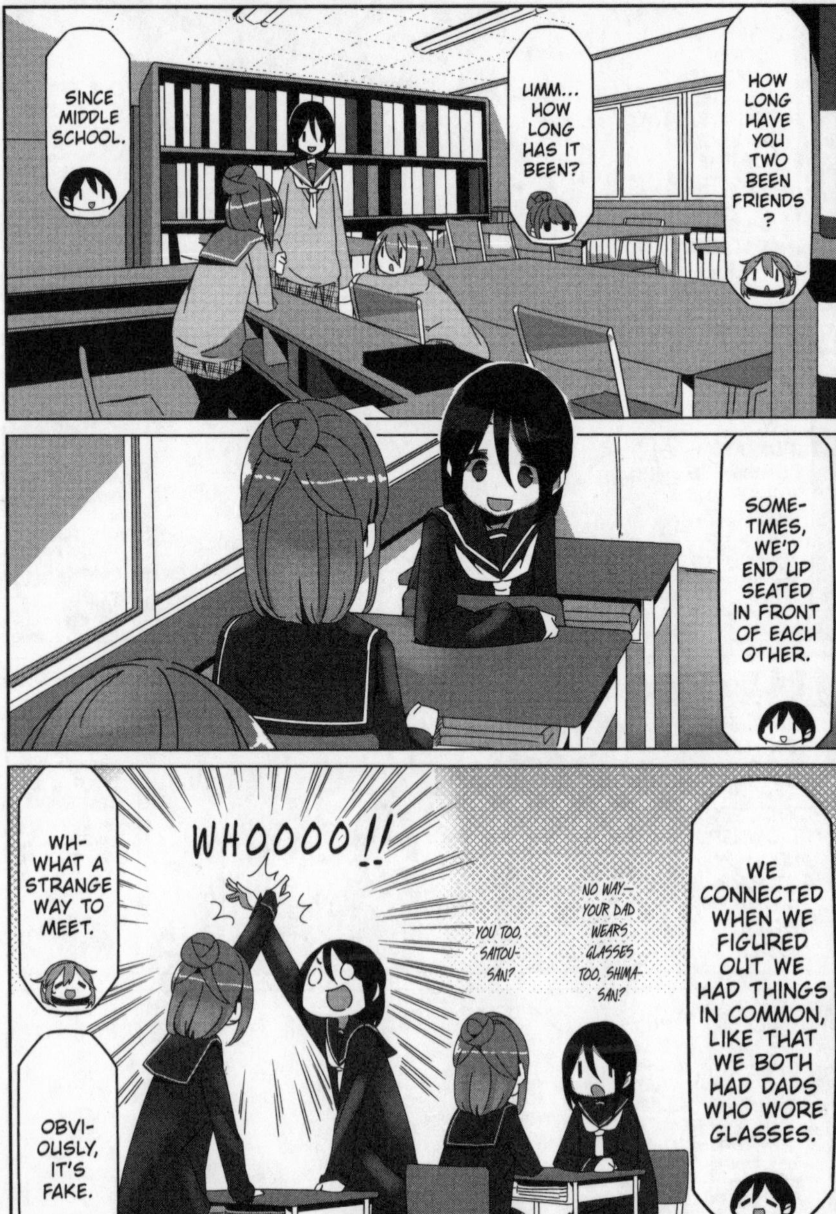
HOW LONG HAVE YOU TWO BEEN FRIENDS?
UMM... HOW LONG HAS IT BEEN?
SINCE MIDDLE SCHOOL.
SOMETIMES, WE'D END UP SEATED IN FRONT OF EACH OTHER.
WE CONNECTED WHEN WE FIGURED OUT WE HAD THINGS IN COMMON, LIKE THAT WE BOTH HAD DADS WHO WORE GLASSES.
NO WAY— YOUR DAD WEARS GLASSES TOO, SHIMA-SAN?
YOU TOO, SAITOU-SAN?
WHOOOO!!
WH-WHAT A STRANGE WAY TO MEET.
OBVIOUSLY, IT'S FAKE.

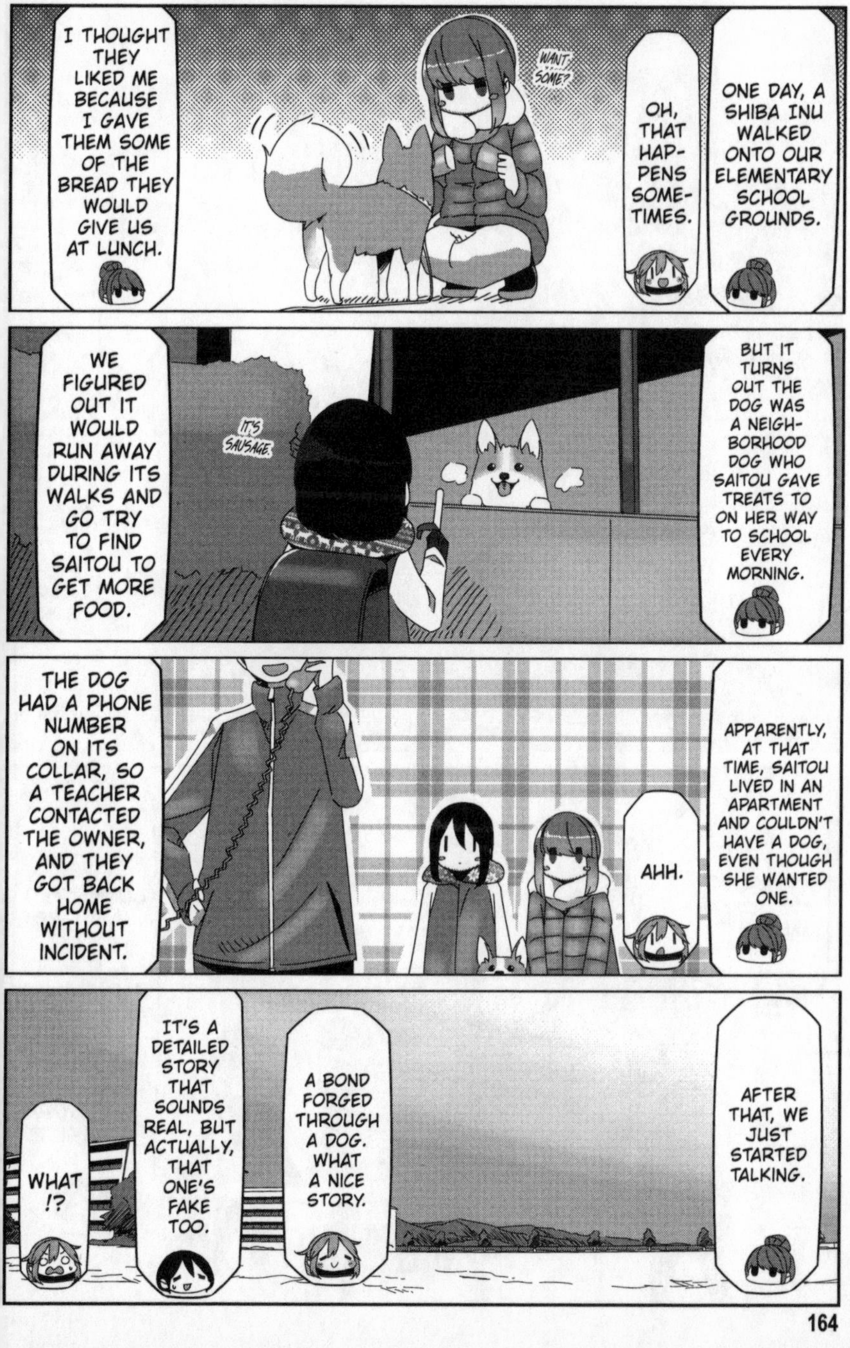
ONE DAY, A SHIBA INU WALKED ONTO OUR ELEMENTARY SCHOOL GROUNDS.
OH, THAT HAPPENS SOMETIMES.
WANT SOME?
I THOUGHT THEY LIKED ME BECAUSE I GAVE THEM SOME OF THE BREAD THEY WOULD GIVE US AT LUNCH.
BUT IT TURNS OUT THE DOG WAS A NEIGHBORHOOD DOG WHO SAITOU GAVE TREATS TO ON HER WAY TO SCHOOL EVERY MORNING.
IT'S SAUSAGE.
WE FIGURED OUT IT WOULD RUN AWAY DURING ITS WALKS AND GO TRY TO FIND SAITOU TO GET MORE FOOD.
APPARENTLY, AT THAT TIME, SAITOU LIVED IN AN APARTMENT AND COULDN'T HAVE A DOG, EVEN THOUGH SHE WANTED ONE.
AHH.
THE DOG HAD A PHONE NUMBER ON ITS COLLAR, SO A TEACHER CONTACTED THE OWNER, AND THEY GOT BACK HOME WITHOUT INCIDENT.
AFTER THAT, WE JUST STARTED TALKING.
A BOND FORGED THROUGH A DOG. WHAT A NICE STORY.
IT'S A DETAILED STORY THAT SOUNDS REAL, BUT ACTUALLY, THAT ONE'S FAKE TOO.
WHAT!?

AFTER-SCHOOL 102 OUTDOOR KOTATSU

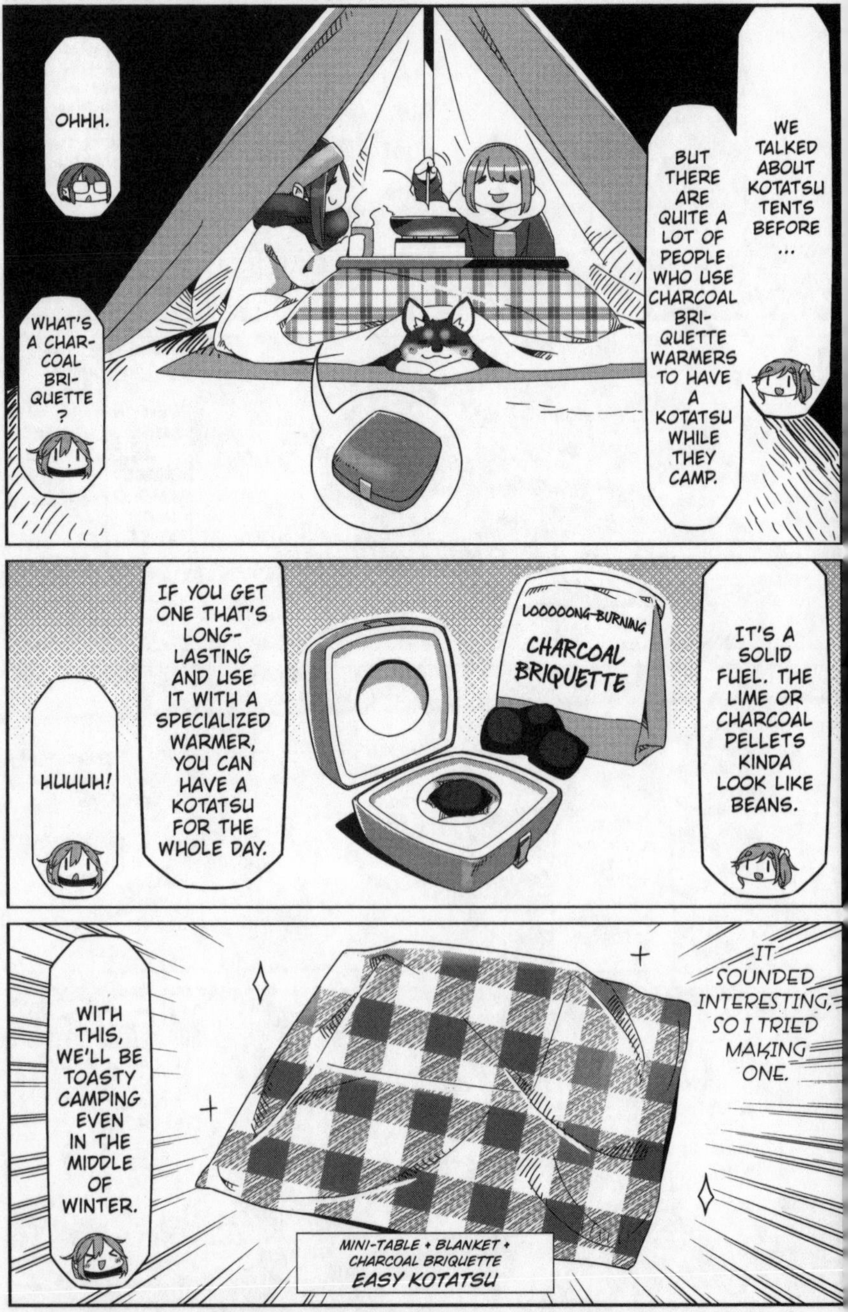
WE TALKED ABOUT KOTATSU TENTS BEFORE...
BUT THERE ARE QUITE A LOT OF PEOPLE WHO USE CHARCOAL BRIQUETTE WARMERS TO HAVE A KOTATSU WHILE THEY CAMP.
OHHH.
WHAT'S A CHARCOAL BRIQUETTE?
IT'S A SOLID FUEL. THE LIME OR CHARCOAL PELLETS KINDA LOOK LIKE BEANS.
LOOOOONG-BURNING
CHARCOAL BRIQUETTE
IF YOU GET ONE THAT'S LONG-LASTING AND USE IT WITH A SPECIALIZED WARMER, YOU CAN HAVE A KOTATSU FOR THE WHOLE DAY.
HUUUH!
IT SOUNDED INTERESTING, SO I TRIED MAKING ONE.
WITH THIS, WE'LL BE TOASTY CAMPING EVEN IN THE MIDDLE OF WINTER.
MINI-TABLE + BLANKET + CHARCOAL BRIQUETTE
EASY KOTATSU

※ WHEN USING CHARCOAL BRIQUETTES, PLEASE BE MINDFUL OF FIRE OR CARBON MONOXIDE POISONING.

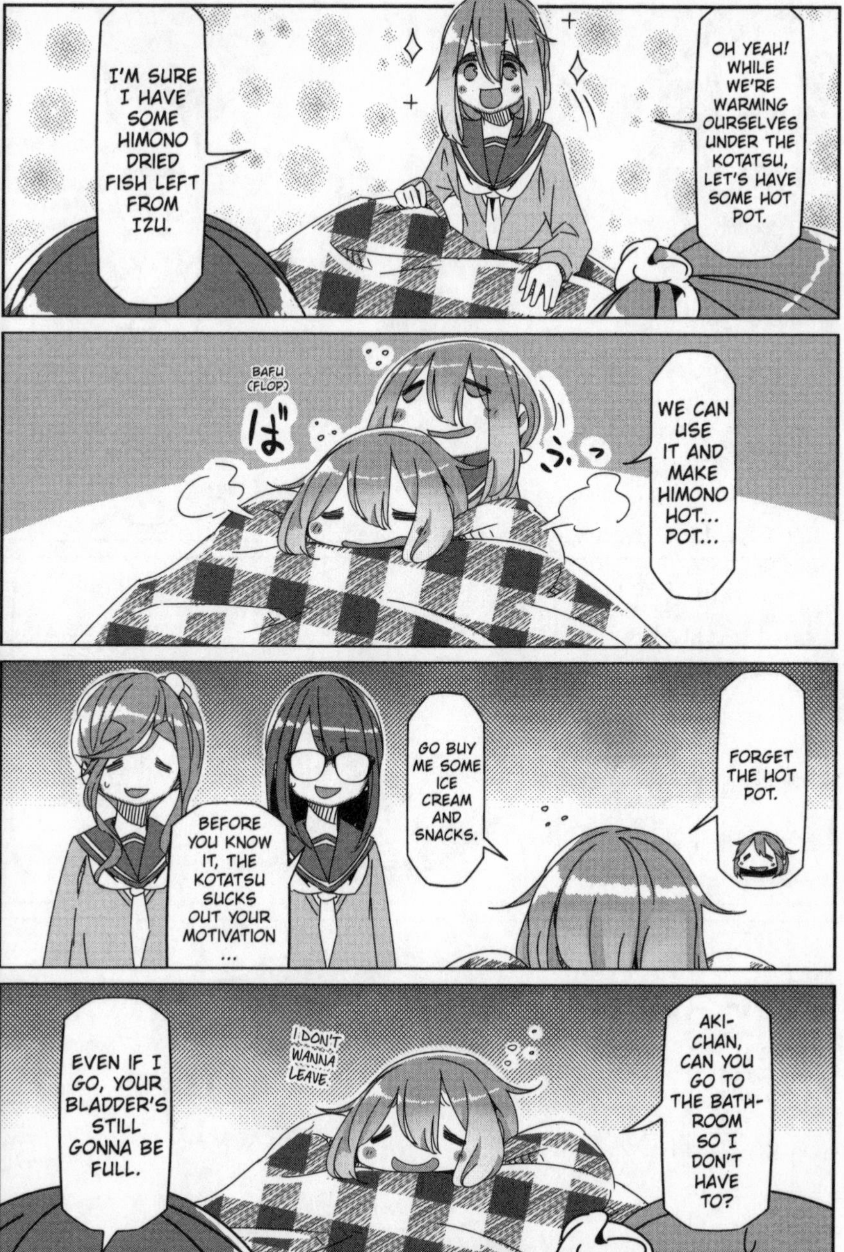
OH YEAH! WHILE WE'RE WARMING OURSELVES UNDER THE KOTATSU, LET'S HAVE SOME HOT POT.
I'M SURE I HAVE SOME HIMONO DRIED FISH LEFT FROM IZU.
WE CAN USE IT AND MAKE HIMONO HOT... POT...
BAFU (FLOP)
ば
FORGET THE HOT POT.
GO BUY ME SOME ICE CREAM AND SNACKS.
BEFORE YOU KNOW IT, THE KOTATSU SUCKS OUT YOUR MOTIVATION ...
AKI-CHAN, CAN YOU GO TO THE BATH-ROOM SO I DON'T HAVE TO?
I DON'T WANNA LEAVE.
EVEN IF I GO, YOUR BLADDER'S STILL GONNA BE FULL.

AFTER-SCHOOL 103 CHIKUWA AND MR. SAITOU

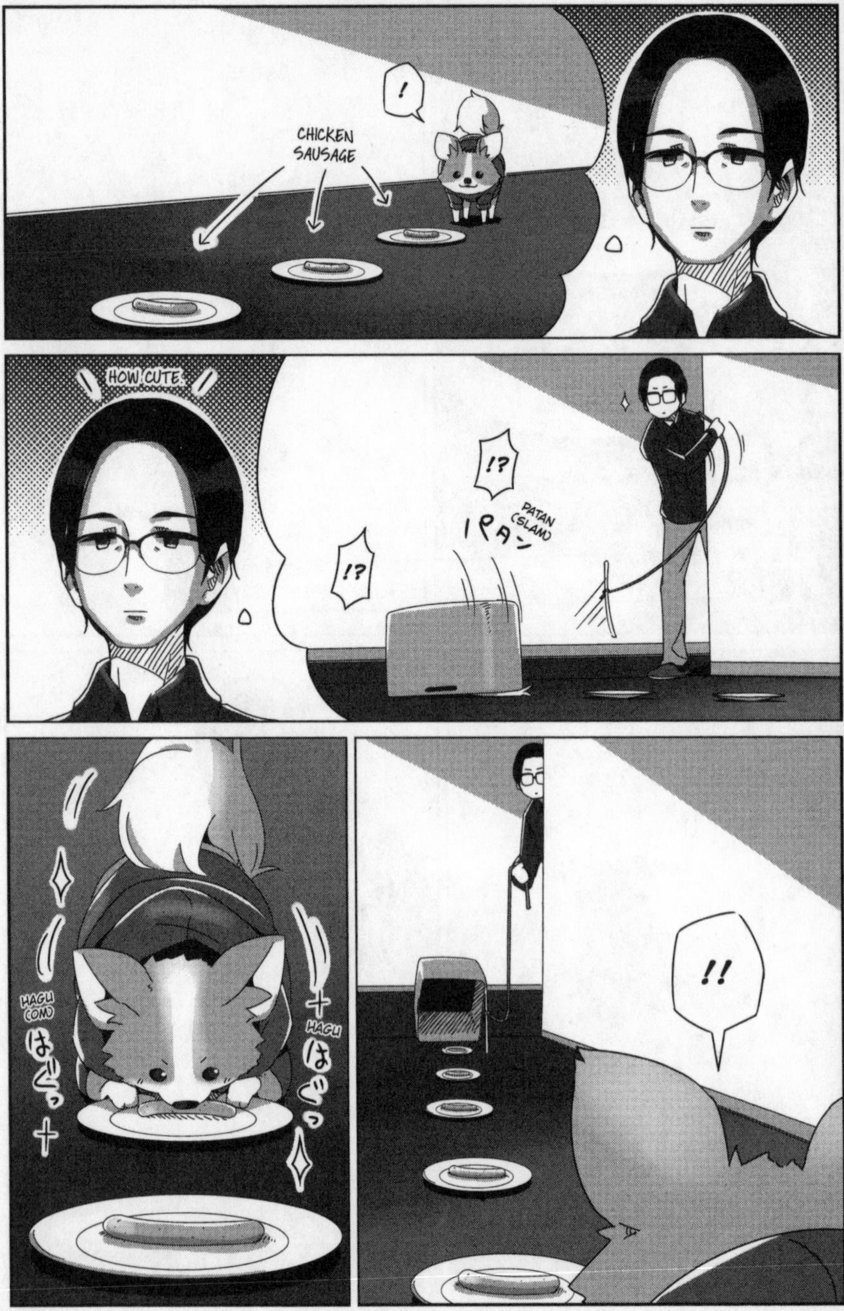

!
CHICKEN SAUSAGE
!?
PATAN (SLAM)
パタン
!?
HOW CUTE.
!!
HAGU
はぐっ
HAGU (OM)
はぐっ

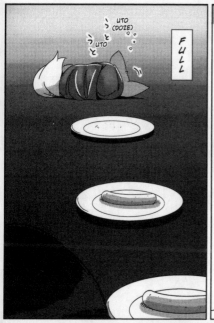

UTO
(DOZE)

UTO

UTO

FULL

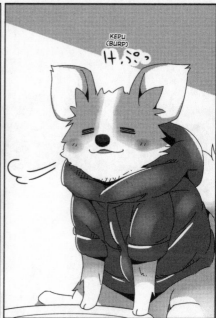

KEPU
(BURP)

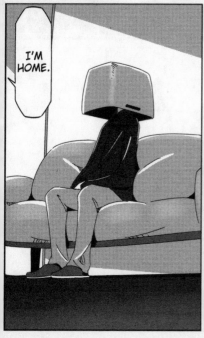

I'M
HOME.

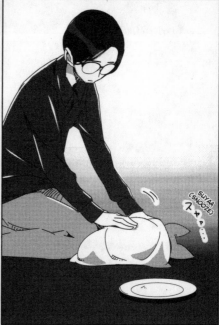

SUYAA
(SNOOZE)

AFTER-SCHOOL 104 YOU CAN EVEN EAT THE PLATE

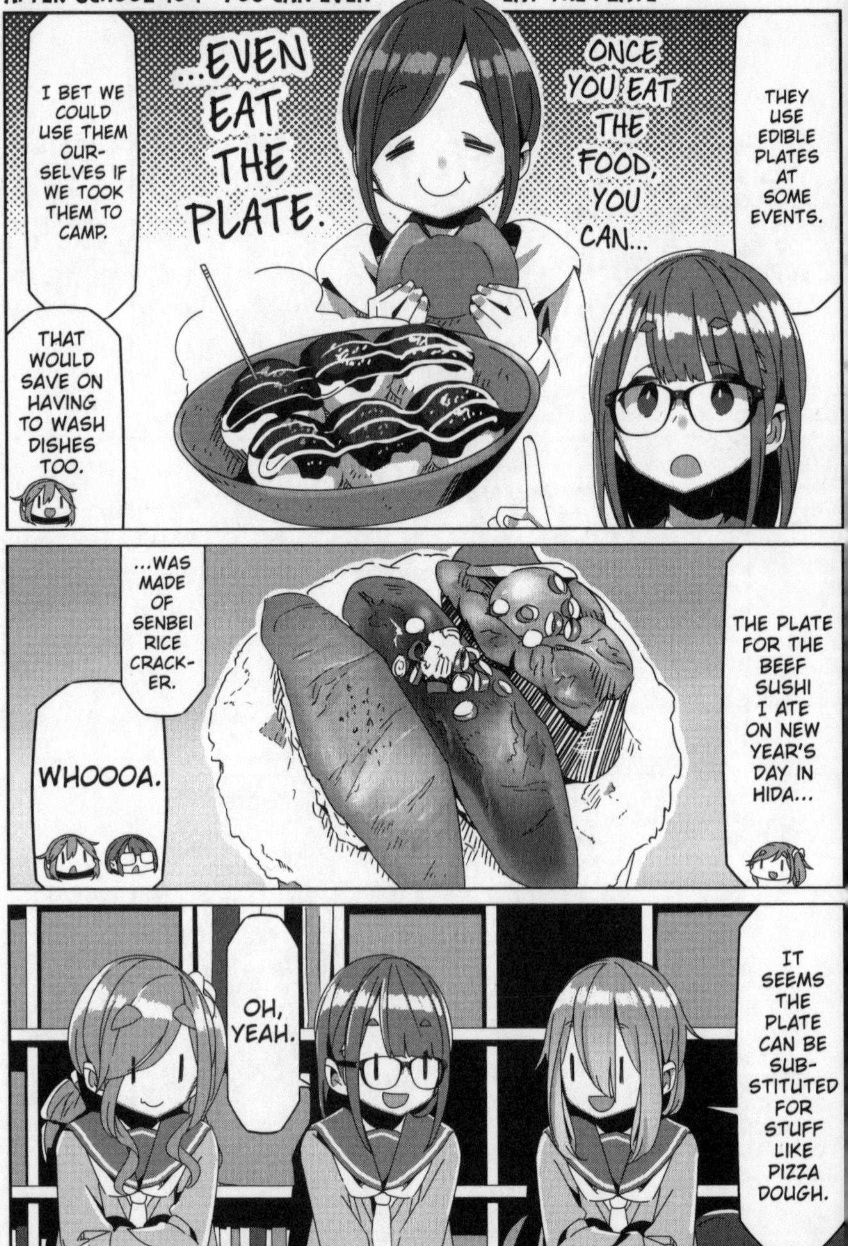
THEY USE EDIBLE PLATES AT SOME EVENTS.
ONCE YOU EAT THE FOOD, YOU CAN...
...EVEN EAT THE PLATE.
I BET WE COULD USE THEM OURSELVES IF WE TOOK THEM TO CAMP.
THAT WOULD SAVE ON HAVING TO WASH DISHES TOO.
THE PLATE FOR THE BEEF SUSHI I ATE ON NEW YEAR'S DAY IN HIDA...
...WAS MADE OF SENBEI RICE CRACKER.
WHOOOA.
IT SEEMS THE PLATE CAN BE SUBSTITUTED FOR STUFF LIKE PIZZA DOUGH.
OH, YEAH.

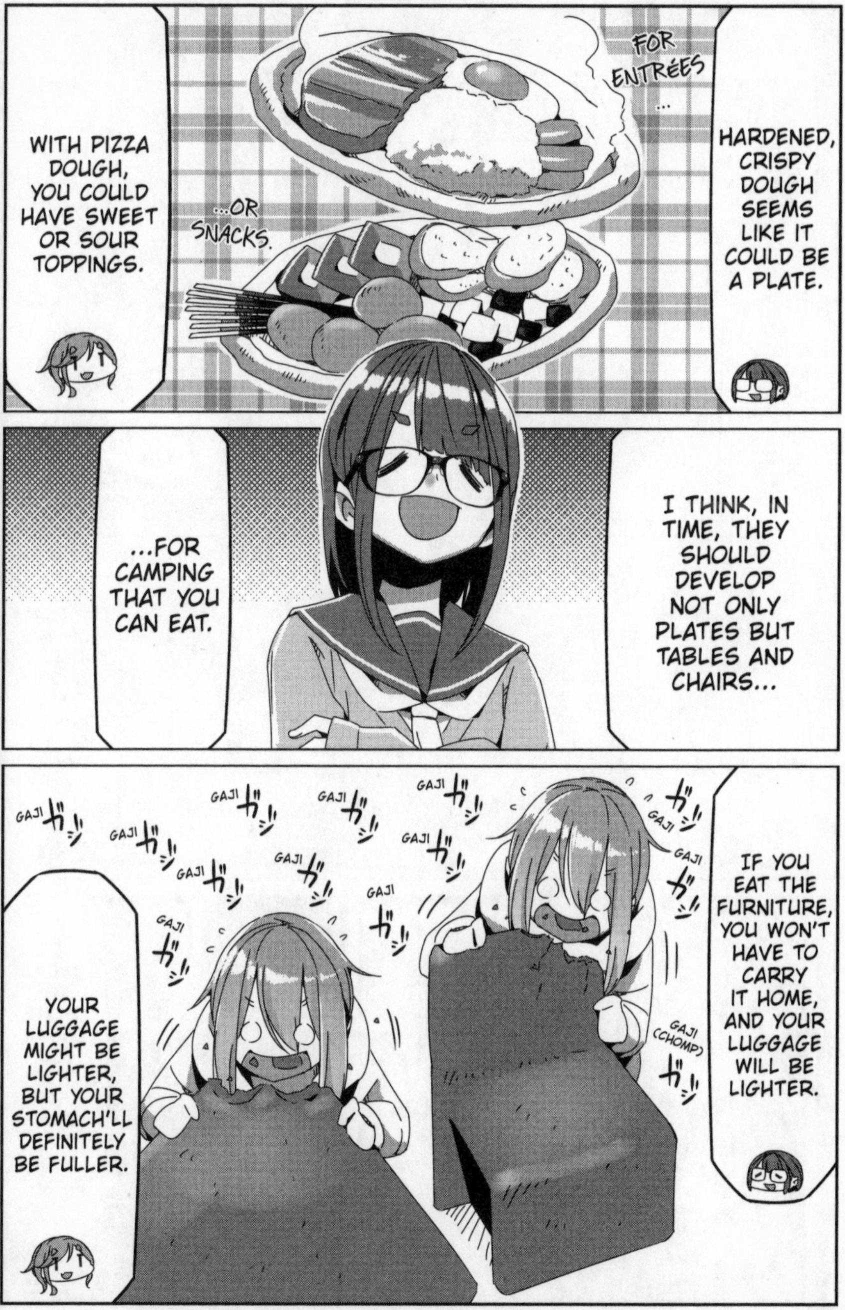
HARDENED, CRISPY DOUGH SEEMS LIKE IT COULD BE A PLATE.
FOR ENTRÉES ...
...OR SNACKS.
WITH PIZZA DOUGH, YOU COULD HAVE SWEET OR SOUR TOPPINGS.
I THINK, IN TIME, THEY SHOULD DEVELOP NOT ONLY PLATES BUT TABLES AND CHAIRS...
...FOR CAMPING THAT YOU CAN EAT.
IF YOU EAT THE FURNITURE, YOU WON'T HAVE TO CARRY IT HOME, AND YOUR LUGGAGE WILL BE LIGHTER.
GAJI (CHOMP)
YOUR LUGGAGE MIGHT BE LIGHTER, BUT YOUR STOMACH'LL DEFINITELY BE FULLER.

AFTER-SCHOOL 105 THE SOUND OF UTENSILS

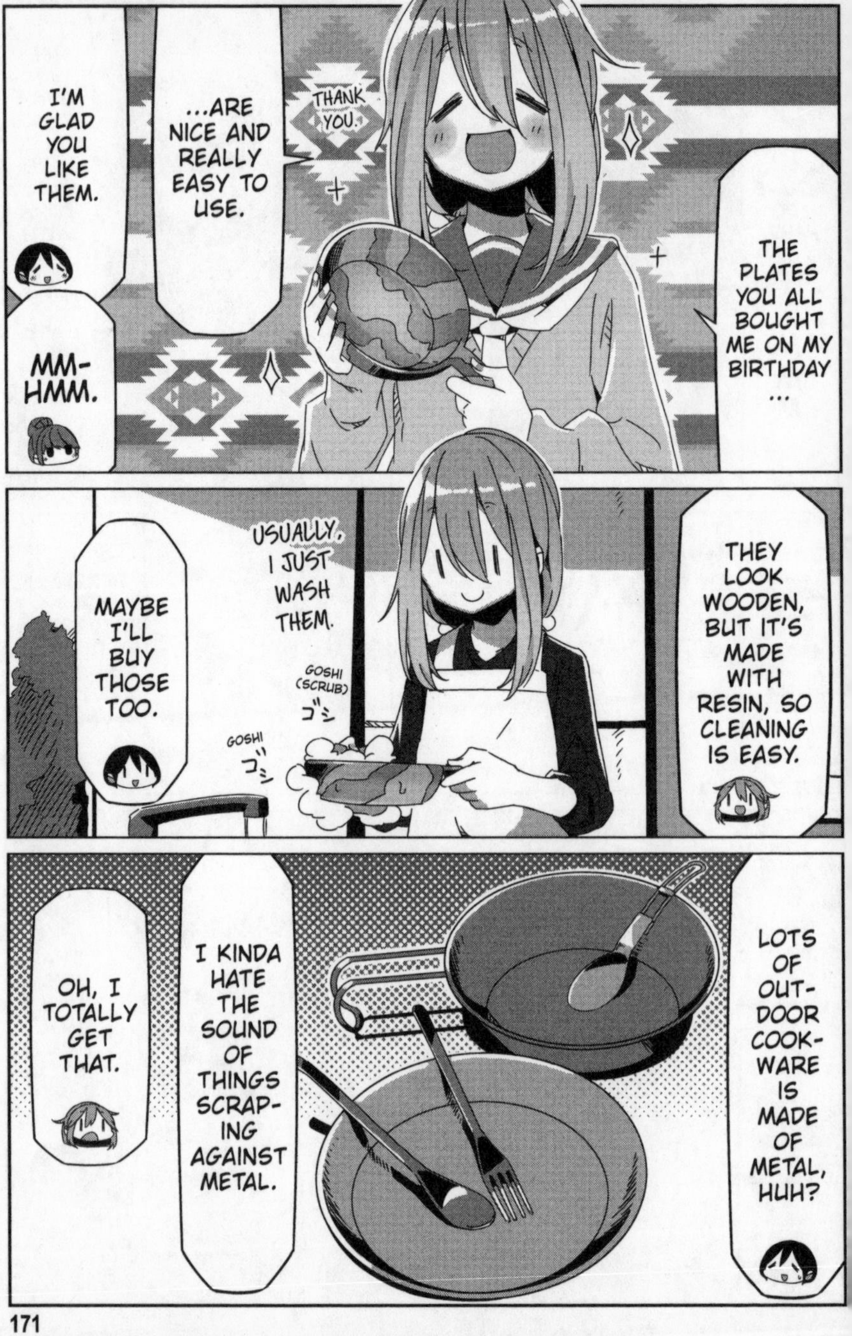
THE PLATES YOU ALL BOUGHT ME ON MY BIRTHDAY...
THANK YOU.
...ARE NICE AND REALLY EASY TO USE.
I'M GLAD YOU LIKE THEM.
MM-HMM.
THEY LOOK WOODEN, BUT IT'S MADE WITH RESIN, SO CLEANING IS EASY.
USUALLY, I JUST WASH THEM.
GOSHI (SCRUB)
ゴシ
GOSHI
ゴシ
MAYBE I'LL BUY THOSE TOO.
LOTS OF OUTDOOR COOKWARE IS MADE OF METAL, HUH?
I KINDA HATE THE SOUND OF THINGS SCRAPING AGAINST METAL.
OH, I TOTALLY GET THAT.

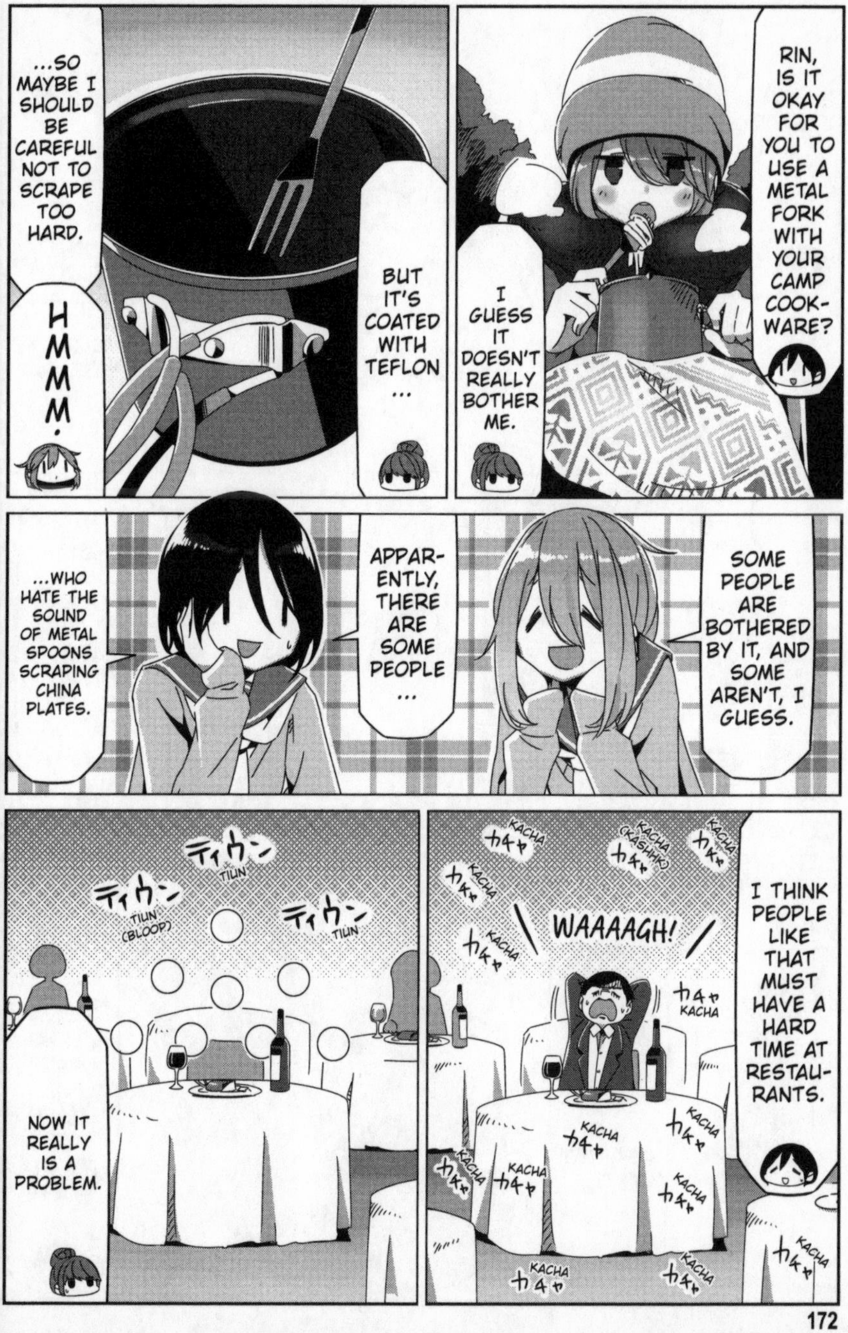
RIN, IS IT OKAY FOR YOU TO USE A METAL FORK WITH YOUR CAMP COOK-WARE?
I GUESS IT DOESN'T REALLY BOTHER ME.
BUT IT'S COATED WITH TEFLON ...
...SO MAYBE I SHOULD BE CAREFUL NOT TO SCRAPE TOO HARD.
HMMM!
SOME PEOPLE ARE BOTHERED BY IT, AND SOME AREN'T, I GUESS.
APPAR-ENTLY, THERE ARE SOME PEOPLE ...
...WHO HATE THE SOUND OF METAL SPOONS SCRAPING CHINA PLATES.
I THINK PEOPLE LIKE THAT MUST HAVE A HARD TIME AT RESTAU-RANTS.
カチャ KACHA
カチャ KACHA (KASHHK)
カチャ KACHA
カチャ KACHA
WAAAAGH!
カチャ KACHA
カチャ KACHA
カチャ KACHA
カチャ KACHA
カチャ KACHA
カチャ KACHA
カチャ KACHA
カチャ KACHA
カチャ KACHA
カチャ KACHA
ティウン TIUN
ティウン TIUN
ティウン TIUN (BLOOP)
NOW IT REALLY IS A PROBLEM.

AFTER-SCHOOL 106 NADESHIKO'S PAYBACK

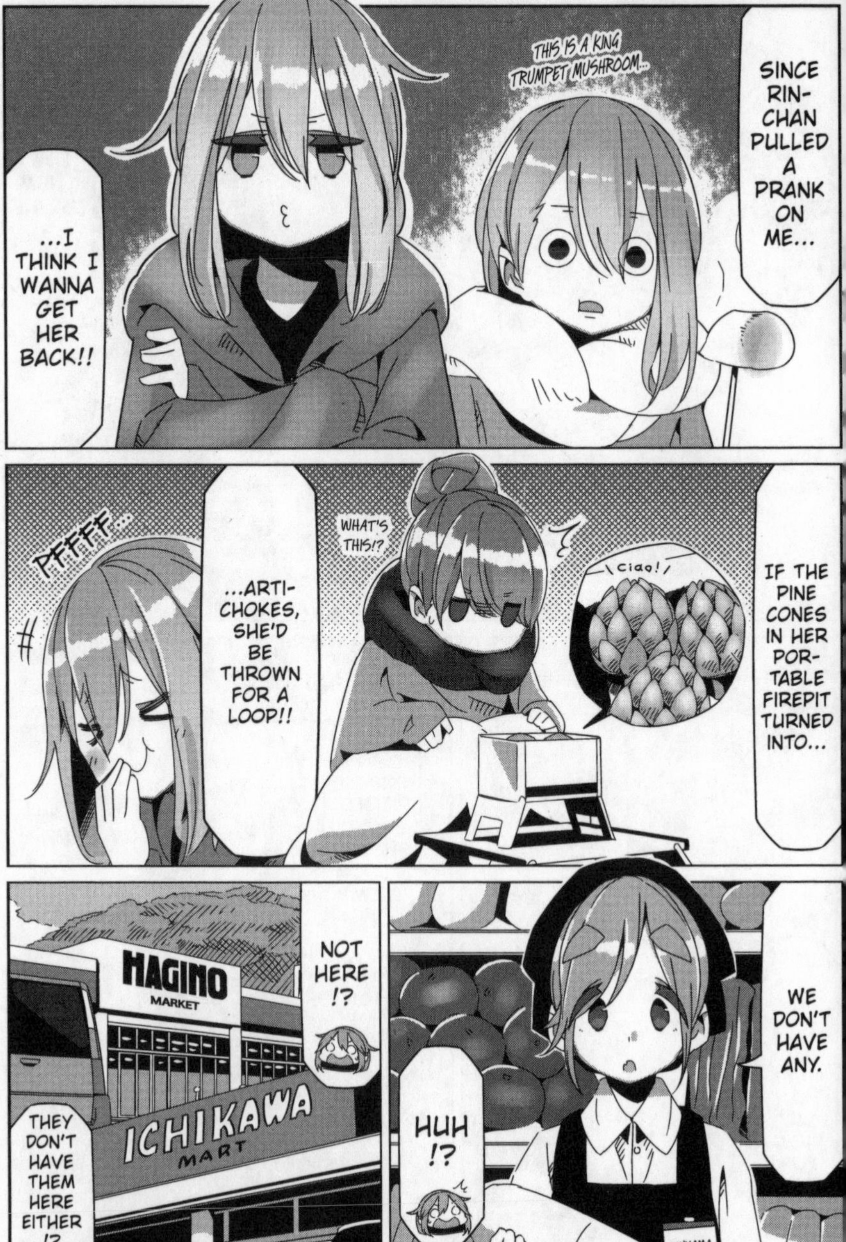
SINCE RIN-CHAN PULLED A PRANK ON ME...
THIS IS A KING TRUMPET MUSHROOM...
...I THINK I WANNA GET HER BACK!!
IF THE PINE CONES IN HER PORTABLE FIREPIT TURNED INTO...
\ Ciao! /
WHAT'S THIS!?
...ARTI-CHOKES, SHE'D BE THROWN FOR A LOOP!!
PFFFF...
WE DON'T HAVE ANY.
HUH!?
INUYAMA
NOT HERE!?
HAGINO MARKET
ICHIKAWA MART
THEY DON'T HAVE THEM HERE EITHER!?

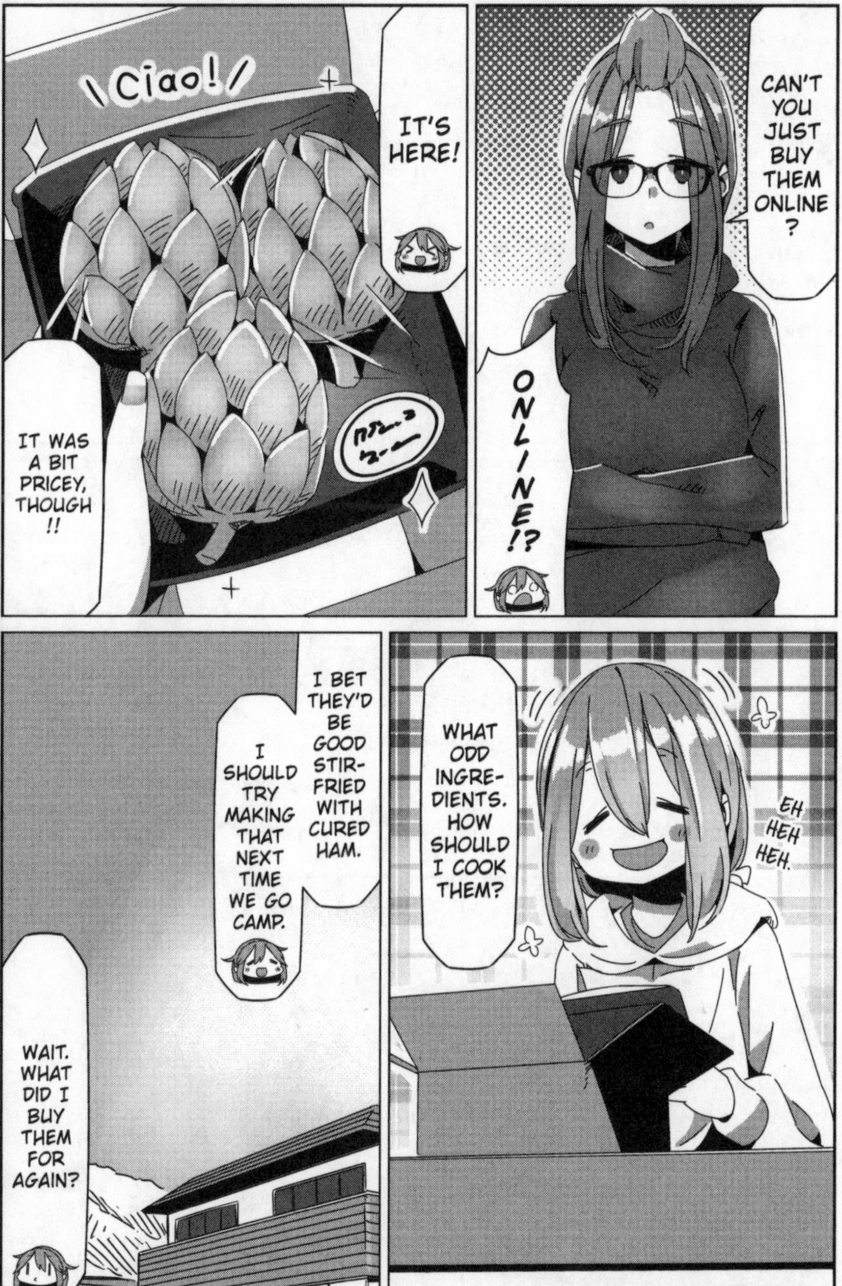
CAN'T YOU JUST BUY THEM ONLINE?
ONLINE!?
IT'S HERE!
\ Ciao! /
IT WAS A BIT PRICEY, THOUGH!!
WHAT ODD INGREDIENTS. HOW SHOULD I COOK THEM?
EH HEH HEH.
I BET THEY'D BE GOOD STIR-FRIED WITH CURED HAM.
I SHOULD TRY MAKING THAT NEXT TIME WE GO CAMP.
WAIT. WHAT DID I BUY THEM FOR AGAIN?

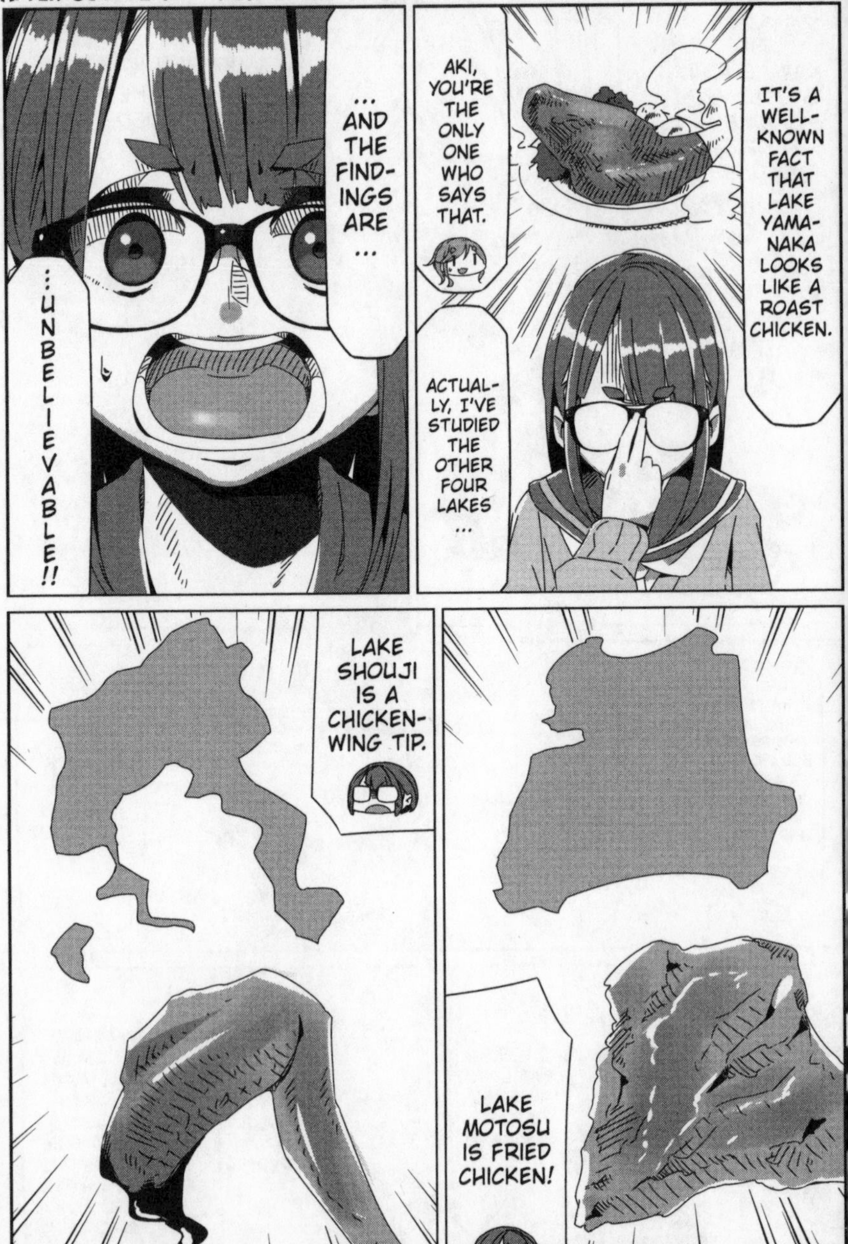
IT'S A WELL-KNOWN FACT THAT LAKE YAMANAKA LOOKS LIKE A ROAST CHICKEN.
AKI, YOU'RE THE ONLY ONE WHO SAYS THAT.
ACTUALLY, I'VE STUDIED THE OTHER FOUR LAKES...
...AND THE FINDINGS ARE...
...UNBELIEVABLE!!
LAKE MOTOSU IS FRIED CHICKEN!
LAKE SHOUJI IS A CHICKEN-WING TIP.

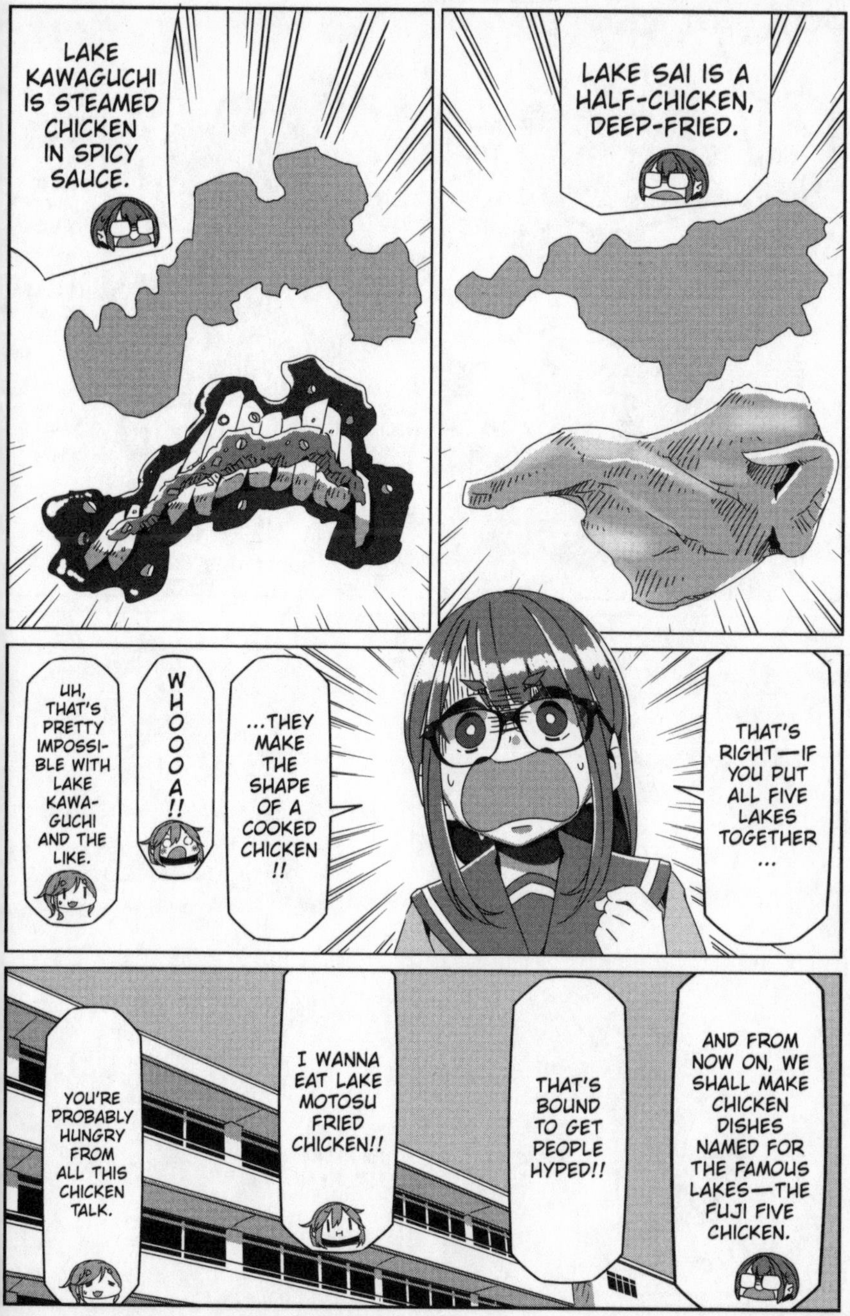
LAKE SAI IS A HALF-CHICKEN, DEEP-FRIED.
LAKE KAWAGUCHI IS STEAMED CHICKEN IN SPICY SAUCE.
THAT'S RIGHT—IF YOU PUT ALL FIVE LAKES TOGETHER ...
...THEY MAKE THE SHAPE OF A COOKED CHICKEN!!
WHOOOOA!!
UH, THAT'S PRETTY IMPOSSIBLE WITH LAKE KAWAGUCHI AND THE LIKE.
AND FROM NOW ON, WE SHALL MAKE CHICKEN DISHES NAMED FOR THE FAMOUS LAKES—THE FUJI FIVE CHICKEN.
THAT'S BOUND TO GET PEOPLE HYPED!!
I WANNA EAT LAKE MOTOSU FRIED CHICKEN!!
YOU'RE PROBABLY HUNGRY FROM ALL THIS CHICKEN TALK.

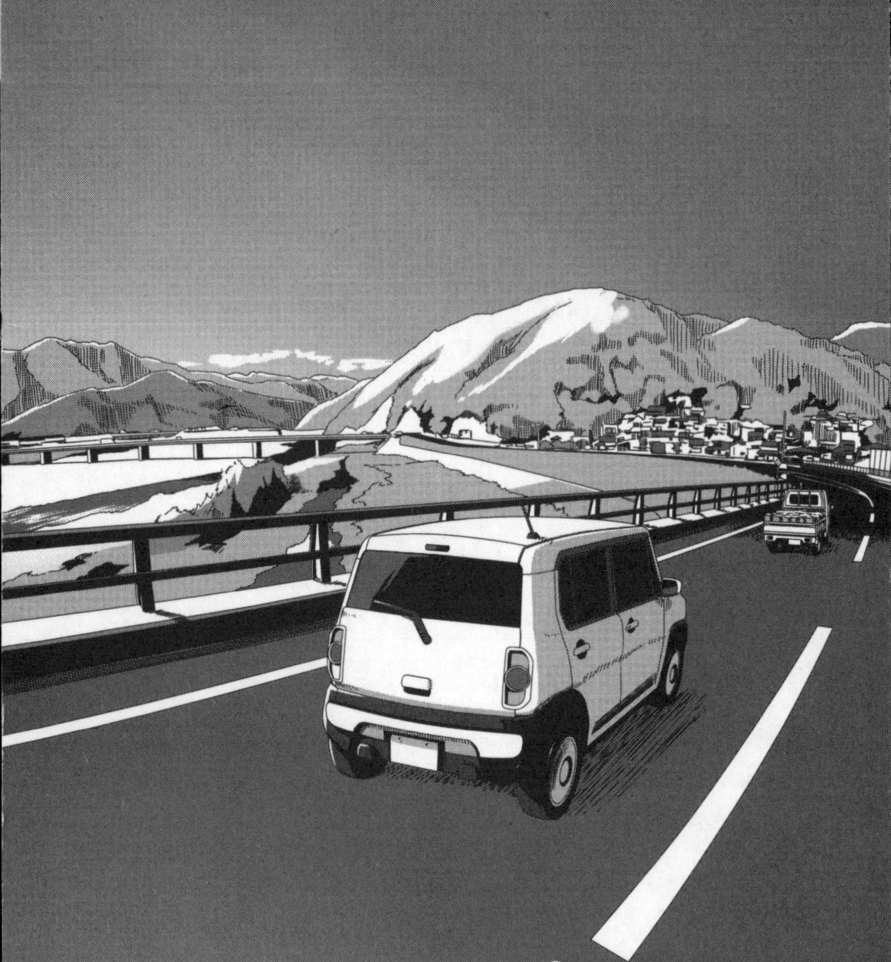

HOW DID YOU LIKE VOLUME 12 OF *LAID-BACK CAMP*?
THIS VOLUME INCLUDED WOOD-SPLITTING AND MIZUGAKI CAMP.

IN THE STORY, CHIAKI AND THE OTHERS VISIT THE MOUNT MIZUGAKI CAMPSITE AT THE END OF MARCH, BUT IN REAL LIFE, THE GATE IS CLOSED UNTIL APRIL, SO BUSES CAN'T GET THROUGH.
THAT, AND THE GODO TUNNEL—NEXT TO THE SIGN THAT CREATED A DISCUSSION—ALSO CONNECTS TO THE NEW GODO TUNNEL FROM THE BEGINNING OF DECEMBER TO THE MIDDLE OF APRIL, SO PLEASE BE MINDFUL.

THIS HAS BEEN AFRO.

[PUBLICATION LIST]
• *COMIC FUZ* NOVEMBER 2019–MARCH 2020, SEPTEMBER 2020–MARCH 2021 ISSUES
• NEW EXTRAS
THE MATERIALS IN THIS BOOK HAVE BEEN COLLECTED FROM THE ABOVE SOURCES.

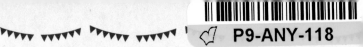

LAID ☕ BACK C⛺MP ⑫
Afro

Translation: **Amber Tamosaitis** ✳ Lettering: **DK**

YURUCAMP Vol. 12
© 2021 afro. All rights reserved. First published in Japan in 2021 by HOUBUNSHA CO., LTD., Tokyo. English translation rights in United States, Canada, and United Kingdom arranged with HOUBUNSHA CO., LTD. through Tuttle-Mori Agency, Inc., Tokyo.

English translation © 2022 by Yen Press, LLC

Yen Press
150 West 30th Street, 19th Floor
New York, NY 10001

Visit us at yenpress.com
facebook.com/yenpress
twitter.com/yenpress
yenpress.tumblr.com
instagram.com/yenpress

First Yen Press Edition: September 2022
Edited by Yen Press Editorial: Carl Li
Designed by Yen Press Design: Wendy Chan

Yen Press is an imprint of Yen Press, LLC.
The Yen Press name and logo are trademarks of Yen Press, LLC.

The publisher is not responsible for websites (or their content) that are not owned by the publisher.

Library of Congress Control Number: 2017959206

ISBNs: 978-1-9753-3776-6 (paperback)
        978-1-9753-3777-3 (ebook)

10 9 8 7 6 5 4 3 2 1

WOR

Printed in the United States of America